AMARI NYLIX

TEMAIR MEDIA

The One…Who Undid Me
Austin Heat, Book One

Copyright © 2023 Tara Delaney (Amari Nylix)
Cover Photographer: Dharmesh Bhakta (Photo by Mesh)
Cover Designer: Staci Hart
Cover Model: James Joseph Pulido

Formatting by: Kim Guidroz

ISBN: 979-8-9885908-9-7

Printed and published in the United States of America by Temair Media

Dedication

To the *ladies* of Austin, thank you for the sass and the heat. You got this!

To the *men* of Austin, you can thank me later 😊 .

To view a selection of fun, saucy videos follow me on:
IG: @author.amarinylix
TikTok: @author.amarinylix
www.amarinylix.com (in Nylix Minxes club there are pix/videos for download)

Chapter One

Jake: (to Dwayne) *Dude, you flying in this afternoon? Mom's asking me if you're coming to the house for dinner...***Send**

Dwayne: *Boarding now. Can't wait to be back in Austin. Tell your mom I wouldn't miss it. Is she making that French Chicken?...***Send**

Jake: *Yep, Coq Au Vin...learn the name since you always gobble it up! And chicken fry for your ass...***Send**

Dwayne: *I love that woman...***Send**

Jake: *How's your mom, sis? You enjoying Ozark City?...***Send**

Dwayne: *Looks like sis is going to Alabama, pre-med. Wants to try out for the cheerleading squad. I said, NO, but you know Eva. Mom's good. Misses seeing you...don't get that* 😊 *...***Send**

Jake: *Wait...cause she loves me. Don't let Eva be a cheerleader at Alabama...NOO!! Those Bama boys!...***Send**

Dwayne: *I know, I know, shit!! Mom says I have to back off sis, let her breathe. But Bama football. Mom's coming this summer...ugh that cramps my Austin fun. Scenery in Austin much hotter than here...***Send**

Jake: *True, this city's got some of the hottest scenery in the country...***Send**

Dwayne: *Whatta they say, 'if you can handle the Austin heat, you'll be rewarded'...***Send**

Jake: *That's what you say, no one else says that. I'm going to try to tone it down...***Send**

Dwayne: *Good for you. Have fun on your own. Not me...Austin is my reward after a grueling season. So watch out ladies 'Pretty Boy' Skyler & 'Sticky Fingers' Bradshaw are heading your way...***Send**

Jake: *It's getting old...all these women all over us just because of the NFL*

*thing…***Send**

    Dwayne: *Dude…maybe that's why they like you, but I have great skills off the field as well…***Send**

    Jake: *BS…***Send**

    Dwayne: *Pretty Boy, you getting all noble on me?…***Send**

    Jake: *No, tired of being used…want a normal girl…***Send**

    Dwayne: *Waaah…nobody feels sorry for you…***Send**

    Jake: *I knew you wouldn't get it. I'm heading into the gym to meet Jordan…***Send**

    Dwayne: *Tell big brother hi…***Send**

    Jake: *Safe flight. See you soon. I'll warn the women of Austin…***Send**

Jake: *Mom, Dwayne's on for dinner…make double chicken…***Send**

    Mom: *I love you too Jake. Yes, I'm having a great day. Thanks for asking. Will do…***Send**

    Jake: *Come on Mom. Love you…***Send**

"Great season Jake! You guys were the bomb!" someone yelled as Jake sprang up the stairs, so happy to be back at his hometown gym Lift-ATX, the most badass gym in Austin.

"Thanks, dude!" he yelled back.

He didn't recognize the guy, but he'd become accustomed to being recognized himself, especially here in Austin. Jake made it a point to try to get to know some of the most dedicated local fans, especially because most Texans were Cowboy or Lone Star fans. So when the rare Texan rooted for him because he had played for UT in college, he made sure to acknowledge them warmly. Jake tried to make a point of being grateful, even humble. There was some acting involved with that, but the NFL had knocked him off his perch early on. When he hadn't gotten drafted in the early rounds—his dream of being drafted by the San Antonio Lone Stars or the Iowa Tornadoes denied—he'd learned that nothing was guaranteed and that humble pie did not taste good. But he hadn't really learned the lesson he knew he should have. That would take a few more failures, a shitty reputation and, of course, his parents' continuous lectures to prompt a change. At some point, he had no choice but to bury some of the arrogance that accompanied making more money than he could have imagined way too young. Before joining the new Sacramento team, he'd played backup quarterback for Seattle. That had bought him time—time to mess up his personal life but also time to stew and figure out a new course.

After two years with Seattle, he heard that the Iowa Tornadoes were scouting for a backup quarterback, so he had his agent reach out. But Iowa leaked it out that their quarterback, Randall Adams, was not a fan of Jake's reputation. He shook his head thinking about that, how he'd looked up to Randall when he was in high school football, how every woman in America loved Randall. And he was scandal-free to boot: Randall didn't have any compromising stories out there about him. Somehow, this guy—a guy who'd dated his share of actresses and models and the hot brunette who was the first woman to compete in Formula One—was America's wholesome quarterback. How did he pull that off?

Jake scanned the gym.

"Gentleman Jordan, my man!" he yelled across the gym to Jordan, addressing his friend by the nickname Jordan had garnered at the University of Texas. It suited him. As big as they came, even in the football world, Jordan conducted himself as if he was born in a tuxedo, which confused his opponents and, of course, the media, who wanted to see him as a beast. He was far from it, a realization that tended to come after only a short time in his presence.

Jordan had been a senior at the University of Texas when Jake was a freshman, and he'd taken Jake under his wing. Jordan played offensive line and was the first-round draft pick for the Miami Dolphins. After five years in the NFL, he'd returned to Austin to marry the love of his life, Delilah. He'd gone back to nursing school and now worked as an emergency room nurse. Jake laughed wondering how patients reacted when they looked up to see an almost three-hundred-pound giant attending to them. During the off-season, Jake and Jordan were a constant presence at the gym, often joined by Dwayne, the Sacramento Condor's number one wide receiver, who, like Jake, had his home base in Austin.

"Jake, my man—you're late. I was beginning to wonder if you were going to make it. Get your cocky ass in here so I can put you in your place, young man." Jordan opened his arms, and they hugged like it had been years since they'd seen one another. At six-feet-four and two hundred seventy pounds, Jordan made Jake's six-two, two-hundred-twenty-pound frame seem thin. Within a few years after his retirement from the NFL, Jordan's ample muscles had faded into memory, replaced by fat. For a couple of years, he ran around with a middle-aged man's beer belly. But Dr. Delilah, his wife and a renowned cardiologist, wasn't having it. He did as she instructed, getting himself back to the gym and cleaning up his diet.

The two men settled in, discussing the latest local news. Jordan filled Jake in on Jasmine, his three-year-old daughter. Jake, Jasmine's godfather, had been receiving weekly pictures and videos, but he still couldn't wait to see her in person. Even a couple months seemed like a lifetime in toddler time. Jake's brain scooted back to Jasmine's birth, the day he felt the world shift, like somehow life mattered more. When he'd held that small bundle, he'd smiled, thinking, *Someday this little baby girl will rule us all*, taking comfort knowing that. Then when Jordan and Delilah asked him to be her godfather, his brain sparked with fleeting thoughts of who he would be to her and how he'd make sure whatever else happened in his life, Jasmine would be a priority. The feel of her small nose on his lips when he bent to kiss her was indelibility imprinted on him, along with the few tears he couldn't prevent slipping from his eyes. When he looked up, Delilah's lip protruding to fight back her own tears, she winked at Jake as if she knew they'd made the right choice. God, in that moment, he'd felt so proud.

Thirty minutes into their weight routine, Jake walked across the gym to refill his water bottle. As he approached the fountain, he couldn't help noticing the girl in front of him bending slightly as she filled her bottle. Her long, dirty-blond hair was pulled into a high ponytail. Her powerful, long legs and high, round butt were covered by a thin layer of light-gray leggings. Hell, that was only the back view. Then she turned and smiled. Jake took in her big, green eyes framed by long, dark lashes under dark eyebrows. Her encompassing grin made Jake forget why he was standing there. She smiled big enough to show all of her white teeth, and Jake noticed that her top-right eye tooth was turned out—a flaw that only made her smile more interesting. Jake couldn't stop staring.

She held up her bottle. "Ah, sorry it took me so long, mate," she said. "Completely dry." Her voice was husky with a definite accent. It seemed to possess tentacles, which teased the skin on the back of Jake's neck.

"Um, yeah, no problem. Take as long as you need," Jake stammered. Later, he wouldn't remember what he said to her.

Her wide grin settled into a softer, smaller smile as she stepped away from the fountain, her eyes flicking over Jake's body and back to his face. "Well, good day to ya," she said as she walked off.

Jake stared openly at her backside until someone came up behind him and impatiently cleared his throat. He stepped aside, letting the next guy fill his bottle while he watched the woman walk to the back of the gym through a set of two doors. In the five years he'd worked out at this gym, he'd never bothered to look at what was behind those double doors on the other side of the free weight room, but now he was curious.

As he walked back over to Jordan, he wondered what kind of accent she had—English, Scottish, Australian, maybe South African? He couldn't be sure, but God did it ever sound adorable and so fucking sexy all at once.

"Jordan, have you seen that tall, crazy-beautiful girl? The one that just walked by to the back?" Jake was pointing to the double doors. "Have you seen her around?"

"Yeah, I've actually seen her lifting. She works out hard. Not sure when she started here, but it's been a while. Come on, Jake, you're not even home twenty-four hours and you're already scoping. Don't you think you need a break after Jessica?"

Jordan was referring to Jessica Ortiz, the rising movie star from LA that Jake had dated for almost eight months. The one who had been cheating on Jake with her more famous co-star, Bernardo Cappuccino. Jake had found out a few months before, when his friends sent him screenshots of the Instagram photos of her and said star making out at an LA hotspot. He'd known something was going on with her because her communication with him had seemingly dropped off out of nowhere. Still, he didn't like the way it happened. He never spoke to Jessica again after he saw the pictures. He simply texted her *END*, and that was that. He blocked her and unfollowed all her social media and never revisited.

He had been drawn to Jessica, the way her large brown eyes seemed to light up when he first met her. They'd been able to spend a lot of time together when he first met her at a bar in Sacramento, where she'd been shooting a movie. He'd fly down to LA, and she'd fly up to Sacramento, or sometimes to Austin, when he moved back during the summer season. But he'd noticed the more time they'd spent together that their conversations became more stilted. She seemed uninterested in his life outside the NFL. When she visited Austin during his bye week in October, joining him and his extended family for a get-together at his parents' house, she was removed, barely talking to anyone, including Jake. She shook her head when his family had invited her to play cornhole or horseshoes, choosing to entertain herself with her phone. He caught his parents' concerned looks and knew their relationship was short-lived, but it was the way she announced it to the world the following week without even reaching out to him that burned.

"Dude, I'm over the whole Jessica thing. Kinda think I'm done with the whole famous-girl thing, or trying-to-be-famous thing. You know, up-and-coming actresses, models, NFL cheerleaders…all of them. I hate taking selfies, and all they care about is making sure every fucking moment is part of some kinda storyboard. So sitting around watching TV in sweats or hanging out with my parents is out. It has to be some super cool bar or place with a view, so there's a spectacular backdrop for the Instagram reel. Even kissing a girl has to be practiced to get the best angle. It's ridiculous. I'm sick of those parties where I have to make small talk and act impressed by people I don't even know."

"Uh, I think that's part of the whole famous-NFL-quarterback thing, don't you?" Jordan said as they moved to the pull-down machine.

"Let's be real, man," Jake said. "I'm not famous. In Austin, people know me just like they know you, 'cause we're UT kids who made it big. Outside of Austin or Sacramento, I rarely get attention, and I'm good with that." He sat at the pull-down machine and groaned, tightening his core, pulling the weights toward his chest so that it was his lats working to pull the bar back. Jordan kept talking, saying something about how it was just a matter of time before Jake became as recognizable as Drew Brees. Jake pulled hard, groaning, eking out one more rep before releasing the bar back to the starting position.

"Damn, that was tough. Haven't been lifting heavy this season."

Jordan adjusted the weight. "I'll need a little more," he said, winking at Jake. "Don't worry, lollipop, you'll get that strength up in no time. Stick with me." He chuckled.

"Ha, thanks," Jake replied, stepping back from the machine, relishing the ease that was his friendship with Jordan. A big part of Jake envied the hell out of Jordan: settled down, with a great wife, a beautiful daughter, and a job that made him happy. What some referred to as a simple life to Jake seemed more like a dream. After six years of being in the NFL, that life felt so far away from the one he was living now. He enjoyed the off-season. He was so grateful that his father insisted he buy a home in Austin right away, a place to come back to that he could call his own. The time he had with friends and family always ended too soon. The closer he got to pre-season check-in every year, the more he questioned what he was doing.

He didn't dread this coming season as much as prior ones, though, if he was being honest. He was about to enter his third season with the Sacramento Condors, and it finally felt like he was maturing into the game, like he had something to contribute to a young team. More importantly, he didn't just respect the head coach of the Condors—he admired him.

He thought back to his first interview with Coach Easton. Jake could immediately tell he'd learn a lot from the man, both on and off the field. Coach Easton was gruff like Coach Mark, who had coached Jake since junior high; both had a no-bullshit attitude when talking to him. Coach Easton also possessed his dad's humility, which Jake didn't often see in a man of Easton's level in the NFL. Coach Easton had grown up playing ball—he'd been a linebacker for Penn State, then gone on to play for the Steelers for eight seasons before coaching at the University of Florida and then Wisconsin. Then he'd accepted his first NFL position for a brand-new team that was forming in Sacramento.

Although he'd learned a lot playing backup quarterback to the star of the Seattle Seahawks for almost three years, Jake craved more time on the field. He was called in for an interview with Sacramento after the recruiters had shown the owners and coaches several football films demonstrating his burgeoning talent. Coach Easton detailed all of Jake's positives and then tilted his head to the side, pulling his lips into his mouth as he studied Jake.

"So let's chat about what's holding you back," he'd said casually, pointing to Jake's head and then to Jake's crotch.

All Jake could think was, *Fuck, I'm never going to escape this reputation.* He was sure Coach Easton had already determined that Jake's well-documented off the field antics—mostly women and sometimes a crossed-eyed slap-happy drunk Jake—would be a liability for the new team.

Jake just lowered his eyes. "I know, sir, that's why I'm looking for a new start. I'd like to work with someone that'll be honest with me instead of just dismissing me like some lost cause." Resting in the back of Jake's throat was a lengthy explanation about how he wasn't the only pro-sports player to enjoy the spoils of money and the notoriety of the NFL. He was sure when he saw into Coach Easton's deep coal eyes that such an explanation would have gotten him curtly escorted out of the office.

Coach responded, "I want you, Skyler, but I need your head in the game, your heart with the team, and your dick to chill out a few years until your brain is strong enough to help make some positive decisions for your life."

Jake's head popped up. "Wait, so I can't date at all?"

Shit, that flew out of his mouth before his frontal lobe had time to reconstruct just how to ask what was banged into his brain after Coach Easton's words. What he almost said was, *What the hell, you want me to be celibate? Not sure you can pay me enough for that.*

Coach Easton chuckled, his voice drifting to the ground. "No, son, but maybe think about sticking with one girl for a while and getting to know her, instead of the harem that seems to swirl around *the pretty boy* and cause so much drama. 'Cause I don't give two fucks about your dazzling smile or piercing blue eyes." He winked, referring to the media's description of Jake. "I *do* care about how it all distracts you, making you less the leader that I suspect you can be. I've talked to Coach Mark at UT. He says he's known you and coached you since you were twelve. He says *you*—" Coach pointed directly at Jake. "Yeah, you were the hardest, and best part, of being a coach. So we can safely say you make an impression."

"Well to be fair, I was in junior high when Coach Mark started working with me."

"Yes, and to be fair, you're almost twenty-five now. Time to outgrow the adolescent stage and control your impulsivity. That is if you want to lead. If not…"

Pulling his lips into his mouth, Jake summoned up the courage to look Coach Easton in the eye and believe the words coming out of his mouth. "Coach, I do want to become a leader, and I think I'm ready for it. And there's no one I would rather…"

Coach Easton put up his hand. "Enough, son. I expect my players to be above reproach on and off the field. And I expect myself and the other coaches to be the example of that." Easton lowered his head, his eyes boring into Jake's, emphasizing his point. "So, son: Do you think you can represent this team?"

Jake responded with a quick "Yes, sir. I'd be honored."

He wondered if Coach Easton's emphasis on being above reproach was because he'd grown up as one of the few Black kids in a rural town in Pennsylvania. He'd also heard that Coach Easton's father had been in the military. It made sense that his sense of honor was both inherited and learned. The thing about working for someone who was an example of what he expected from you was that you wanted to prove to him you had in you what he saw and that you were willing to emulate that example.

Jordan cleared his throat to get Jake's attention as he finished his set and adjusted the weight down for Jake. "Let me lighten that up for you, lollipop," he said, winking at Jake.

"Very funny, animal," Jake shot back.

Delilah always teased them that they were like lovers having a secret affair and their meeting place was the gym. She scolded them that they took three times longer to complete a workout than the average person but accomplished nothing extra except jabbering like a couple of high school girls. There was some truth to her ribbing because Jordan was truly Jake's confidant and counselor, and he always had been. He was also a lot more compassionate about Jake's women problems than Delilah, who pretty much set Jake straight anytime he whined.

They had moved through three more exercises when Jake noticed a few people coming through the double doors, including his new dream girl. "There she is," he whispered. "I'm gonna go say something to her."

"Like what? 'Hey, hot girl. What are you doing back there?' Come on, Jake. You're the one who made the rule that the gym is a demilitarized zone—no fighting, no flirting." Jordan pulled weights off the pec machine. "So if you flirt with her, that means I can beat your ass, right?" Jordan laughed.

Jake watched the woman walk across the gym, her long legs extending in front of her, her ass cheeks tightening as each foot hit the ground. She spread her legs as she got on a machine, the kind that works your inner thighs.

"Mmm, it might be worth it," Jake said, trying to think of a classic line that he'd used before to get a woman's attention. Maybe something like, *I want your workout and the legs that go with it?* No, that sounded stupid. He'd need something more subtle. She didn't seem to be welcoming attention or even observing anyone around her.

"I'm just gonna go say hi or something," he said as he helped Jordan with the weights.

"Don't do it, dude," Jordan replied, shaking his head.

But Jake had an idea. He walked over to the leg machines and headed for the outer-thigh one, as it was facing the machine she was currently on. He'd never used these machines before. He usually worked his inner and outer thighs using resistance bands. Come to think of it, he didn't think he'd ever seen a guy on one of these at all. He understood why as he struggled to get his six-two frame positioned on the machine, praying no one happened to be filming him because he was sure he looked like a male version of Lucille Ball as he tried to move into a yoga-like position on a machine that wasn't designed for a body his size. Finally, he got positioned, pushing his outer knees against the pads, moving his legs in and out like some kind of giant version of Richard Simmons.

He felt ridiculous and must have looked ridiculous too, which was confirmed when he saw Jordan across the room trying to stifle his laughter to the point of tears. Jake shot his friend a dirty look, then looked toward the woman. She had earbuds in, mouthing the words to a song. For the first time, he noticed how full and round her breasts were as they pushed up against the fabric of her sports bra. He'd been so focused on her eyes and her smile he hadn't noticed her breasts, a first for him.

He looked up at her several times, casually acting as if he'd just noticed her. Finally, she looked directly back at him and smiled. God, he thought, he could gaze at that smile all day. He kept trying to look away then back at her and smile, hoping for another one in return… and there it was—a bright, wide beautiful grin to match his own. He was well aware of how his smile changed his face. His sisters and past girlfriends would tell him all the time that without his smile, he looked too serious, almost angry. But when he broke out into a genuine smile, he possessed a disarming quality that drew people in.

Rakell pulled her lips into her mouth, trying desperately not to burst out laughing. She skewed her eyes to the side, mouthing the words to the song that blasted through her earbuds, trying anything to maintain her composure as she watched the tall, muscular guy wrangle his limbs into the outer thigh machine. The sight was like something from a hidden camera show, his torso bending awkwardly, his legs extending up to the side, twisting and turning. Her eyes darted around; she thought there must be a camera crew filming her reaction, as that could be the only explanation for the absurd scene before her. Except, wait—when her eyes did flit his way, he smiled wide, his chin nodding, his piercing blue eyes focused on her.

Oh my God, is this his way of making the moves on me? She was used to staying in her own space at the gym, avoiding eye contact, trying to give off the vibe that she was here to work out, not flirt. She didn't see the gym as a meat market, so she was always cognizant of her non-verbal communication. Her job meant she had to play up to men, so when she wasn't working, she focused on herself. She knew that after this year, she'd have to figure out how to operate in the dating world without a script, but in the meantime, she kept to herself in places like this.

That guy really is full of himself, Rakell thought, watching the hot meathead as he smiled at her like he thought it would make her panties disintegrate. He seemed well aware of what he had: stunning good looks matched with a rugged air. The kind of guy who thought he could push past the forcefield she'd created around herself to keep men out. It bordered on too much, too sure, too bold. He went from really cute to weird…yet still really cute. She relented, matching his grin almost daringly.

Twisting his torso, Jake lifted his right leg, trying to free himself from the contraption. Fuck, this was definitely some kind of BDSM equipment disguised as an outer-thigh machine. And fuck, his groin hurt as he worked to get the hell off and out of this contraption. Hopefully she would find his vulnerability adorable. *Okay, Jake, whatever you gotta tell yourself, just get off this crazy machine and save some smidgen of dignity.* Finally, his legs made it to the floor, and standing up, he pulled his shoulders back, planting a smile on his face.

She sucked in her lower lip, almost biting it to stop from bursting out laughing. He seemed to regain his swagger as his large but lean form strode toward her. His skin looked naturally tan, as if he'd started with a darker base that was then enhanced by the sun. He wore his jet-black hair shorter on the sides, inky waves of hair spilling from the top of his head, falling around his forehead and framing his chiseled face. His intense blue eyes were enhanced by his amazing smile. He smiled with his whole face. Not necessarily a light up the room kind of smile, but more of an *I got this, I'll make this happen* kind of smile.

She took in his charming fierceness as he approached. His broad chest puffed out, and he had a naturally confident strut to his gait. Internally shaking her head and laughing to herself, she thought she could have a little fun with this. Right now, she was just experimenting with men, learning how to act without a contract, to be Rakell, though she wasn't yet sure exactly who that woman was. All she knew was that it wasn't Marietta, the docile, sweet arm-candy she'd been forced to become when she was on assignment as an escort.

"Hi," he said simply.

"Hi, just a sec," Rakell replied, purposely adjusting her legs on the machine so that the resting stance had them spread wide. She took her earbuds out, looking up at Jake with a small smirk on her lips. Then she leaned forward, reaching for her phone on the floor next to her, well aware that he'd get an extra glimpse of her cleavage.

She couldn't quite grasp it, so Jake reached down and handed it to her. His face came dangerously close to her chest. He stood quickly and looked at her face. She was still sporting that smirk.

Shit, is this girl fucking with me? He wanted to ask if there was some joke he was being left out of.

"Haven't seen you here before," Jake blurted out.

"Well then, you must not pay attention, mate, 'cause I'm here a lot." She smiled up at him. "Doing another set."

She started moving her legs, squeezing in and out slowly. She could tell he was working to focus on just her face before purposely looking around the gym, as if he needed to study the equipment.

Eventually his eyes dropped down, maybe staying a little too long on her breasts before he caught himself, struggling not to look at the apex of her legs as she squeezed them in and out. If there was a camera on him, he'd be recorded being a pervert.

"Okay, sorry, had to get that one out of the way," she said, a little out of breath as she slowly lifted her legs, one by one, out of the machine. He stood there, pleading with his brain to give him something clever to say, but nothing came.

"I reckon you're right. Good point," he finally spit out. "I'm actually the one who hasn't been in for a while." He extended his hand. "I'm Jake."

Rakell shook his hand. "Good to meet you," she said as a smile rippled across her face, his warmth pulsing through her, traveling up her arm. Instinctively, she pulled back her hand.

Her reaction wasn't lost on him. She'd pulled away suddenly, as if there was something threatening about him. He deliberately softened his smile and rocked his torso back a bit, so he didn't seem to be looming over her. Trying to regain her attention, not knowing what to say, he blurted out, "Where's the accent from?"

"Australia, but it's mostly gone," she replied, her tone impassive. "Haven't lived there in a while." Her eyes shifted around, like she was looking for a reason to end the conversation.

"So what brings you to Austin?" he asked, trying to think of any way to keep the sluggish conversation going.

She grimaced. "Jake, right?"

"Yup." He nodded.

"Listen, I'm loving this riveting conversation we've embarked on here"—she made a motion with her hand, waving it in the space between them—"and no doubt you're quite enjoyable on the eyes, but I really need to scoot." She looked down at the phone in her hand intently, as if the text she'd just received was way more interesting than Jake. Then a smile stretched across her face, and her big green eyes popped open, a whimsical glimmer in them as if they were dancing a jig. "Enjoy the rest of your day, mate." She stepped past him. Jake could swear that she was purposefully swaying her hips as a low chuckle trailed behind her.

"Um, you too," he blurted to her backside.

Rakell bit the inside of her mouth, but a chesty laugh escaped. She wanted to whip her head around to see if his eyes were still trained on her. He was so damn cute, tripping all over himself figuring out what to say. She wondered if he was nervous. She hadn't really adjusted to men being nervous around her. She had only been on a few dates, still making sure she stayed in her bubble. As an escort, she was used to her clients dictating how she acted so that they didn't have to work at it; she was either on their arm or in their bed, whatever the agreement was. She had to admit, it was kind of fun watching a hunky guy work for it, fishing to get her attention.

Jake jumped on the treadmill next to Jordan.

"So how did it go, Romeo?" Jordan asked, sucking his cheeks in, trying not to laugh.

"Pretty sure she's in love," Jake said sheepishly.

"Not good?" Jordan's eyebrows arched as he swallowed the burst of laugher inching up his throat.

"She pretty much told me that I'm boring eye candy." Jake shot his friend a rueful grin.

"God, she figured your ass out in less than two minutes. Damn, that's funny, Dwayne's gonna love this." He snorted, slowing down the treadmill because his exploding laughter made it impossible to run.

Jordan halted his laughter, his eyes serious, and Jake knew that he needed to listen to the next words. "Seriously, Jake, you've really started pulling the pieces together in your life, especially your career. Don't get derailed now." He stopped the treadmill, his steady stare boring into Jake.

Jake nodded. "I hear you." He cleared his throat, a *but* hanging on the end of his tongue.

Chapter Two

Whenever Jake returned to Austin for the off-season, he would spend the first few nights eating dinner at his parents' house. His mom, Annette, insisted on it. Jake loved being with his parents, loved that his mom would cater to him for a few days until she got used to having him around. He relished those first few days, when he could do no wrong. She made him his favorite meals, and usually his oldest sister came over with her husband and two kids. Jake often brought his teammate Dwayne along, since Annette had extended an open invitation and Dwayne couldn't resist a home-cooked meal. The meal was usually an assortment of Jake's Texas and French favorites: French onion soup, *coq au vin*, chicken-fried steak, fried green tomatoes, and a dessert of pecan pie. Once the grace period expired—which didn't take long—his mom lapsed into normal mom MO, especially with the lectures and life-lesson discussions.

"Ms. Annette, you make the best fried green tomatoes, and that chicken French fancy thing is my most favorite," Dwayne boomed down the table at Jake's mom.

"Thank you, Dwayne. You know you are always welcome," she said coyly, winking at him. "I consider you my sweet, gracious son."

"Wait," Jake said mid-chew, anxious to jump in. "First, Dwayne, slow down on the damn chicken! And Mom, what was that emphasis on 'gracious'?"

Dwayne cut in: "Your mom knows which one of her boys is most grateful for all her hard work. Come on, Jake, she always puts out an amazing spread, and you're just sittin' here gobbling up her work and talking about football. Maybe you should ask your mom how her dance studio is doing. She's the reason you move like that on the field. Maybe thank her. Like focus on her, you know what I mean?" He slapped Jake on the back.

Annette smirked. She loved the relationship Jake had with Dwayne. They truly felt like brothers, she thought, listening to their back-and-forth banter.

"Ah, thank you Dwayne," she said. "The studio is going well. I just hired another dance instructor, which allows me to concentrate more on teaching singing, which I have enjoyed. I know Jake's grateful. He just doesn't always remember to say it."

"Mom, really, you know how thankful I am."

"Actions, actions… you can clean up after dinner."

"Yep, you know I will."

His dad tilted his head, smiling at his son, and changed the subject. "Jake, we appreciate that James brings Dolly out here every few weeks to see us, and we never mind watching her when he has to travel. I think you and James worked out a nice situation, him living with you and taking care of Dolly."

Jake let out a breath, knowing that the *stay away from women* lecture couldn't be far behind.

"He's definitely a good roommate, easy to live with, and Dolly's crazy about him," Jake said. His roommate, James, traveled a lot for work, but he also made sure he took care of Dolly, Jake's golden retriever, or brought her to Jake's parents' house when Jake was in Sacramento for football season. In return for that, Jake let him live there at a reduced rent.

"So, off season, a time to get things done…" his dad started, his tone a little more serious. "Dwayne, I know renting has been working out for you, but with the housing market in Austin, I think you should look into buying. It would be a good investment. I can help you with that." David never missed an opportunity to give Jake or his other kids (of which he considered Dwayne one) ideas on how to invest their money. "And Jake…"

"Mm…mm," Jake said with pursed lips, a mouth full of food, forcing himself not to roll his eyes, as he knew the lecture that was about to spill out of his father. "That place you bought in East Austin needs a little attention. The renters have called a few times. I think it would go a long way if you contacted them to discuss some of their concerns. They have been solid renters. You have the time, and…."

Jake nodded, smiling at his dad, relieved that his dad hadn't mentioned women yet.

"And," Annette piped up, "you should use this time to heal after the breakup. Don't jump into anything…"

Jake ignored Dwayne's snickering. He'd just told him about the Aussie girl from the gym earlier that day.

"Mom, I'm not crushed from that, and you both have to admit, I've been pretty low-key in the ladies department since I signed with Sacramento."

"Keep it that way, son," his dad said before taking a swig of beer.

Damn, they seriously give me like forty-eight hours before the lectures start. What happened to my grace period, as if I am the same person I was three years ago? Jake thought, annoyed. *Why is it that family is the last to see how hard you're working to become a better version of yourself?*

Jake's sister Melissa marched through the door, her son screaming and her daughter, Cassie, declaring she was going to spend the night at Jake's house soon. "Sorry I couldn't get here earlier. Cassie had piano lessons, and Cameron's speech therapy sessions went long because, well, he didn't cooperate again," she said, exasperation clipping every word.

Jake noticed the drawn look on his oldest sister's face before she continued.

"…and Tom is still in Dallas with work, but he says, 'Welcome home, Jake.'" Melissa threw her arms up in the air in an exaggerated fashion. "What did you guys have for Jake's special dinner tonight, the *fatted calf?*"

"Shit, thanks, sis. Now I am home."

"Jake the mouth…" Melissa said, shifting her eyes to the kids.

His niece Cassie looked up at her mom, her hands on her hips. "It's okay, Mom. He makes bad choices sometimes, but he's trying to make good choices. Right, Uncle Jake?"

"Right, sweetie. Thanks for seeing my potential." Jake winked at his mom.

"And Mom, he's the best uncle ever." Cassie's eyes moved to Jake, who couldn't wipe the grin off his face. "Uncle Jake, can I come see Dolly soon?"

"How about Saturday?" he asked, looking at Melissa, who nodded, smiling.

"Dwayne and I have to clean up, then we can get in a game or two of horseshoes before I head home. We're meeting Jordan at the gym early tomorrow." Jake stood and signaled for Dwayne to follow him into the kitchen.

"Dude, I forgot how rough your family is on you," Dwayne chuckled, grabbing a dishtowel. "I think I'll start being a little nicer."

"Don't. That would freak me out. Then *I'd* have to be nice to *you*. You know my family, making sure I don't get a big head—well, a bigger head." Jake began to load the dishwasher.

From the kitchen, he spotted his mom looking at a picture on the bookshelves in the living room. He knew exactly which picture had her lost in the past, his eyes shifting toward her. "Hey, I'll meet you out back in a few…" Jake whispered to Dwayne.

Nodding, Dwayne stepped toward the back door.

"Mom," Jake whispered, slipping his arm around his mom's narrow shoulders. Tilting her head, her misty eyes moved up to Jake's face. "Sorry I wasn't there…you know Mimi was my world, and I…"

"Shh…I know Jake; there was no way to fly to France right before playoffs. Papi knows it too, and he didn't expect you." Her eyes drifted back to the framed black and white photograph. "I was just looking at that photo thinking, *Jake is looking more and more like my father.* You remind me of him so much."

His hand flexed on her shoulder. He always forgot how small his mom was until he hugged her. Her presence was so large that he always imagined her taller, bigger, when he wasn't near. As he stood next to her, her shoulder hitting him mid-chest, he realized if he wrapped his arms around her, she'd disappear, just like Mimi. His height came from his father, but his girth and olive skin was a gift from Papi, his grandfather, who was born in Morocco before moving to France to study, where he met Jake's grandmother.

"So, Mom, is it the dashing good looks or…" His piercing blue eyes also came from his father, but Grandpa's features came through in Jake's high cheekbones, full lips, and his wavy jet-black hair.

His mom let out a small laugh, her head dropping to his chest. "I think it's your intensity, that fierce protectiveness of those you love. I worry about him without her. She tempered him, kept him in line and made him laugh. I worry about him without anybody there to actively love. Both of you share that as your best quality, needing someone to devote yourselves to…"

Jake bent slightly, reaching for the photo. "Man, they were a stunning couple. I've always seen Mimi as the one in charge."

Annette stood up straight, shifting on her feet to look up at Jake. "Not at first. Papi was controlling, jealous…"

"I get that—look at her." He relished the tidbits of his grandparents' history, especially his Papi, because it helped him understand himself compared to his father. His dad seemed to be the opposite of Jake: calm, seldom raising his voice, and sweet to the point of sedate, whereas his mother was vocal, passionate, the life of the party. He often wondered why and how Annette, his mother, a strikingly attractive and spirited French woman, had fallen for a lanky Texas boy with an accounting degree. Dad was sort-of, kind-of handsome, if you liked that tall, wiry look. How did she decide to marry David? Of course, he was thankful she did, because the yin and yang of the two of them made for great parents.

Someday Annette would share her mom's colorful history, but not today, not at this moment. "Yes, Papi made sure he kept others at bay when they started to date. Once they married, she thought he'd *se relaxerait.*"

Jake quipped: "Yep, quit being a controlling ass."

"So grateful for your formal education," his mom chided. "Yes, I think something like that, but he got worse. But Mimi put her foot down. She told him that if he didn't get a personality transplant, she would have no difficulty leaving him and starting her life anew. Pretty brave for that time period."

Jake roared with laughter. "I can hear Mimi half screaming, *'Relaxe ou je m'en vais!'* He turned toward his mom. "I know Melissa can't leave the kids again, but let's see if Jenae can join us for a quick trip to Strasbourg in a couple of months. Papi loves to give me advice."

Just like that, the idea formed in Jake's head. He knew it would give him a chance to be with Jenae, his sister four years his senior. They were close, but she worked as a lawyer in New York and had recently started dating Winnie, another lawyer; her life in New York was full, making the pull back to Austin difficult.

"I love that idea! He enjoys telling you how not to be exactly like him."

"Good luck with that." Jake gave his mom a final hug. "Let's go beat Dad at horseshoes."

This past season the Sacramento Condors made it to the playoffs. The season had been marked by steady improvement, leading many of football's talking heads to predict this year's successes. He'd heard the scuttlebutt: "Maybe Jake Skyler *does* have it in him after all. Let's see if the pretty boy can actually play ball. Finally leading, finally focusing, finally, finally, finally…Jake Skyler." It got old hearing about your faults, motivations, progress, love life, all through the eyes of social media followers and sportscasters.

Chapter Three

"Come on, Dolly, I gotta meet Jord at the gym," Jake laughed as Dolly came barreling through the backyard. He knew by that run and her high-pitched bark that her intention was to get some play time with Jake. "I'll be back home later," he said, petting her neck and pointing to the back door. "Come on, girl," he said, opening the door. "I swear, James spoils you when I'm gone."

Jake jumped in his truck to meet Jordan at the gym. He usually met Jordan, Dwayne, or both every morning, as well as some afternoons, to work out. As he pulled into the parking lot, he started wondering if he'd get to see the Aussie girl again. Jake parked, got out of his truck, and waited for Jordan outside the gym as he finished his coffee, letting the cool February air wake him up. February in Austin was variable—but often it was tepid, in the sixties, perfect for enjoying some time outdoors.

"Jord, over here." He waved to Jordan as he emerged from his car.

As Jordan approached, Jake caught a glimpse of *her*, the Aussie girl, pushing past the doors out of the gym, wearing leggings and a sweatshirt, her hair pulled back into a ponytail that was threaded through the back opening of an Iowa Tornadoes cap. *Shit, a Tornadoes hat! She follows football?*

"Hey, hi," Jake said as she walked onto the sidewalk.

"Oh, huh, good day." She sounded startled, like she'd been lost in thought. She looked at Jake, then her eyes went to Jordan. "Hey, blokes, are you just getting started?"

Blokes—he loved the way that word sounded coming out of that hot mouth. "Yep, but we'll be at it for a couple hours," Jake emphasized.

She smiled. "Working out or socializing?" Her eyes focused on Jake's face, trying not to let them admire his ripped body. She wondered how the hell these guys had so much time to spend at the gym. Did they not have jobs? They were like walking advertisements for *Men's Health and Fitness* or some kind of bodybuilding magazine. She stared at the cut of Jake's biceps, reflexively wanting to touch his arms. "Well then, so which is it?" she said on a short giggle.

Jordan laughed as he extended his hand. "A little of both. I'm Jordan. I hear you already met my friend here." He tilted his head toward Jake.

"Yes, already had the pleasure." She looked Jake straight in the eye, challenging him. "The only guy I've ever seen do the outer-thigh machine. Probably won't forget that." She pulled her lips tightly into her mouth. "Jason, right?"

Jake cocked his head slightly, trying to ignore Jordan's muffled snicker. "Um, *Jake*. It's Jake."

"Oh, yeah. Okay. I apologize—remembering random names is not my forte." Her mouth twisted as if she was working not to grin.

Random? What woman forgot his name? How did you forget a pretty simple name, tagged to a really hot guy? He scraped together a funny line to hide his confused irritation: "Jake: poor conversationalist, eye candy. Remember?" He patted his chest, trying to get a foothold so he could turn on his charm.

She turned one side of her mouth up. "I don't remember saying 'eye candy.' Must be an American term, but I rather like it. Yes, I do. Okay, that will be my term for both of you. 'Eye candy.' Perfect. But I'd gather Jordan here is probably a better conversationalist than you."

"Absolutely," Jordan chimed in, giving Jake a nudge with his arm.

"And how can you tell that?" Jake's eyes darted to Jordan, then back to the Aussie girl.

"His eyes just seem a bit sharper and brighter; nothing really," she said dismissively.

"Damn straight," Jordan said, puffing his chest up a bit. Then, registering the tightening of Jake's jaw, Jordan moved the conversation in a different direction. "Hey, noticed your hat. You a football fan?"

"Not really. Sometimes I watch the Tornadoes. Well, truth be told, I watch Randall Adams. I don't think I could even tell you the names of any of the other players. Not really into the football player type." She shrugged her shoulders.

Jake quirked an eyebrow, his chest puffing a little at her description. "Football type—what's that?" He cleared his throat trying to cover the challenge in his tone.

Smirking, she said, "Well the meathead type with tunnel vision, I guess—the opposite of the worldly or renaissance man. But Randall, well, how do you not remember the 'Zen Cyclone'?" She made quotation marks in the air, speaking like she was sixteen and had a crush on the most popular boy in school. "Sort of fond of that quarterback. Actually, don't think I'd care what his profession was." Her smile grew as she explained.

Her dad had been introduced to American football from a friend he'd met in London who was from Iowa. It started his obsession with the Iowa Tornadoes. The memory of watching Randall on TV, sitting side by side with her father, generated warmth in her that was soon buried by the regret that would always surround the memory of her dad.

Internally, Jake rolled his eyes. *Great, another Randall acolyte. What the hell does that guy have that I don't—besides four MVP awards, one Super Bowl ring, and enough passing yards to put him in the top ten of all-time?* Oh, and women following him like the Pied Piper on social media. His fucking "grounding" videos, showing the world how he connects with the earth to prepare himself for the day. Was that a Renaissance man, really?

"Who isn't a fan of Randall Adams?" Jordan said, hardly controlling his urge to bust at the seams laughing.

"Yep, America's quarterback. Good ol' Randall," Jake interjected, trying not to sound irritated. "So you don't really get into American football?"

"Not particularly, other than Randall. Not keen on watching a bunch of meatheads in tights grabbing and touching each other all over as if it proves their masculinity. I prefer brains to brawn. That's why I like Randall. He seems smart and down to earth, or earthy—like a thinking man." Her eyes seemed to poke Jake's skin. "Like I said, a worldly man, a man who reads, travels, and is in touch with himself." She bit her bottom lip, her eyes lighting up with amusement as her chin almost pointed at Jake.

What the hell was the inference there? *I read and travel. Damn straight...I'm in touch with myself, and as a matter of fact, sweetheart, I touched myself picturing you just this morning. I worldly-ed you into a shuddering orgasm— well, in my head. Fuck Randall Adams!*

"Sure, of course he's brilliant," Jake mumbled under his breath, then snapped his head up. "So do you like *any* sports?" He wanted to keep her standing there. At least she was talking to them, even if he was feeling a little beat-up. He liked looking at her, listening to the hint of Aussie in her accent, and he got a kick out of her sassy personality. Quite the contrast from the girls that swirled around him, giggling at his wisecracks, even the stupid ones. No, this girl wasn't looking for someone to make her world. It struck him that a rich football player genuinely may not be of interest to her. *Okay, Jake, be completely honest: She made it clear she hates that type.* Damn, he was surprised by how much that notion made him even more drawn to her.

"What your lot calls 'soccer' is fun to watch, but honestly, I really don't have time to get into watching other people being physical. I'd rather do it myself. Well, I need to run…literally." A small smile crossed her lips. "Heading to Town Lake. Perfect weather for a run, so I want to take advantage of it." Her eyes darted from Jordan to Jake. "Have a good workout. Remember: This time, more lifting, less chatting."

They laughed, then Jake quickly jumped in. "I run at Town Lake a lot. I usually take my dog, Dolly." This interjection seemed to come from nowhere, like throwing a ball up in the air with no hands available to catch it.

"Well, it's good to hear you have a companion. Hate to think you'd have to be out there alone." She winked. "Bye now." As she walked away, Jake was sure he heard a low chuckle again.

When she was out of earshot, Jordan made a grunting sound. "Ugh, brother, you are toast! Give it up. You know I don't usually think anyone's out of your league because you seem to be able to charm a freakin' snake. But this one? No way. Quick and drop-dead gorgeous. Clearly brilliant too—did you notice how she picked up on my smarts?"

"You're supposed to have my back. Remember, older brother, I only need one Dwayne giving me shit."

"I'm trying to protect you here. I'm telling you, brother. She's way above your paygrade. You don't stand a chance. Plus, she has no idea who pretty boy Jake Skyler is, and I'm not sure that's going to give you an advantage in this situation." He shook his head vigorously.

"Thanks, Dad, think I figured that out all by myself. Not sure how I tied my shoes before I met you."

Jordan roared. "Delilah says that all the time."

Jordan had been his big brother since Jake's freshman year at the University of Texas. He'd played a big part in quickly reminding the freshman's egotistical self that everyone else here *also* made the Texas team and that most of them had more experience than he did, so maybe he should stop being so cocksure and learn something. And as Jordan made sure Jake knew during summer training, he was just a backup freshman quarterback and probably wouldn't see much playing time, if any. Which proved true, especially his freshman year. He learned all too quickly that he had to make every minute he got on the field count.

It was UT's fourth game of the season. Jake had been sitting on the bench for the first three games, just happy to be there wearing burnt orange; it was all a dream for him. Then the starting quarterback tweaked his knee in the third quarter, and suddenly Jake was in. He never forgot the exhilaration and fear pumping through his veins when he ran onto the home field at Darrell K. Royal Stadium; a hundred thousand friends wearing burnt orange surrounding him, stomping their feet and cheering...for him.

He'd visited that stadium many times before with his dad, a UT alum. He'd always loved the walk through the parking lot, his dad stopping at a few tailgate gatherings to say hi to friends and get Jake a burger, grabbing a beer or two for himself. Jake always felt so big, so connected to his father at those games. When he got older, his dad would try to score extra tickets so Jake could bring a friend, and once or twice, they would leave his dad at a tailgate party, saying they had to go to the bathroom, leaving to sneak in their own beer or two. He figured his dad probably knew what they were up to, but he never said anything.

When Jake ran onto that field, he thought about his mom sitting in the stands. And even though he couldn't hear her yelling, "Dance, Jake! Dance!" He knew she was somewhere up there screaming it. She'd had no interest in going to UT games until Jake got a partial scholarship to play there. Now she'd declared burnt orange her favorite color and made sure they had season tickets, even pushed to go early because she liked the "American tailgate thing."

Jake took the snap, his feet started dancing, and he dropped back to pass. No one was open deep. Then he caught sight of the tight end cutting over the middle, just beyond the linebackers. He heard Coach Mark, his high school coach, ringing in his ears, *Remember son, this is a thinking man's game.* Jake hit the tight end in mid-stride—complete for nine yards! It wasn't a big, splashy play, but he did what Coach Mark told him to do in high school and remembered he was one of eleven. Relief washed over him, knowing he had at least moved the ball down the field.

The commentators raved: "Jake Skyler didn't run it, wow! Okay, so this freshman quarterback might have more than one trick up his sleeve." Another chimed in: "Isn't he known for his running game? Noticed he's got some dance moves," the commenter roared. And another added, "Yes, looks like Skyler is doing a little tap-dancing. Let's see what else he's got. Jake Skyler right out of Bowie High School, not too far from home, is he?" Jake remembered listening to the sports commentary, the men's voices bellowing throughout the stadium, over and over again and how his mom beamed because they'd noticed his feet, the way he moved like a dancer. *That line* made Jake wince, but he'd hear it repeatedly throughout his football career and would learn to love it because it made his mom proud. His dad and uncles had introduced him to the game, but it was his mom who helped differentiate him.

Next play, Jake took the snap, holding the ball as he danced back as if to pass. TCU's defensive line rushed. Jake's heart leapt into his throat, but time slowed, and he suddenly saw a hole down the middle. *Now, Jake!* His feet started moving, doing what he knew how to do best: run. Run, holding that sweet ball. Run, run. Then the sheer weight of body mass, grabbing, pulling as his legs fought to move forward. He was finally tackled after a seven-yard gain, first down. Coach signaled for him to come out, their senior quarterback ready to go back in. The burnt orange-clad crowd cheered, and he was pretty sure he could hear his name emanating from within the roar. He'd done his job and didn't screw it up. He let out a big sigh. UT's offensive line coach shouted, "Nice, Skyler!" as he walked off the field.

A few plays later, UT scored a touchdown. Jake couldn't help feeling partly responsible for the numbers on the scoreboard. The offensive line ran off, and the adrenaline rush permeated the sidelines. Jake felt a massive paw on his arm. "Damn straight, freshman!" He looked up at the mass of humanity standing beside him: Jordan Reyes, UT's best offensive lineman. Jordan was already a football phenomenon, though still in college. He was known not only for his football prowess, but for being a good guy and keeping a low profile.

"Thanks, man! Freaking scared as shit, but at least I didn't screw up," Jake said, looking up at the large legend whose chocolate eyes burst with amusement as he smiled down at Jake.

He sat beside Jake on the bench. "Didn't screw up? You rocked a window of opportunity. Keep doing that, keep your head in the game, and you'll skyrocket. I had your back on that run, and I'd be honored to block for you anytime, brother."

Jake's heart fluttered slightly at Jordan's humble words. "Dude, I need to be thanking *you*—I saw those beasts coming at me. I wanted to cry, if you know what I mean?" Jake spoke quietly.

Jordan let out a loud, guttural laugh, hitting Jake lightly on the back. "Sooo word of advice: don't tell that to anybody else." He looked at Jake and winked. "Some thoughts are better kept in here," he whispered, tapping Jake's helmet.

Jake knocked on Delilah and Jordan's door, excited to see the whole crew. They were his safe spot, after his own family. "Jake Skyler! Boy, get in here and give me a big hug," Delilah said, sounding like an old grandma but looking every bit as hot as she always did.

He gave her a big hug. "Ah, where's my girl?" he asked, looking up to see Jasmine running toward him. He was reminded how quickly time moves as he watched Jasmine, now almost three. It seemed like just yesterday that she was only a baby.

"Unc J! Unc J! Unc J!" Jasmine squealed.

"Jazzie!" Jake bent over and picked up his goddaughter. "Uncle J missed you so much," he said, kissing Jasmine's cheeks. "So much!" He lifted her in the air so that she was looking down at him. Jasmine giggled and stretched her arms out to Jake, so he brought her in close for another hug. He sniffed the air, and the Caribbean spices that he'd come to associate with Delilah's cooking filled his nose. "Something smells good, Delilah. Whatta we having?" He hoped for one of her delicious stews. He loved her fried plantains with fresh crushed avocados, a dish she always made for Jake, especially when he first got back in town.

"She's pulling out all the stops for you," Jordan said, handing Jake a cold beer. "Lots of spices…you'll be sweating up a storm before too long. Probably more than you did in the gym today." His hand landed on Jake's back.

Jake shot him a wide grin, nodding his chin. "Just trying to go slow so the retiree can keep up." Both men laughed, and Delilah rolled her eyes.

"Pepper-pot stew, roti, and of course plantains with avocado," Delilah said over her shoulder as she stirred the stew and let the aroma escape from the pot. "You'll be happy, Mr. Jake." She turned toward them, smiling, and once again, Jake was reminded how lucky and smart Jordan was to realize what an amazing person Delilah was and snag her. Jake had been a bystander to their love affair, with its many twists and turns. In the end, Jordan had retired from the Miami Dolphins, moving back to Austin after Delilah finished medical school. He'd said it was due to an injury, but Jake knew better.

Delilah had the kind of body you noticed mostly because there was a sensuality about her that she didn't seem to work for; it just naturally threaded into the way she moved. She had full, round hips, the base that led into her narrow upper torso, with defined arms and firm, medium-sized breasts. Her beautiful face could melt Jake even when he was super tense. Large, amber-colored eyes, a wide nose, full lips, and smooth mocha skin. When Jake first met her, she wore her hair long and straight, but after she got pregnant with Jasmine, Jordan had encouraged her to let her curls come out. She let it go and cut her hair to her shoulders. She usually wore a hairband to keep it away from her face, with the volume of tight curls rolling down the back of her head to her nape.

"I hear you've been out-leagued," Delilah teased Jake, who was still holding Jasmine.

Jake let out a huff. "Is that the way we're telling it, Jord? That's BS. I haven't even had a shot yet."

"Don't think you're gonna get a shot. Think she's already got your number."

"I just need a chance to show some Jake charm," he said, flashing his wide smile.

"Think she may be too smart for that."

"He's only saying that because she said Jordan's a better conversationalist than me. Now he's convinced she's a genius."

"Well, send her my way. I'll let her know you're both a coupla knuckleheads. Have to be honest, sounds like I'd like her. She's not eatin' up your crap, so that makes her smart in my eyes. You know I wasn't a big fan of that movie-star chick who was always gushing over you, posting pictures with all those love comments…that was nauseating." Delilah put her hands on her hips as she spoke, rolling her eyes.

Jake whipped his head toward her. "Yeah, right. She was *sooo* in love with me that she cheated on me, and now in her interviews she's saying the reason she got out was I was some kinky weirdo. That's rich, since she's the one who initiated anything close to kink…" He stopped himself, noticing Delilah's remonstrative look paired with a hand in the air.

"I know you'd never go public with details about your experiences, but I don't want to hear anything about you between the sheets, and she certainly doesn't need to." Delilah's head tilted toward Jasmine. "Jasmine, Uncle Jake's going to let you go check if your bear is ready to eat."

Jake lowered Jasmine, and she said, "Uncle J, do you want Teo to eat with you?"

"Absolutely. You know I love spending time with Teo," Jake said, smiling as Jasmine ran through the living room.

"Sorry, Jake, but I really don't want to spoil my appetite with all this talk about you and women, and I don't need Jasmine going to preschool talking about her famous uncle's love life. You know that girl hears and repeats everything." Delilah began taking pots off the stove. "Guys, make yourselves useful and set the table."

"I get it. Just makes me think I should listen to my sister and start having women sign NDAs before I get involved with them. Honestly, I'd never do anything a girl didn't agree with or want. I'm out here trying to change my reputation as a womanizer, and now Jessica's dropping hints about something that's not true. So what am I supposed to say? *Hey, that was in bed, and she liked being spanked?* Makes me sound like a bigger jerk."

Delilah squinted her eyes at him, her head cocked to the side. "Best keep your mouth shut, Jake. But an NDA? I know Jenae is a smart attorney, but I can tell you right now, if Jordan had asked me to sign some kinda NDA…"

"You and Jord are different, started dating when you were babies, well, still in college. Besides, what's there to reveal about Mr. Boy Scout?" Jake laughed, looking at Jordan's scowl.

Delilah raised her eyebrows, her voice taking on a seductive air. "Believe what you want. Some things are better left behind closed doors. And you know our story wasn't simple. We broke some rules, well especially in the college library stacks." She twisted her lips, remembering every hot detail of that make-up encounter.

"No more!' Jake protested, scrunching his face up. "Okay, how can I help?"

Delilah pointed to a pot. "Grab that, and—"

"Unc J! Unc J!" Jasmine yelled, running toward Jake with a very beat-up stuffed bear. *That bear's been loved a lot,* Jake thought as he bent down to pick her back up.

"Jordan, you're on your own with the table. Not putting my love down." Jake kissed Jasmine on the ear. She laughed before puckering her lips in an overexaggerated way, giving him a loud kiss on his cheek. "Oooh! See. If this girl loves me, I can't be all bad."

Delilah moved to put dishes on the table. "Not bad at all," she said. "But think about it—that girl at the gym is probably sick of guys coming up to her, trying to get her attention while she's just trying to work out."

"And Delilah would know. It still happens to her all the time. Should get her a T-shirt that reads, 'Married to a 300-pound ex-con.'" Jordan eyed Delilah up and down. "That's mine." He touched the side of her hip.

She swatted his hand away. "Let's eat," she said, scooting her chair back to sit as Jordan made sure Jasmine was secure in her booster chair.

Chapter Four

M att: *Leaving Houston now…be there in a few hours…***Send**
Rakell: *Can't wait to see you…drive safe…***Send**

Rakell had met Matt on an assignment in London. She'd been told a young Texas billionaire needed an escort for a royal engagement that he and his family were attending. It had to be someone who could handle herself well in elite social circles, someone well-versed in the arts, bright, and—of course—pretty. She would be his "girlfriend" for the weekend. He would pay maximum price for the full package: attending the royal event, spending two nights with him, and participating in the all-day activities at which his family would be present.

Rakell read through the paperwork for this assignment sent over by the agency. Every "girlfriend" experience came with specific guidelines: the backstory of how they'd "met" and other information about the client and the image they wished to portray. Matt's dossier dictated that she'd be acting like they'd met a month ago, when Matt had traveled to London for a gallery opening.

When Matt called her on her work number to chat about the details of their arrangement, he'd spoken eloquently and with a long Texas drawl. He introduced himself as Matthew Edward Waterman III. He described his family as a Houston oil family and asked Rakell if she knew what that meant, or if she had ever heard his family's name. She said no to both, so Matthew went on to explain. His family on his dad's side were from multi-generation oil wealth, "snobby Texas billionaires," in his words. His mother was raised in Denver, had an art history degree, and prided herself on her knowledge and taste in art and theater. Matt said his family had big hearts and wallets aimed at the arts. Because of their association with big oil, they had business and social contacts all over the world. Matt and his two sisters were required to attend a lot of swanky black-tie events. He told Rakell that the story he was telling his parents was that they'd met last month when he was in London and had hit it off, going on several dates in only a few short days.

Matt seemed to be jazzed that she was in her last year at the RADO and that she was fluent in Spanish and French and learning Russian. She assured him she knew several ballroom dances and would not embarrass him on the dance floor. He laughed. He told her about the hotel where they'd be staying and that she'd have her own room in their suite, which was not an unusual arrangement for an escort. Clients mostly wanted to show you off. Some paid to get off, but few actually wanted to get close. She was used to the routine by then and liked having her own bed. He let her know that he'd contacted one of the swankiest shops in London and that they were expecting her the next day to outfit her for the weekend. She would be expected to get her hair and makeup done both nights at the hotel salon, which had already been arranged.

As Matt spoke, he peppered her with questions about her life: her favorite food, plays, artists, authors, and her goals for the future. She started to feel excited and was looking forward to spending the weekend with him. She'd already seen a picture of him dressed in a tuxedo and black felt cowboy hat. Dark hair and a dark, thick mustache, grayish eyes to go along with his tall, lanky build. She learned that Matt, his parents' only son, had an undergraduate degree from Rice University and an MBA from Harvard. He'd founded a business consulting firm in Houston with a small branch in Austin. He encouraged her to share a few things with his parents throughout the weekend that would indicate they'd already gotten close.

She started to spit out her normal, completely fabricated history that she'd made up in conjunction with the staff at the agency: that she had been born in Sydney and graduated from high school with honors before finding her way to London to study English literature and

Russian. The Russian part was true, and the agency insisted she include that in her fabricated profile because their clientele appreciated escorts versed in other languages. But with Matt, she couldn't help being put at ease by his sweet drawl and the mild, non-demanding way he talked to her, so she felt inclined to give a more honest version of her history, only leaving out the tragedy that had shaped her.

He told her his father would be intrigued that she'd grown up on a ranch in Australia and could ride horses. "That alone might win him over, never mind your looks and brains. Oh, and in Texas, people— especially young people—refer to older people as 'ma'am' and 'sir.'" She hadn't known that and was glad Matt had told her. He explained that they should act affectionately but didn't need to be all over each other.

After she hung up, Rakell researched his family. They were indeed Texas aristocracy. She found tons of pictures of them in the society pages of newspapers in Dallas and Houston. Matthew was definitely good-looking and clearly wealthy, so she wondered why he even needed an escort. Unless, like a lot of rich men, he wanted arm candy and sex without the emotion. She had learned not to dislike that aspect of her clients. It was the reason she'd amassed a lot of money in her early twenties.

Matt and Rakell instantly connected. He was bright, caring, and easy to be around. The only mistake she made that weekend in London was calling him Matthew, which made his parents raise an eyebrow. His dad finally said, with a dry tone, "He hasn't been Matthew since he was born, except in the papers. He probably introduced himself to you that way 'cause you're a sophisticated Londoner." She tried to be mindful and remember to call him Matt after that. During the weekend, Matt complimented her continuously, kissed her on the cheek frequently, and gave her the most amazing long, deep hug when they parted. But although he paid for her as a "girlfriend" escort, he never touched her in a sexual way. The odd thing was his tenderness toward her and the way he really listened to her when she spoke, making her feel like she was important to him, not just a pretty face he'd hired. It drew her in, and she felt herself aching to be touched by him.

Just when she started to think maybe he wasn't attracted to her, he called her on her escort cell a week later and asked if she wanted to be his "girlfriend" on a ski trip to Switzerland the week before Christmas. He offered to increase her pay for giving up her holidays. She jumped on it. Neither of his sisters joined them on that trip, so they spent a lot of time just with his parents. They had a blast, and she was growing to genuinely enjoy his family. Family was a past concept to her, something she'd made herself stop longing for, but these slices of time with Matt's family felt as close to family as she'd had in years.

His dad was traditional, which he made clear after several glasses of Scotch. He explained that he wasn't upset that she and Matt were sleeping together. After all, Matt was almost thirty. But he hoped that they were at least exclusive. Matt assured his father they were and that he was treating Rakell with the utmost respect. Rakell felt rather uncomfortable during that conversation but wasn't sure how to broach it with Matt. After all, she really was just an escort to him. Typically, they had separate bedrooms, but during that vacation, they'd shared a bed. Matt would crawl into bed wearing pajama bottoms and a T-shirt. He'd say something like, "Thanks for today, Marietta, you were great— my parents truly love you," his tone oozing sincerity. Then he'd turn over facing the other direction, and soon she'd hear the constant of his deep breathing, letting her know he was asleep.

One night after he turned away, she put her arm around him only to feel his body stiffen. Slowly she pulled her arm away, turning the opposite way, barely sleeping, alone in a bed with another human being. Even though she typically had her own room, when they were going to share a bed, she'd pictured this differently. So she truly was just arm candy to Matt? He was probably used to the thin model type, she'd thought, lying still in the suffocating silence, her thoughts choking her. With most clients, she'd welcome the respite from having to pretend in bed, but with Matt, the longing that settled in made her feel empty, spending the night lying side by side with someone that didn't seem to want to be with her.

It wasn't until she met Matt and his family a couple months later in Washington, DC for an exclusive White House party that she would truly understand. His mother, Clarissa, had called Rakell (Marietta) and asked if she could send her measurements so they could have a gown made for the Presidential ball. Clarissa indicated that it would be waiting in DC when she got there. She also added that she and her husband, Matthew Edward II, were delighted to see Matt with such a well-educated, beautiful young woman. Rakell flew from London to DC for the three-day weekend. She was excited to see Matt, but there was something different about their interactions this time, something that confused her. She realized she wanted more from him. She wanted him to want her, which was something she never let herself feel with clients. Matt was different.

The night of the ball, they danced to several songs, only taking breaks to repeatedly have "one more" drink. Rakell had been to some over-the-top events, but there was something electrifying about being at the White House. Something that made her feel especially bold. While they danced, a tipsy Matt told her she really did look like a princess in her lavender dress covered in rhinestone flowers. From then on, he referred to her as "Princess." With his parents' approval, they left the party and went back to the hotel suite. They sat on the couch in front of the fire, Matt rubbing her aching feet.

"Marietta, I want you to know I think you're beautiful and fun to be with." He took another swig of his whiskey and she another swig of her Scotch. They were both drunk, which was one of the strict rules not to break as an escort, but with Matt, she felt safe. "You really are like a dream. I mean, your legs are from heaven, your eyes are like a fairy tale, your hair is like silk and—sorry—I even want to touch your breasts. God they are so beautiful." He sounded so serious, like he was contemplating something.

"Then touch them, please," she implored, looking at him.

He looked at her, his features tightening like he was fighting back a scream or a cry—in her inebriated state, she wasn't sure which. "If only it were that simple. Please know I think you're incredibly attractive, but I'm not…" He looked away from her. She saw a tear slide down his cheek. She scooted down the couch and sat in his lap, straddling him, her lavender Cinderella dress circling around them like a sparkly cloud.

"Hey, Matt." She moved in to kiss his lips before he gently pushed her away.

"Marietta, I'm not attracted to women. Believe me, if I was, you'd be *the one*." He smiled, but the tears started to roll. "I'm gay. Sorry…so sorry."

She gently wiped at Matt's eyes and hugged him, feeling his tears on her face as she held him, not letting him go even when he tried to move back. Then her own tears came out of nowhere. They were both drunk, sobbing and holding each other. But it wasn't the liquor making her feel desperate not to lose Matt in her life. Matt made it clear that he saw her; she wasn't just a piece of furniture designed to make a room look more beautiful. And she wanted him to know her, Rakell, not Marietta.

Finally, when the tears slowed, she arched back, holding his face in her hands, demanding he look her in the eyes. "Matt, you are one of the most beautiful people I've ever met. If you can't be my lover, I am requesting you be my brother." She lowered her forehead to his. "Deal, mate?" she asked before kissing his cheek.

Matt gave her a small nod, and she continued: "We'll last a lot longer as brother and sister than as lovers anyway, and I want you in my life forever." She leaned into his ear and whispered, "My real name is Rakell Marie McCarthy."

He tilted his head back, looking at her blinking. "You're not supposed to…"

Placing her fingers on his lips, she said, "Shh…you're my friend, my dear friend, not my client. Matt, I love that you see me, me, Rakell." She knew the strict agency rules. A client was never allowed to ask an escort's real name, and escorts were strictly forbidden from revealing their true identity. They were also discouraged from being in pictures posted on social media. In some cases, it couldn't be avoided, as in public events with clients, but those pictures could not appear on personal escort accounts.

That night, their branches started to intertwine with shared secrets, past pains, and dreams for the future. His struggle with his sexuality, knowing how disappointed his parents, or mostly father, would be. Rakell sharing about the fire that had taken her family's ranch in Australia, leading to her decision to get as far away from home as she could. A shared bond, resulting in an unceasing protective shield for each other. She opened up to Matt about her goals to move out of the escort world, increase her modeling gigs, hoping as she lost weight, which was a constant struggle, she could land better jobs and achieve her ultimate goal of acting. He smiled, and in typical Matt business fashion, he grabbed a pen and paper, making a list of her goals and then having Rakell detail the steps it would take to get there.

Besides Lana, her best friend in London, Rakell had never let herself speak about her father's death during the fire that took her family's ranch to anyone. Even when she told Lana, she'd said it with a neutral tone, ignoring Lana's pulled-in eyebrows, the strained empathetic look on her face as if she was experiencing it herself. She hated the perfunctory hug. She had to keep the emotion locked away.

It wasn't a few tears that she feared; it was the volcano, that if allowed to erupt, would scorch all the safety walls she'd built up over the years. Somehow, Matt became the moat of protection around the searing pain. When she let herself erupt, telling him the truth (how close she was to her father, his death, and her mother's scorn), when she unraveled, Matt's arms around her cooled the intensity of the wrenching ache in her heart when she didn't stop her brain from traveling back in time.

It was Matt's dad who suggested Rakell move to Texas and work at Matt's new Austin consulting firm, since the firm's focus was on energy companies throughout the world, and having someone as charming as Rakell—who could speak Russian, as well as other languages—would be an asset. His dad seemed to buy his son's story that Rakell had given a form of her middle name when she first met Matt to protect herself. He actually said, "That's one smart woman."

Matt proposed the idea to Rakell of moving to Texas and working very part-time at his firm, saying it might be a way for her to eventually leave the escort world, as well as have time to pursue more modeling gigs and auditions. He would get an apartment for them in Austin, but he'd stay in Houston most of the time. She'd be his pretend girlfriend, but she could continue seeing her clients in Europe. However, she had to agree that any dating she did in the US would be low-key, so as not to make Matt or his family look like fools.

When Matt first made the offer, laying out all the details, Rakell was reluctant, partly because it was an outrageous amount of money, but more importantly, it meant moving to Texas. Matt assured her that the money wasn't nearly enough to ask someone to give up a big portion of their life so that he could continue to live a lie. She researched Austin and thought about the fact that more and more modeling opportunities were coming her way—not to mention that her modeling agent, based in London, had sent head shots to several other agents in London, Los Angeles, New York, Paris, and Amsterdam hoping to land her more lucrative opportunities. Maybe Austin would be a good place to launch a new life. She wasn't going back to Australia, that was for sure. She rarely talked to her mom and had only been home once since she'd left. She knew how to pretend, and being Matt's girlfriend came with a lot of perks, namely spending more time around Matt.

Rakell wrapped her arms around Matt's neck. "Missed you! Seems like forever since you've been in Austin." She loved it when Matt came home to their shared apartment, even though she knew it was just for show. A calmness settled over Rakell; it always did when Matt was here.

"Missed you too, Princess," Matt said, kissing her cheek. "Let me put my stuff away, then we can figure out dinner." Matt carried his small suitcase and briefcase to his room.

Matt opened a bottle of white wine and poured a glass for himself and Rakell. Since Rakell only worked part-time at Matt's satellite office in Austin, they caught each other up on the week. He updated her with goings-on at the firm in Houston, and she told him about her new gym stalker. Matt rolled his eyes and said, "Another one? God, how do you stand it?"

They both laughed.

"Well, where do you want to go tonight?" he asked.

"I'm craving oysters—how about Eddie V's?"

"Sounds good, but since we don't have reservations on a Thursday, we may have to wait. So I might have a friend meet us there." He smiled at her.

"Oh, do tell."

"I met him at a club in Houston, but he's from Austin. Not sure where it's going. He's kind of young."

"How young?"

"Twenty-four."

"So!? You're only twenty-eight. That's not bad at all. Besides, I'm almost twenty-four, and look how mature *I* am." She winked and took another sip.

"That's exactly what I'm afraid of." He laughed and touched her chin.

"Hey! Okay, I'll go get ready."

Rakell walked out of her room almost an hour later in a short black wrap dress that tied in the front. The low-cut neckline showed just the edges of her black lace bra, which pushed her breasts up and center. She slipped on a pair of four-inch black pumps. Matt helped her fasten the clasp of a silver necklace adorned with a small drop of gemstones that slid into the crease of her healthy cleavage. She put on some simple silver hoop earrings to match. Her long hair rolled back from her face in loose waves, reminiscent of a modern Farah Fawcett look.

"Cleavage for days! Do I need to make sure I have my pistol with me?" Matt teased.

"Better watch your friend's eyes." She winked.

"Pretty sure his eyes are more interested in my pecs than yours," he said, smiling, looking at the text that popped up on his phone. "Is it okay if I drop you off a little early at Eddie V's for a drink and then go pick up Nate?"

"Sure, I can put our name in and buy time with a martini."

Chapter Five

Eddie V's in downtown Austin was alive with people chatting and laughing over jazz music that lingered seductively in the air. It felt so good to Rakell to be *out*. When she wasn't in Europe, she seldom left the apartment at night, unless Matt was in town. She often felt lonely but was committed to her goal of saving enough money to get out of the escort business. She only had to stick it out for a bit longer. She was using this year to set herself up to pursue her passion.

She loved the way this dress made her feel—sexy, bold, and very feminine. Just as she was pulling out a barstool to sit down, she heard a familiar male voice shout, "Hey! Hey!" She looked to her right, immediately recognizing the hot guy from the gym sitting with yet another buff dude. *Wow, this guy only surrounds himself with other meatheads*, she thought, looking his way and smiling. He started to get up, so she walked toward them, not wanting him to sit next to her.

"Oh, hi," she said as she approached him. He stood up from his stool, and she noticed that even though she was five-ten and in heels, he was still taller. He took a quick, not-so-subtle glance at her cleavage. She had to admit she loved it, having hoped that someone would notice.

He seemed visibly nervous, his eyes darting around as if trying to figure out what to say to her. "Wow… so, well…what are you doing here?" he stammered, his eyes moving up and down her body, quickly, but still not so subtly.

Rakell smiled, reveling in his obvious discomfort. *This is fun*, she thought, becoming acutely aware of her effect on him.

"Well," she said, her voice assuming a stronger accent than usual, "take a guess, mate. I'm not here to fuck spiders. Sooo—am I here to lift weights or drink?" She was surprised by the sarcasm lacing her tone. *Great. I'm reverting to my high school Aussie slang. This guy does not bring out the best in me.*

Jake grimaced, shaking his head and chuckling at the same time. The other guy laughed out loud. "Damn, girl. You know how to cut through it, don't you? I'm Dwayne, never mind this boy." Dwayne stood around six feet with black hair styled into short dreadlocks and facial hair that ran the border of his jaw, accented by large black animated eyes. He wore a permanent smirk on his face. "I'm not here to fuck spiders either."

Rakell smiled at him. "Sorry, just don't like to indulge obvious questions. 'Not here to fuck spiders' is just an Aussie way to say that. You know the kind. The questions you already know the answer to." Her green eyes landed on Jake's face as she raked her eye tooth over her lower lip.

Dwayne's eyes lit up listening to her. "I might have to steal the 'fuck spiders' line." Turning toward a less-than-amused Jake, Dwayne hit him on the arm lightly. "Schooled."

Jake shot Dwayne a slanted look before turning back to her. Damn, he knew this girl was pretty, but she looked insane right now. Plus, she had a brainy, sarcastic edge to her. Even if he was the target of her quick comebacks, he liked it. But he was squirming, scrambling to get a foot up in this situation. "Okay, fair enough. How about…what are you drinking? Can I buy you a drink?"

"That's two questions, mate," she said, holding up two fingers. "Though I'll acknowledge that the questions are improving." Her face broke into a huge smile, like she was trying not to laugh. "No, thank you. I'm meeting…"—she hesitated, not knowing how to say it—"someone. In about thirty minutes."

Jake heard, but blew by, the "someone" part and pressed, "Okay, well, that's long enough to have a drink. What are you having?" he asked again, standing and gesturing toward his stool for her to sit.

She nodded, mouthing *Thank you* as she scooted up on the stool.

He pressed, "Drink?"

"Vodka martini. Tito's please. Extra, extra dirty." She looked at Jake, her eyes wide. Marietta knew that it was time for a soft smile and furtive upward glance at her client as a silent thank you. But she didn't have much experience with flirting as Rakell, so she wasn't sure how to proceed in a natural way.

"Got it." He repeated the order to the bartender, thinking, *Of course she would order that, and of course her breasts are practically spilling out over the top of her dress, and of course she's meeting "someone" tonight, and of course Dwayne is here as my not-so-flattering wingman. Maybe I should order a few tequila shots.*

He started to hand her the very full martini, but she put her hand up and said, "Wait, can you steady it so I can slurp off the top sip?" An amused sultriness infused her tone.

He and Dwayne quickly found each other's eyes, trading a look before they focused on her as she slowly bent toward Jake's hand, arching her back slightly so the tops of her breasts were on full display as her lips seductively opened.

Jake's eyes recorded every minuscule second of her plump, glossy lips meeting the edge of the glass, then her eyelids fluttered upward as her catlike eyes sported an *I got you* look, obviously reveling in Jake's surprised expression as she loudly slurped the liquid into her mouth.

From deep in his throat, a guttural "daaamn" rumbled out. Jake flexed his arm muscles, willing himself not to drop the glass.

Her big green eyes challenging him, she asked, "Did you say something or just grunt?"

"Mmm…humorous, aren't you?" he threw out on a heavy breath. Fuck, she knew what she was doing to him, probably knew exactly what he was visualizing as her plump lips touched the glass, followed by the loud slurping sound. Yep, he could definitely picture her hot mouth all over his cock.

As she stood, she murmured, "Thank you. Now I know I won't spill." A not-so-innocent smile curved her lips. Reaching for the glass, her long fingers grazing Jake's. He willed his hand to open, releasing it to her.

The whole thing seemed like foreplay to Jake. And goddammit, did he ever have something he'd like to feed her, keep that mouth occupied, maybe shut her smart ass up. Grab a fistful of that hair, guide her head back and forth while watching her mouth engulf his cock. Oh yeah, he could picture it! He shuddered. *Jesus, Jake, stop,* he reprimanded himself as he steered his thoughts away from her lips, her cleavage, her hair, and what it would be like to touch her.

"Damn, you know how to tackle a martini, don't you?" Dwayne said, grinning from ear to ear, the whites of his eyes growing bigger as he raised his eyebrows, mouthing *Wow* to Jake.

Jake tried to shake off what he'd just witnessed, subtly shifting his legs as he silently told his cock to give it up. "So I never got your name." Jake looked at her face, hoping for a little inroad, begging his weak self for some modicum of control so he didn't seem like a bumbling fool. God, it had been years since he'd felt so discombobulated by a woman. Wasn't he the one that made women swoon? Made them forget their words as they tried to steady their nerves?

"That's because I didn't give it to you." Her chin tilted toward him. "Got a bit of a creepy stalker vibe from you." Her eyes shifted to Dwayne, who was chuckling. "Is Jacob here a stalker? Be honest," she chided, purposely using the wrong name again and having a hard time stifling her own laugh as she continued to poke at him.

Jake shook his head. "It's *Jake*. Jake." He tried to sound calm, like it didn't bother him. He kept getting the feeling she was fucking with him.

"That's right, how could I forget?" she exclaimed, theatrically placing her hand on the upper part of her cleavage. "I'll try harder. Well, Dwayne, is your friend here a creepy stalker? Because I saw him doing the outer-thigh machine at the gym, and I'm pretty sure only creepy stalker guys do that so they can stare at the women around them doing the inner-thigh machine."

Jake had the feeling he'd regret that ridiculous move for a long, long time.

Dwayne smiled up at Jake, who was standing between him and Rakell.

Jake squinted his eyes, slicing him with a death glare.

"No, not a stalker. Just not a lot of experience with women, so he may seem clumsy. Be gentle on him, okay? He's kinda fragile." Dwayne gently touched Jake's arm before Jake swatted him away.

Rakell laughed, her chin rising up as she threw her head back. Jake couldn't help but catch the trail of honeyed skin going from her chin down her long neck and spilling into the mounds of flesh pushed together. His eyes dropped to her breasts. That image would stay with him. He caught himself, attempting a forced laugh to mask his irritation with Dwayne.

"Dwayne here is not my best wingman," Jake said, trying to sound lighthearted but thinking he'd like to strangle Dwayne later. On the field, he was the best wide receiver out there. Off the field, though, he sucked ass.

"So do you *have* a name, or were you sent from another planet to straighten my man Jake out, take him down a notch or two? Because I can definitely see someone upstairs"—Dwayne looked up to the ceiling—"wanting to see that happen."

"I'm Rakell," she said, extending her hand toward Dwayne while tossing Jake a smile. "Definitely not here to reform your friend."

Rakell touched Jake's upper arm, gently squeezing his bicep. He held his breath for a few seconds as her hand ran down the length of his arm and stopped at his wrist. "Don't have the time or energy to fix a man," she said, lightly squeezing his wrist before her hand dropped away.

Reflexively, Jake shut his eyes, then quickly opened them. Her touch seemed to snake down his chest, working its way between his legs. He shifted his stance, hoping nothing was showing. "*Rae*-kale. Pretty name."

She smirked, caught off guard by the way he drawled her name out. "Ra*kell*," she repeated.

The side of his mouth shot up. "Got it. *Rae*-kale."

Dwayne shook his head. "Rakell, Jake here struggles with English. He speaks Texlish, some combo of Texan and English. It's hard to adjust to, but eventually, you learn to decipher it."

Rolling his eyes, Jake moved to the bar behind her and ordered them all another round. He leaned into Dwayne, handing him his drink. "Here you go, jerk, an oleander mule. I'm going to miss you," he growled under his breath. Then he steadied the new martini in front of Rakell.

She looked up at him. "Really, I have to go, so you shouldn't have—"

"Take it with you. I don't care where you drink it," he said, an edge to his voice, anxious lust threading his tone. "Do you want to slurp off the top?" he asked, his mouth tight, his blue eyes taunting her. Purposefully sliding his gaze from her green eyes—which were outlined in a thin black liner and black mascara, giving them an almost cat-like look—then gradually inching down her neck to the drop necklace embedded in the top of her cleavage. "Nice necklace," he commented, his tone coarse. He stared back at her wide eyes, meeting her surprised stare with a wicked look. "Waiting...go ahead and slurp it," he repeated, a slight demand in his voice. "Don't want you to spill a drop, making sure it all ends up down your throat." His voice dropped an octave as he inched the glass closer to her. *Let's go, sweetheart. Two can play this game.* "Whenever you're ready, bend forward. Now that I know what to expect, I'll steady it even more firmly." His eyes bore into her as she looked up at him nervously.

"Jeepers," he heard Dwayne whisper just before he drew in an audible breath. Jake didn't look his way, instead digging his gaze into hers, letting her know that he was controlling this show now.

His intensity pricked the surface of her skin. She could feel herself losing the control she'd had. "Yes, yes," she said between a couple of forced breaths before slowly bending her head to slurp the top liquid out of the martini glass, her eyes caught on his fingers holding the stem. Then the visual converted to the sensory input of those same fingers working her wet folds. *Oh God.* Her chest moved up and down just a little more than it had been. Her head popped up as she cleared her throat, squeezing her thighs together.

Jake twerked his lips, raising an eyebrow, not moving his eyes off her. *Gotcha, sweetheart.*

"Damn, that was hot." Dwayne's comment cut through the tension. "Who are you meeting here tonight?"

"A friend," she said, her voice tremulous, again unsure of what to say.

"A guy?" Dwayne looked at Jake, who was unabashedly staring at Rakell.

She could sense his eyes on her profile. "Yes—two," she said weakly.

"Damn...two. Jake and I are up for that anytime." He grinned before he felt Jake's smack on his arm. "Hey," he jolted, his eyes narrowing on Jake.

Rakell laughed, thankful for the levity. "Not sure you guys could handle it," she said, winking. Just then, she caught sight of Matt and his friend walking by the window to the front door. "Oh, sorry—I do have to go." Grabbing her purse in one hand and her drink in the other, she placed a foot on the floor, shifting forward on the stool.

Jake cupped her elbow, steadying her as she slid off the stool. She couldn't help but absorb the strength in his hand, a power she knew wound up his arms, through his torso and permeated the muscles of his long legs. "Ahh...thank...I..." She sucked in quickly.

"Thanks for hanging with us," he stated graciously, absorbing the nervous expression that suddenly washed across her face. He'd broken through that smart-ass façade, hadn't he? A Cheshire cat grin sprang to his lips.

"Um, yeah. Thanks for the conversation," she said, tossing Dwayne a glance. He smiled back. "And for the drinks." She held the martini glass up to Jake. "I owe you." Her tongue slid over her right eye tooth, teasing the tip.

Was it a nervous or seductive gesture? Jake couldn't tell.

She stood up straight, taking a couple steps past Jake.

"Yeah...you do," Jake drawled out in a low, gruff tone, turning to watch her hips swivel past him.

She glanced back, not sure what he'd said, but it sounded dirty to her. His commanding voice had registered between her legs as his stare, heavy, hung on her. Quickly she turned her head away from his blue-eyed, almost invasive, gaze.

She steadied herself against the heavy ache consuming her pelvis before greeting Matt. He introduced her to Nate, then they followed the hostess to their table. Thankfully, they didn't have to walk by Jake and Dwayne. During the dinner, Nate could hardly keep his hands off Matt, even though Matt sat beside Rakell.

As another oyster slid down her throat, her mind clung to the imprint of Jake, his penetrating eyes, his husky voice, and his powerful form. Between bites of seared tuna, Rakell told them about the guy at the gym, and another guy from Dallas with whom she'd had a couple dates, but it wasn't really clicking. Nate took a bite of sea bass, then teased her, making it clear she wouldn't click with someone until they jumped between the sheets. She nodded, agreeing with Nate, ignoring Matt's cautionary look. She knew Matt's story—*Rakell's like a sister to me*—and felt sure he wouldn't break out into big-brother lecture mode in front of Nate, a guy he barely knew.

The truth was that she wasn't really looking for a relationship. She just wanted to get some experience flirting and dating. And maybe some authentic sex, not interactions where she was only pretending to be into something. Anything deeper, she knew, was not an option. Other escorts shared horror stories of trying to simultaneously work in the escort business and engage in a serious relationship. Most of the time, it ended disastrously. Most escorts gave up on the emotional aspects of dating altogether. Most guys weren't going to accept that the way you made money was by being some rich guy's plaything.

Dwayne looked at Jake, who was staring at him, clearly pissed but slightly amused.

He realized that having Dwayne along had probably helped lighten things up.

"We gotta debrief on that," Dwayne said.

Yeah, Jake needed to debrief. Debrief in bed with his hand wrapped around his cock.

Dwayne continued, "Dude, I'm telling you right now. Stay away from the flame, far, far away. Damn, that is way-waaay too hot—you'll get burned. I'm afraid *for* you, brother, because I can tell you're already drawn in. Like a butterfly…I mean moth to a flame. Yikes."

"Got it! Enough," Jake said, wanting to disagree with Dwayne but knowing that there was a lot of truth to his words.

Dwayne knew him. They were like troubled brothers when it came to women. They'd first met in Jake's senior year in college (Dwayne's junior year), in Miami, when UT played Missouri Bluff University at the Mojito Bowl, sponsored by the largest rum company in Florida. Their worlds had intertwined with a weekend Miami tryst involving two girls from Brazil nearly ten years older than them. Jake always knew he wanted to play ball with Dwayne after that bowl game. Even if they had been rivals, watching Dwayne from the sidelines was like getting a glimpse of a god among mere mortals. He'd never witnessed anyone with such an instinctive sense of where a flying football would go. Combine that with sticky fingers, and you had an all-star wide receiver.

When Dwayne graduated, Jake was stuck in the shadows as a backup quarterback in Seattle, and Dwayne ended up in Buffalo, NY. They stayed in contact, Dwayne visiting Jake in Austin during the off-season, sprinkling in a few Miami and Vegas trips.

Dwayne grabbed Jake's forearms. "Just saying, she's not a get-over-Jessica kind of girl. I can tell there's a lot there." He dropped his serious tone. "But heh, she did perk up when I floated the idea of both of us…"

Yanking his arm away from Dwayne, Jake said, "Bullshit, Dwayne, she's just quick. Anyway, this is not one of those situations…not looking for that kinda fun right now. I'm trying to behave myself."

Back at the apartment, Rakell drank some sparkling water to offset the alcohol during a brief conversation with Matt and Nate. She then excused herself to bed, clearly a third wheel in the "after dinner" plans. In her room, she turned on her air purifier. It acted as white noise to block sound. She was too horny to listen to the sounds of their physical tryst. She ached to get herself off, thinking about his blue eyes, hard biceps, and God, whatever he'd said to her when she walked by. She wanted to lie in bed picturing what could be next with that cocky meathead.

Jake declined Dwayne's offer to go to another bar, explaining that he'd started drinking earlier so he needed to get home before he couldn't drive anymore. He just wanted to get home and get off. The vision of Rakell in that form-fitting, cleavage-baring dress with those big green eyes looking up at him as she seductively put her mouth on the edge of the glass and unabashedly slurped the first gulp of martini while he was barely able to steady the damn glass was searing in his brain. His cock loved it and begged him to imagine what would be next.

Chapter Six

Jake figured out Rakell's gym schedule and tailored his own to match. On days that Jordan or Dwayne weren't available, Jake would go twice. Jordan told him he'd lost his mind, and he agreed. He was still going out with friends and had had a couple of dates during the past few weeks, but he became increasingly focused on seeing and talking to Rakell, which Jordan and Dwayne noted was becoming an unattainable obsession. Dwayne had suggested more than once that it might be time to let her know that he was Jake Skyler, NFL quarterback, but Jake had a sense that would be the wrong move.

Jake signed up for Pilates class on Tuesday and Thursday mornings, knowing that was when Rakell would attend. But he wasn't prepared for the torture of Pilates or for the teacher, Olga. She made him bend in ways he didn't know were possible and contract muscles he was pretty sure didn't exist. Olga was a drill sergeant like no other.

Fuck Pilates, she should coach an NFL team, Jake thought as her finger poked his flesh.

"You're not in your core. If you were, your butt would be smiling, right here at the crease," she barked, her index finger digging into his upper leg just centimeters from his ass. "Make it smile!"

"Okay, got it," he murmured, trying to ignore the giggles of the women in the class.

His goal was to watch Rakell, but the mental and physical energy it took for him to get through the classes made it almost impossible to even glance her way. When he could, she either wasn't looking at him or was literally rolling her eyes. A few times, he could tell that Olga and Rakell were exchanging looks as he struggled to figure out a move on the reformer, which to Jake looked like some kind of S&M torture machine.

Rakell watched Jake walk out of the Pilates class, a defeated look on his face. She had stayed back to let Olga know when she would be out of town and when she'd be back. She pushed through the double doors leading to the main part of the gym and walked past Dwayne and Jake, who were both huddled around the T-bar. Dwayne waved just as Jake turned his head, his grin growing as he caught her small wave in their direction. His smile penetrated her as he said her name in a hushed shout, gesturing her toward them.

"You two working out or gossiping?" she said with a wink.

Dwayne chuckled. "Neither. I was just telling Jake here that this Pilates thing is bullshit. When you're doing things called 'downward dog' on a machine that moves, you're gonna get hurt. If he hurts himself, then what good will he be to the world?" He laughed loudly, shaking his head. He wanted to shout, *The dude is an NFL quarterback, go out with him already, will you!* But Jake had made it clear he didn't want her knowing yet. Dwayne shook his head, marveling at Jake's stupidity.

Crossing her arms just below her breasts, she said, "Well, it's not bullshit. It's actually really good for you. Especially good for core strength, which helps with lifting. But Jake, you have to actually pay attention *to the Pilates*."

"I do." Jake jumped in. "It's not that I'm scared I'm going to hurt myself, but shit, that woman is tough. Not sure if she makes everybody feel this way, but I kinda leave the class feeling like I have an IQ of a frog. The way she calls out my name with her German accent and says, 'Jake! I can tell you are not in your core, you are not paying attention!' Jeez, give a guy a break."

Rakell let out a snort, quickly covering her mouth.

Jake's face pinched up. "Hey, not funny. She should try to be a little more supportive."

Rakell's eyes darted to Dwayne, and they both burst out laughing.

"What?" Jake retorted.

"Dude, you're whining. Shut up," Dwayne said, amused at how childish his usually confident friend sounded. Dwayne shot Jake a big-eyed, eyebrow-raised look, indicating that Jake sounded less than impressive in front of the girl he was chasing. "Seriously, you sound like a kindergartner on a T-ball team—or better yet, the *mom* of a boy on a T-ball team who wants to make sure her baby feels good about his nonexistent skills."

"Shut up! I'm just making the point that I *do* pay attention. Maybe the sadist teaching the class could cut me a little slack."

Rakell crested her head, giving him an admonishing look as if to say, *You're not fooling anyone.* "Let me rephrase, mate: you need to pay attention to your *own* body and what it's doing, not the bodies of others in the class. And for the record, Olga is Polish." She spread her legs slightly, taking an authoritative stance.

"Hey!" Jake protested in the midst of Dwayne's laughter. He had the fleeting thought that he didn't have a clue how old Rakell was. Sometimes she seemed almost child-like the way she toyed with them. Yet now, with her arms crossed and her face stern, she appeared older and more mature.

"Rakell," Dwayne said, grinning, "can you do us all a favor?"

"Mmm?" Her eyebrow twitched up.

"Dwayne..." Jake warned.

Dwayne pressed, ignoring Jake's narrowing eyes and jutted jaw. "Go out with him already. Have dinner, then dump him, so we can all move on, so he can stop this Pilates bullshit."

Jake squeezed his eyes and shook his head, wishing he could grab Dwayne's neck and squeeze hard for about two minutes. Quickly, he opened his eyes to take in her reaction.

She grimaced, her arms unfolding and dropping to her side. "He hasn't asked me. Was I supposed to just guess that the gym stalker wanted to take me to dinner? And by the look on his face, it seems..."

Dwayne's hand shot up. "Believe me, all he does—"

Jake stepped toward her. "Shut up, Dwayne," he growled before rearranging the features of his face into a casual smile. "Okay, not how I was planning on doing this..." he started, catching the confusion on her face. "But Dwayne's right. I've been wanting to ask you out."

Her shoulders went up. "Then why didn't you?"

"Cause I wasn't sure you'd say yes?" His face fell, vulnerability edging in. Something he hadn't felt around a woman in a long time.

"So dinner?" she asked, a thick feeling settling in her lungs and making it hard to breathe. "Just dinner?" She blinked.

He nearly blurted out, *Unless you want more,* as a joke, but he picked up on the hesitancy in her expression. "Yeah, would you like to go to dinner with me? Just dinner." He repeated the original request, unsure of her reaction. It was as if there was something threatening about his offer.

His voice sounded strangled, an air of guilt to it that he hadn't intended. Of course, he wanted more, but he made a practice of waiting, adopting the three-date rule Jordan had drilled into him after Jake's second year in the NFL. He wasn't always successful, especially when a woman pushed, but he tried.

Dwayne cleared his throat. "Jeez, I can go with you if he freaks you out that much. Dinner, that's all. Not like he's expecting a favor after." His fingers formed quotation marks as he chuckled the word *favor.*

She whipped her head toward Dwayne, her cheeks suddenly flushed. "It would take a hell of a lot more than that," she spat out as she turned to leave, her breathing ragged, striding away as if she'd been spooked.

Dwayne's eyes sheepishly glazed over to Jake, who stood motionless, stunned. "Dude, that was…shit, sorry…I was just…"

"Enough," Jake hushed, shutting his eyes then slowly lifting his lids, trying to absorb what just happened. *What just happened?*

"Sorry," Dwayne said again cautiously. "I didn't mean…shit."

"I know, wow. That was…" Jake murmured, his eyes bouncing in the direction she had marched off. He was pretty sure she'd turned the corner and headed to the treadmills.

"Damaged," Dwayne whispered. "Not saying she is, but…"

Jake exhaled, scrambling to figure out a way to fix this. "I know. Seems like someone must've done something to her."

Dwayne touched his arm. "You don't do well with damage, man. You don't have the energy or time."

"Hey," he said, stepping back, his eyes dropping over his friend. "I think I actually care what she thinks of me and like really care if she's okay. I'll be back. I need to talk to her."

"Okay, tell her I'm sorry. I was just…"

"Got it," Jake said before turning his torso in the direction she'd gone.

Rakell stepped onto the treadmill, rubbing her temples and regaining her composure. The shock that vibrated inside her chest was at her own biting reaction to Dwayne's joke. Something she'd buried had emerged, seemingly out of nowhere. She shook her head, embarrassed and stunned by the way she had reacted. She pushed the speed button to "walk."

After nearly eight months in Austin, she'd started to entertain dating, experimenting with who Rakell was with men, but only for fun. She hadn't planned on feeling so attracted to someone she'd just met, some random guy from the gym. Jake's potency was not lost on her. Her body registered him at a primal level she'd never experienced before. She decided it would be best to stay away. She didn't quite trust herself around him.

"Hey, you," came his low, husky voice, sprinkled with compassion, from behind her. She turned to see him walking toward the treadmill. His steps seemed too robotic, as if he had to think about how to place his feet as he approached.

She winced self-consciously before forcing a stiff smile to her lips, willing the heat to leave her cheeks. Nothing came out of her mouth as she searched for something to say.

He cocked his head. "The correct response to 'hey you' is 'yeah you,'" he said, smiling, trying to suck the tension out of the air.

She raised her eyebrows, grateful that he'd infused a lightness into his voice. "So is that another version of the Texlish 'Hi y'all, hi back at all y'all'?" she said, trying to imitate his Texas drawl.

"Wow, you're a quick study," he said, moving in front of the treadmill. Because of the height of the machine, they were eye to eye, and his cobalt blue eyes flowed over her, catching for a second on her chest then scooting up, landing solidly on her face. He cleared his throat. "So I wanted to apologize for how that went down."

Rakell shook her head. "No, me. I'm sorry. I just overreacted." Her casual tone sounded a little forced. "It wasn't a big deal."

"Nah, it wasn't cool. Dwayne got carried away. He wanted you to know that—"

"Can we not?" she said ruefully. "I'm over it." Again, she forced a smile.

He cocked his head, trying to keep his face impassive, confused by her brush-off. He made a concerted effort to breathe a light air into his voice. "So then, back to dinner with no strings?"

He smiled so big it pierced her, and she drew a breath. "Um, Jake? I just learned your name…"

He wrinkled his nose, still smiling. "Nope, you just *remembered* my name. Finally. Which is a solid start."

She laughed as the heaviness dissipated into a mellow vibe between them.

"So, dinner?" he prodded again gently.

"I'm really not in the market to—"

"Eat?"

She shook her head, smiling. "I mean, the whole dating thing."

"Umm…you seeing someone?"

"No, not really, just starting to date. But…"

What kind of answer is 'not really'? Are you or not? 'Just starting to date'? What? Her convoluted answer ricocheted in his head.

Registering the bewildered look on his face, she blurted out playfully, "Do you always ask so many questions?"

He caught himself, masking his confusion with a small grin as he nodded. "Yep, pretty much my only flaw. So if you agree to dinner, we can set a limit on the number of questions I'm allowed to ask. Deal?"

"That's a given. Not sure I could last through an interrogation dinner." As her eyes took in his taut, muscular frame leaning toward her, she wanted to add *or get through dinner with all of our clothes on.* She kept walking slowly on the treadmill, wondering if she should just tell him she traveled a lot for work and would be gone for a week—oh, shit, and by the way, she was an escort. She shook the thought from her head.

"So—we're on?" He inquired, his tone laced with trepidation but trying to push past it.

"Let me think on it."

Jake registered her conciliatory tone as a nice way to let him down.

He swallowed a flash of irritation, unaccustomed to begging. "Fair enough," he said thickly. "You know where to find me." He searched his brain for something to say to shift back to casual, as if the letdown didn't burn. He tapped his hand on the front panel of the treadmill. "Gotta eat, so might as well have company." He forced his lips up in a contrived smile, turning, then letting it drop.

His brain began replaying the earlier scene, her insistence on *just dinner*, her fierce reaction to Dwayne's joke. He started to speculate on what the hell her story was, wondering if he really wanted to know. Dwayne was right. He was drawn to her in a way he didn't feel in control of, and that scared the shit out of him. But there was an equal amount of intrigue that made it impossible for him to get her out of his mind.

Chapter Seven

When Rakell emerged from Pilates, Jake was already doing crunches on the decline bench. She greeted him with a friendly, "Hey, Stalker Jake," a greeting she made up on the spot. She came to stand over him, noticing his eyes were closed in concentration. But she wanted to get his attention, maybe ask him casually what he'd done last night. She'd caught a glimpse of him at the grocery store, and he wasn't alone—he'd been with a cute brunette.

He knew who it was by the citrusy smell. "Can we just keep it to 'hot stalker'?" He stood, smiling. "Tough workout? Honestly, I had no idea the torture I was getting into when I signed up with Olga."

"Yes, Olga is the toughest, but she's the best teacher. So at least you're learning things the right way. She won't let students move to the next level unless they show competency. And it really will tighten and help stabilize your core." As she spoke, she touched his upper abdomen with her right hand. Jeez, she couldn't believe how rock hard his stomach was; he probably didn't really need to worry about his core, she thought, pulling her hand away.

"I've been meaning to ask, so what was all that about 'this is working on your Kegel muscles'? I wanted to pipe in and let her know there were a couple guys in the class, and we have different equipment," he said, winking.

A giggle left her mouth, and she quickly cupped her hand over it. "Olga would have ripped you apart. Jake, not sure how much you know about anatomy, but you, yes *you*, big guy"—she pushed on his chest with her pointer finger—"have a pelvic floor, so you, yes *you*, have muscles that control peeing and your erection, so consider working them out before you're an old man popping Viagra…"

"What the hell. Of course, I know that," he said puffing his chest out. This girl was challenging his future manhood…what the fuck? He raised his eyebrows, teasing her. "So what makes you such an expert on male anatomy?"

Her finger dug into his breastbone. "I took high school biology, so I can read a diagram. You should try it." She spread the fingers of her hand on his chest.

Jake sucked in a quick breath as his stomach tightened from her touch. "Just so you know, I'm pretty sure my future wife will be happy *well* into old age."

Rolling her eyes, she said, "Not if you don't learn anatomy."

He bit down on his bottom lip, the corners of his mouth pulling up, fighting like hell not to give it to her, but a quick bark of laughter escaped his mouth.

She tossed him an exaggerated wink. "Just watching out for your future wife," she said through a laugh, her hand pushing into his chest. Her fingers trailed from his breastbone to his stomach before she pulled them away.

More, more, please…was all he could think.

"Sure, okay." He wanted to add *smartass* but thought better of it. "So what's next on your workout agenda?"

"Legs, probably squats, leg extensions, and hamstrings. I have to travel to Europe tomorrow, and doing legs the day before a long flight makes me feel better. I don't know, more grounded."

"Europe? Vacation?" he asked.

"No, work."

"Oh, that's cool. What do you do?"

"Business consultant as an interpreter," she answered, her eyes moving off him.

"I'd like to hear more…" Her responses did not invite further questions. Shit, this was like playing a close game in a torrential downpour; you couldn't move because you couldn't see what was ahead, and the rain was dragging you to the ground.

She twisted her body, turning away from him. "Well, I'd better get to this."

"Hey, I'm doing legs, too. Wanna work out together? I could give you a few pointers."

Really?! You don't even know anatomy, she wanted to say. "Nope, that's okay—don't really need pointers." Rakell turned and started to walk toward the Smith machine to do squats. She'd spent the past four years pretending that men knew more than she did, but she got paid to do that. He wasn't paying, so she wasn't willing to indulge him.

"Hey." He walked after her. "How about just a partner, someone to spot? I didn't mean to insinuate that—I mean—"

"That you know more than me? Good, don't," she said pointedly as he walked behind her.

Jake caught up with her as she got to the Smith machine, which was situated in front of a large wall of mirrors. He held up his hands in a placating manner. "Hey, you."

"Yeah, you?" She turned, twisting her mouth, almost smiling.

His hands were still up. "I'm sorry, really. Just trying to be—"

"Helpful? Okay, we can work out together, but I don't need or want your help." Her smile flattened.

"Got it." *God, she's tough*, he thought. He felt like he was constantly mis-stepping with her. He'd never had to monitor himself so closely with any other woman.

He asked her how much weight she usually used and then loaded up the bar. She got in position and started to squat. As he watched her, he knew he could give her some pointers that would help protect her back, but he bit his tongue during her first set.

Jake then loaded up the bar for his own set. While he did his squats, Rakell couldn't help but stare at his muscular form. His legs were so powerful. *They grow them big in America*, she thought. *Must be all the meat.*

Jake and his friends were built differently than European men. European men were, in general, narrower. They were still muscular but lean, like the builds seen in bikers or runners. She'd never been near this much muscular power in one body, and there was a part of her that wanted to touch it, explore what was beneath that T-shirt and shorts. God, that was exactly what she needed to stay away from. She couldn't get drawn into anyone right now, and she wasn't sure he was the kind of guy who she could just have some physical fun with and move on.

"Hey," he said, waving his hand after he finished taking weights off the bar. "You're up."

"Oh, yeah—okay," she said, bringing herself back to focus. She approached the bar and bent underneath, centering it on her upper back. When she looked at him, she saw that he was staring at her with a concerned look on his face. "What? Why are you looking at me like that? Am I doing something wrong?"

"I said I wouldn't interject, but I kind of know what I'm doing when it comes to lifting. The way you have your hips and legs positioned could hurt your back. That's all."

Rakell blew out a sigh, remembering that she'd tweaked her back a few months ago, costing her two days in bed, and then said, "Well, I don't want to hurt my back" with contrition in her tone.

She saw him move behind her as she looked in the mirror. "I'll go down with you and guide you." She couldn't help registering the coach-like way he spoke, reminding her of her father giving her volleyball pointers when she was in high school. She clenched her jaw, willing the memory of her father away.

"Make sure you keep your feet out a little more, at shoulder width, with the tips of your toes angled slightly outward. It's important to keep your core tight so you alleviate pressure on your lower back. Okay?" During this explanation, his hand rested on her lower back, distracting her from fully listening.

Her skin tingled from his touch, her flesh tightening around it, making it hard to concentrate. "Ah, huh," she said, stilling her voice, trying to imagine he was just a trainer and not the guy she was picturing when she got herself off at night.

Rakell watched in the mirror as Jake placed his legs on either side of her just behind her legs, his large hands on the side of her hips, with his thumb behind her hipbones and his long fingers wrapping around the fronts. She steadied her breath, wanting to tell him to get his hands off her, at the same time loving the feel of the stabilizing power in his hands.

"Let's go down together, and I'll steer your hips so you can feel what you need to do. Okay, ready?"

"Yep." First stabilizing the bar on her shoulders, she bent her knees, moving her hips back and squatting slowly, concentrating so she could show him she knew what she was doing. She tried not to look at him in the mirror squatting behind her. As she went down, he went down. When she stood, he stood, never taking his firm grip from her hips. She'd never paid this much attention to her form before, her body aware of every muscle, every nerve, every move.

After her set, he asked her if she felt the difference. He explained that she'd have to mentally adjust to the proper mechanics as her body had grown used to her improper form.

"Our bodies develop routine motor plans," he explained. "You can change it, reteach your muscles, but it takes a lot of mental focus and practice." He began to load weights on the bar for his set.

As Jake completed his set, he verbally walked Rakell through his body mechanics, explaining that sometimes feeling it and then seeing it helped. He was clearly knowledgeable about lifting, body mechanics, muscles, and how to reteach the body. She was impressed and wondered if he were a trainer, though she'd never seen him working with anyone. *Guess I should rethink his knowledge of anatomy.*

Jake did the remaining sets with her, once again standing behind her and holding her hips. She was focused and serious, intent on maintaining proper form. By the time they got to the last set, the sensation of his skin brushing against her, leg to leg, had become almost unbearable. Whenever their legs touched, Jake would try to adjust his, but not before she registered the sensation, which licked at her thighs before traveling up, forcing her to tighten her lower belly.

As they squatted for another repetition, she smiled internally before pushing her bottom back enough to brush by the stiffness between his legs. "Hey," he said, using his large thumbs to rotate her hips slightly forward.

"Oh, sorry. Wasn't paying attention for a minute." Rakell spoke softly, her body noting the hardness under his thin shorts, making her ache to feel it again.

He steadied himself. "It's fine. One more." His voice was stern, all business.

As they began to squat, she took a step back, sticking her round ass out, swiping the whole of his crotch before she felt his hands dig into her hips, tilting them away from him.

"Not cool—you're going to get us both hurt," he scolded, grabbing the bar from her, then removing and racking the weights.

Internally, his body begged for more of the feel of her against him. He wished they had a few more sets. He looked at her, watching her fingers pull and twist her bottom lip like she was unaware of what had just happened. *Bullshit*, he thought. *I'm totally being played. Don't give it to her. Don't let her know you were even fazed. Don't even mention it.* He wanted to say, *You know what we call girls like you in America? "Prick teases."* He buried that thought, yanking himself together. "Okay. Next, leg extensions."

As they walked across the gym, she thought again about seeing him last night at Central Market shopping with a cute girl. She'd almost said hi, standing behind them at the meat counter as they ordered two grass-fed filet mignons, but she didn't want to make the girl feel uncomfortable. They were clearly a couple, at least for last night. Rakell was getting the idea that Jake dated a lot, that between his ripped, solid body, striking face, and outgoing personality, he had no problem getting women. That thought niggled at the back of her brain whenever she thought about him, an occurrence that was happening with greater and greater frequency.

Rakell stood beside the machine while Jake did his extensions. During the third set, as he gritted his teeth and extended his legs, she looked at him, smiled wide, and asked, "How was dinner last night?"

"Huh?" he grunted, blowing out air as he strained, his blue eyes shifting up toward her from his seated position.

"The filets—they looked good. Nice juicy big ones. And the asparagus, how did you cook them? Grilled? Sautéed?"

He finished the last rep, rubbing his cramping thighs. "What the hell? Now who's the stalker?" He feigned irritation, masking the amusement in his tone as he moved off the machine so she could get on.

"Not stalking, just happened to be standing behind you and your girlfriend at the market last night," she said, maneuvering her legs under the machine and reaching down to lower the weight. "Just happened to notice what you two were having for dinner. Wine looked a bit cheap. Might want to up-level on that, mate." A small, closed-mouth grin crossed her face.

"Get to work," he barked, anxious about how to explain to her what she'd seen.

Rakell stuck her tongue out at him before starting her extensions. *Oh great, now I'm reverting to my grade school self,* she thought. *Real mature, Rakell.*

Jake cocked an eyebrow, his mouth twisting as he looked at her. "Wow, really? First of all, that wasn't cheap wine. *And,*" he emphasized, "it's what she picked out. I would have bought a different bottle, but I was trying to be nice and let her pick it. Second of all, she's not my girlfriend. If I had a girlfriend, I wouldn't have invited you to dinner," he said pointedly.

She kept her eyes downward, not acknowledging him.

His eyes focused on Rakell's face. "Hold it at the top for a few seconds, then you'll get more burn and"—he touched the top of her thigh, running a finger over the ridge of her quad muscles—"you'll develop even more definition here."

She got off the machine, and he got on. Once her breath steadied after the strain of the lift and the tingling of his touch on her thigh, she continued, "You two looked really cooozieee. So what is she?"

"Friend," he blurted out, his face getting redder, straining, legitimate annoyance dominating his tone.

"Oh, okay. So are you that cozy with all your friends? Because me, I'm only that cozy with the ones I'm fucking or thinking about fucking soon. So which is it?" She wasn't telling the truth, but it was fun goading him, and there was a part of her, a big part, that wanted to know what he did when he wasn't at the gym and if his interest in her was sincere.

"Shit!" Jake let his legs drop, the weights slamming down, his eyebrows tugging together. "What!?"

Rakell got on the machine for her last set. "Which is it? Currently fucking her or thinking you'll fuck her soon?" She started her set, looking down at her thighs, biting the inside of her mouth and trying not to look at him.

He'd never met a girl he wanted so desperately to swat or maybe full-on spank, at least not unless they were in the middle of fucking. But this girl...what a brat, pinning him like this. What was her fucking end game? And why was he still standing here, wanting more? Maybe Dwayne had been right, after all. He should've stayed away.

"We're friends, period." His eyebrows were still knitted together, his mouth straight and his electric blue eyes steeled on her face when she finally looked up at him.

The side of her mouth curled up. She was enjoying getting under his skin. By now, she was sure that he was sort of a player, the kind of guy her friends talked about, guys who charmed women into bed but never committed to them. She already entertained men like that, but that came with a lot of money. Not just dinner and conversation with a bodybuilder.

Rakell got off the machine, following him to the hamstring machine, staring at his muscular thighs and ass. He adjusted it, lying down on his stomach, starting his set, explaining to her how to keep her pelvis on the machine so her hamstrings were doing the work. He finished and started adjusting the weight and the leg-length on the machine to fit her.

"So friends? Is that what you Americans call 'friends with benefits'?" she asked, making quotation gestures in the air between them.

Jake stopped what he was doing, glaring at her. "Yes, that's what we call it in America. And yes, that's what we are. Now get on," he said, an exasperated, rough quality seeping into his voice as he pointed at the bench. "Let's get this done."

She flinched at the way the command in his voice titillated her skin, as if he'd slowly run his fingers from her knees up her inner thighs and was now using his big hands to open up her legs. She climbed onto the machine, a theatrical innocence threading her tone. "So just trying to understand—basically friends that fuck, correct?"

He steadied himself, answering with a flat tone. "Yep. Lie down and get on with it."

He watched her firm, round ass flex, straining along with the hamstring muscles to bring the weight up and down. Damn, he loved women's asses. Asses with flesh. This girl was sporting a high, fleshy ass he'd love to get his hands on. He didn't even correct her when it popped too far off the machine. He just stared at it. As she twisted to get off the machine, he couldn't help but notice how her breasts crushed against the padding, as though trying to escape from the black and purple sports bra she was wearing.

As he finagled his large torso onto the machine, Rakell kept talking, probing. "So all you have to do with a friend like that is buy a couple of steaks, a cheap bottle of wine, and then you get to fuck her for free? Nope, no way."

"Again, she picked out the wine," he huffed, contracting his glutes and hamstrings. He clenched his jaw, sure he had ground the enamel off his back teeth. Damn, she was a bawdy little wench, like a character from an old western movie.

"Still, cheap. Not hardly worth a free fuck. She got the wrong end of that deal, for sure," she needled, mirth winding through her tone.

"How's that? She had fun too," he blurted out defensively, his large frame sliding off the machine. He was getting tired of this, irritated with himself for falling right into her bullshit. He felt like he had nowhere to go. Like she had already painted him as some kind of womanizing asshole. Just imagine what she'd think when she found out who he really was and googled all the articles about him.

"How do you know? Seriously, because you're good-looking and muscular? That wouldn't be enough for me to spread my legs." She lay down on the machine.

Jake cleared his throat, yanking himself in, wishing Dwayne was here to say something funny and inappropriate to alleviate the tension.

This time when her ass kept popping off, he moved to the side of the machine and firmly placed his hand on her lower back. "Keep your pelvis on the bench. Don't let it pop off." Still applying pressure with his hand, he said, "Go again, but think about that bottom." He purposely dragged the vowels out into a sultry drawl. "Keep it still, sweetheart." He heard her pissed huff. Keeping his cool, he let his hand slide a little lower so that his pinky and ring finger were touching the top of her leggings. He bent down so he could talk in her ear. "Can you feel the difference when you keep your pelvis glued to the pad? Then you really have to use your glutes and hams. Makes it harder to cheat using your hip flexors." He kept his voice purposely low and husky, like he was picturing more than her legs flexing. *Yes, I do know anatomy, sweetheart, and yours is fucking hot.*

Her face flushed. It was very pink, and he could tell it wasn't just because of the workout.

"Um, okay. I got it." She sounded breathy, and for the first time today, he started to see a little crack in her demeanor. An amused thought hit Jake. *Not so bawdy now, are you?* He really wanted to swat that ass as he watched her. What a brat. A crazy, beautiful, funny brat—but still a brat.

"We're done," he declared as she finished her last repetition.

"Great, I need to…leave, go—" She started to twist as if she was preparing to make a mad dash away from him.

Swiftly, he cupped her elbow and gently moved her in front of him, putting his hands on her shoulders and looking directly in her eyes. "Wait, I wanna answer your questions more fully," he said. "I was really concentrating on lifting, so I'm sorry I blew off your questions. I think they're important." He wasn't completely clear where he was going with this, but he knew she wasn't going to have the last word.

"Don't worry about it," she responded, her eyes darting to the side, now in a state of near panic. She could hear the thump of her heart beating against her ribcage.

Jake could tell she was uncomfortable, which gave him a modicum of satisfaction.

"No, no. If I'm going to keep stalking you, I think I should be a transparent stalker," he teased. "So let's clear the air," he said, a sober tone returning to his voice. "The girl you saw me with—"

"Jake, really. I don't…" Her eyes widened, her skin prickling from his proximity. She tried to block out the warm, heavy scent of sweat emanating from him. Her nostrils swelled, and she had the fleeting thought of wanting to bury her face into his hard chest and lick the wetness off his skin. She needed to get a grip, but his presence yanked at her senses. She tightened her jaw, trying to move her eyes from his, shifting them over his shoulder.

"No, you pressed. You wanted answers, and I want to provide them." He squeezed her shoulders so she couldn't move without effort. "The girl you saw me with is a girl I dated for a short time, years ago. We are both between relationships. Mine ended more than three months ago. And yes, we are both horny, so we are *enjoying* each other. For the record, we both know it's for fun, and we both know it's temporary. Does that make sense?" Her green eyes were growing wider as he spoke, and he could see her chest lifting and falling more than it did when she was working out. He shifted his head slightly to the side to catch her eyes that were trying to avert his. "Seem fair?" he added when she didn't answer.

"Uh, yeah. Fine. Whatever." Rakell hunched her shoulders, but his grip got firmer. Her skin absorbed the imprint of his fingers on her bare shoulders, making her back stiffen. She wanted to get away, not because of his words, but because the nearness of him swirled beneath her skin, making her feel something foreign, something she had learned not to feel with men.

"Please let me finish," Jake implored as he leaned down, his mouth right next to her ear. "To answer your other question about how I know she's having fun, I try to judge a woman's fun level in bed by three things." He spoke slowly, his warm breath stroking her ear, making the muscles and tendons along her neck and jaw feel like they were being pulled tight. "Number one, how wet she gets. Two, how loud she screams during orgasms. And finally, how much she begs for more. So by those measures, I guarantee you—she's having fun."

Her whole body flinched as his illicit words tunneled into her brain, making the muscles from her asshole down to the apex between her legs reflexively contract. A barely audible short whimper escaped her mouth. It felt like a hand had reached between her legs; her whole lower belly jerked in before she realized she was holding her breath.

"Breathe, sweetheart," he said in a gruff whisper, just before loosening his hold slightly. He seemed to loom over her. "One more thing," he said, ignoring her shaking her head and her hushed *No*. "I get that my smile and muscles aren't enough for you to, as you so elegantly described it, 'spread your legs.' I wasn't asking for that, just looking to hang out. Maybe friends *without* benefits, since that doesn't seem to interest you," he said, opening his fingers and releasing her shoulders.

Taking a step back, a small smirk crossed his face when he looked at her pinched, visibly pissed expression.

"Don't pretend to know what does or doesn't interest me. You don't know me," she gasped, defensiveness masking her arousal, simultaneously wanting to grab the back of his neck, yank him close, and bury her tongue in his mouth, working him up like she knew she could, but also wanting to push him away and tell him to fuck off. Twisting her torso sideways, she stepped around him, desperately needing to get free of the stimulation his energy generated.

"Point taken," he said, still smirking as she turned, almost stomping away.

He watched Rakell descend the stairs, and the certainty that there would be a sincere apology in his future dampened his momentary victory. This girl...she really knocked him off his game. His Texas charm had evaporated, taken over by the cocky, crude, superstar. *Damn*, he thought, shaking his head. *Fuck. Grow up, Jake.*

Chapter Eight

Francesco, one of Rakell's regular clients, had requested that they meet in Santorini, Greece, this time instead of their usual spot: his villa in Milan. Rakell knew something was up by the way he spoke to her over the phone. He had always been a very confident and natural conversationalist, but during their last call, he'd been neither. Francesco explained that he'd gotten tied up with some issues at home, so he would have to fly out a day late. She'd been his escort for many events and luxury trips over the past two years, but recently, he'd been requesting her less frequently. She hadn't seen him in nearly three months.

Francesco was the reason Rakell had pushed herself to learn Italian. She'd been taking classes at UT and found that it wasn't that hard to learn because she was already fluent in Spanish and French. Her mother had been a model in Europe and learned French there, insisting Rakell learn it even though her father thought it was utterly useless. Her father had instead mandated that she learn Spanish, so she'd studied both from a young age.

Francesco acted like it was impossible to keep his hands off her body no matter what they were doing or where they were: having dinner, dancing, going to an opera, or at a party. Other women would comment on how clearly attracted he was to her, how lucky she was to have such an adoring boyfriend.

Rakell arrived at the luxury hotel on the outskirts of Imerovigli, perched above the expansive Aegean Sea, knowing that she'd have the first night to herself. The staff knew to expect her, handing her a pale blue envelope from Francesco. It was his love note to her, telling her to enjoy the spa and roomy suite, instructing her she could take the bedroom with the soaking tub, and he'd be there soon to make it up to her. Looking out over the veranda, she took in the seemingly unlimited shades of blue that kissed the sandy white beaches. The hotel's location offered an impressive view of the caldera, with Santorini's half-moon shaped bay at its center, surrounded by white-washed villages perched on reddish cliffs entreating the vibrant swirls of blue.

She sucked in the Mediterranean air, the smell of the sea filling her nostrils. In less than a year, this would all end: the men, the exotic hotels, the expensive gifts. She would no longer need to transform herself, performing for men as Marietta. She would leave all this behind. With that thought, she sighed, closing her eyes, giving herself permission to see the future. Would she miss this, this world she'd learned to inhabit for almost five years?

Once she and Matt officially broke up to the world, she'd be put to the test as Rakell, and she'd be alone. Would she be able to make it as a model, an actress? Her dream was shared by so many, and the competition was fierce. It was overwhelming when she thought about all the talent that tried but never made it. Then it came back to her— her dad's insistence that she acquire languages, that she would always have that to fall back on after trying her hand at a career that was equivalent to winning the lottery.

The image of her dad sitting beside her on the couch, his green eyes as intense as his words, caused a film of tears to blur her view of the sea. She'd done what he asked, pursued an education, but he would be heartbroken to know some of the decisions she'd made in order to set herself up financially. All to make sure she fulfilled not just her dad's wishes, but also her own dreams.

The next morning, she ate a light breakfast, worked out, and went to the spa before returning to the palatial suite to get dolled up for Francesco. Clients' preferences varied; Francesco's requests were light makeup with loosely curled hair, and he insisted that she be waiting for him in lingerie. He'd been married for almost a decade before his wife left him for a man—wealthier than he—whom she'd met vacationing in Dubai. Francesco's family owned one of the largest and oldest shipping companies in Europe, and Rakell couldn't imagine that *anyone* was richer than he was.

In his early forties, he kept fit and had a thick head of brown hair with silver creeping in at the sides. When he'd first requested Marietta, the agency let her know that he had been a long-term client. She learned through other escorts that he had a voracious appetite for women. To ensure he did not get "stuck" with a girl from a less than satisfactory upbringing, his father had started arranging escorts for him in his college years. After Rakell was treated to several lavish trips where he pampered her and acted like he was making love to her, he shared with Marietta that the thing he regretted about his marriage was that he hadn't demanded any offspring early in the marriage. Rather, he'd tried to be understanding that his young wife wanted to pursue a career as a designer like her famous grandfather.

Although he was from an old-world family, he recognized that his grandfather and father were backwards in their views of women, especially wives. He wanted to be a progressive husband, so he'd set his young wife up with a studio in Milan so she could pursue her dream with the agreement that she would be open to getting pregnant as soon as she turned thirty. On her twenty-ninth birthday, however, she'd gone to Dubai with friends to party.

Rakell wanted to ask if Francesco's wife had known about the escorts sprinkled throughout their marriage, but Marietta shook her head sympathetically and tried out her newly learned Italian on him. *"Mi sento triste per voi."*

The door opened, popping her back into the present and her current role.

"Bellissima ragazza," Francesco cooed, kissing her lightly on the mouth as he entered the multi-room suite. He was followed by two young Greek men, one carrying his suitcase, the other a tray with an assortment of cheeses, fruits, and a bottle of Prosecco. The two young

men tried to divert their eyes as she greeted Francesco in nude high heels and a black and nude lingerie set allowing a shrouded glimpse of her nipples. She'd come a long way from the newbie escort who turned red from embarrassment and tried to hide, learning quickly that the wealthy didn't try to hide what their money afforded them, but rather brazenly showed it off to highlight their power. She was what money could buy.

"*Mi sei mancato, Francesco*," she whispered into his ear. This was the start of their routine every time they met. He'd have specific lingerie and clothes sent ahead and waiting for her wherever they were staying, with specific instructions dictating what he wanted her to wear the first time he saw her. It was one of the reasons he always found a reason to arrive later than she did. They would kiss quickly, he'd say, "Beautiful girl," and she'd always tell him she'd missed him, while staff bustled around them, setting the table, pouring wine, and putting his clothes away.

"Quickly, store things away and make sure this beautiful specimen has a glass of Prosecco in her hand *ràpido*," he commanded.

He sat in a chair with a full glass of red, turned on some Italian music, and then, as she knew he would, directed her to stand in front of him. When he had finished his wine, he held his empty glass for a moment until one of the young bellmen poured his wine. Francesco relished their stolen glances at her lace-covered privates, revealing enough skin to wind up the curious onlookers. Many times, he would brag to them, "Yes, she's beautiful, but it doesn't compare to how she feels to the touch." A knowing smirk would spread across his lips as the young bellman nodded.

She kept her eyes cast downward, allowing a small smile to cross her lips, feigning a demure shyness she no longer possessed. Yes, in the beginning, the staff's eyes on her while her client perused her body made her internally shrivel, but she'd become accustomed to the idea that these men, her clients, saw others' desire to have what they had, as yet another way to stroke their egos. Her defenses slowly shed, and now she relished their fleeting glances, the longing of these men toward her. If she were honest, it was more titillating than the touch of the men who had bought her.

While the men went about putting things in their proper places, his routine was to ask her to open her robe first, then stare and nod his head approvingly. He'd then make sure to clear the room, indicating with a gesture for staff to exit, his eyes to the door then back on her. He was blatantly letting them know he was seconds from getting his hands on something that they never would.

"Let me see," he said, signaling for her to drop the robe to the floor and turn around so he could stare at her backside. Next, he'd put his wine glass down and run his hands up and down her ass before asking her to open her legs and bend forward so that her sex was exposed from behind through the crotchless panties. Sometime, early in the routine, he'd pull his pants down, lowering them to just below his balls, stroking his cock while he watched her. By the time she backed her sex into him, his cock would be hard. He'd slip a condom on, stand, and slide himself into her while holding her hips. Then he'd pump her until he came, screaming in Italian about how beautiful she was.

The routine was the same this time, but Francesco seemed distant. His enthusiasm for her lacked his typical sincerity as if, like her behavior, it was rehearsed, making her question what was going on. Of course, Rakell knew he had other women, mostly escorts, but since she'd entered into a contract with him a year ago, he'd always declared her his favorite and, perhaps naïvely, she thought there was truth in his words. But was there ever truth in these men's admirations, their declarations, or, for that matter, hers back to them? Her faint intake of breath when they kissed her neck, the deep moaning when they inserted themselves into her, the soft giggling at their attempts at humor or the sadness she feigned at the end of their contractual agreement? Of course, there were some men whose companionship she enjoyed, but she'd learned to *disassociate* years ago. She'd studied their reactions to Marietta embracing that character completely, but after five years of living a double life, she wondered if she could figure out who *Rakell* was with men.

His cock pumped her sheath from behind as his hands gripped her hips; his legs stiffened as his strokes grew more intense, harder.

"Marietta, come for me," he yelled.

Knowing he was close, she shut her eyes, imagining the young Italian bellmen sitting on the couch watching her, stroking themselves at the sight of her arched back and extended ass as Francesco fucked her, giving her an audience for her upcoming performance.

"Yes, *si* more, *di più*," she screamed back, knowing how it turned him on when she threw out Italian in the midst of what he thought was her climax, but she wasn't there. She so wanted to rub her clit, fucking come for real, not fake it. Quickly she reached under her belly for her crotch, her fingers finding her hard nub. "Yes, I'm…"

"*Ora dolce troia, ora…*" he barked, bending toward her back, one hand digging into her hip while his other hand roughly jerked her hand from between her legs. He pulled it behind her back, her arm bending unnaturally as he jammed her wrist into the small of her back. "*Nessuna troia!*"

Slut! Had he just growled *slut* in her ear as he stopped her from her own pleasure? Trying to recover from the air bursting from her lungs, she winced. His voice had shifted from lust to something breaching on sinister.

"*Troia ora, this moment!*" he hissed as he thrust hard into her again and again, squeezing her wrist roughly.

Shit, shit, he had said *slut*, something's wrong. *Marietta, do this, get it over with*, she pleaded with her brain to let Marietta perform. To stop Rakell from standing up to him. *Just fucking perform…end this!* Stiffening her legs, arching her back, shaking her head so he could see that she loved it, Marietta loved it.

"Yes, I'm coming for you, coming," she screamed into the air between loud shrieks of pain concealed as ecstasy. She performed for him, knowing in seconds his cock would give way and he would have gotten what he wanted.

She heard his deep guttural grunt before his cock grew, then softened inside her as he went limp, letting her arm drop. He wrapped his arm around her waist, pulling her up to standing. "*La mia bella ragazza,*" he murmured into her ear.

He wrapped his arms around her shaking body. She knew he would interpret it as hurt, but the shaking and the tears were not hurt, but anger. He had been a good man to her, treasuring her, but not now. She was what she was—his bought toy.

"Shhh, shh," he whispered as he turned her in his arms, his eyes lowering to hers. God, she couldn't look at him without wanting to spit on him.

He lifted her chin so she was forced to look in his eyes. "Baby… *Scusami tanto. I wish you were mine. Sorry.*"

She wouldn't show him anything, no emotion, nothing! *Fuck these privileged men, I can't! This all ends soon and then you'll be on your own, just Rakell, no more Marietta. Just do this.*

She coaxed her eyes wide, her bottom lip out and soft. "I'm yours, you know that."

"Beautiful baby…no, no, soon it won't be…shhh…not now," he gushed, pulling her closer, her face buried in his chest hiding the twist in her features from disgust. "I will show you how much I am…so…*scusami tanto.* I will lavish to you this week, everything, anything before…"

She felt a couple drops of moisture hit her cheeks. Was he fucking crying? How could he know she would be leaving the business in several months? No one but Matt knew. She hadn't even told the agency yet. They would know as soon as she refused anything beyond this year.

Squeezing her eyes shut, she willed herself not to shove him away and use all the Italian she'd learned to tell him what a fucking bastard he was, how he sucked in bed and that she never came with him, it was all an act. *Why in the hell do you think I touch myself? So I can eke some pleasure out of this!*

"*Nessun problema,*" she mumbled into his chest.

They pulled apart, going to the separate bedrooms for showers. She begged sweetly for room service after he suggested they dine downstairs. She wasn't really hungry and couldn't stomach the acting required in public. He usually had his hands all over her, commenting to everyone how beautiful she was. She didn't trust herself not to roll her eyes.

She let her back fall against the shower wall as the hot water sluiced down her body, meticulously running the bar of soap over the skin of her forearm where his hand had gripped her without care for any pain she may have experienced. She didn't care, either; they had both been playing a role. The redness on her skin was a reminder of who she was, his paid-for toy. She could have stopped him and ended this night, but the consequences—lost money and an agency investigation—were never worth it. Escorts learned to bury certain things so as not to appear as troublemakers because the agency would consider removing her from her current assignments. She would be ending her escort life on her terms. She just needed to get to the end of the year.

Gripping the lavender soap, her hand traveled down her torso to the crevice that ached between her legs. She started to rub her clit. Her eyes closed as she pictured Jake, the smile that morphed his face from threateningly fierce to a young boy. His charm, the way he almost seemed hurt by her jokes, and the way he had apologized for Dwayne's comment in earnest. What would it be like to have him between her legs because she wanted it? Would her needs matter to him? Was that how it worked when you dated someone? Your needs, your desires, your preferences mattered to them? Rubbing herself, she quietly got off, as her body shuddered, silent tears dripping down her face and mixing with the hot water. Her brain drifted back to her first time as an escort.

I thought I understood the sacrifice I was making; I thought it would only be for a few years, just acting as armpiece for a little while. Well, it started as that but soon drifted into more. I was selective, primarily agreeing to long-term, fake-girlfriend scenarios. It would only be a few years of my life, and the work would provide me with enough funds to finance my education and explore my dream of acting. It ended up allowing me to pay my way through school and start to amass what would become a sizable savings. But I was too naïve to understand that there are certain life events or decisions that you never return from. I've heard it said that life is merely billions of moments that form one picture, that no single moment defines us. But there are moments that set us on a different course, and it's impossible to reverse time. I wondered then but couldn't know: If I hadn't lost my dad, would I have made the same decisions? Would I be here in this moment, using an alias, smiling at some rich man that paid to bed a woman while his new fiancée waited at home?

Instead of slipping on a sexy robe, which she usually did when they decided to dine in, Rakell dressed in leggings and a large zip-up cardigan. He glanced up at her as he ordered room service, a questioning look on his face. Pretending to ignore his scrutinizing eyes, she went to the balcony to absorb the air emanating from the sea and listen to the crash of the waves hitting the shore, praying he hadn't taken a Viagra.

Something was off with Francesco. He did as he said he would, lavishing her for the next few days, treating her like his most prized possession. But the sex was detached, more perfunctory than usual. She didn't try to get herself off after the first night, thinking it had triggered him. Every evening he'd retire to his room (he seemed to be forgoing the Viagra), and she could hear the low murmurs of words exchanged on the phone, a sweet tone arising from behind the door.

Rakell learned on the fourth and final night of the trip that this would be their last time together. He'd gotten engaged, he told her across the table at dinner, after a few glasses of wine. He added that if she'd only been born to a different family, she would be the one he'd be marrying. He made it clear he would still be paying for the year.

"I'll fulfill the contract with the agency," he assured her, and then insisted that she accept a gift of a diamond and aquamarine necklace. She politely tried to refuse but ultimately accepted it. She had learned over the years to accept gifts, even when she didn't want them, that men hated it when you refused their gifts.

She acted as if she was heartbroken about Francesco's engagement, but of course she wasn't. She never fantasized about marrying any of her clients, even though many of them were the most eligible bachelors in Europe. She knew who they *really* were. How steeped in insecurity, how removed from the everyday life of most people, how careless they were with the things—and even more so, with the people—in their lives. No, she did not see her happily-ever-after in any of her clients.

That evening, he asked her to strip in front of him, to put on a show. He drank three glasses of Grand Marnier, purring on about how fucking beautiful she was, his words crossing over from Italian to English and back again, demanding she step forward between his legs. Unsure of what would be next, her pelvis felt queasy as she did as he requested, internally wincing, but he simply ran his hands over her body, as if trying to capture the feel of her for his memory, sliding his hand between her legs, gently inserting a finger before declaring she had the softest, wettest pussy.

"*Come il velluto,*" he murmured, inserting two fingers into her. He slid his fingers out, looking at her solemnly, telling her he had to be on his best behavior for a year, but once he got his young wife pregnant, he'd call for her again.

Rakell felt her dinner turn over in her gut as she stood there naked, listening to his words, a declaration of planned betrayal. *I never want to be that woman, beholden to some monied man, pregnant while he relishes his dalliances.*

Hard no, hell, fucking no.

She swallowed hard, forcing a small smile toward him but with no words. She didn't have anything. Then she said she was feeling under the weather and needed to retire early. She gathered her clothes and rushed into the hot shower, scrubbing him off her.

On the long flight back to Austin, Rakell thought about how her view of men had been shaped by her years as an escort. In some ways, it was simple. They had requests; you said yes or no to those. There was a contract; both parties knew what to expect. Those expectations were set up beforehand, so you knew what you signed up for.

Early on, she'd worked only as eye candy, with some clients requesting that she try on lingerie while they watched and stroked themselves. Most of those were lunch meetings or after-work encounters so the client could slip in a secret show before a business meeting or before rushing home to their wife and children. Those assignments were easy and safe: The meetings were mostly held at a handful of high-end lingerie shops in London and Paris. In the industry, they were called "lace plus skin," which sounded more seductive in French (*dentelle plus peau*). Once Rakell made the jump to sexual escort, the money really began to flow. Some clients wanted a quick blowjob or an evening tryst, but most wanted her for weekends and trips. Soon her weekend clients became long-term clients, which was where the real money and a sense of security came.

Since beginning to dip her toes into the dating world, she'd been asked out here and there. She had even been going on a couple of dates with a guy from Dallas because she could meet him there and stay under the radar in Austin. She didn't really know many people in Austin, but she had promised Matt she'd stick with normal guys and steer clear of the network of rich Texas kids that might know his family. She hadn't been drawn to anyone except Jake. But she wasn't dating him. He was so unlike the men she'd become accustomed to. There was something about him. Her mind couldn't reconcile Jake, the cocky but yet sincere, down-to-earth guy. Her body's response was undeniable when he was near her, but her instinct was to step back rather than let him in. There was a comingling of arrogance, compassion, and something genuine— something she hadn't seen in most other men.

Once Rakell was back in Austin, Matt reminded her about the gallery opening in Denver they would be attending with his family. The driver would pick her up and take her to the airport, where she'd fly on the family's private jet to Houston. There they'd join her and head on to Denver. They'd be going directly to the art gallery, so she would need to board the plane ready for the event. This trip would be a quick turnaround, but the owner-curator of the gallery was the son of one of his mom's best friends from high school, and Matt's mother was insisting that everyone be there to support Jonathon.

"How was Greece?" Matt asked.

"Beautiful as usual. This was my last time with Francesco. He's engaged, and he was pretty disconnected this time. I hope it works out, but he's sort of a playboy."

"Ya think?" Matt laughed. "Were you upset? Just want to make sure you're doing okay, Princess?"

She sucked in, remembering the humiliation. "Not really upset. You know you're the only one I've fallen for."

"Ahh, but I want you to have a life too. I promise once we get good news on my dad, I'll have a sit-down with my parents. I'm kind of going crazy myself."

"At least you're still seeing people, even if you have to keep it under the radar," she said.

"Well, why don't you sleep with someone? I mean it. Maybe that guy from the gym or the Dallas guy? Jim, right?" Matt sounded serious.

"Not sure I can just give it away after selling it for the past four years. Seems counterintuitive to me. Plus, I'm not even sure I know how to act when I'm not acting."

Matt lightly chuckled.

"I'm serious, Matt," she scolded as she drew in a breath, thinking about how Francesco had turned on her in the middle of fucking her the first night in Santorini. She couldn't tell Matt, or he'd lose his shit, probably call the agency himself, getting them both in trouble since she had signed a contract with a solid non-disclosure and non-compete clause. She was not to take any clients on without contractually going through the agency. Technically, she was working for Matt at his firm, but he paid her three times more than she would probably garner on her own. They had worked out their own agreement, so in the agency's system, Matthew Waterman was simply a past client with whom she should not have any contact.

Other escorts broke this rule, too, usually when they thought that the client would take them under their golden wings forever. Yet that dream seldom manifested, and they usually found themselves broken and jobless. She'd watched it happen many times, and she knew that if the agency suspected outside fraternization, she'd be ostracized by the most exclusive agency in Europe. Managers there relished the stories of models, actresses, or others who tried to go off on their own, only to find themselves begging to be put back on the agency roster, and the answer was always a hard no. She could not afford for Matt to rock the boat.

Chapter Nine

Rakell had only seen Jake in passing since she'd returned home five days ago, either as she was leaving the gym and he was entering or vice versa. She'd seen Dwayne more than Jake. Dwayne had apologized for his crass joke from before, and she assured him she had overreacted. They'd had a couple of good laughs, and Dwayne spotted her on a few exercises when she'd asked.

"Hey, girl." Dwayne waved at Rakell as she approached the free weights, dripping with sweat from the hour she'd spent on the treadmill.

She waved back, using her other towel-draped hand to wipe sweat from her face and chest. "Dwayne!" she yelled with a smile as she moved to the dumbbell area. She grabbed both a thirty and a twenty-five-pound weight to do bent-over rows and triceps combinations, since she needed to wrap up early. She'd had to drag all her stuff to get ready for the art opening to the gym; her apartment building had shut off the water due to plumbing work. *Of all the days*, she'd thought when the building manager told her last night.

She leaned over the weight bench to do dumbbell rows with her left arm and leg on the bench and her right leg on the floor. Bracing, she held the thirty-pound weight in her right hand before leaning over and moving the weight from in front of her, concentrating on keeping her back straight.

"Your back's arching a little," Dwayne said.

"I'm really concentrating on trying to keep my back straight. Will you watch me do the set on the other side and tell me if I'm arching?"

"Gotcha," he said, sitting on a bench close by. "Yep—right there.

Arching. Do you feel it?"

"Yeah, I kinda do. It happens when my mind drifts," she said guiltily.

"We all do it." Dwayne shrugged his shoulders in understanding. "What ya gotta do is imagine there's a rod down your back. Don't think about your back, think about not breaking that rod. Do another one. I'll show you where the rod should be. Don't worry—no funny business." He let out a soft chuckle, but she heard the sincerity in his voice.

She bent over to do another set, and Dwayne ran his finger from her neck between her scapula and down her spine. He stopped when he got to her leggings. "Do you get what I'm saying?"

Rakell felt his presence before she heard his deep voice.

"She doesn't like help. Believe me—I've tried," Jake declared as he walked up, stopping in front of the bench.

She looked up at him from her bent position. "Really?" she murmured reproachfully, trying not to roll her eyes or better yet, flip him off. But the part she wasn't willing to show was how giddy she was to see him.

"Jake, my man—the girl's smart. Knows that, unlike you, I don't got any ulterior motives. I have a pure heart." Dwayne put his fist over his chest.

Standing up, Rakell put the weight on the bench. "Actually, it did help, Dwayne. And I know you have a pure heart," she said with alacrity.

His hands on his hips, nodding toward her smugly, his biceps bulging, Jake was wondering if there was a way he could apologize for their last interaction. But he didn't want to bring up the whole "friends with benefits" thing again. Better to leave that behind them and see if he could nudge things forward.

"Sure," Jake spat out, looking at Dwayne. "Pure. He came here straight from Bible study this morning."

Dwayne threw his hands up. "Fine, join me over there when you're ready. Jordan's on his way."

Jake shifted his attention to Rakell, who was lying down on the bench and ignoring them, holding a weight with both hands, doing triceps extensions. Her arms were back, both hands on the weight, lowering it behind her head.

His eyes grazed over her, her blondish-brown long pigtails hanging on either side of the bench, her large breasts squeezed together, the tops pushing up toward her chin as she strained against the weight. Her taut, honey-colored abdomen and long legs made Jake shudder imperceptibly.

He forced himself to look away, then moved in front of her. He waited until she finished. "I'll get it," he said, reaching to grab the weight from her hands so she could get up.

"Thanks." She sat up.

He put his hand out to help her stand. To his surprise, she took it. "Thanks again," she said sincerely.

"You look like you got a little sun. How was Europe?"

"Nice." She looked away briefly, almost as if he'd asked a personal question.

Her anxiety was not lost on him.

Jake buried his mild annoyance at her reaction, wanting to get back to an easy footing with her. "Where in Europe did you go?" He was trying to sound light.

"Greece, Santorini. It was beautiful. The weather was perfect, but I'm glad to be back." She rambled uncomfortably, her green eyes focused on him. "You? How's the whole 'friends with benefits' thing going?"

A tight smirk took over her face, as if she was containing a roaring laugh in her throat.

His eyes pricked up at her question, her taunting expression. *The balls on this girl had no limit.* Stilling himself to control the features on his face, he said, "Well, she moved on to a real boyfriend. Nice guy." He spoke evenly, not offering any hint of irritation.

Grinning, Rakell lightly swatted his arm. "So I was right all along. That cheap wine did you in."

God, what he wouldn't give to pull both her pigtails at the same time. "Again, she picked it out." He did not sound as controlled as he intended.

"A girl's not going to keep giving it up for a twenty-five-dollar bottle of wine. No way. Just a little advice." Her expression danced with giddiness. "Dig a little deeper in your pockets next time."

She's fucking loving this. Don't give it to her, don't, Jake. He snorted hard, throwing his arms up. Damn, he had no control.

"How about this? I take you out, and you order any bottle of wine you want? Don't worry about cost—anything." He looked at her, his chin jutting forward, an *I dare you* look blanketing his face. He forced himself to ignore the tangible tension that gathered around them once again. God, how could he simultaneously be so drawn to her and want to swat her at the same time?

"I'm the wrong girl to make that offer to. I can guarantee you that. I want you to make rent this month." She protruded her bottom lip feigning concern. "I wouldn't do that to you." Her tone was overly patronizing, but mischievous; he was sure she was testing him.

Jake had an overwhelming urge to grab her at the small of her waist and the back of her head, to cover her mouth with his. Suck the haughty attitude out of her. Something about her—not just her hot body and beautiful face but some subtle vibe she exuded—made his body flex, like an electrical signal innervating the muscles down his spine. His ass and crotch twitched.

The desire to grind into her, knowing she would respond to him, was getting hard to bury. Mentally, he reined himself in, remembering that he'd been stroking his cock nearly every night while picturing her, the look on her face when he told her how he knew when a girl was enjoying him in bed, sure that her pussy had flooded with his words. Right now, he wondered if his fantasies might be skewing his impression of her. Why fucking bother with a girl who was so difficult? There were others, easier ones. He didn't want or need a challenge in his personal life. He had enough to deal with on the field.

"Shit, I'm not fucking kidding. Any bottle. Deal?" He wanted to say, *I'm an NFL football quarterback making seventeen mil a year. I can afford whatever fucking bottle you pick out.* Yet he had the sense as soon as those words flew out into the air, he'd wish he could bottle them back up. He wasn't going to sully whatever this was with fame or money. Besides, with her, he wasn't even convinced his status would bode in his favor. Maybe even the opposite.

"Um, let me think about it." She wanted to say yes but forced herself to hold off. "I have to finish up because I have to get ready for work here. The plumbing is shut off at my apartment, and I have a big event later. Worst day for it, so it makes my morning crunched."

"All right, well, think about it," he grumbled.

"Jake," she said as he walked away. He turned back around. "I'm not having sex for a bottle of wine, no matter how much it costs. Just wanted to be clear."

"Got it. You're clear. Believe me, loud and clear." He turned again and let out a forced breath. He stopped himself from shaking his head, wanting to yell, *What the fuck!?*

Rakell took more than an hour to get ready in the locker room. She had to use two lockers because she'd brought her overnight bag with her containing everything she'd need to get ready for the gallery opening. She'd already called the driver and told him to pick her up at the gym. She was dressed in a couture suit of turquoise brushed silk. The pants were straight-legged, the waistband buttoning just below her belly button. The matching jacket was the most unique part of the ensemble: a short blazer with one large black button that fastened below her breasts. The blazer then split to the sides, purposely showing a small part of her stomach, including her navel. The color and cut looked appealing with her tan, she thought as she looked in the mirror. She wore a black lace shelf bra because the jacket was designed to show an undergarment, preferably lace, as the women at Saks Fifth Avenue had explained to Rakell. The bra also pushed her breasts up, adding to her ample cleavage. Her hair was pulled up in a loose bun with ringlets falling around her face. She completed the look with black stilettos and black gem-drop earrings. She didn't like big jewelry; she wore enough of that show-off shit as Marietta. Rakell opted for a less-is-more approach. After finishing her makeup—daytime smoky eyeshadow and a pale lipstick—she packed up her things and headed out.

Rakell entered the café carrying two bags and rolling an overnight suitcase. She ordered a protein shake, explaining to the girl behind the counter why she was dressed like this and had so many bags.

"What a drag," the girl replied. Rakell nodded, agreeing, before peeking out the window to see if the driver had arrived. She took a deep breath. Everything had worked out; she wasn't late. Then she heard them, all three of their deep voices behind her as they entered the café.

"Damn, is that you, Rakell?" Dwayne said from behind her.

She took a breath. "It's me. Had to get ready here. They're working on the plumbing at my apartment." She felt like she had to explain it to everyone she talked to, like she was doing something wrong.

"You clean up like a freaking supermodel," Dwayne kept going. She could feel the heat creeping up her neck.

"Thanks. Amazing what happens when you hose off," she replied, trying to move past the comment.

"Come on, Dwayne, leave her alone. Let's order. You do look nice, Rakell," Jordan said in classic polite Jordan style.

Rakell's nervous system winced from the sharpness in Jake's stare. His eyes stayed on her, not blinking, until he finally said, "That's what you wear to work?" She registered an accusatory note in his rough voice.

"Uh, yeah—well, not to the office, but this is an event with the owner's family, and we're flying to..." She stopped herself, her consternation over his tone overriding her awkwardness. Why was she explaining anything to him? Her spine stiffened, and she narrowed her eyes at him, feeling the urge to lay her palms on his steel chest and push. "Like it's any of your business? Some people *do* have jobs and responsibilities. I know stalking is your hobby, but how about getting a real job?" she said contemptuously. She could hear snickers from his friends but kept her gaze hyper-focused on him.

"Yeah Jake, a *real* job," she heard one of them chide.

Jake forced himself to pause, not taking her bait. He smiled. "I have a job, actually. Kinda seasonal work." He heard Dwayne snicker and Jordan shush him. Jake was amused; he thought it was a pretty damn funny retort.

Rakell gave him a raised eyebrow. "Like a ski instructor?" she said, her tone softening a bit.

"Something like that," Jake shot back, just as the girl behind the counter handed Rakell her shake.

"Well, I gotta go. See you around." She scrambled to gather all her stuff together in her arms and carry her drink.

Jake stepped forward. "Let me help." He grabbed the handle of the rolling suitcase and slung one of the bags over his shoulder. "Be right back guys," he said, moving to follow Rakell.

He walked past her, opening the door out to the parking lot, leaning against it so she could scoot past him.

Slowly, she stepped by him sideways, purposefully looking up, her big green eyes staring tauntingly at his piercing blues.

He swallowed a thick knot in his throat. "I wanted to say in there that you look beyond fabulous."

She stopped just in front of him. "I wanted to say that I kinda like having a hot stalker. Gives me something to think about at night." She turned and walked toward a black town car.

Jake focused on taking slow deep breaths as he strode behind her, the charged air between them tingling his skin. Was he reading this wrong? Her messages were all over the place: *stay away from me, chase me, back up, come on, boy, look at me.* And here he was like a fucking puppet on a string…whatever string she pulled, he responded. *Damn this girl,* he shook his head, *No, sweetheart, this isn't how this works. In my world, I'm a lion, and the gazelle lies down for me. In my world, I don't even have to sneak up on my prey. I smile, and they offer themselves to me. So not sure what the hell she's doing to me; it's exhilarating and frustrating. I need therapy or maybe just a bottle of tequila.*

The driver hopped out of the car and took the bags from Jake and Rakell. "Jimmy," Rakell said, hugging the older man. "Jimmy, this is Jake—my hot stalker."

Jimmy rolled his eyes and said, "Another one?" Laughing, he shook Jake's hand, then his eyes widened. "Hey! You're…yeah."

"Nice meeting you, sir," Jake said, shaking Jimmy's hand, pleading with his expression and a shake of his head not to reveal him. Jimmy gave him a subtle chin nod.

Before Jimmy could open Rakell's door, Jake grabbed the handle, standing with his arm on the top of the door, his other hand waving her to get in while Jimmy went around to the driver's side. He hoped that Jimmy wouldn't ask about him—and then it struck him, what the hell kind of job Rakell had that warranted a driver. *Who in Austin has a driver? We're not talking LA or New York here.*

Jake smiled down at her, determined to find out more about her.

Rakell slid past his illicit, intense stare, staving off the twinge between her legs. Twisting onto the backseat, she slid in as she looked up at him fleetingly. "Jake, thank you for all your help." Her tone suddenly deviated from playful to formal, as if he was a bell check at a hotel, trying to put a damper on the energy that was pulsating between them.

Hand still on the door, Jake leaned in toward her. "Just so you know, I work for tips," he stated, a greedy grin on his face. She would not get the upper hand.

She swung her legs to the side so that she was facing him and looked up, purposefully making her eyes big. She crooked her index finger, signaling for him to lean in closer. "I have a tip for you, mate…" Her hands scooped her breasts from below, pushing some of the flesh over the top of the lace.

Fuck, he couldn't believe it! His cock stiffened, registering the beautiful mounds of flesh making their way above the black lace.

Rakell leaned toward him so he could get a closer look. He could almost see the edge of her dark pink areolas. "Here's my tip, mate: Take a *cold* shower, sweetheart," she cooed, imitating his Texas drawl. And just like that, she swung her legs back in, jerking the door closed.

"Dirty pool!" he yelled as the door slammed shut. "You don't play fair, sweetheart," he grumbled into the air.

Jake heard her laugh from inside the car.

"I am definitely being fucked with. Damn that girl," he said out loud before adjusting his firm cock, which had started to push against the front of his gym shorts. Shaking his head, he walked slowly back into the gym. The image of her full breasts pushing up over the lace flashed in his brain. He shook his head again, willing himself to think about anything but those delectable mounds of honey-colored flesh and how much he wanted his face smothered in them. His brain couldn't stop touching her body. Damn, this girl was a brat. A brat he desperately wanted.

Chapter Ten

Electric Mix—Denver's newest art gallery—was over the top, even more than Rakell had expected. She'd never seen an art gallery so closely resemble a '70s nightclub. Most of the gallery openings she'd attended in Europe were like museums with champagne, filled with people trying to out-intellectualize each other, striking pensive long looks at the works blanketing the walls as they nodded intently as if they saw the "real" meaning behind the splattered paint. Rakell had had to bury laughter one too many times while playing eye candy to some banker, hedge fund dude, or CEO who knew nothing about art yet led her through the gallery as if they were experts. All of it was laughable.

But this? This gallery was like a party surrounded by art. She looked around at the old warehouse that had been converted to a space with a vast array of sculptures, glasswork, paintings, and live-humans-as-art. A jazz band played as hors d'oeuvres and champagne were passed around by hunky men wearing electric blue leotards with painted torsos, the depictions ranging from classic to modern art. It was the liveliest gallery opening she had ever attended. She looped her arm through Matt's and whispered in his ear, "For once, a fun art opening; feels more like a party on the verge of getting out of control. Like any minute the mushrooms are going to come out." She laughed.

"Lord, I hope not. I can tell my dad is already overwhelmed," he said, "but this is a great way to pull in the rich millennials."

She squeezed his arm. "This is amazing. I can't wait to meet this gallerist. What was his name again? Jonathon?"

"Jonathon Donaghy. I've only had to hear his name from my mom a thousand times. He's her friend Judy from college's son. They recently reconnected. I guess he was a real handful early on, and his mom was worried about him until he found his passion in art. Now he's a huge success. Just named a 'Top Entrepreneur Under Forty' in Denver's *People on the Move* magazine. My mom says this is the first of four galleries he wants to open this year, including one in San Antonio or Houston. My mom has already committed to help finance his next gallery." Matt sounded bored reciting his mom's words.

"Ooh, is he cute? That could work. I'd love to have a boy-toy who's sophisticated in the arts and lives in Denver. That way we'd definitely stay under the radar."

"Yeah, I've seen pictures. You're gonna think he's cute. Can't tell for sure from the pictures, but I'll warn you: He might be shorter than you," Matt said, looking at Rakell in her four-inch stilettos. She stood a bit taller than his six-foot frame.

Rakell winked at him. "I can lose the heels for a cute art guy."

"You need to get laid…by someone who cares if you get off," Matt said.

"I've been thinking the same thing. At this point, I can safely say the French socialite has been my best experience…and I still don't think I'm a lesbian or bi, but she made sure I was taken care of, even though she was paying just like the men. I think women are just better…more giving…" She halted at Matt's arched eyebrow. "You're different, and I know I'm not super giving…"

His arm went to the small of her back. "Hey, Princess, you're just guarded and with good reason. It's okay to guard yourself; that doesn't make you selfish…" He leaned toward her, putting his lips softly on her forehead. "Someday, I hope you find the one you don't have to guard against," he whispered.

Her eyelids slid down slowly. "You, Matt. You're the one that protects me."

He tilted his head up. "I mean that forever person. You'll always have me."

"Ugh, I just think men and I don't mix…"

"I'd venture to say that the issue is you've only been with bazillionnaires who are dropping a lot of cash to get…" His eyes scrunched up. "And who are accustomed to the world revolving around them—even in the bedroom."

"So I need to aim for a normal guy who can't pay for it. That's my plan."

"There are plenty out there who would be grateful to have you."

"By the way, Matt, *you* look super handsome tonight. Dark blue tux—kinda shaking things up, aren't you?" She pulled him close as they walked through the gallery.

"You think I'm *so* boring, don't you? "

"No, you just have your routines. Everybody's like that, me included." She squeezed his arm. "Let's see if we can both shake up our routines tonight. Maybe we'll both pick up a couple of cute boys," she murmured conspiratorially.

"You're scaring me," Matt said, raising his eyebrow. "Maybe giving up all your sex clients isn't such a good idea for you."

She lightly hit his arm. "Hey!"

Then came one of those moments in life a person never forgets. The crowd seemed to move to either side of the room as if in slow motion while a lean, blond man who looked to be in his early thirties strode through. He was wearing a maroon tuxedo with matching tie and cummerbund and a smile that could cure anybody's bad day.

He thrust his hand out to Matt. "Well, well. I just spoke to your mom and dad," he said, his eyes shifting to the end of the gallery where Matt's parents stood admiring a sculpture. "They are lovely people. My mom talks about your mother all the time and her handsome son. So you must be Matthew Edward Waterman III?" He sounded slightly amused, his eyes leisurely roaming up and down Matt before returning to his face.

Rakell couldn't help noticing that Matt's long legs swayed slightly as if trying to figure out how to remain standing. "Yes, and you must be Jonathon Donaghy." Matt extended his hand. "This is really impressive." The words rushed out of Matt's mouth, accompanied by a loud exhale. "I've heard so much about you from my mom. Uh, yeah. A lot of great things. She loves your taste, and the pieces you've been able to find for her have made her quite happy." Matt smiled, looking down, realizing he was still holding Jonathon's hand. He reluctantly let go.

Jonathon grinned. "Somehow you are even more dashing in person than in your pictures. Didn't think that was possible." His eyes slowly shifted to Rakell. "And who's the beautiful model on your arm tonight?" He reached for Rakell's hand.

"I'm Rakell," she said as Jonathon gently brought her hand to his mouth, lightly kissing the top.

"You make a beautiful couple," Jonathon murmured. "I'd love to hear more about your relationship later. But I do have to make my rounds, as much as I'd like to stay right here."

"We really loved meeting you, too. And yes, we'd love to connect with you later. We really do enjoy your gallery. This is the best opening I've ever been to. You should be proud. I am so grateful we made it." Matt spoke in a halting manner, sounding unsure of himself, which was unusual for him. "We, we…" Rakell nudged him, looking at him as a mother would trying to hush a child.

Jonathon grabbed Matt's elbow, squeezing it. "We'll connect later—I can guarantee you that, Matthew Edward Waterman III. And very nice to meet you, Rakell," he added, still looking directly at Matt before walking off.

Somebody spray this place down with cold water, she thought, laughing to herself, remembering her words to Jake. Rakell nudged Matt. "Well, there goes my fantasy about an artsy boy-toy," she laughed.

"Yeah, sorry. Can't see that happening." Matt was lost in thought, following the maroon tux as it made its way back through the crowd.

A few minutes later, Jonathon was at the microphone, thanking everyone for coming, naming some of the artists that were present, and thanking the painted waiters, the band, and the generous donors, which prominently included Matt's family. He exuded a magnetic personality, and it was clear why people were drawn to him.

Matt's parents made their way over to let Rakell and Matt know they needed to retire early. His dad wasn't feeling well; the chemotherapy treatments had zapped his energy. He explained that they had been able to connect with Jonathon and that he seemed like a truly charming, bright, hard-working young man. Then his dad leaned in close to Rakell and whispered, "I think he might be gay."

Rakell laughed, cupped her hand, and whispered back, "I think you are correct, sir," winking at Mr. Waterman like the two were conspirators. Matt always said that Rakell could get away with saying anything to his dad, way more than his dad would tolerate from him or even his sisters, but he had a soft spot for Rakell and tolerated, or maybe even enjoyed, when she poked him.

"I'd just like to say no judgment here. Clarissa and I are fine with that, his choice to be gay."

Rakell saw Matt shift on his feet and try not to wince.

"We are accustomed to gay people. For some reason, you find a *lot* of those people in the arts and…"

Matt's jaw tightened, and his face started to redden.

Rakell's hand went up. "'Those people'?" She made quotation marks in the air.

"Choice?" Matt jumped in, seeing the red creeping up Rakell's face, knowing feisty words were about to emerge. "Dad, she's right. You say it like they're lepers...or some deviant to society."

Mr. Waterman grew more erect. "I most certainly did not. My point is that they don't have to be so out there, so obvious. Just thinking a little more discretion is warranted..."

Matt's mom looped her arm around her husband. "Matthew, would that look like the discretion *you* demonstrated when I ran into you at that Duke fraternity party?" she said, her eyes squinted in an accusatory look juxtaposed to her wry grin.

"We shouldn't..." He tried to stop her, but Matt was grinning big, knowing that look from his mom; she wasn't going to stop.

"Well, you two, it's too forward to repeat, but it's safe to say that your father"—she raised her eyebrows at Matt—"*lacked discretion.*"

"Got it," Matt said, watching his father squirm.

Rakell nudged Mr. Waterman. "I guess your lack of discretion worked. Would anyone like more wine?" Rakell said, looking toward the bar.

"We are fine here. The wine vintage isn't..." Mr. Waterman started.

Rakell laughed. "This isn't the Cattle Baron's ball, sir. I'll grab you a glass, Matt."

When she came back, she didn't see Matt. She walked through the gallery clutching the two glasses, taking in the art while searching for him. Thirty minutes later, she wandered to a hallway at the back of the gallery, looking for a bathroom. She heard Matt's low voice and his distinctive guttural laugh coming from a closed office door. She knocked hard on it and heard scrambling noises. Jonathon finally called out, asking who it was, and when she announced herself, he opened the door. Something had definitely been going on.

"Okay, you two. Jonathon, you're supposed to be the host. And Matthew Waterman, what the hell? Totally out of character." She put her hands on her hips, adopting her best teacher's voice. "Both of you—save it for later." Matt scrambled to fix his tie as he and Jonathon exchanged guilty looks.

Later, they snuck Jonathon into their hotel suite, which was just down the hall from his parents' own. They sat around drinking wine and chatting about nothing and everything. Matt was unusually talkative, Rakell thought as she sat on a chair watching the two lovebirds on the couch cuddling. Rakell could immediately tell that they were meant to be together. She could see that Matt had possibly met someone capable of appreciating all he had to offer. She wanted to be sappy and tell them just that, but she was afraid Matt wouldn't approve of her honesty in front of Jonathon.

As they chatted that night, Jonathon made it clear he knew Rakell was a poser, so he asked Matt why. Matt was open with Jonathon about his and Rakell's relationship and how he planned to talk to his parents soon, that he was waiting until his dad made it through the chemotherapy sessions. Rakell took note that Matt didn't call her an escort, saying only that they were friends. But she knew eventually Jonathon would know. This double life she was so hoping she could just slip out of seemed like something that would linger. She slept on the couch that night, ceding the bedroom to Matt and Jonathon. In the morning, Jonathon snuck out early to avoid detection by Matt's parents.

Chapter Eleven

Rakell stared at her Guy Forsyth tickets. She loved his blues music, and his wife Jeska was supposed to take the stage with him tonight. Yet again, she was alone for the weekend. Matt was spending more and more time in Houston, especially since Jonathon had announced that Houston would be the perfect place for his next new gallery. She'd met a couple of guys, but it was simultaneously dull and excruciating to go out on what were essentially blind dates. She couldn't do it, she was realizing more and more. She was pretty much trapped. Matt did his life in Houston, and she sat home in Austin. Even if she wanted her escort life to end, it seemed way more appealing than the everyday lonely life she seemed to be carving out in Austin.

She called Lana and Levi, but they were busy. Lana, her old flatmate from London, had been concerned when Rakell moved to Texas almost a year ago, but when she came to visit three months later, Lana fell in love with Austin and in lust with the city's newest newscaster, Levi. So on what seemed like an impulse, she moved to Austin to be with Levi. They'd grown to become Rakell's closest friends apart from Matt. She trusted them both, since they had a non-judgmental approach to people and life. Lana's spirit and feistiness could set even the biggest beer-drinking Texan straight.

Rakell then tried Matt, but it was too late in the day for him to make it to Austin from Houston. Besides, Jonathon was coming into town in a couple of days, and he wanted to get ready for him. Matt encouraged her to just go by herself, have a few drinks, and enjoy the music. Maybe she'd even meet someone to give the extra ticket to before the show.

"Kells, just go. My God, it's not like you're going to have a hard time meeting people," he said. *He doesn't get it. How am I supposed to do this, pretend to be his girlfriend when he's never here, just go out by myself? Matt isn't grasping how hard it is to try to date under the radar.*

Sipping from the glass of wine she'd poured herself as she searched Netflix for the latest saucy series, it hit her how much time she'd spent being Marietta. She needed to start living as Rakell. *What the hell, I'm going for it*, she thought as she went to the bathroom to turn on the shower.

An hour later, she walked into the Driskill Hotel bar wearing a bright blue and cream lacy bohemian-style backless dress with bell sleeves. It was cut mid-thigh with a full skirt that moved when she walked. She wore caramel-colored suede boots above the knee and a matching fringe leather jacket. Her hair was down, and for fun, she'd rimmed her eyes with bluish eye shadow, stepping into her best Daisy Jones meets Dolly Parton persona. Cream-colored feather earrings completed the look. This laid-back bohemian style was truly her; most of the other styles she wore for work felt like she was playing pretend—which she was.

She sat in one of a pair of large leather wingback chairs arranged around a coffee table in the expansive hotel bar. Her eyes scanned upward to the iconic copper ceiling, the dark wood paneling, the massive bar on one end, cowhide chairs accenting rich brown leather chairs. A symbiotic dance, where rugged Old West meets luxury, the stories this bar could tell.

Oh, she could only imagine. The chiseled cowboy entreating the glances of the daughter of a Texas socialite, her casting her eyes away, then stealing furtive glances, his mouth twisting as his dagger-like piercing eyes made promises that he'd later keep as they stole away to one of the suites, courtesy of her daddy's money. His callused hands taking her soft body, showing her just how un-ladylike she truly was. *Damn it,* she thought. *I really need a date with my lipstick.* She shook her head, forcing her thoughts toward the art in the room.

The star of the show commanded the middle of the grand space, a cupula of stained glass illuminating a grand copper sculpture depicting a cowboy's boot caught in the stirrup of a runaway horse, another rider behind him with his gun pointed forward, making the observer wonder which one he'll shoot. She studied it, remembering that Matt had told her the piece was called "The Widow Maker." What an excruciating choice the second rider had: kill the horse or watch the man be dragged to death.

Shutting her eyes, she thought about the artist, his story, a former dentist who retired early to pursue the arts, Barvo Walker. *People do it all the time, Rakell—reinvent themselves, start second lives. I can do this. I can start over.*

When the waiter approached, she asked for the wine list, inquiring about French Bordeaux. She landed on a bottle of Chateau Pichon-Longueville Baron. The waiter returned with a 2010 and two glasses. He opened the wine, letting her taste and approve, poured her glass, and then looked to the other. She told him it wouldn't be needed and added a cheese and charcuterie plate to the order.

It was a surreal feeling to be dressed up at a bar, drinking expensive French wine by herself. It felt liberating, like she was doing something she should have done a long time ago. Like she was taking back control of her life, something she hadn't realized she'd been missing. Her plan was to enjoy the wine here and then walk a few blocks to Antone's Nightclub for the concert. Rakell loved Jeska Bailey's sultry voice; the kind of smooth seduction that oozed from her mouth could entice anyone into "the mood." The first glass of Bordeaux went down way too fast. The waiter poured a second when he brought the charcuterie plate, which was large enough to feed a small group.

"I don't know if I can handle a whole night of your shit," Jake jabbed at Dwayne as he swallowed the last of his second beer.

"Come on, Jake, give your wingman a break," one of the other guys sitting around the couches and chairs at the Driskill bar blurted out. Most of them were buds from UT, together for a guys' night out.

"On the field, best wingman ever. Off the field, he sucks."

They all burst out laughing as Dwayne pretended to cry.

Jake got up. "I'll be back."

"Can't wait, lover," Dwayne chortled, blowing Jake a kiss.

Exiting the bathroom, Jake's eyes caught on the familiar bronze sculpture of two horses in the middle of the expansive bar, then shifted to a woman with long blondish hair sitting by herself on the opposite side of the bar. He took a second look. "Can't be," he grunted. He stood for a minute, watching, his jaw shifting as her "tip" comment rang in his head. *You little minx. You owe me after that tease. Better be some damn good wine.*

She had chosen a spot around the corner from the bar as if she didn't want anyone to see her, much less pay attention to her. She appeared to be alone…odd. He went to the bar and asked for a wine glass.

He came up on her side and set his empty glass next to hers. "You owe me," he said sternly, hiding his bemusement. His eyebrows knitting together, he leaned toward her, relishing in the surprised "Oohh" that sprung from her mouth as her back jolted.

"Yep, time to pay up, sweetheart," he challenged, plopping down in the chair facing her.

Rakell jerked in her chair, startled. "Jeez, Jake! Don't sneak up on me like that." A warm smile crossed her face, trying to hide the sudden flush of heat she felt on her cheeks in his presence.

"That's the only way I can get close," he replied, offering her a heavy-lidded stare as the corner of his mouth inched up. He slid his glass forward, his eyes pasted to her face, trying to control the desire to drop them to her breasts, the top edges of which were making an appearance. "Like I said, you owe me. Your tip didn't work."

"What?" She took in his *give me a break* expression. "Oh—maybe it wasn't cold enough?" The side of her mouth twisted as she picked up the bottle and poured him a generous glass.

"An ice bath wouldn't have helped. So, no, it wasn't," he said, a lusty weightiness to his voice. He took a long, savoring sip of the wine, lifting the bottle to look at the label. "Wow, good taste," he said, offering her a small nod of approval. He wondered what woman sits at a bar alone and orders a two-hundred-plus dollar bottle of wine. He almost felt guilty about the generous pour.

Rakell felt her sex flex under his stare, twisting in her seat uncomfortably from the moisture wetting her crotch. *God, it's as if he's fucking me with his eyes. Stop that!* She sucked in air, reining in her thoughts. "I told you, mate—I was the wrong girl to offer *any* bottle to." She lifted her glass to him and took a long sip.

Her throaty voice teased him, winding down his chest before wrapping around the root of his cock. He shifted in his chair. "Offer is still out there…any time," he said pointedly. He lifted his own glass, his eyes still focused on her.

"Are you here alone?" she said, almost challengingly, trying to clear the sensual fog that seemed to be descending over them.

"Buds just left," he said as he got out his phone and started texting the group.

Jake: *Leave without me and use the 7th Street exit…***Send**

The roar from the direction of their table signaled that they'd gotten the message. Rakell raised her eyebrows, a definite question in her stare.

Sean: *Loser…***Send**

Bobby: *WTF…***Send**

Dwayne: *Jake's good buds–0; Spiderwoman–1; Pussy over your devoted friends?…***Send**

Jake: *Who?...***Send**

He rolled his lips into his mouth, burying a chuckle as he put his phone down.

She looked so different to him tonight, so wild compared to the other outfits he'd seen her wear. He didn't know if it was the dress, sort of a gypsy style, laced up the front from her waist all the way between her breasts with leather shoe-string ties. He could tell she wasn't wearing a bra because of the flesh peeking out from in between the laces.

"You?" His eyes were on her before taking another sip.

"Yeah, I have tickets for Guy tonight at Antone's, but my date bailed. He thinks I'm seeing other…" She reached for her glass, taking a quick sip.

"Well…are you?" He sipped his wine before lifting his eyes to her, gauging her reaction to his direct question. One that he had probed before tonight without an answer. She didn't appear bothered, but rather thoughtful, as if she had to sort out the answer before responding.

"I guess. I mean, I wasn't planning on just dating him. So yeah, he wouldn't have been the only guy I was seeing, just one of them." She took a long drink, and then poured herself another glass. The bottle was almost empty.

He arched an eyebrow. "As in plural?"

"That's more than one, correct?" she added, grinning from ear to ear, toying with him.

Cocking his chin to the side, he slanted his eyes toward her. "Mmm, okay. I kinda see how he might have gotten spooked. But he may have jumped the gun on the exclusive relationship piece, especially if you guys hadn't—" Jake stopped himself because he knew he was fishing. He waved the waiter over.

"No, we didn't fuck. We barely even kissed. I couldn't see myself voluntarily signing up to fuck him. I guess that should be one warning sign for the future," she chuckled to herself as if she just had a realization.

Jake's throat convulsed with the frankness of her words. He had to concentrate not to choke on the sip of wine he had just taken. "Uh, okay. Thanks for the details." The side of his mouth twitched. "Yes. Since it should be voluntary. If you can't picture it, move on."

The waiter arrived, and Jake asked him to put another bottle of the Bordeaux they were drinking on his tab. When the waiter explained that was the last bottle, Jake asked about another one, Château Montrose. The waiter affirmed that he had some. Jake told him to bring the oldest vintage they had.

Rakell noticed he pronounced the French name perfectly and had ordered a wine slightly better than the one they had been enjoying. She felt bad that he was spending that much money to impress her.

"Jake, you didn't need to. I mean, with the wine…"

"Wanted to. I wanna help you drown your sorrows over this guy you couldn't picture fucking." He sported his familiar smart-ass grin. "So any other plans? Or are you just gonna spend a hell of a lot of money getting drunk?"

"Well, I was weighing my options when you sat down."

"Let's hear them." He leaned back in his chair, willing his eyes to stay focused on her face instead of the honey skin that was peeking through the crisscrossed leather laces between her breasts. The base of his cock tightened just thinking about pulling one of the laces and exposing all the goodness underneath.

"One, I could do as you said and spend a hell of a lot of money getting drunk on great wine, nibble on some cheese, go home and order

Chinese take-out, then end the night with my trusted lipstick…"

He cut her off. "Lipstick?" *Damn, is she inferring…*

"Let's move on to option number two, and this was the one that I was seriously considering. I could try something new and bold…"

"All right, let's hear it," he said nodding.

The depth of his voice, tinged with his Texas drawl, made her nipples spike, as if his hot breath was dragging across her chest. The wine seeped through her, mellowing her, and she could feel herself wanting to shed the constraints on her actions, her life.

"One-night stand," Rakell said assuredly, boldly sitting up straight, anticipating his reaction.

"One-night stand?" he questioned, keeping his features impassive, wondering what kind of response she was hoping to elicit. Toying, teasing, taunting…this girl was a wanton queen. And he was court-jester just trying to get her attention. *Bullshit, babe!* he wanted to spit out. *I'm a cunning warrior. Just let me get those clothes off and that smug queen smile will be gone, replaced with an open, screaming mouth, begging for more.*

Damn it, his chest tightened, and he felt her saucy words between his legs. "Like, just pick up some random guy? Or someone you might already know?" He tried to control his voice to sound casual, his hand flexing slowly, willing himself not to react to her sassy mouth.

"No, I don't think it counts if you already know them, does it? Like, see that cute guy with the blazer at the bar? Just going up to him and saying, 'Do you want to get a room here and fuck tonight?' He doesn't have a ring on. I checked." She bit her bottom lip hard.

Jake arched an eyebrow. "Uh, might be a little abrupt."

"Okay, I'll buy him a drink first."

"I don't know. I don't do one-night stands, so I can't really recommend them." He kept his expression somber to match his tone. He wasn't being altogether truthful, but it had been a rule he'd been trying to stick to, especially the more well-known he became. Jordan had pointed out that Jake had earned that reputation, and Jake needed to work hard to create a new image to replace the old. The gift of social media being that the old one never really gets replaced. What a relief that this girl didn't seem to know him, wasn't kissing up to his fame. So here he was just being Jake from Austin. It surprised him how that made him breathe easier, feel lighter, even if it was a shit ton more work than he was used to with most women.

"Never?" she taunted.

"A few times when I was younger, until Jordan got hold of me. His rule: at least three dates before jumping in bed," Jake explained, pouring more of the recently arrived wine for each of them.

"So you don't think he'd do it?" Her eyes slanted toward the guy at the bar.

"Not sure, but I know I wouldn't," he said, sounding a little too preachy.

"Oh, okay. So let's say hypothetically speaking..." She stood up, holding her glass of wine.

Where was she going? She seemed on edge to him tonight, in a way that made him nervous. Then she put her hand on his shoulder and her legs in between his legs as she lowered herself onto his thigh, his quad muscle turning to stone as her bottom made contact. *Jesus*, he thought. *I wonder if she's had too much?*

"So hypothetically, a girl comes up to you at the bar and asks to buy you a drink..." Rakell murmured, looking down at him.

Jake tried to still his visceral reaction to having her so close, knowing he should get her off his leg. "Okay, I would probably insist on buying her a drink, first of all..."

Slowly she placed her long finger into the cleft of his chin. His eyes crossed, watching it as if it was happening to someone else, but it was his balls that were growing heavy from her touch. *Jesus.*

"Nope, this is the kind of girl that's bold. She's buying your drink. Do you say yes or no?" she asked, letting her finger trail down his chin before pulling it away.

God, just that simple touch felt like too much, in a good way.

"Is she hot? Just wondering." He forced a smile, his body on fire, wishing he could twist himself out of the chair before she could feel his growing bulge against the side of her thigh. Her leg was way too close to his crotch, waking up every nerve from his sternum to his toes. Here he was, being slowly tortured in the middle of his favorite bar as if all the women he had seduced amongst these dark paneled walls had melded into this powerhouse. He was paying for all the times that his piercing blue eyes had purposely traveled up and down their bodies, just as his fingers trailed the edge of their chins before lightly playing with their ears, relishing the tell-tale signs of arousal, knowing they'd ask him to bed before he could even hint at it. Now, at this moment, he was paying the piper.

Rakell slid her arm around his shoulders to help brace herself.

"Yeah, I would say pretty. So what do you say to the drink?"

"I'd say, 'Yes, I'd love a drink,'" he murmured back, sucking in a breath through his nose, gripping the sides of the chair, desperately trying to control his body's urges.

"Okay. After a couple of drinks, she puts her hand on your leg and starts to rub your thigh. This most definitely gets your attention, right?" Her focus settled between Jake's legs. "So *hypothetically*, do you feel aroused?" Her lips partially opened.

He wanted to scream. Jake sucked in another sharp breath. "Okay, *hypothetically*...does she have big breasts?" he asked, trying to sound amused, desperately wanting to pull her attention up so her eyes would move away from the apex of his jeans. His brain was begging his cock to stand down.

"Yes, she has big breasts, and you can see the tops of them." Rakell let out a little laugh as her torso bent slightly, just enough to make Jake's whole body tighten. His toes were curling in his boots as his body fought the onslaught of her touch, her smell, her warm breath, her languid throaty laugh, and the way she shifted her ass on his leg.

Bending her head, she moved her mouth up against his ear, her voice purposely low. "Then she leans over and whispers in your ear, 'Let's get a room. I want to suck your cock and have you fuck my brains out.'" She popped her head up, looking at him. "So what would you say to that, Mr. No-One-Night-Stands?" Her eyes expanded into saucers as amusement oozed from her tone.

Damn her! The shaft of his cock firmed against his stiff jeans. His balls felt like they were filled with jumping beans. *She knows exactly what she's doing.* He moved to stand, put a hand on the side of her waist, and pulled her to her feet, then took her hand and led her the two steps back to her chair. His hands slid around her waist so he could lower her gently into her seat, bending down as he did. He lowered his face to hers, glaring, his inky waves falling forward as he spoke. "I'd still say no."

Rakell made a purposeful pouty face, protruding her bottom lip in an overexaggerated fashion.

He put his index finger to her lip. "Eh, eh...but what I *would* say to her is, 'You're the kind of girl I'd like to get to know. Let me buy you a drink, hear your story, and take you on a couple of nice dates. Then if you still wanna blow me, I'll let you. But only after I get my tongue between your legs. If that all works out, I'd gladly love to, as you put it, 'fuck your brains out.'" His hand cupped her chin, her mouth lax as she stared at him. He pressed his thumb to her mouth, running it over her bottom lip, absorbing her saucer eyes, leaning in, catching himself when he heard her gasp. Then he dropped his hand to the side of the chair. Bracing himself, he leaned into the side of her face and spoke to her hair where her ear was hidden.

Rakell was breathing so hard her chest looked like it was going to cave. He loved it. "So *hypothetically* speaking, do you think Ms. One-Night-Stand would put off her lusty self for a few dates? Or…would she move on to a different guy?"

He moved his lips so close to hers that she could feel his breath on her face.

"Well, uh…" she stammered, not sure where to go. Gently, she put one hand to his chest and pushed. He stood and moved back toward his chair.

"You don't have to answer right away." Finally, he'd gotten the upper hand with this girl. *Checkmate, sweetheart,* he thought, pleased with himself. "What was option three?" he asked, the stiffness between his legs forcing him to lower himself slowly into his chair as if he had pulled a muscle in his lower back. "Option three?" he repeated.

"Yeah, uh…three…Oh, I have two tickets to Guy Forsyth in my purse, and I was going to ask some random person if he wanted to join me. But, um, I mean, would *you* like to go with me? You probably…I mean, your plans…" She struggled to get a coherent thought out, and it wasn't the wine; it was the rush that had taken over her body.

"I'd love to go with you. Guy is one of my Austin favorites," he said, picking up his phone and texting the group.

Jake: *Have fun without me, have other plans…***Send**

His phone blew up, but he ignored it. Looking at his watch, then to her, taking in the flush in her cheeks, he said, "We have time to finish the wine. We can walk there. I'll just leave my truck here."

Rakell nodded, not speaking.

"Hey, you?" he said, concerned he'd gone a little too far.

Her mouth relaxed. "Yeah you?"

"You good?"

"Mmm-huh," she murmured, taking him in. Dark denim jeans, black cowboy boots, and a midnight blue button-up shirt, untucked but perfectly tailored to his broad shoulders and narrow waist. She wondered if he had to get things specially made because of his size. His jet-black hair tossed around his head, paired with his piercing blue eyes that made him look somewhere between a sinister villain and a fashion model. Then add in the cowboy boots. It was all too much, she thought, looking away. Needing to cool off, she reached for the glass of ice water that was next to her wine.

Chapter Twelve

As they walked the few short blocks from the Driskill to Antone's, Jake didn't attempt to hold Rakell's hand or put his arm around her, even though he wanted to. It didn't seem like she was inviting it. He was getting seriously mixed signals from this woman. Or was it him? Did he want this too much?

Antone's buzzed with people and background music. It was an Austin music staple which always attracted great acts. Even though the place had a typical small club vibe—the black walls and stage lending it an almost cave-like feel—there were plenty of tables and a large open space for people to gather. Guy Forsyth was a huge attraction—the show had been sold out for weeks—especially with Jeska joining him on stage tonight.

Jake tentatively put his hand on the small of Rakell's back just under her fringe suede jacket to guide her past the crowd to the bar. He loved that the backless dress let him feel her soft skin as he steered her body through the throng of patrons.

After waiting a couple of minutes at the bar, they got the attention of the bartender. "I'll take a double tequila on the rocks," Rakell shouted over the din.

"Make it two Tequila 512's," Jake added. His hand caressed her lower back. He could feel her muscles tighten under his touch. He knew he needed to temper his excitement. The fact that she'd invited him tonight gave him hope, but he knew he had to approach with caution.

"Got it," the bartender said, looking at them both and smiling. "Gonna be a good night," he shouted as he poured the tequila, letting generous amounts spill into their highball glasses.

"Absolutely. Guy is playing—can't get better than that," Jake offered, smiling, instinctively pulling Rakell close to his side. He was going to have a really hard time keeping his hands off her tonight. He took the glasses from the bar and handed her one. He slid the bartender cash, instructing him to keep the change.

The place was packed. All the tables were taken, so they wiggled themselves forward while people were still shifting around the large room. As they sipped their tequila listening to the Guy Forsyth Band, Jake tried to constrain himself, badly wanting to pull her into him. Then she took a small step backwards, her back bumping his full chest. That's all he needed to touch her, one hand slipping gingerly around her waist, following her lead, moving with the music. The crowd sang along and hooted for Guy and his band. Then Jeska made her entrance, slinking on to stage. Her legs moved slowly, like a panther stalking its prey, as she stared at Guy. The crowd went crazy. The boisterous cacophony that had been bouncing off the black walls quieted to a hushed murmur when she started to sing. The electric intimacy that strung between Guy and Jeska seemed to quickly permeate the crowd, and a rapt stillness ensued, as if a channel had been changed.

Rakell leaned back on Jake, the back of her head resting against his chest.

Shutting his eyes momentarily, Jake took in the feel of her against him. Sucking in a slow, long breath through his nose, he coaxed his nervous system to engage warily. Laying his hand across her belly, his fingers opening, he flexed his arm, snugging her deeper into his body. He could stay here all night, drinking in the floral scent from her hair spun together with a citrusy fresh scent that he wasn't sure whether it was lotion or perfume. All he knew was that her smell, the feel of her against him swaying, her upper ass brushing against his crotch, her husky voice singing softly, were all sucking him in. So much so that he felt like she was his…and always had been. He shook his head, yanking himself back to reality. God, he needed to get a fucking grip!

Guy's low voice, intertwining with the music from instruments, swirled in Rakell's ears as the tequila warmed her bloodstream. Both intoxicants teased her, plucking her nerve-endings and imploring her to absorb the feel of Jake's hard chest against her back, his pelvis shifting with the music, the stiffness of his arousal subtly apparent. All of it ganged up on her resolve, her fight not to lose herself in the moment.

Breathing in and out, she surrendered, letting her sensory system win, falling into the here and now. She allowed herself to be just a normal girl liking a guy, not Marietta, the high-end call girl, whose personality was defined by a man's desires. Rakell, *Rakell*, that's who you are; the daughter of a rancher, at a bar in Austin Texas, listening to blues. You define who you are with this guy, a cute guy you met at the gym. At the gym… what a normal place to meet.

Her senses overrode her rational brain. She wasn't looking for anything, just fun. Why did he feel like more than that?

"Hey," Jake whispered, lowering his head to her side, "hand me your glass." She extended the glass toward him. He grabbed it, brushing his fingers against hers. "Do you want another one?" he asked, a little too breathlessly. *Jesus, Jake, you're asking if she wants another drink, not what you really want to ask: 'I want to bury myself in you; do you want that too?'*

Rakell turned, stepping back from him. "No, I'm feeling it." She wrinkled her nose, smiling. Lifting up on her toes, she whispered in his ear, "Thanks for coming with me. Are you enjoying it…the music?"

He held a glass in each hand, preventing him from wrapping her up in his arms and showing her how much he enjoyed it… and her. "God, of course. And the music is great too." He tilted his head back, flashing his giant Jake grin. "I'll be right back." He stepped away and sucked in a long breath, entreating himself to chill out, reminding himself that he wasn't some horny teenager who melted any time a girl got close.

Forgoing another desperately needed tequila, Jake put the empty glasses on the bar, then moved back across the room to find Rakell. He stared at her in her gypsy dress and Dolly Parton-style fringe jacket, swaying and singing low as Guy and Jeska sang "The Things That Matter." Jake came up behind her and put both arms around her waist, pulling her back into him a little snugger than before.

Then she twisted in his arms, her hair a little messy from dancing, her chest covered in a thin film of perspiration. Her green eyes were glossy, wide, searching. She was still singing, "Don't give me diamond rings…those so-called finer things…they don't matter when they're not there." Her pink lips, partly opened, smiling up at him as she continued, "I only want the things that matter…only want the things you can share." She broke off from singing, moving up on her toes so she could whisper in his ear, "I love that song." She craned her head back, looking up at him.

Her voice, her touch, those eyes—they all enveloped Jake. He cupped her chin in his hand, wanting to say, *And I love you.* But he didn't. He knew better, knew he didn't know her. Yet here he was aching to know their "together story," to have the end written somewhere he could read it now. He leaned down, laying his lips to the side of her cheek, close to hers.

She turned her head, bringing her lips to his. Without thought, Jake let his mouth cover hers, gently pulling her lips in. Then firmly, his control evaporating, he took her mouth in whole, his tongue rushing in and she sucking it as her head craned back, her chest pushing into his lower chest. He couldn't get enough.

Rakell could still hear the music, the murmur of the crowd, but it seemed distant, like a recording playing at a low volume. She wanted to crawl into Jake's skin and make this last, never let it stop. She had never been kissed like this, never had what felt like her whole being sucked up in a kiss.

Guy thanked everyone and announced the last song. The crowd started to break away. Rakell pulled back, shaking, laying her head on Jake's chest as he squeezed his arms around her. Neither said anything, as if they were both holding their breath, waiting for the cold air of reality to wake their lungs up.

Jake took her hand and pulled her outside, walking briskly down the street before stopping short and pulling her into him again, his hands on either side of her face, dipping his head to kiss her again. His mouth captured hers, absorbing her light moans. He couldn't stop. *I can't let this go,* he thought as his hand went to her shoulders and peeled her body back, looking down at her red, puffy lips and the confused softness in her eyes as she stared back at him.

Rakell closed her eyes briefly, breathing in deeply. She yanked herself back. "What are we doing? I mean…"

Later, when he lay in bed running through the night in his brain, would he register an imperceptible concern, or was it confusion in her tone when she asked him that? But at that moment, he was solely focused on wanting more, more of this, more of her.

"We have a few options," he said, pecking her lips, tilting his head back, trying to stop himself from attacking her mouth again.

"Okay, what's option one?"

A small smile crossed his lips as his senses started to connect again. "I reckon it's the best option. You come home with me, and we don't waste any more time clothed."

"Second option, mister? Because that's a one-night stand, and a really wise guy once made a strong case against one-night stands. I agree with him." She was tempted, but she'd have to face him again at the gym, and she wasn't sure how to navigate that.

Jake yanked her against him harder. "*That* guy? You bought all his BS? He's an idiot, talks way too fucking much. Grrrr, that guy will be the end of me." *Pull back, Jake, slow down, slow time, just like you do with that football in your hand, give your brain a second to make the right move.*

She rolled her eyes. "Next option?" she pushed as the departing crowd began passing around them on the sidewalk.

"Pancakes at Kirby Lane?"

Rakell made a face. "If I'm eating this late, it better be killer tacos."

"Better yet, we head down the street to the Roosevelt Room for a drink, then we can grab some tacos at Velvet Tacos," he suggested. Thinking about how the dark bar with its black leather secluded booths made it easy to run his hands up and down a woman's legs, and perhaps a little higher, with no one the wiser to the goings-on beneath the table.

"Sounds so good, but I'm spent. I'd probably fall asleep at the table," she answered, the words leaving her mouth slowly.

"Another night?" He hated the anxiety dominating his tone, not wanting this to be just one night.

Rakell nodded. "I'll take an Uber from here. Are you walking back to the Driskill or Ubering?" she asked.

"No way, you're not taking an Uber alone at night. Let's walk back to the Driskill, and I'll drive you home." A sternness threaded through his voice.

"Uh, I'm perfectly fine taking Uber by myself. I do it all the time," she replied, her body waking up in defense.

"I don't care; not with me you don't. Seriously, let me drive you." A pleading aspect entered his tone as he tried not to sound too controlling, reminding himself they weren't actually dating. But this was a hard rule for him with any woman: He was directly responsible for making sure she got home safely. It was a lesson his dad had pounded into him.

Normally, she'd lecture a guy like this with the fact that she'd been independent since she was seventeen and didn't need to depend on any man, but she was fighting fatigue and the desire to stay close to him a little longer. "Okay, but I'm not sure I have the energy to walk back to the Driskill, so maybe we Uber together?"

Jake had another idea: a bicycle carriage ride. Before Rakell could object, he pulled her to one of the many waiting along the sidewalk. They climbed in, and he wrapped his arm around her as the bicycle glided through downtown Austin. The cool air made it necessary for him to wrap both arms around her. She buried her head in his chest.

She looked up at him as they rode down 5th Street. "Jake?" She didn't know how to say what she was about to say, but the night air, the liquor swirling through her bloodstream, along with the nerves that had been pricked awake by his lips, made it impossible for her to hold her thoughts.

"Mmm?" His eyes moved to the hooded lids of her own as he stroked his thumb lightly over her cheek.

"I've never been kissed like that. I mean…well, no one's ever kissed me in a way that made my whole body pay attention. I…" She trailed off, feeling silly, overly dramatic.

The sincerity in her tone tugged at his heart. He wanted to ask her if she really meant it because it was the sweetest thing he'd ever heard. Instead, he smiled at her and joked, "I need a billboard that says: *Jake Skyler—kisses that make your whole body pay attention.*"

"Shut up," she said, nudging him gently.

"Mmm, that's what your kisses do to me, too." His mouth went to hers, nibbling her bottom lip until she arched into him. His lips instinctively pressed on her mouth. Her tongue made the first move, and his tongue responded firmly. His kiss grew aggressive, possessive, as he heard her soft mewl. His chest pushed against hers.

When the carriage stopped and the driver looked back, they peeled apart from each other, both gasping lightly like the separation was work. They walked to his truck, and she sat next to him, letting her head drift to his shoulder.

Jake heard the steady breathing of her sleep during the ten-minute drive, thinking that he'd love to hear that sound all night, for many nights. He pulled up outside the main doors to her apartment complex where he could see faint shadows of a couple of people through the frosted glass of the lobby, he assumed a doorman and security guard. He knew this complex well—some of his buddies had lived there before they'd gotten married. Because of its location, it was a pricey complex—she must do well, Jake thought.

"Rakell," he whispered, gently moving her shoulders to sit her up.

"Oh...sorry." Rakell blinked her eyes rapidly before looking at him. "Didn't mean to...Just tired, then add in the drinks and..."

"Anytime my shoulder can be your pillow, I'm in," he replied softly. "And just so you know, if you had gone home with me tonight, technically it would not have been a one-night stand."

"How's that?" She gave him a one-eyed, sleepy look.

His eyes were genuine. "Because it wouldn't have been one night—it would have been the start of many, many nights. That I can guarantee." He brushed his lips on her forehead, puckering softly against her skin.

"Ah, but there are no guarantees," she said, sitting up straight. "Except me passing out if I don't get upstairs. I had a great time." She reached for the door.

"Wait." He jumped out and ran to her side of the truck, opening the door. He hugged her and asked if he could walk her up to her place. Emphatically, with an air of panic in her tone, she blurted out, "No!"

Her reaction made his spine stiffen. What the hell? Tightening his neck to control the features of his face, he didn't want to argue. Not tonight, not with the newness of her and him. He watched her walk into the lobby, and it hit him that he had never even gotten her number.

Chapter Thirteen

Sunday passed with no sight of Rakell at the gym. Monday morning, no Rakell. Monday afternoon, no Rakell.

"Jake, not another word about that girl," Dwayne lectured him between sets. "Damn, brother, you are spiraling. Listen, I already worked it out with my girl, Jenn. She's gonna set you up with her best friend, also a realtor and a sweetheart, next weekend. Somebody, I guarantee, who will take your mind off this one."

"First of all, 'your girl' what? Like two dates and you're already laying claim? Dude, you act like *I'm* jumping the gun…really? Also, not sure I want to be set up, Dwayne." Jake spoke solemnly, his tone distant.

"Jenn knows I'm only here for off-season. She doesn't have any ideas of long-term…makes it easier. So, dude, you're going. This girl is already on board and excited about going out with *Pretty Boy Jake Skyler*. You saw her picture, so you know she's hot. What do you have to lose?" Dwayne prodded.

"Yep, probably right," Jake murmured almost to himself, but his mind flashed back to Antone's and the way Rakell's lips melded to his, as if they'd spent a lifetime figuring it out.

Tuesday morning, Jake sat in his truck outside the gym, drinking coffee, while he waited for Jordan to arrive for their morning workout. He planned to go by Rakell's apartment to leave a note with his number after they finished. He couldn't get her out of his head. His mind dug into Saturday night—the look in her eyes after he'd kissed her, her willingness to open herself to him, the things she'd said about his kisses. His whole life he'd been able to categorize women, but he wasn't sure where she fit in. She wasn't innocent; instead, she was some unusual mixture of bold and vulnerable. Definitely not as sure of herself as she appeared, but at times she seemed almost aggressive about standing up for herself. To call it an odd combination grossly understated the contradictions.

Jake saw the Tornadoes cap, and his eyes darted to the swinging doors. *She's going for a run. Maybe Town Lake?* Just then, Jordan pulled up, and Jake called him as he was backing up his truck. "Sorry, but you're on your own this morning," Jake told him.

"What the hell? I'm looking at you right now. I'm sitting in my car watching you drive off. Where are you going?" Then Jake watched Jordan notice Rakell walking across the parking lot. "Oh, right. Jake, my man—you are messed up. You're really gonna follow her?"

"Yep, and I know I'm fucked in the head."

"Got that right. And I'm really close to sickin' Delilah on you." Jake heard a note of concern in his voice as he hung up.

Rakell got into her car, a yellow Camaro convertible with a black top, as he pulled out. The car, just like everything about her, was unexpected. He wasn't sure what he thought she'd be driving, but a canary yellow Camaro?

He had guessed right. She pulled into a parking lot near the Town Lake trail. Jake pulled in a few spots away and got out of his truck. He knew this was too much, that his actions really did border on stalking, but he couldn't reason with himself. He couldn't help it.

Rakell pulled a thin sweatshirt over her head, grabbed a water bottle from her back seat, and walked through the parking lot to the trail. Jake jogged up behind her. "Hey, you," he called, trying to sound casual.

Rakell whipped her head to the side. "What the hell?" she exclaimed with a barely controlled yelp. "Jeez, Jake. Again with sneaking up on me?" She was obviously irritated.

"Sorry. I just…well, I wanted to see you, and I didn't have any way to get in touch," he blurted out.

When she looked back at him, she couldn't help but notice the little-boy smile pleading *forgive me*. That sweet smile framed by black hair, a chiseled jaw, and fierce blue eyes, seemed incongruent with the force the rest of his person exuded. His thin athletic shirt catching on the lines of his muscular chest and back, his powerful legs below his shorts—this guy went after what he wanted. She shook her head, taken aback by his bravado to just show up.

But she had to admit, there was a part of her that was almost giddy. She had thought about him constantly since Saturday night but didn't know how to make sense of her feelings. She had committed to Matt and had a few more escort clients she had contractually agreed to through the end of the year. She knew if she could hold on, finish out all her contracts, she would be financially set and could finally wholeheartedly delve into her life as *Rakell.*

"Well, since you're here, you think you can keep up with me?" she said, smiling as she playfully punched his arm. Jake grinned as he noticed her initial irritation fading.

"And if I do?" he said, his mouth curling up. "What do I get?"

"Um, the pleasure of my company." She winked as she moved close to him and pushed her hip up against his leg.

His arm went around her shoulders. "I'll take that and your number."

"Deal," she shouted as she turned away and took off running along the trail.

He caught up and ran beside her. "What are we aiming for today?"

"Five."

"Got it."

They ran the five miles with few words. Jake told her how Dolly, his golden Lab, usually came with him, so he'd normally run a few miles and then take a break so she could have water. It was unnatural to hold back on his life. He was eager to talk about anything but what he did for a living, hoping he could avoid the NFL player thing for as long as possible. He wanted her to like him for him. He told her about Dolly, how he'd adopted her from a shelter, how she was pretty demanding attention wise. The next line—that he missed her so much when he had to be in Sacramento—he swallowed.

He finally shut up when Rakell looked at him oddly. "I got it, Jake. You love Dolly, she's your life. Please bring Dolly next time. I'm eager to meet the girl that has your heart." Her lips curled up. She had grown up with animal lovers, but the amount of detail about Dolly's life was bordering on ridiculous. *God, next thing you know he'll be referring to this dog as his fucking "fur baby."*

After they finished the run, both sweating and out of breath, they grabbed coffee and more water at Mr. Grinds across the street. They sat on a bench, drinking and talking mostly about Austin and working out. He loved how she looked in her camo leggings and army-green sweatshirt, which almost matched the color of her eyes. Every time he looked at her, he wanted to kiss or embrace her. The ache to be close to her, touching her, strung through him.

Jake pulled out his phone. "I gotta get your number so I can quit stalking you."

She slid closer to him on the bench, draping one leg over his, looking at his phone as he typed in her number and sent her a text so she'd have his contact.

Jake: *Me wanting you, Jake…***Send**

Rakell looked up at him. "Well, I'm here. What are you doing about it?"

That's all he needed. He put down his coffee and wrapped her up in his arms, leaning down and gently kissing her lips, softly feeling her mouth against his.

Her mouth opened as his tongue moved inside. It started gently, but an urgent passion quickly took over. Instinctively, their tender morning kiss became a rapid, greedy frenzy. Rakell invited it with her quiet moans while her hands moved up and down his hard chest, touching, grabbing, wanting more.

The sound of children giggling in the distance brought them both back from the storm of desire they'd been caught up in. Rakell took a couple of quick breaths, distracted by the thought of what it would be like to have sex with him. If just kissing him did this to her, she couldn't imagine what it would be like to be with him completely. So contradictory to her life as Marietta—could she compartmentalize with Jake, have fun, not connect?

"Hey, we're dangerously close to giving those kids over there an early lesson about the birds and the bees." He craned his head back, watching her fight back a smile. He wanted to lean down and nibble on those smirky lips but knew he needed some public self-control. "Guess we'd better wrap up this make-out session. Kinda putting on a show here." He brushed his thumb over her cheek, then her red lips, caressing them, thinking he'd gotten a little carried away with her mouth.

She lifted her leg from his thigh. "Yeah, I'm not into indecent exposure in public and really need to get going to work. I have a big lunch meeting." Matt had texted her yesterday to see if she could meet his team today at lunch to help on a big deal with a wind energy company in Texas. They needed an interpreter because the wind farm they were looking to purchase was owned by an older local farmer in Costa Rica who spoke limited English.

Jake stood and pulled Rakell to her feet. They walked on the path with their arms around each other. She wanted to ask him so many questions about what they were doing; she wanted to know what she was supposed to do next. She wished someone could give her a book about how all this worked. If she let him in, would she need to tell him what she really did for a living? She couldn't do that. He couldn't know about Marietta. This was why most escorts didn't really have personal dating lives; it was too complicated. But couldn't she just date and have some fun?

"So what are we doing? I mean? Are we...?" She hesitated, not sure what to say next. He was so easy to be with, but she couldn't get into anything serious. How could she tell him what her main profession was? It was true that she worked for Matt as an interpreter partly as cover, but also because he had a lot of contracts in Central and South America, but still...

Jake quickly kissed the top of her head. "Dating? Or starting to see each other...right?" He treaded carefully; there was something fleeting about her.

She looked up at him. "This is dating in America? Just meeting up at random times and making out? I thought dating was going to the movies, playing putt-putt, holding hands—stuff like that." Smiling, she added, "Sharing an ice cream cone."

He laughed, squeezing her shoulder as they walked. "So you're looking for the high school dating experience?"

"I didn't know that was high school. What were you thinking?" She was thinking that her high school dating experience had come to an abrupt halt when her dad died.

"Nice dinners, great wine, flying you to Cabo for the weekend, taking a helicopter ride over the Grand Canyon that ends with a champagne picnic, a weekend in Napa..."

Rakell jumped in. "That's not dating, that's trying to impress someone." His ideas were sounding way too close to her escort life, making her wonder what he did for a living or if he was just saying those things to impress her.

"Well, that's exactly what I want to do," he said, not hiding his bemusement.

"I'd rather be impressed by you as a *person*. I've had so many experiences that—" The words jumped out of her mouth, and she wished she could take them back. "I mean, not with anybody that I wanted to be with." *Stop talking, you're making a mess out of this*, she thought, sucking in air. "I think the point is that I want to try the normal, everyday experiences with a normal guy and see if I like, really like him for who he is and just have fun." Her words twisted out, jumbled, as she tried to explain.

"Shit, no pressure," Jake said as they approached her car, thinking that what he wanted was a normal girl, and that he yearned to be what she wanted—a normal guy. Moving into her so that her body was pressed against the car, he studied her, wondering about her past, especially her past with men. He lowered his head, touching his forehead to hers, and whispered, "What if you don't like the normal guy—me?"

Rakell stared up at him. "And what if he doesn't like the normal girl? I'm tired of being—um, always having to be somebody else." Her eyes dropped from his as panic mixed with her words. She immediately wished she hadn't said that. She obviously couldn't tell him the truth, but her inexperience dating men without contracts showed whenever she tried to relax.

He put his thumb on her chin while his hand enveloped her left jaw, his eyes brimming with concerned confusion. "*Rae*-kale, I already like the normal girl, you. Period. You don't have to pretend to be anybody else. I don't know what your dating experiences have been like, but I don't need you to pretend with me. Believe me, I've been in enough pretend situations myself."

"I just meant that—that I have to travel all over the world for work, and I meet some pretty amazing people, but...I'm expected to act a certain way." Her speech was halting. "You know, in business, I told you I work as a business consultant mostly when they are working on deals outside of the US. Mainly as an interpreter, but I have to create a certain image... anyway it's not the Austin me. That's all," she explained.

"Your job sounds cool, but I like the Austin you. I'd like to hear more about your work sometime." He kissed her cheek lightly, looking back at her face. "But…"

"Okay, but what?"

"Just want to assure you that I'm definitely more your normal guy than any of those exotic, amazing men you're meeting on your business travels. So, okay, let's get on with 'normal dating' in America. Are you up for putt-putt tonight? There's a fun place called Peter Pan Mini-Golf on Barton Springs."

Rakell pushed past the "exotic men" comment, wanting to say, *Not really. They're just really, really rich men that like to see themselves as exotic.* She got a jolt thinking about doing normal couple stuff with Jake, clapping her hands together, an open-mouthed grin on her face. "Yes! You know…I've never played putt-putt golf before. What time?"

Jake laughed, shaking his head. "Does six work? I have to warn you—I'm a pretty bad-ass mini golfer."

The smile still shone on her face. "It's fine if you're better than me at one thing." She stood up on her toes, pecking his lips. "Can we get ice cream too? Maybe go to one of those ice cream trucks?"

She sounded so young and giddy that Jake couldn't help but chuckle. "Sure, I'll even share a cone with you. But another warning—I have a big tongue." He looked at her, amused, as he continued, "So a few good licks and it could be gone."

She eyed him back. "Well, you've met your ice-cream-licking match. I have a big, fast, well-practiced tongue, so I'll challenge you and win. My tongue is better than yours," she teased, breaking out into laughter.

His wide grin falling into a wry smile, he said, "You turn everything dirty. I love that about you." He leaned down and gently bit her bottom lip, then pulled away, leaving her mouth open, begging for another kiss.

She protruded her bottom lip, obviously pouting. "Ah, not fair. Who turns everything dirty?" She turned, unlocking her car. "I have to go. See you at six. Text me when you're on your way. I'll meet you out front." She slid into her car.

Jake drove back to the gym, knowing he had to lift today. Off-season didn't mean lying around, eating like shit and drinking beer. It meant a certain amount of resting, but also preparing for another season. He'd have to fly back to Sacramento next week for a few days since Coach wanted to plan for next season, analyze some videos, and chat about potential draft picks. It was strange not to talk to Rakell about what he did, not to have led with that since it was what most women knew about him right away. And yet at the same time, the connective energy that strung between them enticed him even more. *This is real, there is no pretense with her* rang in his head.

Rakell caught Jake staring at her ass more than once as she bent over trying to putt the ball. She purposely made sure her hips wiggled back and forth as she positioned her body over the club. A few times she heard him blow out a breath that sounded like it was combined with a sigh. She wore white skinny jeans that sat low on her hips, a chambray cropped top with elbow-length puffed sleeves that was gathered around her breasts, and white Converse tennis shoes. Her goal had been to look sexy without looking like she'd tried too hard, so she wore only a little bit of mascara and sheer lip gloss with her hair pulled back in a loose low ponytail, wisps of hair falling out of it and framing her face. She'd skipped the jewelry altogether.

There were two eighteen-hole courses at Peter Pan. Jake explained that it was family owned and had been there as long he could remember. He'd even had a couple of birthday parties there when he was a kid. Jake filled a plastic cup with wine that he'd poured into a cooling sleeve before he picked her up. "Here you go," he said, his eyes glancing up and down her body as he handed the cup to her.

"Thanks. Can't believe they let you bring in wine," she said, sipping from the cup.

"Yep. No glass allowed, but it's still pretty cool. There are actually a few places in Austin that are BYOB," he said, grabbing his club.

"Being good at putt-putt probably helped in high school. I mean, with the girls, right?" She offered him a goofy grin.

Jake nodded, cocking one eyebrow. "Sure, that's what all girls are looking for: a putt-putt master. I could give you some pointers, but I know how much you hate direction."

"Hey, not fair! I just don't like men bossing me around." Rakell turned to grab her club, and under her breath, she said, "Had enough of that for a lifetime."

"Huh, what was that?" He laid his club down, then stepped toward her, putting his hand on the edge of her hip, easing her into him. "Not nice to whisper shit about someone when they're standing right here."

"Not talking about you. Just men in general."

Leaning into her, he said, "Um, if you haven't noticed, I'm a member of that species." His face moved close to hers. "Have you noticed?" he growled before pecking her lips. Jake shifted her hips so she was facing him, her cup in one hand and her club in the other. Rakell took in his smell, a combination of pine, the outdoors, and something muskier: a masculine smell, something that made her want to breathe in deep.

His hand moved to the small of her back, spreading across the bare skin above her jeans. Rakell sucked in sharply. She couldn't wait to feel him arching into him as his lips touched hers. She opened her mouth. She'd never felt like this. Hungry, almost aching for a man's touch. She could feel her effect on him push against her lower belly. She thought about Jake a lot, in the middle of everyday activities, work, working out, driving. And when she did, her lips would pucker as if trying to capture the feel of his own on hers when he kissed her. He started softly, then swiftly the intensity of his lips grew fiercer, seeming to demand more. She suddenly remembered they were in the middle of a putt-putt course, and she could hear the milling of people, families talking, laughing.

His intense stare bored into her as he leaned back slightly. "Well, did you notice?" he repeated, a cocky grin surfacing on his face.

Rubbing her lips together, her head arching back, Rakell looked into his sharp blue eyes. "Ah-huh, I noticed." Her mouth turned up. "Well, sort of."

"Really?" Jake barked, releasing his firm hold on her low back. He stepped back, abruptly, both hands in the air, as if he had singed his hands while touching her. "Let's get back to the game or we'll be playing till midnight," he said, watching her pick up her club.

"Yes, let's." She walked to the next hole, and he followed behind her.

Rakell wanted to turn around and say, *Okay, give me the fucking rule book. What are we doing? I'm having fun, but this feels like much more, and we just met.* Jake would know the answer. She could tell that he'd touched many, kissed many, and that many had fallen for him. But she knew she wouldn't be one of them. No, her life wouldn't allow for it. This had to be just fun. It didn't matter how her sensory system lit up when he got close, how much she wanted to bury her face in his chest, suck in his scent, feel the firmness in his lips.

Bending, she aimed the club and swung, apparently too hard, because the ball hit the edge of the green and popped onto the walkway, rolling downhill. She dropped her club and ran after it. Walking back to the hole, she saw him standing at the tee laughing. "So ready for me to give you some lessons?"

"No, because I'm poised to win," she replied.

"Eh, no. You have to start from the tee again. What the hell are you doing?" he said, chuckling.

Rakell stood by the hole, bending slightly, with her hand extending just above it, the ball between her first finger and thumb.

"Hell no," Jake said. "That's called cheating, missy." He approached her with a wide grin on his face. "You know I'm winning, so you're gonna go and cheat?"

She lifted her eyes up to him as he stood close. She couldn't help but notice that his eyes got stuck on her cleavage. From his vantage point, she was sure he got an eyeful. "So are you the breed of mate that has to prove his manhood by beating a girl?"

Jake snorted, "What the hell?" He bent toward her, so his face was inches from hers. "Are you the kinda girl I gotta let win?" He squinted his eyes at her, his mouth straight, fighting back a smile.

She breathed in his smell once again. His straight mouth, challenging jaw, and piercing blue eyes made him appear ominous. But she knew once he smiled, his face would alter to a bright, boyish flash that had the power to disarm.

He saw the teenage boy a few holes in front of them, turning around, staring, then turning back to his dad. *Shit, had that kid recognized me?* He wasn't ready for the other Jake to come out yet. "Well? Wait…" He leaned a little closer, his warm breath on her face, his eyes catching the kid in the distance. He'd stopped looking, but Jake needed to ease them out of here quickly, just in case. "What do I get if you win?"

"Um, what do you get?" Rakell watched him nod his head as his eyelids drew down over his eyes, a lusty gaze staring back at her. "A kiss…and?"

"And…" he croaked out, as if he was having trouble speaking.

"And if I lose, a hug and a thank you." She smirked.

"I'm holding you tight during that kiss, really tight." His voice was thick, taking on a gravelly tone. "Drop the ball. A hole-in-one." A smile blazed across his face as he stood laughing. He grabbed the score card and pencil. "Two more holes. Pretty sure you're going to need a hole-in-one on both of those to beat me," he said, marking something on the small card.

She dropped the ball in the next hole, then picked it up, her body oozing sass as she walked and dropped it in the next one. "Damn, I'm good," Rakell said, picking up the ball. "So we're done?"

"Yep, you beat me. And you're good. But those are two different points." He picked up his cup, walking toward her. "Let's get out of here," he said yanking her hand, his eyes flitting to the teenager who had moved with his family farther away. "How about a burger at P. Terry's before ice cream?" he said, trying to disguise his urgency to get out without someone saying something. Most of the time, folks kept to themselves even if they knew who he was, but with her by his side, the pea of paranoia seemed to be sprouting leaves, tangling in his chest.

Chapter Fourteen

He pushed for dinner the next night, thinking that the more time he spent with her before telling her what he did, the better chance he had for her to accept him—to see him as Austin, Texas Jake instead of NFL Jake. He knew his weekend would be tied up with his niece and nephew, so he kept insisting that she let him take her out sooner.

She pushed back, trying to say she was busy, but Jake insisted on seeing her again, and she really didn't have a solid excuse. He wouldn't let up after she said she hadn't seen the sunset at the Oasis, an indoor-outdoor restaurant perched high above Lake Travis on the edge of Austin. The restaurant provided what some would argue were the most spectacular sunset views in the world.

As he helped her out of his truck, he took in her outfit: high brown boots that rose to just above her knee, a tight denim skirt with a front slit that traveled up her leg exposing her honey-toned thighs. *Damn he could imagine his hand taking that same path to the sweet center of her.* Then the cream-colored, thin-ribbed short-sleeved turtleneck top. It was tight enough for him to make out the edges of her bra, making it hard to keep his eyes off of her nipples as they pushed against the thin material. She wore her hair down and straight.

She shimmied off the seat, trying to keep her legs together as she took his hand.

Jake diverted his eyes back to her face. "Don't worry. I'm trying not to see how high that slit goes up," he said, bracing her arm. "I'm a gentleman, after all," he uttered as if he were trying to convince himself.

Rakell squinted her eyes at him, trying to fight back a smile. "Are you?" she replied as her feet hit the pavement below.

Taking her arm in his, tightening his hold, he coaxed her into his side. "Actually, I am. But I'm also human, so I'm subject to temptation. And you seem to bring that in spades, Sweets." His voice sounded gravelly, like he was trying to control his tone.

Her eyes roamed his face with its wicked grin. The black, long-sleeved T-shirt he wore seemed to highlight every line of his muscular chest and arms. "Well, you're pretty tempting yourself," she gushed back at him.

Jake stopped, gently pulling back on her arm, swooping his hand behind her back, rotating her so she was facing him. His hand on the side of her face, his thumb on her chin, tilting her head back, he lowered his head until it was inches from hers. Her eyes went wide with surprise. "Just so I'm clear," he whispered, "I'm not trying to tempt you. It's yours for the taking, whenever you want it." His eyes locked on hers, and when she tried to divert her gaze, he gently moved her face back toward him.

"Um, okay," Rakell murmured back, her voice breathy. She could feel her pulse in her neck and wished she could pull back from him. She was pretty sure he'd fight to keep her close, as she could feel his arm flexing on her back.

After a long minute, Jake released her, taking her hand as they walked toward the entrance. He'd texted his friend who worked there, asking if he could possibly get them an out-of-the-way table on one of the lower decks. He wanted some alone time with her, and also didn't want to risk someone recognizing him. It wasn't common for people to recognize him on the street, but he did know a lot of people in Austin, since he'd grown up there. And the folks he knew, well, they knew that he played in the NFL. He'd been interviewed several times by a local newscaster, Levi Storm, so even if it wasn't someone he knew personally, he'd become more recognizable to the general public. He knew he would eventually need to tell her if they moved forward, but for now, he liked that she didn't know who he was. It made him feel like her attraction to him was genuine.

He'd run through the scenarios in his head. What if someone *did* out him? What would he say—*sorry, just wanted you to like me*? Fuck, this felt precarious. He would have to tell her sooner rather than later. He'd already worked out his sincere speech explaining to her that he didn't want to use his job to get her attention. Surely she'd understand that—

maybe even be more endeared to him for not showing off.

Rakell was quiet as they walked to the table, breaking her silence only to say the view was beautiful. Jake scooted his chair a little closer to her, both of them sitting on the side of the table that allowed them to face the lake. He sensed her stiffness as he put a hand on her knee. She visibly flinched, and he was pretty sure he heard her suck in air. "Hey, you," he whispered, still staring at her side.

A stiff smile emerged on her face as she turned to face him. "Yeah?"

"I hope...."

Just then, the waiter appeared. "Can I start you all off with some drinks?"

"What would you like? They have great margaritas here," Jake said, looking at her then back to the waiter. "I'll take a mango margarita."

"Can I please just have a double Tequila 512 on ice?" she said, her eyes on the waiter.

"Sure. Do you all know what you want for apps?"

Rakell shrugged her shoulders. "That's up to you, I don't know what's good here, but I like anything with avocados," she said, her eyes on Jake. Jake ordered something, and the waiter finally walked off. She knew she had to be careful with what passed her lips; the modeling industry and food did not coincide, and she'd been told many times she was beautiful, but...

Jake moved his hand on her lower thigh. The warmth of his touch ran up her leg, her muscles tensed, and her legs instinctively parted. God, this guy was making her crazy. All she could think about was how amazing it would be to feel his body on hers, to just let herself go with him, encourage his hand up her skirt between her legs, Jake getting her off with his hand the way she got herself off every night thinking about him. To feel his mouth moving down her body. She wanted to give in but wondered what that would mean to him. She winced, snapping her legs together.

Jake yanked his hand away. "Hey, sorry," he murmured his eyes bouncing from her face to the lake, then back to her, taking in the stiffness of her jaw.

Rakell let out a rushed sigh, willing herself not to be so jumpy, on edge, fuck, just plain horny. "No, sorry. I was just..."

"*Rae*-kale," he drawled out cautiously, "I don't have any expectations. I mean, I know what I said earlier. I was just letting you know that I'm available—shit, I mean…"

"Okay so you're available…for what?" She smirked, turning to face him, feeling herself coming back to her senses, her breath slowing.

He felt the heat on his neck. Damn, this girl had knocked him off course. "Just sayin'…"

The waiter returned and placed their drinks, chips, guacamole, and queso on the table.

Jake grabbed his margarita. "So where were we?" He smiled, noticing her smile.

Rakell lifted the tequila to her lips, her eyes peering at him over the glass. She swallowed, watching him take a sip of his margarita. "I think you were telling me you're available, like a precious piece of sought-after artwork that's finally come on the market." She altered her muted Australian accent into an animated British one. "When does the bidding start? I've been saving up for the ideal piece."

Hit by her sarcasm and bite, he almost spit his drink back into his glass. "Piece? What? That's not what I'm saying. I just…hell," he stammered, all Jake's charm evaporated into the sticky Texas air. "I was just saying I'm really attracted to you." He looked down as she placed her hand on his knee, wiggling herself on the chair a little closer to him. He guffawed. "I'm sure that's not the first time you've heard that from a guy. I swear, I'm usually better at this."

She leaned toward him, pushing herself up and using his leg to brace herself, moving her lips to his. She pecked his lips, then nibbled on his stiff bottom lip. "Well, I'm usually not better at this, so you're doing well on my scale. I'm not sure what to do," she whispered close to his mouth, her forehead bent toward his.

"God," he murmured before his lips parted, matching her lips. He let her lead, and she did. She had one hand on his knee, the other grasping at the crook of his elbow, moving her fingers onto his lower bicep, like she was trying to gain traction.

Rakell kissed him firmly, working her lips to his. Then he felt her hand slide up to his shoulder as she pushed back. Her green eyes met his, her chest heaving ever so slightly. He heard it but forced his eyes to stay on hers.

A gradual change of her lips, a tight smile, her eyes still locked on his. His sternum felt like it was being crushed with the weight of a car, the pressure inside to control himself when she was near insufferable.

"Jake, her lips a whisper from his.

He could smell the sweet scent of tequila emanating from her mouth. God, he just wanted to taste her again, but hard, fast, his tongue in her mouth and his hands taking over her body. *Jesus, Jake—you're acting like a wound-up teenager.*

"Mm-hmm?" he said, eyes still locked on those gorgeous green orbs. "Yeah?" His tone was laced with restraint, like he was driving during a bad Texas ice storm, focusing like mad to keep the truck out of the ditch.

Then she abruptly leaned up and pecked his cheek. "Can we both just, you know, act normal…just be ourselves?" she said, leaning away from him, sitting back in her chair and taking another sip of her drink.

If I could just get you naked and be inside you, then yeah, maybe I could act normal again, instead of this insecure teenager who's fucking inhabiting my mind, he thought, his eyes dropping to her full lips, wondering what it would feel like to have them wrapped around his cock.

Jake forced a wide grin to his face. "Yep, let's do that. Whatever the hell normal is."

Rakell let out a jolt of laughter, nodding her head like she agreed. He wasn't sure on what, but her laugh was genuine, making him laugh too, letting him release the air that was stuck in his lungs.

Their ease continued through dinner. They both ordered another round of drinks and watched as the sun set over Lake Travis. They stood, cheering with the rest of the crowd who'd gathered on the decks of the Oasis. He clinked his glass to hers as the last of the yellow globe disappeared behind the hills surrounding the lake. As the lady of the light lowered herself behind the lake, she painted the sky with an expansive color palette, shimmering pink, bright yellow, fiery orange, and electric purple.

Taking in the beauty, Rakell let out a quiet gasp. It was so intricate that even the most skilled photographer couldn't capture what her senses absorbed. Her eyes worked to take in the kaleidoscope of colors as they danced and morphed in the sky, the sound that wove through the onlookers, the hushed gasps, the excited claps, plus the feel of the sky giving up a smidgin of heat as the sun waved goodbye. The overwhelming sense that experiencing this moment with someone she wanted to be with made her crave a simpler life. "I loved that! It was amazing," she said, turning her head to see all the other people standing and cheering.

Jake chuckled. "Glad you liked it."

"Yes, loved it." She nudged him. "I was thinking about how I've seen pictures, beautiful photographs of this very sunset, but some things are better in person, and this is one of them. Amazing!"

"Agreed, some things are better in person. That's especially true about the Texas sky." He snaked his arm around her shoulders, snugging her into his side. "You're easy to please. I love that you loved it." There were *more* sensory experiences he'd like to please her with. He wasn't sure he could compete with a Texas sunset draping over Lake Travis, but he'd damn sure enjoy the challenge.

"Mmm…hmm," she said, shifting her drink to her other hand and letting herself lean into him, savoring the last bit of color before the night sky took over, the diffused pink hue of the horizon hanging on. How utterly happy she was made to feel by something so seemingly simple.

Turning her torso toward him, her hand going to his face, she let her fingers trail from the side of his forehead down to his chin, watching his eyes grow more intent. She felt a comingling of confusion and need as her hand cupped his chin, her index finger inching up the cleft of his chin to his bottom lip. Smiling as his breath hitched in his throat, she said, "I like you. In a world where everyone is trying to be more or extra, you're not. You keep it simple."

He was sure the feel of her index finger would be indelibly imprinted on his lips. "So *simple*…that's what you like about me?" He purposely sounded light, trying to cut through the thick, heated tension building between them, clutching his groin. "As long as you add 'simply' handsome, sexy, brilliant, and funny, I'll try not to shrink at the word *simple*."

Smirking, she let her finger drop from his lip, tracing his neck over his Adam's apple, feeling the strain in his throat. "And cocky, did I mention cocky?" Her hand stilled on his upper torso. "What I'm trying to say is that *simple* is appealing, *just Jake*, that's nice. In a world where burgers are now 'gourmet' food: Wagyu beef with Havarti cheese, covered in sundried tomatoes smothered in a special pesto cream sauce. That's not a burger, it's a commitment. I just want a burger; *just a burger*, you know what I mean?"

Jake leaned back from her touch, biting his lip, and said, "Okay, smartass, you just compared me to a menu item at Whataburger. I have been referred to as lots of things, but never…" He stopped himself, picking up on the lost expression taking over her face. "Wait, you *have* eaten at Whataburger…?" He said, not hiding his shock.

"No. I drive by one every 100 yards, but I've never…"

"Shhh…stop…." Holding his finger up to his lips, he leaned in close, whispering, "They'll hear you. You cannot tell anyone that you haven't eaten at a Whataburger…the Texas Marshals will arrest you and throw away the key."

He laughed, shaking his head. "Justa Burger is their smallest, most boring burger on the menu, so I'm feeling great right now. Just great." He exaggerated his expression to make the point. Watching her lips curl up made him smile wider, made the edge in his chest soften. She had just made it crystal clear that Jake, the emerging NFL star, was not what she was looking for. Even if that made him like her more, which it did, the fear of her finding out made his heart thump against his chest. How long could he keep this from her? And could he make sure she fell for "just Jake" before she knew, before she found out, he actually was "extra"?

"I like your truck. Reminds me of something my dad would drive," Rakell said, buckling her seatbelt. She didn't say it in the past tense because she didn't want Jake to ask questions about her dad, forcing her to lie.

"Yup," Jake said. "My dad bought it in 2010, so it's more than a decade old now. He gave it to me my senior year of high school. Just don't see a reason to get rid of it. Still drives well." He turned the key.

"A Ford F-150, right?"

"Yeah. I'll probably get another one when this one is done. But I like the front bench seats in the older models." He rubbed his hand on the bench seat next to him. "The newer models aren't as roomy up front."

"I bet you do," she goaded. "Makes that high school dating experience easier, huh?" Her hand stroked the middle seat between them as they drove down the road.

His eyes shifted to her. "Not when my date sits all the way over there by the window and I can't reach her. Kinda defeats the purpose of the bench seat." He chided, eyes back on the road.

Jake heard her seatbelt snap off, then she scooted in next to him, fishing for the middle seatbelt. She shifted her long legs slightly to the side to avoid the dash as he moved his right arm around her shoulders. "Yup, definitely not getting rid of this truck."

His long fingers dangled just above her breast, the tips moving around the top of her large mounds. Rakell arched. "Um, so what's next? I mean, in the high-school dating experience? Do we park some-where and make out?" she asked, turning her face toward him and biting the inside of her mouth, trying not to laugh.

Chuckling, he moved his hand to her shoulder, gently massaging it. "Well, I have a house with a couch, a kitchen counter, a hot tub…even a bed."

She started clapping her hands as if she were a toddler, cutting him off and laughing. "And a kitchen table?! Oh, and walls, floors, a bathtub too!?" she said with over-the-top enthusiasm. Oh, she did like fucking with him.

Jake swallowed, not sure where this was going, though he knew where he wanted it to lead. "Yep. My house has got all that, so if parking and making out is what you're seeking, we can do the adult version there."

"No, we agreed to the high-school dating experience, and you have the perfect truck for it." She pecked his cheek.

"I'm *so* getting rid of this truck," he grumbled, shifting his eyes to her, then back to the road.

"Come on, it'll be fun," she said, almost giddy as she leaned in, pecking his cheek a few times. "Come on."

"When I used this truck in high school, I was five-eleven. Now I'm six-two and you're like, what?"

"Five-ten," she said seriously, trying not to laugh.

"Okay, so I can't see that working." He turned the wheel again.

"Not even for making out?"

"What does that look like for you?" His voice was thick, gruff, burying the irritation he was starting to feel, realizing they weren't going to his place.

"Well," she murmured whimsically, "finding a secluded spot off a quiet road and kissing more, maybe 'copping a feel,' as they say." Rakell waved her hand over her body.

Jake wanted to reply, *Jake going home with blue balls—that's the experience you're looking for? Well, I guess that was my actual high school dating experience.* He cleared his throat. "I know a place."

Chapter Fifteen

"So, just checked, we're out of that tequila," he said, his big brown eyes looking at Rakell. "Let me make you something I think you'll like. You good with a little spice?"

"Spice? Sure, I like spice."

"Mmm…bet you do," he said under his breath, casting a cocked grin across the bar. "I'll be right back."

She shook her head. What was that? What the fuck was up with men? As if a woman sitting alone in a bar could only be here for one thing. Yanking her top up to diminish the cleavage, she reached for the blazer she had hanging on the back of the bar stool. Then she took a sip of the water the bartender had put down.

Rakell felt the tap on her shoulder. "You beat me here," Lana said, her arms out.

"God, I'm glad you're here. The bartender thinks I want to get it on with him in the back room."

Lana threw her head back. "Well, you are oozing horniness," she said, laughing and scooting onto the barstool next to Rakell at Whisler's, an East 6th Street Texas-hole-in-the-wall-meets-upscale-craft-cocktail bar.

"I *am* horny. But I'm not oozing it," Rakell said, eyelids drifting down and her bottom lip protruding. She put on a sultry pouty expression, twirling her long hair with her fingers, and said, in a falsetto, "Why, Mr. Bartender, I *do* like spice, if *you're* the one giving it out."

Lana started to laugh, widening her eyes. Rakell giggled, then dropped her voice lower and adopted her best Southern accent: "So you got some spice for me behind that zipper, ooh, ooh, let me have it.

Just thinking about getting some spice from you has me all hot and..."

Shaking her head, Lana grunted, "Stop," her head tilting toward the bar, just as Rakell heard someone purposely clearing their throat.

Rakell's eyes followed the voice, and there he stood with a Cheshire grin and his hand still on the glass he was sliding toward Rakell. "Here you go, tequila made right here in Austin with a touch of jalapeño syrup. Let me know if it's too spicy for you." He sucked his lips into his mouth, eyebrows arching.

"Oh, sorry," Rakell said sheepishly.

"Ahh, no problem. I've probably never been so flattered being made fun of in my life."

"I wasn't..."

"Rakell, shh..." Lana said. "She was—it's just the whole insinuating you have something to add to her life thing—she's tired of men thinking that."

"What?" Rakell scrunched her nose up.

"True?" Lana said, nodding at Rakell.

Rakell nodded.

"Okay then, I get it. What can I get you, miss?" he said looking at Lana.

"Suggestions and no spice. She's the spicy one." Rakell cleared her throat, but Lana kept her eyes on the bartender, who was trying not to laugh.

"If you like Bourbon, try Operation Flood 14."

"Sounds good."

"Thanks!" Rakell said, grabbing Lana's knee. "Now that guy thinks I'm some slutty manhater..."

"Actually, I think the credit for that goes to the sultry speech you were giving while he stood as a single audience. By the way, great acting."

"Super, let my agent know." She bent her head, taking a sip of the drink. "Shoot, this *is* spicy..."

"But you can handle it, right? I'd hate to disappoint that cute bartender, those chocolate eyes..."

"All right."

"How's it going with the Austin agent?"

"I like her a lot. She's in LA more than half the time, but we meet up every few months. She's in touch with Nicole, even flew to London so they could meet in person and coordinate. It makes sense to have an agent both in Europe and in the States. I know they are in talks with a French lingerie label and...I don't want to jinx this, but I may have a shot at *Sports Illuminated*. Probably buried, but who cares if you get to grace the same pages as Camille? I'll take a postage stamp picture in SI."

Lana excitedly clapped both her hands together. "Rakell, that's amazing!"

Rakell put her finger to her mouth. "Shh...haven't said anything because it's not for sure, but a couple models dropped out, one to take an acting job. We'll see. Honestly, everyone wants to know what I've already done to make a name for myself, and plus-size catalogue modeling doesn't make industry elites swoon."

"Stop, you've lost a lot, and—"

"I'm finally in single digits, an eight, but get this—that's considered plus-sized." Rakell took another sip. "Let me correct that: Eight is considered average, and there's nothing worse in this business than average. I may have been better off in the plus category."

"That's just another reason women have fucked-up perceptions of themselves," Lana said, a little too loudly, as the band ended. The bartender slid Lana's drink over cautiously as if he was afraid to get bit.

"Thank you, we're just venting," Lana offered in explanation, leaning toward Rakell as soon as he was out of earshot. "He's cute! He may be fun to hang with, do more Austin stuff. You could just say you're not looking for anything because you're just getting out of a relationship."

Rakell shook her head. "I'm struggling just to keep this gym guy at bay. He doesn't strike me as the type that would be okay with me living with a guy. And no way can I open up about what I do...You haven't told Levi, right?" Levi was Lana's boyfriend.

"I've only told Levi that you're Matt's pretend girlfriend until he can come out to his parents and that you fly back to Europe a lot for modeling."

"Levi seems fine with me pretending to be Matt's girlfriend. I don't get any weird vibe from him."

"Levi really doesn't care what other people do. He doesn't judge at all. I think he'd shrug his shoulders if I told him about what you do, but you asked me not to, so I won't."

"Thank you."

"I may have to, though, if he keeps pushing to set you up. He's telling me about a couple of people he's met interviewing. Thinking they may be fun for you."

"No, not yet. I can't seem to just have a fun fling without it feeling complicated. I haven't talked to Matt too much about it. He wants me to have fun, but he's also super protective. Meanwhile, he's always in Houston, but he did say he and Jonathon were coming for karaoke next week. You guys have to come. I think I sound better—well, better than the last time you heard me a few months ago. I've been taking lessons at a new studio here. It's just another way to open myself up for different parts."

"I'll tell Levi. But listen, either decide to have fun with the guy from the gym or move on to someone else. There are plenty of Austin guys who would welcome a casual, no-strings-attached relationship."

"True, he's sort of simple, like in a slow way." Rakell shook her head at Lana's laugh. "I don't mean slow as in his brain, but he has this way that just seems like an old blanket or something familiar, somebody that's trying to learn and absorb life. He—not sure how to describe this, but remember that furry, heavy blanket Mandy's mom gave her?"

"Oh yeah, it weighed about a stone right? I spent too long in London, twenty pounds? Mandy's mom always said it was better than Xanax. Not sure I agree with that, but it did have a calming effect. Especially with a glass of Scotch."

"Yes, that blanket and a glass of Scotch together remind me of Jake. Just feels like things move slower when he's in the picture. Sounds silly, I know."

Lana scrunched her nose, slightly tilting her head toward Rakell. "Wow, impressive. He sounds like a winner, a *slow* old blanket. Sign me up for that excitement. Sounds like he'd be easy to have fun with and move on."

She shook her head, smiling. "I don't know, it doesn't seem like he'd be easy to end with, and I really don't know what I'm doing. I've been pretending for so long, laughing while men say stupid stuff thinking they're funny, acting like I'm smitten, so impressed with their money, power, and even—"

In true Lana fashion, she spat out, "Faking it in bed!"

Rakell's face flushed, but she let out a laugh. This was Lana, after all. "Yes, pretty much every time, makes it go quicker. Thinking they like that too, because then they don't have to say awkward things about how much they really like me. I mean, you know the stories. I'm not saying it's always like that, but I am definitely acting most of the time."

"This might be hard to believe, since you've never had a non-payment boyfriend—" Lana covered her mouth, her eyebrows shooting up. "God, shit, sorry. That sounded awful."

Rakell pulled Lana's hand down from her face. "It's okay. You're right. Besides my horrible high school boyfriend, a few wankers that I met for beers when I first got to London, and the few times here meeting people for coffee, I've literally never been out with someone who wasn't paying for it, and never anything long enough to declare it boyfriend status for sure. Honestly, I'm not sure I want that. I see how much women give up, and I'm not doing that, not after everything I've done to finally do my thing. But I do know I am fucking tired of faking it, especially in bed, all the time. I'm just tired of the double life."

"Just so you know, it's like that in the 'real' dating world too…until you meet that person, the one. Believe me, I would not have hauled my ass from London to Texas for someone I had to fake it with."

Rakell agreed, "No, especially with the modeling career you had in London. Did you ever think about trying acting?"

"No way. You and Mandy are both great actresses, but I can't act, it's not in my blood. Take now, I'm doing student teaching in a rich school in Lakeway, where every kid, according to them and their parents, is above average. I've almost lost it so many times with those little brats, and don't even get me started on the parents."

"Well, that's what I deal with with these men from über-wealthy families who told them how blessed and gifted they are from day one or who hired a nanny to do just that. Then they grow up and expect that to continue."

Lana raised her glass. "To the end of limp-dicked egomaniacs!"

Raising her glass, Rakell gently tipped Lana's. "Not too much longer and I'll be focused on my career."

"You'll do it," Lana said with a wink.

"Come in, crazies!" Jake yelled through the back door to the pounding at the front door. "Get in here, door's open." Turning the grill on, he set the burgers down next to it, giving Dolly a look. "Not yet, girl. Treats later," he said, walking into the house.

"Uncle J, Uncle J, we're here!" Cassie, his six-year-old niece exclaimed, one hand in the air, the other wheeling a suitcase that looked big enough to hold enough clothes for a week, not the planned two nights Jake had agreed to so Melissa and Tom could get away.

Cameron, his two-year-old nephew, held his sister's hand but still managed to hide behind her legs.

"Go on, Cameron, give Uncle J a hug," Tom urged but was met with a shriek from Cameron.

Melissa whipped her head around, glaring at her husband. "Tom, damnit, don't! I told you what the therapist said. Don't force him."

Tom's hands went up in resignation. "So we're not supposed to encourage social interaction, correct him, we're just…?"

Melissa barked, "Shh, stop."

Jake sucked in a short breath, trying to still the features of his face so his sister wouldn't see what he was thinking. This didn't seem like a great start to a couple's getaway.

Melissa bent down in front of Cameron. She spoke softly and paired her words with signs she'd learned from the speech therapist Cameron had just started seeing. "Cameron, buddy, remember how we used the iPad to count down the days before you could come to Uncle J's house and see Dolly?"

"Meee…" He nodded. "Dhhh…" he grunted as his dad and Jake stood there watching.

It struck Jake that while this little guy really couldn't get his words out, his eyes seemed to take in everything. "Melissa, can I?" Jake asked softly. She turned her head, meeting her brother's eyes. He saw her utter exhaustion, the threads worn bare.

Her eyes filmed over as she let her head drop. "Sure, but"—she looked at Tom—"might not be able to leave him."

Jake felt the collective room sigh. Shit, they needed this. He hadn't registered this level of tension between Melissa and Tom before.

"Cassie, can you open the back door and let Dolly in?"

"Yes, yes, Uncle J," she said. Cameron threw himself to the floor, his fists balled up.

Jake went to his knees next to his nephew, whose tears were pooling in his eyes, accompanied by a high-pitched squeal.

"Dolly, over here, girl," he said, patting the floor by his nephew. Dolly sat next to the boy, then lay next to him and started to whimper. Jake had counted on Dolly doing exactly that. She always whimpered when she heard children cry or scream, like she wanted to fix it. "Lay down, girl," Jake said, laying his large frame on the living room carpet next to his nephew. Dolly lay between them and, as if Jake had instructed her, she put her paw out to Cameron and whimpered again.

"Hey buddy," Jake whispered, "Dolly needs some love, maybe a gentle hug."

Cameron shifted his face toward Dolly, touching her paw with his finger. He let out a small sigh. "Ga…ga…wolgee," he said before sitting up and petting Dolly's back. Dolly's whimpers changed, letting out a sound that reminded Jake of the sound he made when he stretched his muscles after a game.

"Ahh, you made her feel better. Do you think you can keep her company for a couple days? She gets lonely because Uncle J is gone a lot." He made sure he spoke slowly and kept his voice neutral, but he could hear his sister and husband, who had moved out to the backyard, speaking in urgent, angry-sounding whispers.

"Mea c—n," Cameron said, looking at Jake, then back to Dolly.

Cassie bent over to Jake. With her hand cupped to her mouth, she whispered, "He says 'me can,' which means he can keep Dolly company. Which means, I think he'll be happy staying here, which means Mom and Dad might stop fighting, which means…"

"Yep," Jake whispered back. "Let's see if we can get them out the door so the real fun can begin. Burgers and, don't tell anyone, but I got us one of those giant chocolate chip cookies with frosting."

Cameron jumped up. "Eeeeee," he squealed. Pointing to the backyard, he tried to say something, but Jake couldn't make it out. Jake could tell how frustrated he seemed, his arms out, motioning.

Quickly, he turned to Cassie for interpretation, and she was on it. "Oh, he really wants to swim." She pointed to her suitcase. "His floaties are in there. I'll get them. I brought everything; all his toys, his blankie… he'll be okay, Uncle J. I'll help so Mommy and Daddy can go away and like each other again."

Jake winced, watching her walk toward the suitcase she'd placed by the couch.

Melissa walked into the house with Tom following behind. "Jake, I think…" she started.

"Again, we're cancelling…" Tom grumbled.

Jake raised his hand, nodding toward where Cameron stood, his hand on Dolly's collar. "Well, we're getting ready for a swim, and we kinda got this weekend planned without you two, so I'd get lost if I were you." He winked at Melissa as Cassie giggled in the background, whispering *get lost* to herself.

"Thank you, Jake," Tom said with a guttural choke, as if everything that Jake had just witnessed was only the tip of what was going on. "Come on, kids, let's bring Dolly outside. Mommy needs to talk to Uncle J."

"Tom, can you turn the grill off for me?" Jake called as they walked out the back door. He turned back to Melissa, who was brushing away tears from her face.

"Hey Issa, Sweets." He moved toward her, pulling her tall, thin frame into him. "Issa, what's going…"

Her chest expanded with his words, his name for her growing up *Issa* and as an adult, he reserved, *Sweets* for his sisters and his mom. She knew he was trying to reach into her by his tone. "Stop, 'Jake the Snake'," she said into his chest. "You don't get to adult me. I take care of you…remember, you little snake?"

"Not so fast, Sweets…I owe you a lotta hugs and an ear, for all the times you didn't kill me for bugging you and your friends, for that matter. I thought I outgrew 'Jake the Snake'."

Wrapped in his arms, she tilted her head up. "Sorry, little brother…never…when you throw a live snake in your sister's room the night of her fourteenth birthday slumber party…basically ruining it…it never dies. Some things you can't live down."

"Yep, I'm learning that the hard way."

"You never took the easy learning route." She smiled. "But I'm still not sure about leaving Cameron…"

"Give me a chance. And anyway, I've got Cassie…"

"She's taken on role of interpreter. It's just been too much with Tom's promotion. He's traveling a lot, and now the speech therapist wants us to have Cameron evaluated by a psychologist."

"Because he's having a hard time speaking? He's still young."

Melissa stepped back, drawing in a breath, then blowing it out. "She's concerned that some of his behaviors may be due to…" Her jaw tightened. "God, I just…"

"What?"

"Autism." She shut her eyes. "Tom is really struggling with the idea." Then Melissa's eyes teared up. "And I guess it's pretty obvious that it's not good with us."

"Hey, I am not a relationship expert, obviously." He smiled. "But people have hard times and…"

"It's more than just Cameron. I started my business right after Cameron was born."

"Mom says it's going great, really growing. That several small businesses in Austin are turning to you for publicity, and you and your company were written up in the newspaper."

"Yes, it's great, but with Tom traveling so much, I'm the one solely responsible for the kids, and the business needs a lot of attention right now. It's not fair that just because I'm a woman, his job gets priority, even though my company is on track to make more than he can make."

"Whoa…I, I, just…I mean."

"Sorry…"

"This is even more reason you guys need to go, take the weekend in Fredericksburg, drink wine, eat, and get nasty."

Melissa's eyes popped open. He was blunt with his sister Jenae but not Melissa. She was more like a second mom, with seven years between them, but he was tired of their roles. He could be there for her too.

She swatted his arm. "Not appropriate!"

"Hey, you know I'm right. Don't even try to talk clothed; men are stupid that way. We hear criticism way different when it comes out of a naked woman's mouth."

"Great, this is who I'm leaving my kids with?" She laughed, then stepped forward, hugging him, "Okay, but you *have* to agree to send me pictures every few hours, and if Cameron gets to be too much, please, please call. And…he's back sleeping in our bed, so I don't think he'll stay in the guest room in the playpen I have in the car, might have to have it in your room." Jake wanted to squeeze her and yell, *Go! You need this and you've already told me all this three times over the phone,* but he just held her. "Cassie's fine, she sleeps anywhere. Cameron sometimes wakes up screaming…and…"

Jake let out the breath stuck in his chest. His oldest sister hurting implicitly settled in him. It was a sadness he couldn't resolve. He just had to stand by and hope.

Chapter Sixteen

Rakell bent over, blow drying her hair and trying to stave off the sexual tension penetrating her nerves. Her evenings now ended with her in bed alone, her hand between her legs, thinking about Jake's hard body pressing against hers, his hard cock pushing into her slit as she screamed for more. Last week, when they parked, making out and running their hands over each other's bodies, she'd seen the outline of his cock in his jeans and couldn't stop fixating on it all weekend.

Several nights, she'd stopped her spinning brain by picturing sucking her lips around his cockhead as her hand wrapped around the hard shaft. She pictured his face as she sucked him dry, first working her hand between her legs, then using her lipstick vibrator to bring herself off, dissipating some of the pent-up friction and allowing her to sleep.

In the morning, Rakell saw Jake while she was leaving the gym. He confirmed the time he would be picking her up that night, and the tension crawled back into her body and seemed to ebb and flow all day until it was just a steady throb between her legs.

She dressed in a white eyelet off-the-shoulder short sundress. A ruffle around the top covered her breasts, so she felt free not to wear a bra and put on only white lace panties. She finished the outfit with leather gladiator sandals. She wore her hair in a loose braid that spilled down one shoulder and small pearl earrings. Staring at her reflection in the mirror, she reached under her dress, slipping her finger under the crotch of her panties, working her clit until a spike shot through her pelvis. She pulled her finger away, a gasp escaping her mouth, knowing that wasn't enough, that the ache would linger.

Rakell gathered a backpack and a couple of blankets, her sunglasses, and a wine carrier. Her phone buzzed with a message: "*On my way.*" Just reading his text made her twitch, and now she was wondering how she was going to get through the night.

She met him out front. Jake opened the door and helped her into the truck. He wore a light gray crew-neck shirt, faded jeans that hung low on his hips, and flip-flops.

He watched her, unable to keep his eyes off her long legs or the way the short white dress moved up and exposed the edge of her white lace panties as she crawled into the seat. He wanted to lean in and pull the dress down, to ask her why the hell she'd wear something so short for a picnic. What was she trying to do to him? His cock hurt from him pulling on it every night (and some mornings) as he pictured everything about her. Rakell on top of him, from behind, lying with her legs splayed open while he kneeled between them before plunging into her wetness, her lips spread beneath his hungry mouth. A new scene entered his repertoire after her little tongue display with the ice cream on their first date: her with her mouth on his cock. Now he had a picture of her sucking and licking his cock the same way she went after the caramel butter brittle ice cream as they walked on South Congress; him glancing at her then scanning the passersby to make sure no one recognized him. All of it was crazy-making. He had warned her then to be careful with her visual teases, but she seemed to be fearless when it came to tormenting him.

The make-out session in the truck last week had nearly done him in. Rakell squirming against his touch. Moaning as his tongue fucked her mouth while his hands cupped her breasts over her ribbed top. The feel of her body arching into his touch, the way her knees shimmied together like she was fighting back an orgasm, paired with the sounds emanating from her, all of it made his balls swell and his cock lurch in his jeans.

Almost an hour into their high school parking lot make-out session, Jake had firmly told her that he had to take her home. They drove in silence, her head on his shoulder, breathing a little faster than normal, the sound of it filling up the truck. When he'd pulled up in front of her apartment, he'd asked to see her following his weekend of uncle duty, and she said with a small smile, her eyebrow cocking like Jake would get the message, "We probably need some time off, but I have tickets to the concert in the park Friday night, if you want to go." Matt had gotten tickets for her and him, but he was too wrapped up in Jonathon to break away and make the trip to Austin. They were in that cocoon phase where they just wanted to stay at Matt's place in Houston when Jonathon flew in from Denver and devour each other.

Jake jumped at the chance, wondering if he could take another night of being taunted into a frenzy. He was shaking his head as he slid into his seat and started the truck. "Jesus. What are you trying to do to me, seriously?"

"Huh?" Rakell replied, sounding innocent, her big green eyes on him.

Jake shot her a *give me a break* glance, but he questioned how aware she was that she was teasing him. She had an incongruous naïveté, cloaked in brazen sensuality. The mixture was maddening or captivating, he wasn't quite sure. But he knew he didn't have the self-control to back away from her, no matter how crazed she made him feel.

"So you thought that dress was appropriate for a picnic? A dress that covers your ass and your...ass by a few inches?" he said with a skeptical tone.

She arched her eyebrows. "You're saying a white summer dress isn't appropriate for an outdoor concert? Should I have dressed warmer?" A coy smile shaped her mouth.

Shaking his head as he drove, he replied, "Um, pretty sure you know what I'm talking about." He squinted, sporting his best *not buying your bullshit* grin, letting her know he was on to her.

"I'll make sure I don't bend over too much so no one will see my panties, and I'll make sure not to let the top be pulled down"—she looked at him pointedly—"so no one will see my bare tits. Okay?"

"Fuck," he growled under his breath, trying to get that visual out of his head. Then came the idea of her over his knee as he pulled up the white sundress and pulled down the white lace panties, exposing her bare ass and swatting it for being such a taunting brat.

They picked out snacks at Whole Foods—cheese and crackers and a few pre-made salads. They sauntered over to the wine section, and Jake started to grab a bottle before pulling his hand back. "No, I'm not choosing. Not taking any chances in the wine department," he grumbled, his eyes slanted toward her. "You choose. Whatever you want."

Rakell laughed. "Come on, I'm not picky," she jabbed back, biting her bottom lip, then smiling.

"No, not at all. Only when it comes to men, right?" Jake narrowed his eyes at her, his lip curling up.

"Very, very choosy then." She winked. "This looks good," she said, reaching for a California chardonnay from Merryvale Vineyards that Jake recognized.

"Damn, you have superior taste in wine *and* men. Grab two," he said, taking the first bottle from her hand.

He'd brought the rest of the picnic supplies in his backpack, as well as a flashlight and bug spray. He'd been to enough outdoor events in Austin to know the drill.

They had to park in the back of the lot, near woods, because many of the spots had already filled up by the time they arrived. He was always surprised how early folks showed up for events like this, but again, it was a beautiful night, and after South by Southwest, people were still craving outdoor music. And what better place than Zilker Park?

They found a spot to set up toward the back of the grounds, on the opposite side of the food trucks and bathrooms, where there was less foot traffic. They could chill and enjoy the music as the sun settled around them, making room for the night sky. Rakell spread out a blanket, and Jake poured them both white wine in red plastic cups. "Do you want to wait on the snacks?" he asked. "I brought a couple of waters too, and if you want anything from the food trucks, let me know," he added.

"I'm good with wine for now," she said, taking off her sandals and setting them on the grass just past the edge of the blanket. Jake did the same with his flip-flops. Then she pulled another blanket from her backpack. When she sat, her legs stretching out in front of her, her white dress rode up to an inch or so below her crotch. Jake was right—this *wasn't* the best choice. But she had wanted something loose and short, something he could slide his large hands under if they made out again in his truck. His touch felt like no other, as if he was the first to really touch her, to take her in. She craved more of it.

Jake's eyes fell over her legs and moved directly to the edge of the dress. "Thinking you should have just worn a nightie, sheer with crotchless panties to boot," he said gruffly.

Rakell squinted her eyes and met his gaze. "Shut up. Seriously, I didn't think it would be this bad." Raising her red Solo cup to his, she said, "Just wanted to make sure you were paying attention," tapping her cup to his before taking a drink.

Jake's eyes moved back to her crotch, then slowly, lewdly slid up her torso to the ruffle covering her breasts. "You've got my attention. The question is whatta you going to do with it?" He leaned in, pecking her cheek and trailing a row of kisses to her ear before tenderly biting the edge of her lobe. "You got what you wanted; my attention is all yours, so what comes next?" He aimed his pointed stare at her, practically demanding an answer as the tension coiled around his groin.

Rakell's eyes widened, and she could feel her pulse throbbing in her neck. She hoped he couldn't see what she felt. "Um…" God, he had a way of saying things with his thick lusty drawl that made her inner thighs flex, as if he was between them staring at her pussy when he talked, challenging her for an answer as his mouth captured her intimate flesh. "Um…"

The band stopped playing, and the lead singer thanked everyone for coming out, telling the crowd to expect a great night. Jake hadn't seen either band play before, but he'd heard great things about them. They both clapped, and he noticed that her dress had traveled up even farther, the white material shifting on her apex as her arms moved back and forth clapping. Jake leaned across her and grabbed the other blanket.

His hand brushed her stomach as he did, sending an electric stinging sensation up her torso to her breasts. Her nipples responded, stiffening against the light fabric. His eyes caught the sudden change in her chest, which jerked forward just a bit.

Rakell kept her eyes on the stage, not wanting to confirm his observation. He spread the blanket over her legs, covering her, letting it rest in her lap as he moved behind her and spread his legs, squeezing his thighs gently against hers. "Hang on to the blanket. I'm going to move you back so you can lean on me. I'll be your chair," he whispered. He slid his hand under the blanket from behind her and rested it on her upper thigh, just on the edge of the valley that led to her sex.

The heat from his fingers touching her skin and slowly, gently rotating, made her sex clench deep inside. God, she was so raw, so edgy. It ate at her control. She wasn't used to this kind of touch, the intimacy of it, even if it was only her thigh. Its effect was far more intense than when her clients grabbed her breasts or ass before sliding themselves into her for their own gratification.

They listened to the music as the sun dwindled away, leading to twilight. Then darkness settled in, softly illuminated by the stage lights. She took a long swig of her wine and scooted back into his spread legs a bit more as she pulled the blanket up to her chest, grateful she had brought an extra one as the fading of the sun sucked some of the daytime warmth out of the air.

Jake moved his hand from her thigh, and she almost whimpered, then he crossed his arms over her chest under the blanket. "Sweets, you getting cold?"

She heard people shuffling around, singing, even laughing, yet it felt as if the two of them were strangely alone.

His hands traveled to her rib cage, gently massaging, responding to the rise and fall of her ribs with quicker, more exaggerated caresses. His breath followed hers, his cock growing firmer. He moved his hands to her hipbones, swiftly yanking her ass back, meeting his crotch, wanting her to feel what she was doing to him.

Rakell flinched, registering his rigid zipper against her backside, she grabbed her cup and swigged again. "I need more wine," she said, a little too breathy.

Jake moved back. "I'll fill us both up." He didn't bother asking about food; he wanted his hands back on her and didn't give one fuck about eating. "Here you go," he said, handing her the cup.

"Um, thank you." She looked up at him, her eyes soft, and wondered was this Marietta or Rakell? No, this wasn't Marietta. She was here with a guy, just a guy from the gym. She was Rakell. *Do what you want, Rakell,* she thought to herself. Her mind had linked with her body, wanting only a release from the twisted tension that strung from her chest to the moist hole between her legs.

His legs spread, and he pulled her in again, purposely grabbing her hip bones and pulling them back into his open crotch. "Pull the blanket up to your chin, okay? I don't want anyone to see what my hands are doing under it. Do you, Sweets?" he purred in her ear.

"Huh, no," she said, on a whispered whimper that was barely audible.

Jake's hands slid under the sides of the blanket to her ribcage, then inched up so that his thumbs grazed her breasts, slowly feathering along the bottom of her full mounds and relishing the feel of how her chest caved and expanded like her lungs couldn't get enough breath. His mouth found her ear. "Breathe, Sweets. Slowly, slowly, so no one knows what I'm doing to your body under this blanket. Can you do that?"

"Not sure." God, the way he said *Sweets*...dragging the long 'e' over her ear.

"Shall we try?" His fingers molded to the bottom of her breasts, lightly squeezing. "Tell me yes or no before my fingers find your nipples." His voice was strained as he whispered in her ear.

"Mm-mm."

His hands were cupping her breasts under the ruffle over the white cotton of the dress. "Taking that as a yes," he said, as his thumbs found her hard nipples and worked circles around them before lightly pulling on them, causing a soft "Ahh" to leave her mouth.

Jake stilled his fingers on her breasts. "Can you keep quiet, or do I need to stop? Do you want me to stop exploring your tits? 'Cause I'd like to get to know them," he growled in her ear.

"Please...I'll try." Her eyes shifted around the grassy area that circled the stage. Everyone was engaged with each other or the band. Most of the foot traffic was contained to the opposite end of the grassy area, and since they were in the back, they were now bathed in darkness. She let her head drop back on his shoulder and put one hand under the blanket and over one of his own, guiding one of his fingers under the elastic of her dress. Hooking his finger, she urged it down, bringing with it the cotton fabric.

He hooked a finger from his other hand and popped the elastic band of her dress over her large breasts so that it rested beneath them, pushing her flesh up and creating a shelf for her boobs.

Jake's gruff sigh reached Rakell's ear as his flesh touched hers. She tilted her hips back more. His hands were kneading her flesh, molding it to his large hands, almost big enough to encompass her ample mounds. "God, how did you get so lucky? That face and these...God." His fingers circled her round flesh, then his hands held them, his thumbs gently feathering her nipples. "So hard...I want them in my mouth," he whispered with heavy breath in her ear, his fingers gently plucking her stiff nipples, then letting them bounce back. He ran his palm over them, barely touching skin, sending a shiver of ache down her belly to her groin. Her need was becoming unbearable. She had never done anything in public like this, but her body was pleading for it.

Rolling her head on his shoulder, Rakell sighed, "Please... I...please," urging his touch. His hands obliged. He began man-handling the mounds of flesh and plucking at her nipples harder, twisting them. She pulled the blanket even tighter around her chin, biting the edge, muffling her cries. Her body absorbed her nipples' stinging eruption, tightening into hard nubs. "I need...please...I..." she whimpered, not hiding her need.

Jake's chest was rising and falling like he was at the end of a close game and couldn't get his breath. Her body's responsiveness made him even crazier than her body itself. He'd never touched someone that was simultaneously so sweet and downright lusty. The way her entire body stiffened with her nipples, the sweet way she almost begged for more. He could feel her legs straighten, almost plank-like against his own, pushing out, then opening up. He needed to get out of here, get to his house so he could do this right. He would stop, they would leave, and then he'd make her head spin. He'd finally find relief, he thought, as one hand squeezed her tit while the other drifted to the crevice between her open legs. His hand found wet panties, cupping her sex over the lace that covered her crotch. "Sweets, so damn wet, just from touch?" A low grunt left his throat. "Damn. So fucking receptive."

Her sex arched up against his hand, and she knew what he was talking about. She could feel the soaking between her legs; she was right there, pre-cum lubricating her lips and seeping through the thin layer of lace in the crotch of her panties. "Yes, please. I have to..." She moved one hand down from her chin and pushed his hand under the blanket. "Please."

Jake slipped his fingers under the narrow thin material covering her outer lips, discovering soft wet hair covered in her juice. *Just one finger,* he thought. *Feel that hot pussy, then stop and get out of here.* He'd allow himself just a sample of what he would devour later. His fingers moved around her outer sex, opening up the folds of wet flesh, finding her clit, gently stroking the engorged nub. He wished so badly he could see it, see all that wetness soaking her panties, her pussy hair, her flesh. His thumb took over stroking her clit while he slid his middle finger gently into her slit. Rakell gasped, biting the blanket as he steadied his finger just inside of her, wishing his cock was his finger. He couldn't imagine how crazy it would be inside that taut fleshy wetness. He felt her pelvis tip forward, urging him in. He slid his finger in farther. She whimpered into the blanket, stuffing it farther into her mouth.

Jake knew he should stop. He scanned the area around them; no one was paying attention to them. But he knew they should get out of here.

He began to withdraw his finger but stopped when she shouted through a stifled whisper in his ear, "No, no—don't stop!"

He sucked in a thick breath. "Not stopping, Sweets," he said, twisting his finger deep inside her, working past the taut flesh while his thumb feverishly moved back and forth on her throbbing clit. His finger stroked the inside walls of her vagina, moving deep in her so that his other fingers were touching the inner part of her ass cheeks. He slowly stroked her insides, feeling her tilt her pelvis up, rocking into his finger. Then her inner walls clamped down on his finger, driving him deeper where he could feel the spasm starting. Her whole body shuddered against him, her spine and shoulders, shaking under the blanket. He grabbed her under her breasts and steadied her as she shook and moaned into the blanket, a ball of fabric in her mouth. As her shudders slowed, he gently slid his long finger out and adjusted the crotch of her panties. His other hand slowly pulled up her dress, covering her breasts. His body absorbed her weight as she fell back against him. Moving his hand from under the blanket, one arm wrapped around her, he brought his finger to his mouth, sucking her juices off of him. No way was he letting a chance to taste her slip by, no way.

Rakell's sluggish eyes popped open when she heard the sound, just in time to see him sucking the finger that had been inside her. She'd never seen anyone do that before. It made her chest pull in. Quickly, she shut her eyes to fight back tears. She wasn't sure why, but it struck her as so deeply intimate, as if it were her, the essence of her, that he cared about. She couldn't make sense of it.

He wrapped both hands around the front of the blanket. "You taste amazing. I need more of that, Sweets," he whispered in her ear, again that long 'e' tunneling in her ear, titillating her spine. Then he turned his head and repeatedly kissed her lips with soft quick puckers, the sensation lavishing her whole body.

Rakell's mouth stayed lax, unable to respond. The way he said "*Sweets*, as if it were her new name, mingling with the vision of him sucking her juices off his fingers, squeezed her heart while simultaneously sending off a warning blast to her brain: *Dissociate!*

"Where have you been all my life?" he asked playfully, trying to cover the weightiness he was feeling being with her, touching her.

Her eyelids fluttered, her head felt heavy on his shoulder, like she couldn't lift it; knowing exactly where she'd been—with Francesco and the others like him, who dictated how she acted while they fucked her. Images rippled through her brain, but she shoved them away, a learned strategy to preserve her psyche.

She willed a soft smile to her lips, her eyes looking up at Jake sideways, those wide, docile Marietta eyes that could disarm any man. "Mm...mm, being bad," she whispered sweetly.

Jake's arms flexed, squeezing her tightly as he lightly bit the edge of her ear. "Be bad with me. I got you."

If only he knew that being good at being bad meant making money in her world. Her brain snapped—she hadn't pleased him. He had gotten her off, but she hadn't done anything for him. As her senses reconnected, Rakell become acutely aware of his hard length pressing into her from behind. She desperately wanted to take care of him, to relieve him, to make him feel as good as he'd made her feel. Abruptly, she sat up, looking around, her eyes wild. The concert would be going on for a while. The second band was only a few songs in, long enough for her to suck him off. She twisted her body around. "Jake, let's get out of here. I want to talk to you about something in the truck." She moved the blanket over his lap as her hand reached under it, squeezing the space between his legs. Reveling in the stiffness of his erection, her fingers stroked the long shaft of his cock. "Let me take care of you. Pleasure you. I should..."

"Whoa, Sweets. Shit." His lower abdomen contracted, his hand grabbing her hand, moving it away. "Not now, you're going to make me embarrass myself."

Rakell turned all the way around, crouching on her knees, the blanket draping over her. She whispered in his ear, "Let's get packed up. I want to suck your cock. I don't want you blowing your cum in your pants. I want to feel your hot cum down my throat. Let's go." Her tone was sweetly urgent. The usual taunting tease in her voice was gone.

What the fuck? He'd never heard a woman say anything remotely that fucking intense, except in a porno. His crotch lit up, begging him to let her. "*Rae*-kale," he drawled, "you don't need to please me or take care of me." But she was already standing, putting one of the blankets in the backpack, then tugging on the one on the ground. "Okay, slow down. I'll help." He stood, steadying himself. Her words had tweaked the nerve endings throughout his body, from his toes to his jaw. His brain kept repeating them, playing her voice over and over. *I want to suck your cock. I want to feel your hot cum down my throat.*

Rakell wrapped one of the blankets around her shoulders as they briskly walked to the truck. The parking spot was pretty isolated; she probably had a good thirty minutes before people started streaming out of the park. He opened her door, watching as she climbed in.

God, she's adorable. The thought popped into his head as he helped her stuff the blanket in the truck so it wouldn't get caught in the door. He slowly moved into his seat, his cock so erect that normal movement felt cumbersome.

She scooted in close to him, the blanket still around her shoulders. "Turn on country or whatever you listen to when you jerk off at night," she said coyly, her teeth raking over her bottom lip, one hand on his chest and one hand on the long stone pushing against the zipper of his jeans. "I'm going to make you smile."

Jake covered her hand on his chest, his cobalt blue eyes narrowing, his mouth straight. "Rakell, please. You don't have to do this, not here. Jesus, not at all. You don't owe me…" He felt her hand leave his cock, and a finger pressed up against his lips.

"I know…me, I'm making this decision," she said as if she were coaching herself. "I *want* to do this. I want to please you. I want the satisfaction of knowing I made you twist in ecstasy as I get to swallow all that hardness." Her finger lifted. Her hand was back on his crotch, but now her fingers were grappling with the button on his jeans. "I want all of it. Whatever you can spew, I want to swallow," she continued, moving the other hand to his zipper.

"Fuck, fuck. You are. God, you are…"—he struggled for the

words—"making me crazy."

"Turn on the radio now and help me get this hard cock out of here." Yanking on the zipper before she pulled his black briefs down, she released his cock as it thumped against the ridge of his bunched-up underwear. "And there it is," she said, her big green eyes gleaming as she looked at his swollen cock, pre-cum glistening from the end.

She wanted to taste it, taste him. She hadn't tasted a man before because her clients always wore condoms. Escorts were coached to set the rules for exposure to fluids. She opted for safety even if a client offered more money. It hit her that she didn't have a portfolio on Jake with his medical report, that he hadn't been vetted, and that his preferences weren't listed for her to review. "Jake..." Her eyes lifted to his face. "Um, are you clean? I mean, I really want to do this without a condom, I'd love to *taste* you."

His cock lurched at *taste*. Jesus, he'd never heard a girl say that before, then his brain backtracked on her words. *Do this without a condom? What?* Sucking in air, he said, "Yes, I get tested, and I always wear..." he sputtered, barely audible.

Rakell bent forward, kissing his cock, her big green eyes looking up at him. "Good, I can't wait," she said almost to herself. A hushed giggle left her mouth, then she said, smiling, "I'm really good at this, so lean your head back and enjoy."

Again, what? *Really good at this?* Jake felt her hand wrapping around the base of his hard shaft and her lips opening up around the top of his cockhead. The tip of her tongue licked the pre-cum from the slit. He winced from the softness of her tongue on his head, the word *taste* ricocheting around his brain.

"Jake," she hushed, her hot breath wisping across the bulbus head, making his pelvis contract, "I want to know your preferences...I mean what do you like...?" Her hand was still wrapped around his shaft, her mouth centimeters from his cockhead. She spoke softly, as if his cock was a microphone.

His eyes cast down to her head. "Preferences? *Rae*-kale?" He couldn't mask the confusion in his voice.

Her eyes lifted to his. "Yes, do you like a lot of soft licking around the head, vigorous sucking with fast hand motion, aggressive, deep throat? I can..." Her sincerity was evident in her tone.

He knew she wasn't fucking with him. Shit, he'd never, never had a woman ask him what he liked in that way, as if it was part of a menu he could choose from. His cock pulsed in her hand from her words. "Jesus, whatever you do I'll love, but if you keep talking like that, it will be a moot point. I'm a really controlled sorta guy." He smiled at her. "But my cock is still an impulsive teenager, so one more word about…"

She giggled against his sensitive cockhead, her hot breath making him wince. Then her open mouth encapsulated the head as her hand moved up and down aggressively.

His brain let go of everything.

Her lips clamped down on his swollen member as she took him into her mouth before opening her throat. He could feel himself deep in her throat. His brain told him to pull her head up, but his cock demanded he push her head further down, so he didn't do either. He just ran his fingers madly through her hair, intertwining them into her loose braid, gently pulling it apart and then letting her hair fall freely into his lap. He then grabbed it loosely, holding it up so he could see her beautiful mouth entrap his cock.

Rakell pulled up, licking, circling her tongue around the ridge of his cockhead. Then her tongue was on his balls, licking and taking one up into her mouth and creating a light sucking motion with her tongue. He cried out as her mouth moved to the next ball, repeating the sucking pattern. A gravelly groan escaped his mouth as his head rolled back and forth on the headrest.

She moved up, reaching toward the dashboard, turning up the radio to muffle his moans interlaced with cursing shouts, all of which she recognized as the building frenzy that was gurgling within him. It spurred her on. Her hunger for his release was more intense than she had ever felt with anyone else, making her more ambitious, more rabid.

Rakell knew how good she was at this. Luke, one of her early long-term clients, had instructed her, detailing different techniques with the utmost patience. They'd spent hours in front of the mirror, him giving her pointers as he watched her, urging her to watch herself. "Look how beautiful you look with your lips on my dick," he'd say, letting her know that with her looks and the ability to suck cock like this, she'd become one of the most sought-after escorts in Europe. She'd be able to choose her clients and demand more money. Both were true.

She moved her mouth on his cockhead again, sucking hard, then opening up to take his cock in, determined to get as much of it down her throat as she could. She leaned over his lap more, supporting herself with one hand as the other hand pumped his base. His cock pushed down the back of her throat. She relaxed her jaw, making it go lax, lowering down another inch, swallowing more of his cock. Wishing she could get to his balls.

"I'm fucking crazy about you. I lo—I'm fucking nuts about you," Jake shouted between moans, his head arched back. She didn't take anything he said as truth. She'd become accustomed to men screaming all kinds of things when she'd held them strongly in the grip of her mouth and throat. Men who shouted, "I love you!" but who wouldn't remember her name in a month. But they'd remember her mouth, the way her tongue swirled around the head, her throat's ability to relax and take them in, to "deep-throat" them, as she had learned it was called. But they wouldn't remember or care that they'd professed love in those minutes before their cock let go. And she didn't care either; she told herself that over and over. She didn't care.

She gagged, water leaking from the sides of her eyes. Instead of pulling off, she breathed through it. "No, please… I'm going to…No, Sweets." Jake's hands cupped the sides of her head. She tightened her lips, moving her mouth up, then back down, making his cock go deeper. Her eyes watered, and her jaw ached, but she loved the feeling of his cock as it started to let go.

"Ohhh, I'm—no, no," he jerked, spewing liquid deep in her throat as she moved her tight lips up his cock, sucking all of him up into her mouth. She swallowed his musty essence, surprised by the taste of it and how powerful it made her feel. Jake was the first man she'd ever tasted. There was a lot to consume. She tried to get it all, but there was so much that it spilled out of her lips and down her chin as her mouth circled around his cockhead for one last suck. Then one final small lick into the slit at the top, her tongue relishing the last drop. She couldn't have imagined enjoying this with another man. But she wanted to absorb as much of Jake as she could. Her lips brushed his cockhead; her watery eyes looked up at him.

Jake studied her with an expression that looked like a mixture of awe and release. What the hell had just happened? His brain short-circuited as he looked down at her beautiful face. Her lips kissing the tip of his cock. Her mouth, with its swollen red lips, managing a sweet smile as she lifted her chin up. He couldn't make sense of what he'd just experienced.

Jake's chest rose and fell hard, but he willed himself to steady his breathing. His cock lay lazily against his leg and lowered briefs. She snuggled in next to him; he put his right arm around her shoulders, holding her. He wanted to say thank you, but he was unsure if thanking someone for the most explosive blowjob of your life was cool. Speaking slowly, his tone caring, he said, "Sweets, that was amazing." He moved his hand to her cheek, rubbing his thumb against her soft skin.

"I'm so glad you liked it," she whispered into the air.

He sat up, pulling his pants and briefs up with the other hand. Rakell sat up too, moving away a couple of inches while he fitted himself and zipped his pants, using the time to gather his thoughts. He looked over to her. She had wrapped the blanket around her shoulders again, and her hair, wavy from being trapped in a braid for hours, was now loose around her shoulders. Her lips were puffy, her eyes still a little watery. He started the engine so he could turn on the heat and noticed that some cars had already left, and others were moving toward the exit.

When Rakell turned to take him in, he put his arm up, beckoning her. "Please, come here," he drawled, his Texas accent surfacing from his lax jaw as he slid toward her a bit. She met him as he hugged her, pulling her head into his chest, not knowing what to say, just wanting her to know he cared. He loved that she cared that he liked it.

His chin rested on the top of her head. "Um, just for the record—I loved that. 'Like' is something I reserve for a good ice cream. That blowjob reached the level of love." His tone was purposefully light.

"Don't call it a blowjob—it's called 'cock swallow.' 'Blowjob' doesn't sound as appealing. Makes it sound like work." A small giggle left her mouth.

"Sweets, I'll call it whatever the hell you want me to," he laughed. "Cock swallow it is."

Jake tried to talk her into coming home with him, promising he'd just hold her through the night, no advances, but she refused. She said she wanted to go home, get to sleep. But Jake couldn't bring himself to take her straight home after that moment of heaven. Plus, they hadn't eaten. He wanted to take her out for a late dinner, so he suggested Casino El Comino for a burger. But she didn't want to go anywhere.

"Honestly, Jake, I look like a girl that just got fucked or swallowed cock. Everyone will know when I walk in. *What the hell happened to that girl?* They'll be whispering," she explained, her tone playful but purposeful. She was not going out to eat. She had to absorb what had just happened: she, Rakell, pleasing a man because she wanted to.

To him, she looked like the most irresistible combination of hot and adorable. He grabbed his backpack. "Picnic in the truck sound good?"

Rakell nodded, smiling.

Chapter Seventeen

J ake: *Can I beg off from the date tonight?*...**Send**
    Dwayne: *No way, dude, it's the day of*...**Send**
    Jake: *Not up to it*...**Send**
    Dwayne: *Get up to it! She's hot*...**Send**

The last thing Jake wanted to do after the previous night, was go on a blind date. He wanted to see Rakell again, but she had plans tonight as well. Hell, she was probably on a date, too, but he wasn't about to ask her. He couldn't get her and last night out of his thoughts. His mind pulled him back to the park, her reactions and some of the things she'd said. She didn't add up to him. He constantly felt at odds with how he perceived her. She was so independent but also skittish, as if she was unsure of him, or maybe her reaction to him. She didn't fit neatly into a box, that was for sure.

Rakell fought herself to get out of bed. She wanted to lie under the covers, dreaming about Jake's hands on her body and his response when she went down on him. It wasn't the sexual act itself so much as the intense emotion connected with his touch, his words, his orgasm. It was so foreign to her to connect emotion to sex. Jake had settled into her in a way she hadn't expected. Now her mind was grappling with how to keep him from becoming more intertwined within her psyche.

Rakell heard Matt and Jonathon enter the apartment while she was in her bathroom getting ready for karaoke. She threw on a robe to greet them. "Hey, you two. You're on time." She smiled and hugged them both. They'd already put their stuff away in Matt's room he seldom used, except for the occasional overnight for business. She peppered them both with a few questions about Jonathon's gallery opening in Houston as they made themselves at home opening wine they'd brought.

"Would you like some, Princess?" Matt asked, holding up a glass.

"Short pour if you guys expect me to sing tonight."

"Well, that's why we're in town, isn't it?" Jonathon piped in. "How are the lessons coming?" Jonathon always took an interest in her life. Since his and Matt's connection in Denver, Jonathon was working on plans to open a new gallery in Houston; still, Jonathon and Matt made a point of getting to Austin to see Rakell. She had moved to Austin nearly seven months ago, but still didn't know many people, and Matt sensed she was lonely.

"Ms. Annette is amazing, but since I travel so much, my lessons are hit and miss. I'm so-so, but with more work, hopefully I'll be good enough to audition for some parts in the next year. That's my goal, anyway," she explained, making sure Jonathon didn't have high hopes for her karaoke performances tonight. They always went to the same place for karaoke, Penny Lane Street Bar, so the staff knew Rakell and frequently pushed her on stage. She usually went with Matt and Jonathon, Matt posing as her boyfriend and Jonathon as her friend. They always sat on either side of her when they went out. It was awkward, but there were worse things in life than being sandwiched between two hot gay guys that loved cheering her on when she sang. Tonight, Lana and Levi were coming too and bringing a few of their friends. Even if Rakell wasn't totally into it, still reeling from last night, she figured it might be a good way to get her mind off Jake.

"I'll change so we can grab a bite before meeting the group at

Penny Lane," Rakell said, carrying her wine to the bathroom. She put on tight jeans, her over-the-knee brown suede boots, and a cream lace-front blouse. It was getting warmer but was still cool at night, so she grabbed her fringed leather jacket, which Matt called her "Dolly Parton jacket." She wore her hair straight, pulling back the crown into a clip with a few wisps of hair falling out. She didn't have a lot of energy for getting ready tonight, so she skipped the makeup. Usually, she would be made up if she was getting on stage, even at a local karaoke bar. But tonight, she had a fuck-it attitude.

"Girl, you going to church!?" Jonathon squawked when she walked out.

"What?"

"That top. No, no. With you dressed like that, we'll be lucky to get you married off before forty," Jonathon teased. "Come on—we are revisiting that closet. You have boobs like that and you're trapping them under some *Little House on the Prairie* blouse? Ugh," he said, grabbing her hand.

Rakell let herself be pulled down the hall, yelling 'help!' back to Matt, who was laughing.

Jonathon rummaged through her closet until he found a rust-colored sequin halter that was structured like an apron top, with ties around her neck and her waist, leaving her entire back exposed. The top fell loose to just below the top of her breasts. She couldn't wear a bra with it, so it was, to say the least, suggestive. She had forgotten about this top; she'd only worn it once at a party in Barcelona with one of her clients. She'd paired it with a short black leather skirt and black stilettos. She had been hired as an escort that night, but once the client had seen her, he called the agency to buy "add-ons," which is what sexual acts were called when a client had originally requested a simple date. It was always up to the escort to accept or refuse. Rarely did she accept. For her, it depended on how decent the guy was and how much money was being offered. Her client in Barcelona was charming and made it clear he would make it worth her while.

"This may be a little over the top for an Austin karaoke bar," Rakell said, looking in the mirror and turning to make sure that there wasn't any side-boob sticking out. She had to admit it looked cool with jeans and boots and would be a fun look on stage.

"You're wearing it. Now let's do something with that face. I get natural beauty, but we can highlight it a bit instead of hiding it."

Jonathon pulled out a bathroom drawer and began looking through her makeup. "Sit down. I'm good with makeup. Matt said you're dying to get laid, so let's put a little effort in here."

She sat down, laughingly giving in to Jonathon's orders. "Um, I'm pretty sure the fake boyfriend thing is more of a hindrance than the lack of makeup." She made a pouty face. "I'm just saying."

"Hook someone, and we'll work around it. You can say you're sick of Matt and need a break."

"Not sure how that would work. I just wish I could be honest about things. It's not just Matt; it's my whole life right now. I mean, how do you let someone you like know that your main profession is as an escort to billionaires? Is it really better than being a prostitute, just because I'm making a lot of money?" she asked rhetorically.

"Matt says you've always seen it as a means to an end, financing your future and other goals." He put his hands up in the air. "No judgment here, girl. I mean, I've slept with several women, knowing I was gay, because I was trying to 'un-gay' myself in college. How fair is that? You know what you're doing, and you've become wealthy at a young age. Keep to your plan, get out at the end of this year. You're still young, twenty…what?"

"Twenty-three."

"That's right, don't you have a birthday coming up soon? The next time I'm back in Houston, aren't we planning on a couple nights out to celebrate?"

"You'd better make it. Who's going to dress me?"

"Oh, I'll be there. My point is you're young and still have plenty of time to enjoy men without money. You may find they're not any better than the ones with it. Hell, you'll probably find yourself sleeping with people you wished were paying for it, because they suck."

"I don't know, Jonathon, just the little bit of normal boy fun has already made me want more."

"So maybe he knows what he's doing or actually cares that you get off."

She cooed, "I'm thinking I won't have to fake my academy award-winning orgasms with this guy. But I just want to have fun. Maybe that's all he wants, too, and I'm reading too much into his eye gazes and sweet stuff he says…"

"That's the shit guys say so you'll fall for them, take your clothes off, and want more. Seriously, you're just used to guys that are paying big bucks, so they know they're getting it at the end, hell at the beginning of the night, if they want, right?"

She nodded, rolling her eyes.

"So this guy from the gym's brain isn't wired like those rich guys' brains. His brain has to calculate the right moves, words, touches, to make you feel safe so he can get what he wants. Which, we all know, is hands on that sexy-as-hell body. You're just not used to what normal guys will do to be in you. I am…and I can tell you that they'll do pretty much anything." He threw his hands up. "Anything, but then sometimes they change once they get it. Unless you've snagged their heart, and that's probably not a good idea in your situation, cause that, honey, is another whole level of complications."

Rakell laughed, clapping. "Oh my God! What would I do without Jonathon's speeches? I definitely don't have room or the mental bandwidth to snag someone's heart and do the boyfriend thing. Most escorts don't…we know it's too complicated. Especially once they have to tell whoever they're dating; it gets messy. I'll tell you some horror stories sometime, boyfriend types threatening to mess clients up. It's not worth it."

"So it's settled. You're in the market for fun. The guy from the gym can just get in line with the other guys lining up tonight, after my artwork…." he said, his hand making a circle in the air in front of her. "Pretty easy with a stunning canvas. You got this, girl."

She bounced up on the toes of her boots. "Okay, I'm rocking this top and your makeup job."

Jonathon clapped, too. "Bravo! That's my girl."

They met the rest of the group at Penny Lane around eight and grabbed a table close to the stage. After hugs and introductions, everyone ordered drinks. Rakell knelt between Levi and Lana so she could catch up with them, feeling like it had been ages since they'd hung out. She found out that Levi had received a promotion to lead reporter at the station, which meant he would now be assigned to more interesting stories. Lana had finished up her teaching certificate and was in the second half of her first year of teaching middle school. So far, she was loving it. She couldn't help but laugh at the thought of the boys in

Lana's class and what they'd be thinking while she was teaching if they ever found her lingerie photos.

"Dude, snap out of it," Dwayne whispered to Jake as the three couples walked into Penny Lane after dinner.

"Jenn, we'll meet you guys at the table. Getting drinks…" Dwayne shouted over the music. "Seriously, Jake, this girl is great. She's hot and a total sweetheart." Dwayne sounded almost like he was pleading with his friend.

"I know, sorry, man. I'm just distracted. Cindy's nice. I'm just not into it."

"I don't want her feeling bad, or Jenn's going to have my ass, because she's the one who arranged this. She told Cindy what a good, down-to-earth, blah, blah, kinda guy you are. Believe me, I sure couldn't have sold all that shit with a straight face," Dwayne laughed.

"Ha, ha. Okay, I'll give it a little more energy, but I'm not sure there will be a second date. Just to warn you." Jake shrugged his shoulders, as if apologizing.

Dwayne offered him a sidewise look. "Dude, the Jessica thing was a fucked-up mess. You're still reeling from it, so this Aussie girl is a distraction, but you and I both know if she was into you, you would not have to work this hard."

"I think she's just cautious. Maybe something in her past like you said, maybe somebody hurt her. You know I usually run from complicated, but I like that she's not all over me, not thinking I'm something great and then I have to live up to that. It's bad enough trying to live up to whatever public persona I'm supposed to have. Or, in my case, *undo* a public persona.For instance, Cindy…" He tilted his head toward the table. "Super nice, but honestly, during dinner she just kept praising me. Like why? She doesn't even know me."

The hostess found them a round table toward the back of the room, away from the stage, so they could talk. They could still see the stage, but they were far enough away that they weren't right on top of the speakers, where it would be too loud. When they returned from their restroom trip, Jake sat next to Cindy. He could see the stage over her shoulder, which was good enough, since he wasn't a big karaoke fan. Some of his friends knew he had taken singing lessons for years because his mother taught singing and dance, but no one had managed to get him up on a karaoke stage yet. Dwayne ordered a round for everyone, getting Jake a double Jack and Diet Coke. Jake could tell Dwayne was trying to loosen him up.

A tall guy with a deep voice took the stage and sang Johnny Cash's "Ring of Fire" and a couple other Cash songs that were pretty good. After his set, the manager came up to the mic, telling everyone to enjoy the acts and to be sure to take care of their servers. Then he said, "One of our favorite performers is right here in front tonight. Kells, get up here." He motioned to someone at a table near the stage. A group at the table started chanting, "Kells! Kells! Kells!"

Jake turned back to Cindy and asked about her real estate business and if she thought home prices would continue to climb; he owned several properties in Austin and was thinking about investing in a few more. Cindy assured him that, within the city limits, prices would continue to go up, even if they stagnated for a period in the suburbs. They began discussing how people were buying houses in the '04' zip code only to tear them down and build multi-million-dollar homes. Then he heard her voice. *It's her. Shit!* he thought, turning to look at the stage. *God, she looks incredible—can she sing?* Thoughts were whirling through his head. *Shit.* He shifted his seat toward the side so he was slightly more concealed. *Damn it, what the hell?* God really short-changed him in the luck department. *Rakell?*

"Hi! Never mind them," Rakell said, waving her hand toward her table. "I'm going to sing one of my favorite Linda Ronstadt songs, 'Love is a Rose.'" She smiled and launched into the song. *"Love is a Rose, but you better not pick it. Only grows when it's on the vine...."* She sashayed around the stage, her hips moving to the beat while her free hand tapped the side of her thigh as she sang. She finished the tune and bowed, a big grin on her face. Then she sang an Emmy Lou Harris song, "Beneath Still Waters." This was his parents' music, the music he'd grown up with. Hearing it come out of her, while she sauntered around in her sparkly top, was too much.

The crowd cheered as she finished, and a couple of guys

approached the stage to help her off, chatting her up as they each took a hand. Jake watched her walk off. He had no idea she could sing like that. She was dressed like a country singer, he thought, and even from a distance, he could tell her top was backless. All he could think about was putting his hands on her, the way her body responded to his touch. God, he wanted to feel her again. He could feel eyes on him across the table, and turning, he saw Dwayne's laser-focused eyes burning a hole in him. Jake shot him back an innocent look.

Rakell returned the high-fives of her tablemates, then offered to get them another round. She wanted to walk around a bit and scout out the scene without Matt by her side. She made her way to the bar, surveying the crowd. *I really need to get out more*, she thought, looking around at all the twenty- and early thirty-somethings packing the bar. Then her eyes landed on Dwayne at the round table near the back, followed by Jake, who was looking right at her, though clearly, he was with a date. Quickly, she shifted her eyes to the bar. She swiftly approached it, getting in line behind two other people. Shifting on her legs back and forth, she tried to swallow past the constriction in her throat. She hated the way she felt. *He's having fun, you're having fun...that's dating. Stop, you can't do anything more than this.*

Jake swigged his drink, pushing his chair back and asking if anyone else needed another one, explaining he didn't want to wait on the waitress because the place was so crowded.

"Yep, I'll take another," Dwayne spat out through tight lips as Jake stepped away.

"Hey, you," Jake said from behind her.

"Yeah, you?" She kept her eyes straight ahead.

"Beautiful voice. Didn't know you could sing." His own voice was flat, low.

"I've been taking lessons for the past few months, but I still have a long way to go," she replied, her eyes still focused forward.

"Are you going to look at me?" His voice was still steady.

"Really don't want your date to see us chatting it up," she said, matching his flat steady tone.

"Dwayne already told the table you were a friend of ours from the gym. Plus, she can't see the bar from where she's sitting."

Rakell turned, not smiling, but she wasn't sure why. She had no claim to Jake, yet irritation and embarrassment were creeping into the façade of calm reserve she was putting forward. "So what did you tell them? We're friends with benefits?" She spoke pointedly now.

He looked around tensely before turning back to her, regret seeping through him. He knew he shouldn't have agreed to this date. He didn't want to explain it here, not like this. "I didn't say anything about you. Didn't think here, now, was a good time to explain anything to anybody," he insisted, shaking his head. He wanted to say, *Stop acting like a fucking brat*...that the benefits comment wasn't warranted. She threw him off balance with her statement, but it was more than that. The surprise of learning that she could sing, the jolt of seeing her looking so damn hot, and the realization that there were so many men in the room hearing and seeing the same thing. "And for the record, we're not friends with benefits."

Jake signaled for her to move forward in the line. She did and turned back to him, her eyebrows pulled in. "We're not? Then what are we?" She sucked in a quick breath. "Sorry. Honestly, you don't owe me an explanation. I'm not some silly little girl. I'm not under any illusions about us." She turned back and stepped up to the bar to order.

Well, sometimes you act like an immature little girl, he was tempted to say but swallowed it. Jake moved beside her, thrusting his credit card out toward the bartender. "Let me get this round," he said contritely.

"No way. Get your drinks, go back to your date, and be the man I know you are." Her tone was authoritative.

His mouth drew in tight as he raked his fingers through the sides of his hair. "You're right," he said, thinking, *She jumps from bratty little girl to intelligent mature woman. Make up your fucking mind so I can figure this out!* Then his mouth broke into a slight smile. "I hate it that you're smarter than me."

Her face softened slightly as she picked up the drinks off the bar. Her chin angled toward him to move on when she saw Lana approaching. She didn't want to face an introduction—*here's the hot guy from the gym, he's here with his date*—and he moved past her, brushing her bare arm.

The surprise of seeing him on a date with someone else had jolted her. She swallowed, trying to bury the angst that had crept up her throat. It shouldn't bother her. Her life choices didn't make room for anything deeper than having some fun and then moving on. Lana walked up behind her. "Hand me a couple; there's no way you can carry all those drinks."

Jake eyed Dwayne, signaling him to help carry drinks back to the table. "Dude, I'm feelin' you right now. I know I give you shit, but this is tough," Dwayne said, grabbing a couple drinks off the bar.

"Yep. Just my luck. A dozen karaoke bars in Austin, and I land in the one *she's* singing at," he said as he picked up the drinks.

"Let's head out after these drinks. I'll just say I'm tired, plus you and I are working out early tomorrow. Jenn will get it, but you're driving Cindy home; it's up to you to come up with an explanation dude. You're leaving a pretty great girl because you're caught up on one that doesn't seem to want you right now. Not sure I'd waste my time." Dwayne registered the angst in Jake's nod and then added, "I have to admit, she sounds amazing and that top…wow!" His eyebrows arching, blowing his bottom lip out.

"God, I know." Nodding, Jake let out a forced breath before they made their way back to the table.

He handed Cindy her drink and sat down behind her. A few more people took the stage to sing, two not so good, one decent. Everybody was a little looser by now, which made some people better and some worse. Cindy asked Jake about the Sacramento real estate market and if he planned to invest there as well. He could tell she was working to keep the conversation going, and he kicked himself for being so distracted by Rakell.

He watched as Rakell climbed back on stage. Cindy turned around. "Your friend is good."

Jake didn't register any irritation in her tone, so he made sure he answered neutrally. "Yeah, Dwayne and I didn't know she could sing. We just talk to her at the gym."

As Rakell spoke into the microphone, her mouth a little too close, her accent thicker than normal, Jake could tell she was buzzed. She had a huge grin on her face, and her body swayed as she soaked up the energy of the crowd, cheering for her, as her table chanted, "Kells! Kells! Kells!"

"How about a little Pat Benatar?" She looked toward the MC, who started the song. "*Heart breaker, dream maker…*" she sang, moving her hips as she strutted back and forth across the stage.

His eyes were fixed on her as he gulped down half his double Jack and Diet Coke, wishing he could go to her.

The bar crowd cheered as she finished, screaming, "More! More!"

Rakell performed a mock curtsey, smiling wide. "Okay, how about more Linda Ronstadt?" Her eyes shifted back to the MC, who cued up "When Will I Be Loved." As the music started, she scanned the bar, her eyes landing on someone at the front table. Jake couldn't see who it was from where he was sitting, but her eyes were fixed on him, and she was smiling. Damn, was that some other guy she was dating? Fuck, he hated competition off the field.

Her voice sauntered across the room, stroking the back of Jake's neck like velvet hands, teasing, gently tugging his ears. A shiver ran up his spine, his mind going straight to her knowing smile after she'd sucked him off in the park.

His eyes were fixed on her. He couldn't pull away. He listened as she passionately sang a song about heartbreak, begging for love.

When she got to the line in the song asking when she'd be loved, her eyes darted around the room and locked with Jake's steady stare.

His eyes flicked to the back of Cindy's head, then he did it. He answered Rakell, discreetly pointing to his chest and mouthing, *me*. She broke their stare, nodding her head as she sang. She was tipsy, but she saw that, Jake thought, as he joined the crowd clapping for her and egging her on for another song. She begged off and thanked everyone for letting her practice and always encouraging her.

Jake saw him again, the tall dark-haired guy with a thick mustache, extending his hand toward her, helping her off stage with a big proud smile smeared across his face while another guy, blond, stood clapping madly. Damn it, she probably had a harem of men begging for her attention. He didn't like just being another guy in her circle of men. Maybe being "just Jake" was not going to work after all.

The NFL player card was always a sure bet, but not with this girl...*Damn, I have four aces and I'm still going away empty-handed.*

Chapter Eighteen

The ride to Cindy's house was chilly. After several stiff minutes, Jake said, "Thanks for going…"

Her head snapped toward him. "I could tell you were really into it," she said, not hiding the sarcasm in her voice.

"Sorry, I'm just…"

"Jenn assured me that Dwayne said you were over the actress and would enjoy some company in Austin."

"I'm not…" he started to explain he was over Jessica, but he let it sit between them as the excuse he needed and walked her to the door in silence.

He poured himself a glass of Nine-Banded whiskey on the rocks. His go-to when he needed to yank his anxiety down a notch or two. Sitting on his back deck, he couldn't get the vision of her on stage out of his head. She unsettled him, but the only answer that seemed to make sense was more of her. Just past midnight, with too many drinks in him, he picked up his phone.

Jake: *I want you*…Delete.

Jake: *I wish you were here with me*…Delete.

Jake: *Who were those guys tonight?*…Delete.

Jake: *For the record, didn't touch my date*…Delete.

Jake: *You were great tonight!*…**Send**

Handing Rakell a glass of wine, Jonathon gushed, "I'm telling you, you rocked it tonight. And the top? Forget about it! Did you see how guys were dying over you? Did you *see* it?" He beamed.

She laughed, "Yeah, okay. I did feel a few eyes on me."

"Sure…just a few," Jonathon said.

"Not sure I need more wine, but I do need to get out of this slutty top you put me in," she called over her shoulder as she walked toward her bedroom. She changed out of her clothes and threw a robe on over her panties. She slipped on her Uggs and joined Matt and Jonathon back in the living room.

"You were amazing. You've improved dramatically. I mean, you've always had a good voice, but your tone, pitch—everything just keeps getting better," Matt gushed proudly.

They toasted and sipped their wine. Rakell knew she didn't need any more, but the internal tug of war gave her reason to indulge more than usual. She heard her phone buzz in her purse and grabbed it from the counter.

Jake: *You were great tonight!…***Send**

A grin took over her face as she looked down at her phone.

"What?" Jonathon asked.

"Some guy?" Matt chimed in.

"Yeah, that guy from the gym I told you about. He was there tonight, in the back." She scrunched her nose up, registering Matt's lowered eyebrow expression. "He was with a date, so I didn't point him out."

"Are you upset?" Matt asked, his voice turning tender.

"I don't know, that's what's so weird. I don't have any right to be, but it still felt, felt kind of icky. I mean, I like him, but how far can I really carry this with my life?" she said, looking at both of them. Jonathon sat with his leg draped over Matt's. Matt was rubbing Jonathon's thigh.

"I'm sorry, Princess. Honestly, I want to talk to my parents. Jonathon wants that too." He looked down at Jonathon, who was nodding with a nearly pleading look on his face. "Just want to wait till my dad is through with this round of chemo."

Rakell made a grim face. "I wish it was just this, Matt, just you.

Because I know you'd do anything for me. But honestly, it's the business, my past. I'm down to you and a few other clients, mostly just a pretend girlfriend, escort. Francesco was my last sexual escort assignment, and Amare doesn't touch me. Every few months, I might meet Marco, but that's only sucking cock; he never has sex with me. Somehow, he tells himself that me sucking him off isn't cheating on his fiancée. I swear, these men."

Jonathon laughed. "Girl, you may be the only person I know who is *more* blunt than me."

Scrunching her nose up, she said, "It's you and Matt, so I'm just telling it like it is." Then she cupped her face in her hands. "Oh naur!" she exclaimed.

"What?" Matt asked, bending forward in the chair. "What is it?"

She lowered her hands. "I almost forgot the birthday girl, Brielle, I see her for the last time in January on her birthday, and I have to, her husband already paid for me to be her present for the weekend."

Jonathon wiggled his eyebrows. "Do tell, Princess...this sounds fun."

Matt nudged Jonathon. "This guy loves juicy, but remember that NDA."

"Of course. So, darling." His gaze went back to Rakell. "Details...dish, dish..."

"Well...no details, and forget that I just said her name, but she's a former international model married to a diplomat in France with two children. She happens to be bisexual...well, as you can imagine, that must be hidden, so her husband arranged for me to be her escort for a weekend as her fortieth birthday gift, and it became a yearly thing. So the past three years I've spent the weekend with her."

"Ooooh...please more!" Jonathon squealed.

"No," Rakell said, fighting back a laugh.

"Damn...one question? Do you enjoy it?"

"I was reluctant, but my friend had been the third person for a few couples, and she said it was nicer than being with just a man. Since her husband made it clear he would not be touching me, and this really was for his wife, I agreed. He'd given me her middle name on the phone, but once I saw her, I knew who she was. Her face has been on the front of every major magazine. She's one of my idols because, besides modeling, she's acted in several French films and is a loud voice for human rights issues throughout the world."

"So titillating…" Jonathon rubbed his hands together. "So maybe you're bi? Nothing wrong with that…"

"I know, but I don't find myself thinking about being with women. Instead, I'm dying to get in bed with some meathead from the gym. God, all those years learning how to act around the cultured types, and this is what I'm attracted to…"

Matt cleared his throat. "Wanting to get off with someone doesn't equate love or a lifetime commitment. You are just figuring this dynamic out…"

"Matt's right. Give your vibrator a break, give this guy a chance to make you smile." He raised his eyebrows as if she wasn't getting it. "You know, between the sheets. He might be one of those types that gets a boost to his manhood when he gets a woman off."

She took a sip. "He actually does make me smile…" she said, drifting off, thinking about how he made her laugh. "So no more faking it?"

"Nooo….don't do that!" Jonathon admonished.

"Really? I do most of the time. That's easier because it ends faster, and men aren't threatened. You guys have fragile egos."

"True, but that shouldn't be on you to inflate a man's ego." Jonathon spoke sharply.

"Matt, can you fill him in…? *That* is the description of my job, 'inflate male egos.' It used to be sort of fun, once I figured out how simple men were. But now it's getting exhausting. I guess I'm getting senioritis."

"You're almost there. But I thought you said end of this year was an absolute…so why Brielle…sorry, I mean the lady from France?" Matt asked.

"I like her, and it feels different than the guys I have to see, more like a dear friend that cares about your life. Except Amare, that's starting to make sense to me. It's still tricky, but I'm sort of understanding why he's doing this. Think he needs time to get over the shock of losing his wife and daughter."

"When do you end with him?"

"My contract with Amare terminates at the end of this year. Always amazing trips, but he never touches me. I just have to study a lot before we meet and pretend to be his dead wife, who was an English professor. I thought it would be creepy, but he's really bright and sweet. She died suddenly in a car crash, and since he didn't get to say good-bye to her, he says it through me."

"He actually sounds pretty cool," Matt said earnestly.

"He's a great person, but it's another level of confusion being with him because I am Marietta pretending to be his late wife Elizabeth," Rakell explained.

Jonathon sat up, his curiosity peeked by her story. "So pretending to be in love with a hunk like Matt is easy by comparison."

Smiling, she said, "I never had to pretend with Matt."

"Ahh…Princess, same here."

"Matt's easy to love," Jonathon added. "But I swear you should get to list these experiences in your acting portfolio."

Rakell let out a breathy laugh. "Sure, sure, that would probably get me the right kind of attention on the casting couch," she said, scrunching up her nose.

"But you're out of this in less than a year and still young. You're getting more calls about modeling, and Anna is working to set you up with some auditions. And you know you'll always have consulting work with the firm. I mean, how many employees do I have on staff who speak four languages? Even if it wasn't my firm—you could go anywhere, especially if you were willing to move to a bigger city." Rakell recognized Matt was in big brother mode, lecturing.

She sighed, "Matt, I went to acting school for a reason. The languages are a backup. I still have a contract with the firm, and you know it's not easy to get out, especially with regular clients. Honestly, what do I say to this guy? 'Hey, let's have a naughty, but I can't be your girlfriend because I still have clients'? Somehow, I'm not sure that would play out well. But he seems to be playing the field, so…." She looked down at Jake's message again, smiling. He did have that going for him, for sure—he made her smile. Feeling playful, she decided to respond, even if it was late.

Rakell: *You looked hot tonight. Loved the tight rocker t-shirt* 😜 …**Send**

"I get it. So just have fun with him," Matt said, his hands folded around Jonathon.

"Yup, maybe you're right. Just use him for sex. You two should go to bed. You're making me horny." She smiled at their laughter.

Jonathon and Matt made their way toward Matt's room. "Good night, Princess."

"Good night, you two," she said to their backs.

Jake read her text as he was sipping the last of his favorite local whiskey, Nine-Banded. Damn he loved the smoothness, like something creamy in his mouth. That thought commingling with the image of Rakell on stage was enough to make his cock beg for action. Just a few words from her and his groin tightened.

Jake: *Back at you with the backless sparkly top. Sexy!...***Send**

Rakell picked up her wine and purse, walking back to her room. She sat on the edge of her bed, took another sip and responded, her senses diluted from the wine and the memory of him finger-fucking her last night.

Rakell: *It was for you* 😊 ...**Send**

She giggled to herself as she sent it.

The whiskey settled in him. Instead of stopping, he poured another before answering her. He smiled, shaking his head. "She's so bad," he grunted, reading her text again. Such a bawdy tease. "Bullshit," he cursed into the air. "Bullshit."

Jake: *We both know that's BS. You had no intention of seeing...*Delete

Jake: *Really? You didn't know I'd be there. So, for me? Or all the boys that were ogling you?...***Send**

She read it, smiling, taking another sip.

Rakell: *Fair enough...but what I'm wearing now is for you* 😊 ...**Send**

She slipped off her Uggs and robe and climbed under the comforter, putting an extra pillow behind her back so she could sit up.

Jake, what the hell are you doing? Damn you're a weak man, he thought, knowing he would take the bait as he carried his whiskey and his phone to his bedroom.

Jake: *I hope less (...***Send**

Rakell*: Slipping my panties off now, so is nothing less enough?...***Send**

She took another sip of wine.

He quickly pulled his jeans and T-shirt off as he jumped into bed. Before he could respond, his phone buzzed again.

Rakell: *You? Hope that cock has escaped those jeans.* ...**Send**

He pushed his briefs down, freeing his cock before answering.

Jake: *Free now. Are we sexting?* ...**Send**

Her hand was drawn to her pussy, wanting to feel the wet heat between her legs.

Rakell: *Not sure, never done it...* **Send**

Rakell: *Is me telling you to wrap your hand around your cock and picture last night sexting?...* **Send**

"Holy shit," Jake whispered, leaning in to make sure he'd read her words right.

A few seconds later, her phone rang. "Hellooo, lover," she cooed into the phone.

"Well, hello. You're completely naked?" Jake blurted out, knowing the answer but just wanting to hear it from her.

"Mm...hmm, completely," Rakell mewed.

"Touch yourself." There was a commanding tone to his hushed voice as he squeezed lube onto his palm.

"Already there, lover." Her voice was overly playful as her fingers explored her outer lips, finding her pulsing clit.

"God, you're so hot." He could definitely tell she was feeling the alcohol, but he didn't care; his body yearned for more. "Slide a finger in—better yet, two fingers inside that sweet, hot hole." His voice sounded dark, lusty, as his command swirled in her ear.

Two of Rakell's fingers found their way inside, pushing past her slit as she opened her legs beneath the comforter. "Mm, mm. Are you stroking your cock?"

"Oh yeah, it's so fucking hard. Thinking about you, your tits, your mouth, that sweet pussy. You're all I can think about..." He held his cock tight, running his hand up and down while he held the phone with the other hand.

She set the phone down for a second to take another sip of wine when she heard, "Sweets? Sweets?"

"Sorry, had to have a little more wine, and no way was I gonna take my fingers away from my hole."

"You might not need any more wine," Jake said, wishing he could take it back.

"Um, since that's what's making me brave enough to tell you what I picture at night, you might want to close your mouth, looover." Her tone was animated as she made her point. "You sound like you may have had a few, too."

"Point taken," he said, stroking himself. "What do you picture at night?" he probed.

Rakell slid her fingers in and out of her wet slit, whimpering into the phone. "Just a minute...I'm getting my vibrator," she whispered. Her fingers slipped out, and she set the phone down as she reached into her bedside table drawer for her lipstick vibrator.

She held the vibrator to her clit and picked up the phone. "I'm back. My pussy's so ready." She wished his hands were between her legs.

"Rock hard, ready to go, thinking about what I want to do to you," he growled.

"Tell me. Tell me what you'd do to me if I were there naked," she mewled again. "I want to hear what you'd do to my pussy."

Jake stroked himself again, pulling at his hard shaft, feeling the pre-cum trickling out of his cockhead. "I'd make you sit on my face so I could dive in with my mouth and eat you senseless. Sucking, licking, and fucking your pussy with my tongue, repaying you for last night over and over." His tone was rough, forceful.

"My, my...oh," she managed to get out, his words working with the vibrator, bringing her higher, her clit burning. "So is that a promise?" Her voice was husky with lust.

"Promise? Oh, yes. I promise you're going to sit on my face and I'll work you over till your legs are rubber. I'll suck up every bit of your cream, just like you did for me last night." Jake shook his head at his lewd words.

"Oh, God. I'll hold you to it. Ahh..."

"My mouth is covering your whole pussy before my tongue licks and sucks your clit. Then I'll jab it deep into you and tongue fuck you till you can't take anymore." He spoke harshly, feeling crazed with his own lust as his hand rapidly stroked himself.

"I'm coming!" Rakell dropped the phone, swallowing her scream as her brain reminded her that Matt and Jonathon were down the hall. She arched and whimpered with the sharpness of the quick orgasm, leaving her still wanting more.

"Rakell? Sweets?" She heard his distant drawl as she fumbled for the phone.

"I'm here," she said, her voice barely audible, breathing heavily.

Brimming with his own need, he probed, "How was it? Could you feel my mouth?"

"Mm, hmm. Made me want more. Just a minute." She propped the phone on her pillow and turned onto her stomach, putting a pillow under her belly. Tossing the vibrator to the side, she slipped two fingers into her slit.

Jake could hear her moving around. "What are you doing?"

"Um, just propped the phone by my mouth so I could get on my stomach. Playing with myself, picturing sliding my pussy down on that hard cock you're holding. Would you let me do that?"

"Um, yes. Yes." His cock jerked in his hand. God, she was driving him fucking crazy.

"So right now, I'm grinding my pussy into a pillow with my fingers inside me, picturing riding you. Would you like that?" she asked, purposely sounding innocent, relishing the effect she had on him.

"Fuck, you know the answer to that. I want to hear you as you pretend fuck me. Put the phone by your mouth and go after it," he pushed, sounding urgent. "I'm going to blow soon."

Rakell rocked against the pillow, working her fingers in and out of her hole, letting her breath out audibly, whimpering into the phone, whispering, "Fucking love your cock. I can feel it going in and out of my wet, wet pussy, so hard."

"Yes, I can picture you on top with your huge tits on display for my mouth. Sucking your tits, pushing your hips up and down. I'm…oh God, yes." His cock pulsed in his tight grip, spewing on his hand and belly. He let out a low growl that turned into a moan as the last of his cum shot out.

She let out a muffled cry into the phone as her hips rippled under the intense orgasm that continued in waves. "Oh, oh…again, oh," she muttered between muted cries.

His moans turned into sighs. "Let it go, girl…that's right. I love hearing you come," he urged into the phone, his cock spent from the torrid of pleasure that ripped through him.

The line fell silent, aside from both of their ragged breaths reaching for recovery.

After a few long minutes, Rakell flipped onto her back again and grabbed the phone. "I need to brush my teeth, but I can't get up," she whispered.

Jake smiled. *That's what she says after fucking getting me off over the phone?* Biting back a laugh, he said, "Wish I was there. I'd get your toothbrush, some water, and brush your teeth for you. Then I'd kiss your mouth till you passed out in my arms."

Her chest swelled at his words. "Um, that's…I like that, I'd…"

"You falling asleep?"

"Yeah…" barely audible.

"Good night, Sweets. Sleep good," he whispered, only hearing steady breathing on the line, pretty sure she'd already fallen off. *So what the hell is this girl's story?* he thought, moving toward the bathroom to clean himself up. Why the hell start this up tonight? After being at the club with another guy, seeing me with another girl. "Shit, maybe *I'm* the friend with benefits," he murmured, looking at his disheveled reflection.

Chapter Nineteen

Jake jumped on the Stairmaster next to the one Rakell was on.

"Hey, you," he said, his eyes taking in her pale-yellow sports bra and the valley created by her smashed breasts.

She was covered in sweat and breathing hard. "Yeah, you?" she pushed out, leaning slightly forward on the Stairmaster and offering him a corner-mouth smile.

Flashing his wide grin at her, he said, "Damn…last night…I feel like we should talk about…"

Her mouth straightened. "Which part, the girl or the phone sex?" she forced out between breaths.

"Both. I just wanted you to know that it was a blind date, and I really didn't want to—"

"Jake, you don't have to justify it," Rakell spat out, pushing pause on the Stairmaster. She took a drink of water and continued. "Like I said, I'm not under any illusions about us. We are *both* seeing people, I get that." Her tone was somber, her eyes directly on him, the expression she used in business meetings so men would take her seriously. But as she spoke to Jake, she wasn't sure if she was lying to keep him at bay or to protect herself—or to shield *him* from her hidden life.

Jake shook his head internally, swallowing the exasperation gurgling beneath the surface, the fucking contradictions with her! This girl shifted so quickly. Last night she was a wanton, needy sex siren; today, she was stoic, almost cold. It was as if they hadn't been intimate. Or maybe it meant nothing to her, and they were right back to the beginning. God, he couldn't figure out how to read her.

Jake had planned on telling her today that he wanted to be exclusive, that he didn't want to see anybody else, just her. But the way she said "*both*" made him pull back. Every time he thought he was getting his footing, she said something that untethered him. Damn it, he was hoping for more. He wanted to tell her the truth, knew it was time. But shit, would she walk away because he'd been lying?

Sucking in a quick breath, he shifted his approach. "Okay. Well, let me say that I would like to see more of you," he said, matching her directness, his eyes serious.

Rakell looked away from the intensity.

Just then she heard a loud male voice yell, "Hey, pretty boy Skyler!"

Her head craned toward the voice to see a forties-something man waving at Jake, grinning from ear to ear. A halted nervous laugh spilled from Jake's mouth. The knowing look on the man's face, which made it seem like he and Jake were close, didn't match the edgy nervous way Jake waved at him, as if waving him off. "Sorry, dude, busy here."

Shaking his head, the guy said, "Got it, no problem. Just wanted to say you're lookin' good, real good, Skyler."

"Yep, thanks," Jake quipped, his lips tight, his eyes darting back and forth from Rakell to the guy, then back to Rakell, absorbing her confused expression.

"Who was that guy?"

"He was…." Shit, was he really going to say *He's a fan, I'm an NFL player*? He didn't want to tell her here, right now, not like this. His ass cheeks flexed as his stomach knotted up. He couldn't tell her.

"It's okay, Jake. I don't care, it's fine," she said, a knowing smile crossing her lips. "When were you going to tell me? I mean, it is the kind of thing you should mention, at least." She watched as his face seemed to drain of any blood, realizing she had no right to pin him on not opening up to her, because she knew she was hiding something big. Lowering her voice, she coated her tone with understanding. "Jake, it's freaking 2022, it's okay, seriously, Jake. I'm fine if you like guys too. I just didn't think…"

His head snapped back, his eyebrows arching up. "Wait, what?" He felt the blood that had drained from his face rush back in, heat circling his neck. "Shit, wait…what? I'm not…"

"It's fine. Like I said, it's 2022. People are getting more comfortable with their sexuality; you don't have to hide it. Are you and

Dwayne…?"

Jake bent forward, letting out a gust of air circled by a loud laugh. "Hell no! First, I'm not bi, and if I were, Dwayne would not be in my bed." He cocked his head, grinning at her. "His boobs are too hard. I like a little more soft, sensory input than that."

Rakell laughed. "Okay, well Dwayne brought up the threesome idea at Eddie V's, so I thought maybe…"

"That's just a fool talkin' and hornin' in on my…"

"My?" she clipped, raising her eyebrows at him as she pushed start on the Stairmaster. "I'm not anybody's anything." Her tone was definite.

Jake winced. Damnit, he hadn't meant to sound like a fucking neanderthal, but if he was being honest with himself, he wanted her to be his.

"Understood," he sighed. He was heading to Sacramento in a few days to meet with Coach Easton; he felt desperate to get in another date with her before he had to leave. He shoved her words back, still moving forward, determined.

"So tonight? Are you available? I'd like to take you out for dinner." He lightened his tone but was clearly pushing.

"I actually have to fly out tomorrow for work and still have a lot to do to get ready." She felt herself rambling on, not sure where she was going because the truth was, she *did* want to see him.

"You gotta eat. We can make it quick. Promise." His hand went up like he was swearing an oath. "Hell, I can even bring takeout to you, if that's better."

"No, that won't work." She couldn't have him coming to her apartment. She didn't want the doormen to wonder if something was going on behind Matt's back. "Okay, grabbing something later sounds good. But it has to be quick."

"Perfect! Sevenish at The Odd Duck? Does that give you enough time?"

"Yes, I'll meet you there," she said, thinking again how she was already getting too close to this guy, but also how she'd never been this turned on in her life. When he was near, she felt rabid, crazy, always fighting the urge to touch him. She was sure he got laid often; he exuded sex, and the way he took control made her want to give herself over to him, to let him do anything he wanted because she knew she'd love it.

He nodded, agreeing, even though he'd prefer picking her up. "Okay. Where are you heading?"

"Argentina."

"Wow, Argentina...for work?" He knew his tone sounded a little too surprised. He wondered again about her job.

"Um, yes. Yes, for work. I have a conference..." she said, trailing off. She hadn't been prepared to explain this to him now and felt bad about lying, but she had to. Rakell was meeting her client Amare in Buenos Aries, then flying with him to Patagonia to spend a week on a ranch.

She still had to finish reading *The Alchemist* before she saw him. Amare had demanded it as part of their contract. He wanted to be able to discuss literary works in depth with her, as he would have with his wife before she passed. She'd explained to him that she had been a theater major with a passion for learning languages, not an expert in literature.

"You'll have to spend a lot of time reading and studying to prepare for our trips, then," Amare had said as a matter of course.

She met Jake later at The Odd Duck, a local favorite that fit the "Keep Austin Weird" motto. They sat outside on an old-fashioned, white-washed porch that ran the entire length of one side of the restaurant.

After the waiter set their water on the table, they ordered a bottle of wine and studied the menu. The eclectic vibe translated into a diverse menu.

"Mmm...wow. The food combinations are so different," Rakell said, staring at the menu.

"See anything you like?" Jake replied, lifting his eyes from the menu to look at her, thinking that he definitely saw something he liked and wanted desperately.

"Problem is, everything sounds like something I want a couple of bites of, just to try it." She smiled.

"Let's split a few things. I'm game for anything. The scallops with Portuguese sausage sound good... and the ceviche. You pick a couple, too. The plates are small, so we need to order a few," he said.

Rakell could have stayed there for hours, taking in the heavy night air and talking to Jake. She considered him across the table, noting the T-shirt that hugged his muscular chest and arms, snug on his taut abdomen, before tucking into his faded jeans.

"You said you did seasonal work. What do you do besides work out?" She hadn't probed before because it made things easier, allowing her to avoid questions about her own work. But she was curious. It was weird that all his friends looked like body builders. They had to be in the fitness industry—trainers, coaches? When she'd mentioned it to Matt, he said those kinds of guys attracted each other. "Meatheads are drawn to meatheads," Matt had explained on a laugh. But this guy seemed more intricate than the meatheads she knew from high school.

He looked at her, smiling in the dim light of the porch. He didn't want to tell her. He loved that she knew him only as Jake the Austin, Texas boy. Living his life in view of the worldwide social media audience was getting old, especially after Jessica. He wouldn't forget picking up his phone from the locker after a big win to call her, only to be inundated with texted pictures from friends of Jessica and a more famous actor making out at the see-and-be-seen Malibu restaurant Nobu. Jessica had insisted they go there a few times when he visited her in LA. The whole time at the restaurant she'd snapped selfies, making him pose, smile, kiss her, toast her with a drink as she captioned the images, *My hot player showing me some love.* It was the kind of place young Hollywood or social media influencers went to come out with a new relationship. So Jessica choosing Nobu to announce to the world that she was with Bernardo Cappuccino, the famous, just-divorced actor who'd played opposite Jessica in a forbidden-love-triangle thriller, was hardly an accident.

He really wasn't sure how Rakell would react to finding out he was a football player, much less a quarterback. Would it be easier? Would she fall for him faster if she knew that money isn't an issue for him, knew how he could spoil her? He didn't get that vibe, he had to admit—quite the opposite. She seemed like she could take care of herself. Seemed like she was looking for normal.

"Not sure I want to go into it yet," he said, watching her eyebrows arch in question.

"Is it legal?" she teased, wondering if he was embarrassed to share his job. Most of the men she worked for bragged about what they did—or, more accurately, what their daddies did. Was Jake doing something that forced him to keep a low profile? Her head spun back to the way that forty-something man had said, "Looking good, Skyler!"

Could he be…shoot…an escort. She knew several male escorts in Europe. Many of them entertained older men and women. Looking at him, she backed away from that thought. His personality was too fundamental to be hiding something like that. But here she was, seemingly normal herself, flying off to Europe and Argentina under the guise of business consultant…what if she just told him what she did, would he freak out? But then she'd signed several iron clad non-disclosure agreements. Her anonymity was paramount if she was going to continue as an escort. She knew she would be wrapping up this phase in her life by the end of the year. She would be able to save enough money to purchase the apartment in Austin and be able to live well for a number of years in order to truly give acting a chance.

Watching his face twist as he contemplated an answer made her blood pulse faster.

"So, Jake, seriously, is it legal?"

"Maybe it shouldn't be, but it's definitely legal. It's sort of a means to do what I really want to be doing in the future. So how about I tell you what I'm working toward and my future goals?" he offered, knowing he was skirting past the truth.

"Okay, what?"

"Well, I own some properties in Austin." As soon as he spoke, his cover-up came alive. He knew what to say next. "I like redoing homes, then selling them or renting them out. So that keeps me pretty busy." Damn, he was digging into this lie, but at least it was true, even if it wasn't the whole truth. "But my big goal is to teach history at a high school here in Austin and manage my parents' ranch."

Jake took a sip of wine, watching her face over the glass. He justified his half-truth, telling himself it was the only way to know if a woman liked him for who he was, not his minor celebrity or the money that came with it. He also left out the fact that he had a misdemeanor record that needed to be cleared before he could become a teacher. He'd "accidently" pushed an asshole off a barstool after the guy repeatedly called Jordan the N-word, but the court saw it as assault. So there was that. His attorneys were working on it.

Jordan said Jake was an idiot for doing it, but Jake thought he had been quite controlled. He really wanted to slam the racist piece of shit's head on the bar repeatedly. So relatively speaking, he had behaved with great restraint.

Rakell smiled, thinking about how normal that sounded, how she could picture Jake being a teacher, a good teacher. "I think that's a great goal, but why history?"

"Well, guess I like reading about history, and I had an amazing history teacher in high school, Mr. E. He got me jazzed about it, made me realize that understanding history, like why certain wars started, can help us better understand things that are going on today. I want to teach it in a fun way."

Taking another sip of wine, she said, "So do you read just non-fiction, or do you like fiction as well?"

"Mostly non-fiction, but I am a big fan of old western books." He saw her scrunching her nose. "Hey, they're good! I've probably read all L'Amour's books. Well, all his westerns, not the sci-fi stuff. How about *Lonesome Dove* by Larry McMurtry? We actually had to read that in my high school English class. Did you?"

"Huh no, Jake, I went to school in civilization. We didn't consider old western books, which are typically only read by men over seventy, a part of our educational program." She laughed as she reached for her glass of wine, knowing she was poking him. Where she'd grown up was rural, and Austin was a cultured big city, but its soul still had that "simple life" feel, similar to her home town.

"Really? Well, since it won a Pulitzer, you may want to pick it up and open your world a little," he said raising his eyebrows. "I think when I'm a history teacher, I'd have my students read some historical fiction, because when I read something that is a story, I remember it better."

"History teacher—you'd be good at that. You're already a pretty good teacher, albeit a little bossy."

Jake snorted. "Bossy?"

"Yep, definitely bossy." A wide grin spread across her face.

"Some people have a hard time following directions and need to be bossed around a bit," he retorted, his face matching her grin.

"Really?"

"Yep." He put his hand under the table onto her knee and heard her suck in air. "Did I startle you, or are you just remembering the park?" he asked, his smile turning into a smug smirk.

"Um...you always this cocky?" Rakell chided, trying to hide how her body alerted to his touch in a way she hadn't experienced with any other man. She'd wanted this to just be physical, but she wasn't fooling herself; she might not be able to do that with Jake. She could tell that there was a possibility that he'd take more from her than she was prepared to give, at least at this point in her life. *Why now? Why meet him now?*

His hand continued caressing her knee. His smile straightened, a pensive look flattening the animation in his features. "Just when I'm nervous and trying to be impressive."

Breathing slowly through his touch, letting herself relax into it, she peered at him over her glass, not sure which one of his expressions made her clench harder between her legs. "So I make you nervous? Mmm...I kinda like that," she murmured, smiling, wanting to wring the sexual tension out of the air.

"Bet you do," Jake hushed, squeezing her leg as he spoke. "Probably shouldn't have given you that, but..."

"It's fine. I like vulnerable men." Rakell winked, then let out a short laugh.

"Really? Vulnerable?" He reached under the table and found her other leg, both hands now encompassing her knees, feeling her muscles flinch from his touch. "Well, I can get really vulnerable for the right person." His voice was gravelly as his eyes grazed over her face, dropping not-so-subtly to her chest.

"Mmm...rethinking. Somehow, now I don't see vulnerable being an apt description of you." She smiled, covering up her confusion from his comment. "I was kidding! Actually, I'm not sure what I like in men. I mean, I guess I haven't really thought about what..." She felt him staring at her; she met his eyes. "Sorry, just rambling."

"No, it's fine. I mean...maybe you just haven't met the right person." His tone was serious.

Rakell's eyes shifted nervously. "Of course, of course. I haven't. Um, I should probably get going. I have a little more packing to do."

"Okay." Jake signaled to the waiter for the check. "When do you get back?" He didn't mention he was heading to Sacramento to review some potential draft picks. Or that following that, he'd be scooting down to LA to meet the CEO of a nutrition supplement company his agent was anxious for him to represent because the money was outrageous. He let the truth take a backseat.

"Thursday. Not next week, the following," she said.

"Wow, like ten days from now. Can I snag a date with you Friday?"

"Mm, I'll be heading to Houston for my—" She halted, not knowing if she should tell him it was her birthday. She would be celebrating with Matt and Jonathon.

"My?" he prompted.

"My birthday is March 28th, so I was going to hang out with a couple of friends for the weekend," she explained, looking down at her wine glass.

"Your birthday. Well, will you be home that Sunday? I'd like to plan something for you." He watched as she kept her eyes lowered.

"That's okay, you really don't need to…"

"I want to. Have you ever ridden a horse?"

"Yeah, of course. I grew up on a ranch."

"Really? Where? Okay, before you roll those gorgeous eyes, I know Australia, but it's sort of a big place, so you're going to have to be more specific."

"Now, Jake," she smirked, "would I ever roll my eyes at you?" She watched him nod, sporting a cocky grin. "Southern Australia, about an hour outside of Adelaide, which you may have heard of. It is a very cool town called Prospect Hill. Where I grew up is rural, medium and large ranches."

"So you grew up riding?"

"Yes, my dad taught me to ride young. There are pictures of me and him on a horse before I could walk. I always remember loving being up there with him. My mom wasn't really into riding, so my dad and I did that together…he encouraged me…" She stopped herself; she had drifted off thinking about her dad, her eyes looking past Jake as if he wasn't there. "Oh sorry, just remembering."

Leaning toward the table, Jake reached out and touched her arm. "No, don't say sorry, I like hearing about your family. Do you get to see them much? I mean, living here, it must be tough."

She moved her arm away, reaching up, pinching the bridge of her nose.

Jake registered that he may have hit a painful nerve. "Sorry, I'm sure it's hard."

She squeezed her eyes closed. She couldn't have this conversation. "No, I don't get to go home very often. I need to change that." She left out that her dad was dead, and her mom did not resemble the woman Rakell knew growing up. Grief over her father's death had morphed into anger, justifying her mother's spiral into depression that she medicated with alcohol.

"It's far," Jake said, trying to save the mood, "but thank God we have easy communication now. Hell, when I'm gone, I call home a lot, a few times a week and FaceTime because…."

"Good for you," Rakell snapped. "I don't…my mom is…" Shit, what was she saying? "Anyway, talking to my mom is hard," she said almost under her breath.

He sat up, surprised by her sudden change in tone, her reaction toward her family.

"Wait, you travel a lot?" she asked.

"Well…" Stalling, he wondered how he could explain this without blatantly lying to her. "Yeah, I like to travel and sometimes…"

She started rubbing her chin, a stiff smile emerging. "Your illegal job has you traveling a lot?" She could relate to that. Maybe he *was* an escort. But she still couldn't picture it, even though he really was pretty. Like the man said at the gym, *pretty boy.*

A forced laugh left his mouth. "Something like that. Let's get back to riding. Horses, that is…"

She shifted in her chair, composing herself. "All that to say, I like riding," she said, unnaturally cheerfully.

He definitely felt the urge to probe, but he also didn't want her delving further into why he traveled. And he didn't want to continue to bring up something that seemed uncomfortable for her. His family was such an integral part of his life; he couldn't imagine being so far away. It was the reason he made Austin his off-season home. But everyone should call their mother often. Her reaction when he asked about her family seemed odd to him.

"That's perfect. How about a birthday riding date?" He logged the information that she'd grown up on a ranch, thinking about how this girl got more perfect with time. They had a lot in common. What he knew about her so far made her seem so different from the glam girls who sought his attention. Not once did she take out her phone to check Instagram or ask him if they could snap a picture she could post. He wanted to know more about her—what her family was like, what was going on there, what had brought her to Austin. Was it a job, a friend, or maybe a lover? Jesus, she was a never-ending series of questions. He checked himself, yanking back on his usual Jake bombardment of questions, registering her retreating inward. *Jake, slow this train down.*

"Well, not sure about Sunday. I'll be jet-lagged, and after a couple nights in Houston…" She stalled, buying herself time.

"We can plan for late afternoon, early evening, so you have time when you get back from Houston to nap." He smiled. "Come on, I'd really like to."

"Okay, I'm in," she said. Damn it, she wasn't doing a good job of resisting him. As the waitress reached down to place the check on the table, Rakell grabbed her purse. "I'll get this."

Jake snatched the check from the table. "No way, I asked you."

Her head popped up, "You've already treated me. It's my turn."

"Nope, we don't take turns."

Her back went stiff, her chin out challengingly. "Really, I think in this day and age, men split things equally, correct?"

He laid down a few bills with the check. "I suppose, but I don't necessarily have to go along with this 'in this day and age' stuff. Before you pipe in, it has nothing to do with equality." Once women found out what he did, they expected him to pay, so this was never an issue. But he could say no more to her without blowing his cover.

"All right, Mr. Super-evolved Fucking Caveman. Let's go," she snapped, throwing her purse over her shoulder as she stood, walking toward the exit.

Quickly he scanned the bar following behind her, his new habit when he was out with her, just in case anyone recognized him. "Not easy on a guy, are you?" he said, getting in front of her to open the door.

"Not my goal," she hissed under her breath.

When they got to her car, he put his hand on the small of her back. "I know it's work, but try to have fun."

She nodded as he lowered his mouth to hers, his all-encompassing kiss consuming her again. When he tilted her head back, he paused, his eyes staring into hers like he was deep in thought about her. "What?" she whispered.

"You know the Kenny Chesney song 'Get Along'?"

"I'm in Texas now, so yes, I'm pretty sure I have…"

His hands moved to her shoulders, and with a low voice, he started to sing softly, *"Always give love the upper hand, Paint a wall, Learn to dance, Call your mom…"*

She registered the flash in his eyes when he sang that line. "Jake, please—"

He tapped his forehead to hers, locking her in. "Just a word of advice: Don't let too much time go without your mom and dad hearing your voice. Call your mom, Sweets." He felt her shoulders retract, her pulling away.

"Yes, okay, Jake. I need to go." She whirled around, unlocking her car and jumping in before he could respond. She couldn't think about her mom or how disturbing it was when she did call her. It took all her emotional energy to pick up the phone, only to be shattered by the past and her mom's pain. What did he know about that?

Chapter Twenty

The team did most of their pre-season training in Tahoe, right by Squaw Valley. Jake felt lucky to be able to train in such a beautiful place, nestled in the Sierra Nevada mountains and a short drive to Lake Tahoe. Once the season began, Jake lived in a house with Dwayne and two other guys, Purdy from Nebraska and Rodger from San Diego. Rodger was the old, wise man of the group, having been married since college (he'd met his wife in high school) and fathering two kids by the time he graduated college. They'd all decided to go in on one of the big, older homes with character in the heart of downtown Sacramento, mostly so they could be close to the new stadium. The stadium was built close to midtown, where the old railyards used to be. Rodger had the big bedroom off the living room on the first floor in case his wife was visiting from San Diego. On those occasions, all the other guys were restricted from too much booze and bringing home women. Jake thought that was more than fine, since they pretty much needed to keep their heads screwed on straight during the season.

Jake's dad had been chewing his ear off about buying something in Sacramento. According to his dad, it would be a good investment, since people were moving there in droves. Jake agreed, but mostly he liked the idea of having some privacy. Shit, and the idea of not having to share a bathroom with Purdy, because no one stank up a small space like Purdy—so much so that Jake found himself warning women if he happened to be brave enough to bring them home to that old mansion.

When he mentioned to Ms. June, the owner of the house—an eccentric woman in her 80s who spent most of her time in Paris—that he was probably going to look to buy a place, he told her that his mind was set on getting one of the older homes in the Fabulous Forties. Ms. June insisted on introducing him to one of the artists whose acrylic piece hung in their living room over the mint green velvet couch, telling him she happened to also be the top real estate agent in downtown Sacramento.

So he spent the first morning back in Sacramento looking at homes.

At the end of their last conversation, when Coach had asked Jake to fly to Sacramento, he'd thanked Jake for persuading him to look at Dwayne the previous year. He'd then added that Dwayne was proving to be a missing piece to what Coach referred to as "the team that would take everyone by surprise." Dwayne and Jake were a match on the field; they read each other intuitively.

Dwayne had a sixth sense for knowing, just by watching Jake's body language, where his passes would end up; he could see how high, curved, or direct (according to the plan in the huddle) they would be. And when Jake was rushed, the other team's defenders coming at him, it was as if Dwayne read Jake's mind. When Jake faked like he was going to throw one direction, he'd tilt his chin the other way, and Dwayne would know what to do—follow the point of Jake's chin, jagging right, then left, then running into place, throwing off the defense. It was like dancing with someone that knew where your feet would be before you did, Jake thought, thinking about how his mom had taught him to dance, sensing another's body with the music. Dwayne was that to him on the field. Sometimes it was as if Dwayne knew Jake's moves before Jake knew them, as if they shared a brain.

Coach yelled for Jake to come in before his knuckles even knocked on his door. Jake was surprised to see Rodger sitting at one of the two cognac-colored leather chairs in front of the desk. Both of them looked way too serious. Despite his exhaustion after racing through five homes in East Sacramento, he quickly woke up, his nervous system on high alert.

He couldn't guess what they wanted to talk to him about. He and Rodger had a great relationship. Rodger was the kind of player who just melded into the group; he guided Jake while at the same time letting him shine. An experienced backup quarterback was every rising NFL quarterback's dream. Rodger had seen many days on the field where he was the star, but a lower back injury had put him out for a year at one point. When Rodger came back, he just wasn't as smooth, but he knew that. His plan was to play backup to a healthy, non-egotistical team player that was on the rise. A person that respected his experience and football acumen. *Shit. It's weird for Coach to call us in like this during the off season. Especially without telling me Rodger was going to be here. I thought he asked a few of us players to meet to discuss draft picks with the owners. So where's everybody else?* Jake's brain raced, trying to make sense of it all.

Rodger swiveled around in his chair, his mouth forced into a grim smile, his eyes red with puffy bags under them. Jake knew Rodger didn't drink much. He was cautious of his image because of his family. He'd turned into something of a health nut, too. This guy ate so clean, it almost made Jake feel guilty when he horked down a half-dozen tacos. Jake's mind continued to race. *What the hell is going on? I explained to Coach that Jessica's interviews insinuating I was pervy weren't accurate, and Coach said he trusted me, believed I was focused on the team and that we had potential to go far this next season...*

Coach stood, then Rodger stood. "Have a seat, Jake," Coach said, his voice even lower than usual. "We need to discuss something that can't leave this room. I'm trusting that you'll keep it between us." His hand went to his chest.

That gesture seemed to hold a lot of weight. Jake felt it hit his chest as if someone had taken a twenty-pound weight and thrust it at his sternum. Trying like hell not to let panic show on his face, he stilled his features.

"Of course, Coach...Rog? What's going..."

Rodger gestured for Jake to sit. Coach plopped into his big leather executive chair, and for the first time, Jake noticed Coach Easton's white coarse hair sprouting near his temples.

Jake lowered himself into the chair next to Rodger.

"Okay," he said, looking toward Rodger, then quickly at Coach

Easton. This man had always been straight with him. His brain buzzed. It was past the date for the owners to try to get out of their contract with Jake. What the hell was going on?

Coach nodded toward Jake, then Rodger. Rodger cleared his throat and said, "Jake, I just want to say that you've come so far with this team in only three years. I've been in the league for almost two decades, and I've seen so many guys come and go, guys who think they're better than they are, but you, you don't get how good you are..." Rodger stammered, as if he could only spit out chunks at a time. What the hell, this sounded like a fucking break-up speech. Jake moved his jaw from side to side, trying like mad to stay focused, not freak out.

"Hey, Rog, I know how much you've guided me and I'm..."

"Just listen, Jake." Coach Easton jumped in, his voice stern.

Rodger lowered his head, raking his hands through his thinning light brown hair, the sides showing signs of age, a little more salt than Jake remembered from January. "Jake, I know I said I'd give you five years, but you can't count on me going forward."

"What? Are you okay?"

His long fingers started rubbing his temples, as if whatever he needed to get out was causing a great deal of pain. "Melanie needs help with the kids. The girls are..."

Jake watched Rodger's throat convulse. "My oldest, Sedona, she's not right. She's really struggling... I don't want this getting out to the press."

"God, no..." Jake said on a gusty breath.

He rubbed his eyes. "Sedona's been drifting away from us, and Melanie's been going crazy the last year and half trying to get her back. This asshole guy she's been seeing in college has been telling her things like, she's too fat, she's ugly..." Rodger made an almost choking sound. "Sedona, she's in a bad place. I mean mentally, she's not going to classes or work, she's just sleeping all the time. Her roommate called Melanie. She's really worried...we need to move Sedona home before we completely lose her. She's depressed and we...*we* need to help her." His eyes watered up, his pain so palpable, as if it was something tangible Jake could touch if he reached toward Rodger.

Damn, Jake wanted to twist that boy's neck whose words made this young, bright, kind girl, whom he'd met several times, hurt inside. *Did Rodger fantasize about strangling that piece of shit?*

Rodger kept talking, but his words were jumbled. "My family needs me. My wife can't do this by herself. I know I said, and signed, but…"

Instinctively, Jake scooted his chair right up against Rodger's and put his arm on Rodger's back. He really didn't know what to say: The team didn't have another backup quarterback. They needed Rodger. They had a chance to go even further next season. *Damn,* Jake thought. *We're on fire, but none of that would matter if Rodger lost his daughter to depression.* Who the fuck cared if you got to the playoffs or won a goddamn Super Bowl if your family disintegrated? Jake steadied himself, forging his brain for his next words.

"Hey, we'll figure it out. Your family needs you. Sedona needs you. I know how damn strong you are, Rodger. I totally get Melanie wanting…hell, *needing* you there."

"I'm letting this organization down, but…"

"Jesus, Rog…you're the one that's always talking to me about what matters most. You've said it a million times: family. Your wife and kids. So fuck this organization." Those words were not really the truth in Jake's heart, but he knew that he had to say them for Rodger, and he had to try to believe them. He knew that was how his dad would've responded, but rival thoughts blared in his head: *This was my fucking year to prove to the world I'm more than some impulsive pretty boy with a football, that I have what it takes to pull this team together and march us forward.* But damn, his dreams, his goals depended on a hell of a lot of people's lives holding together, and life didn't always work that way.

Rodger bent his head, pinching the bridge of his nose. "It means a lot, Jake, a lot. I'm not saying I won't be at some of the games, just that I can't be…." He looked across the desk at Coach Easton, who was staring at Jake. "Coach, I know we'll need to rework the contract. You guys can just pay me per game, I'll forfeit…"

"Hell if you will," Jake burst in, throwing his hand up. "No, Coach, take it out of my compensa—"

"Jake, Rodger, both of you…impress me," Coach interrupted. "But Rodger, you're not forfeiting anything. You get back to San Diego, hug that wife and girls. I have videos to show Jake. We'll run some of the draft ideas by you…I have my eye on the kid from Dartmouth…"

What the hell…no way! Jake straight-up jolted. Was he talking about the same kid Jake was thinking about? "Coach, not, shit, the Dartmouth kid…that's not where players go…"

Rodger let out a breath that sounded like a muted chuckle.

Coach jumped in. "Yep, Jake. That's where smart players go who know they're going on to something else, not counting on the game to pay the bills." Coach lowered his head, a smirk emerging, fighting against the serious look in his eyes. Jake knew that look, the look that said, *I'm about to school you, so listen up.* "You may have heard of Ryan Fitzpatrick from Harvard, one of the best backups out there and one of the smartest players the league has ever had, so yes Jake, Ivy Leagues produce good players too."

"Okay. Let's take a look at him," Jake murmured, knowing he should've kept his mouth shut. "What do you think, Rodger?"

Rodger's mouth twisted up to the side, and for the first time since they'd started the conversation, Rodger's drawn lips seemed to relax. "I love watching videos of him walking off the field, the way he gingerly takes off his helmet smiling like a Crest commercial and whipping that long, flowy blond hair through the wind like some kind of Nordic god. You have to admit he would have the best hair and teeth in the league. Oh, and those eyes, Jesus, he could probably make more money as a model than playing backup. If I looked like that, I wouldn't risk it." His eyes shifted to Jake. "Jealous, Jake?"

"Hell no," Jake spat out a little too defensively. Rodger was right: The kid drew the cameras. He sported that white, perfect smile even when the team was losing, which was often, unless they were playing Brown, whose team looked like they'd barely put down their Proust books long enough to suit up.

Coach roared, "Don't worry, Jake. You're not giving up the 'pretty boy' moniker just yet. The kid keeps it clean, like, *really* clean. He's not surrounded by women—well, besides his sisters, five of them, and his mom. I don't see him using his position or looks to…"

"Shit. That's why—five sisters! I have two, and together with my mom they ride my ass about everything, but I wouldn't change it for anything."

Coach laughed. "He talks about his mom the way you talk about yours. Think you guys might hit it off…" He looked at Rodger. "We'd probably pack out the stadium with those two lookers. Can't you just see the poster, the dark-haired brooding quarterback and behind him a ray of sunshine with his blond hair whipping in the wind, you looking at both of them, holding up a mirror?"

Rodger burst out laughing. "Yeah, the balding guy holding up the mirror for the hair commercial…sign me up for that." He looked at his phone. "I gotta catch my plane, but…Jake…I appreciate everything and trust in your confidentiality," he said, standing.

Jake stood, desperately wanting to hug Rodger, but he extended his hand, and their eyes locked. Rodger said, "You're going to go *really* far. I can feel it."

Coach stood, nodding at Rodger. "Talk soon, son."

Rodger nodded as he turned to walk out.

When the door shut, Coach Easton plopped back in his chair, a sigh leaving his mouth, as if *this*, Rodger's life, had taken a real toll on him. Jake thought about how all of their lives probably took a toll on Coach. How he lived his players' ups and downs not just on the field, but in everyday life, too. And how stressful that must be—caring for, guiding, and praying for the lives of an entire organization of mostly men—well, boys becoming men. Hopefully.

Jake remembered Coach's words at the end of a particularly tough game, during which Coach changed offensive strategy because the Steelers' defense had been throwing the Condors around like rag dolls. As he finished his directions, Jake had said, "Say a little prayer for me" as he ran on the field to face off against the Steelers' mammoth defensive line.

That night, after the Condors endured a significant loss, Coach had called him over before Jake entered the locker room. Jake was sure Coach was going to tell him he wasn't worth his weight in salt, that the bargain seventeen mil the team got him for was a complete waste. No, instead he said, "Son, just so you know, I'm always saying little and big prayers for you and everyone else on this team and supporting this team. So you don't have to ask next time."

"I get it, Coach. I guess we needed more than prayers tonight," Jake had grumbled, not happy with himself.

"You're right. We needed more than a few of those behemoths on the Steelers D to get food poisoning, but somehow God didn't answer that prayer." He hit Jake's back, bellowing, "Get it out of your head, Jake. You have the Giants next week. This game is over; we look forward, period, because there's neither time nor energy to look back, especially if you're looking back at defeat. Ignore it and keep your eyes forward. Got it?"

"Yes sir." Lord, he wished he could be that disciplined, but his brain had already started reeling with what he could have done differently. All the what-ifs bouncing around, making Jake second-guess himself.

Rodger was gone, a bomb had dropped, and a man was left riddled with fear: Jake, because he couldn't comprehend doing this year without counting on Rodger. Still, Jake knew Rodger's fear mattered more. Jake couldn't wrap his head around how Rodger and Melanie must be feeling, knowing that they were losing their daughter to depression. A snippet in life, a young girl filled with doubt so great she was retreating from this world. He wondered how it must feel to drown in despair. What would you think once you were on the other side looking back at that dark time?

One thing he did know, after spending a few years side by side with Rodger, was that what he and Melanie had was true love, a commitment based on trust. Rodger had told Jake once that he made sure all his actions reflected his commitment to his wife. That they had met in high school, and no one believed Rodger would ever make it to the NFL, except her. Melanie never stopped telling him he'd get there, and she'd be there cheering him on. He was a walk-on for Rutgers, then once they saw his skill intertwined with passion on the field, the coach folded him in, and eventually, he was Rutgers' starting quarterback.

Jake envied the guys that met "the one" in high school or college, at a time that they weren't famous and loaded, so they didn't question a person's love. He hadn't been looking for "the one." He'd tried to be committed to Jessica, but the truth was, he didn't go to sleep at night with her dancing in his head or wake up smiling from something she'd said or find himself aimlessly touching his skin where her lips or fingers had been, closing his eyes as he could feel her even when she was out of sight. No, he hadn't ached for her, his skin imprinting every touch, and she must have known that when she decided to publicly humiliate him—kissing that fucking famous actor, old enough to be her father, at Nobu, knowing there would be a million pictures.

Then this Aussie girl had strutted by shaking her hips, spouting from that sassy smart mouth, putting him in his place. *She* paraded through his brain constantly. Damn. Now he was acting like a jackass, nervous that she wouldn't like him, as if there weren't thousands of other women he could go for. But there was something different about her—it was as if somehow, she was seeking the same thing he was, someone simpler, someone who cared about her. So here he was, trying to hide a big part of himself—his job—to see if this girl would fall for just him. The irony was that he'd boasted about his job for years in order to attract women. He found himself questioning his life's choices. There was a part of him that wanted what Rodger had, what Howie Long had, hell what Patrick Mahomes had. They knew in their bones that they were loved for who they were without the uniform. But how could he, or a Jimmy Garoppolo, or Randall Adams, know? Well, hell, *Randall* probably asked his shaman, Jake thought, internally rolling his eyes.

Jake's dad always said that was the curse of success: having to question who a woman was falling in love with— the NFL star or the Austin, Texas boy.

Coach cleared his throat, as if to wake Jake up from his reverie. He sat up straighter, blocking out his splintered thoughts. "So, Coach, I guess we've got a lot of work to do. I'm still on to head to Tahoe later and check on the progress of our training camp...planning on getting a group together in Tahoe a few days before we start. What's the word from the higher-ups about the draft?"

"First, Jake, I'm proud of you for how you handled Rodger's situation. I know you're disappointed, but a 'people first' attitude always wins at the end of the day. I want this as bad as you do, but when I walk away from this organization or leave this world, the football win won't matter as much as the people. You get that already, and you're young—must be that good parenting," he said, an earnest smile pushing his full cheeks up to rounded balls below his eyes.

His dad's patience and many of Coach's words were the examples crossing his brain's screen. Jake smiled at this man in gratitude, hoping he'd be that man someday, the man Coach thought he already was.

"Hope I, for my parents' sake, can catch up to the way they raised me, Coach."

"You will. For now, let's comb through these videos. I have several, including Tracy, the hair and teeth commercial boy. Also, a receiver, a junior at LSU. He's incredible, but he's already caused some chaos at LSU. When you read his profile, you'll see he's lacking what you got given to you...he had a hell of an upbringing, and even talent makes it hard to undo the demons of the past. If you think he's worth it, we'll run it by Dwayne, because he'd have to agree to take the kid under his wing. Both of them were fatherless, but polar-opposite dads."

"Okay…"

"What I'm saying is that Dwayne and his family feel the loss of his father every day, but no one misses Jaxton's dad, mostly not Jaxton. You'll have to read the story—it's surprising the kid made it as far as he has, but I'm concerned he's a ticking time bomb. Not sure how we deal with that…but if we don't jump on him, we're turning away from one of the best wide receivers in the SEC. Case in point, Dwayne, Missouri Bluff University…there's only a few that compare to Dwayne, and he's just starting to hit his prime."

Jake said, smirking, "'Cause he's got a special kind of QB…"

"Special, all right…" Coach burst out laughing, and listening to his words thrown back at him, Jake couldn't help but laugh too.

Rakell's job had taken her many surprising places, introduced her to many different cultures, and taught her to accommodate the inflated egos of wealthy men as well as listen to the vapid stories of the women who were clawing to be in the inner circles of wealth. Those circles were still, for the most part, controlled by men. She knew that for most of them, just having her on their arm was a status symbol, a flashing sign that said, *I can afford anything I want, anything.* But nothing could've prepared her for Amare.

Being with him was like having the most profoundly caring professor dedicate his time to infusing you with all his literary knowledge. His wife and his young daughter had been killed in a car accident a little over a year ago. His wife, Elizabeth, had been an English literature professor at Cambridge and the mother of three young children, two boys and their baby girl. And, most importantly, she'd been the love of Amare's life. From what Rakell had been told by the agency, his grief was crippling him at work and home as he struggled to pick up the pieces for his boys.

His therapist had suggested he find someone to replicate, but not replace, his wife. Someone that could be a stand-in for her while he worked through the grief. Apparently, this therapist directed many of his wealthy clients their way. Amare's request was a look type. The rules were she was to wear the clothes he chose when she met him on trips (she assumed the style resembled that of his wife), and she was to have studied the works of fiction he assigned so that they could discuss them throughout the trip. Seeing Amare was like entering another world. She was not the Marietta character Rakell had honed, but Elizabeth, entrenched in the literary arts, descended from British aristocracy, whose grandparents had moved to South Africa to capture land laden with fertile soil. Elizabeth had been raised to be a cultured heiress to a wine and hotel empire and had thrown that away for Amare, the son of the head of housekeeping for the family's boutique hotels that blanketed the wine region near Cape Town. She didn't know how it came to be that Amare and Elizabeth became husband and wife because he didn't talk about it.

Rakell did know that Amare bought and sold rare books to individuals as well as museums. During their first trip together, he had rattled on about some of the books he'd held in his hands. A subdued man, he didn't let a moment of silence pass without filling it with words sputtering from his mouth like a nervous teenager. Somehow his nerves quieted her own. That first trip he'd flown her to Japan to ski, something he and his wife had loved to do. It was beautiful, but being with him was painful, watching him try to see his wife in her, calling her "Elizabeth." All of it stirred her, empathy for him comingling with her own painful past began bubbling to the surface, and she found herself wishing he would meet someone he wanted to rebuild a life with.

Following a day of horseback riding and absorbing the breath-taking view of Patagonia, they sat across the table, candlelight flicking between them. Rakell's hair was twisted into a bun, resembling a hairstyle his wife had frequently worn on special nights out. She wore a scoop-necked, cap-sleeved emerald silk dress that Rakell thought was reminiscent of what the late princess of Monaco would have worn, so far from a style Rakell would have ever chosen for herself.

He raised a glass of champagne with a slight smile, but it was as if Rakell could see the ache in his heart that he was masking with this charade. "Wife, my dear Elizabeth, a day, another breathtaking adventure, seeing the world with you will always be among my most treasured days. When I'm an aged man, the views we shared together will *inevitably* scroll through my mind's movie screen, even as names and dates leave me, the views paired with the smells, sounds and of course your company will stay with me, I am sure of that, my love. Even in the days nearest death, when my mind may fade, my soul will never lose its grip on what we together have seen, the natural beauty of this fleeting world."

Could he see through her forced expression? Her brain was spinning from his words, every one of them so wrought with a deep agony. *Oh God, this, being her, hearing his words laced with grief, it's too much. I would rather take my clothes off and perform for some cocky asshole than have this utterly broken, good man spill his heart before me. How in the hell do I respond?* On the other trips, he had not bared himself like this. On the other trips, they'd discussed previously read literature as if in a graduate class.

He cleared his throat, nodding toward her champagne flute. Her chin trembled slightly as her brain combed through the library of stored experiences trying to find something relatable so she might know how to respond. Finally, she picked up her glass, sucking in her bottom lip to stop the quivering. "Yes, yes, Amare, once again a spectacular trip, made all the better because we were able to share this together."

She saw the question in his eyes, but he regrouped and clinked her glass before sipping from the flute. "So, dear Elizabeth"—he'd say her name, well his wife's name, repeatedly when talking to her, as if the more he said it, the more her face would morph into his wife—"I do so love our tradition of re-reading *The Alchemist* every year, knowing it was the first book I gave to you when we dated so long ago."

Rakell's neck stiffened with the realization of how much this book meant to him and her, his wife, and although she recognized that the book was slathered in life lessons, she hadn't delved into the deeper meaning of every line. *Just smile and nod*, she told herself.

"Yes, I love it too," she said after too long of a pause.

"I know, dear." His black eyes pooled with a depth that she didn't understand. She had to work not to look away from him. "I'll go first. My favorite line this year, I believe, is—" He took a quick sip of air, then his eyes focused beyond her. Speckles of light danced in his dark eyes, and she was sure that if she turned, she'd see him lost in the light of the chandelier hanging in the middle of the dining room. But she didn't turn; she forced a smile on her face and maintained her eyes straight forward on him.

Then he began, speaking with a soft voice, but his tone was professorial: *"We are travelers on a cosmic journey, stardust, swirling, and dancing in the eddies and whirlpools of infinity. Life is eternal. We have stopped for a moment to encounter each other, to meet, to love, to share. This is a precious moment. It is a little parenthesis in eternity."* His eyelids slid down like thick blankets, he took a long inhalation of breath, and then his lungs collapsed, the captured air flowing into the room.

Her teeth clenched behind a sweet upturn of her lips, and her throat tightened, her heart thumping so loud she was sure the sound was ricocheting throughout the small dining room. Soon, she thought, the waiter would ask her to leave because of the disruptive sound emanating from her chest.

Shifting his gaze back to Rakell, Amare said, "Breathe, dear, breathe. I know, I know how much that passage stirs you. I remember well, you chose it for your grandma's celebration of life. That is the reason I can recite it so well, but also, it settled into me during this read of *The Alchemist*." He smiled. "I know I must digest it for its meaning for me, for you, for our shared life, love. And you, dear Elizabeth, what is your chosen passage from this year's reading?"

The quiver in her lips turned into a tremble, the words scrolling in her head because she had read them over and over, knowing they were *truth*. But it was a truth she wasn't prepared to absorb even if the words had etched themselves into her being. So she couldn't force herself to say them out loud. *If you're brave enough to say goodbye, the world will reward you with a new hello.* If she let those words escape her psyche, she knew her façade would crumble. Amare to his wife and she to her father, both of them needed to say goodbye to their past. Just like Amare, she didn't know how. She pushed it deeper, buried all of it, so the quote that came out was safe. She looked at the small bubbles drifting about in her flute, whispering, *"So, I love you because the entire universe conspired to help me find you."* With the word "you," she saw her father in her mind's eye, and a tear spilled down her cheek, wetting the white tablecloth, and then another.

He reached across the table, his hand turned up, inviting her to place her hand in his, so she did. "My dear, dear sweet Elizabeth, that was the first quote you shared with me. How I knew you loved me." His long, thin fingers wrapped around her hand, squeezing.

Sucking in, she swallowed the shock. That line, the one that had jumped out to her from the pages, was his wife's way of saying she loved him? Oh, God. The words were now indelibly imprinted into Rakell's brain.

"Dear, dear…you look, the color is fading from your otherwise rosy skin." Amare's fingers flexed, releasing her hand. Then slowly he dragged his hand across the white linen. "Are you well, my dear Elizabeth?"

Blinking madly, her chin popped up, and she said, "Just a little tired. I think I need…" Scooting her chair back, she continued, "I need to lie down. May I?" Her breaths were short and choppy, her eyes darting toward the door. "All the fresh air, the sun…"

Standing, he signaled for the waiter. "Please charge to Room 101. I'll take care of gratuity later." His hand reached out for Rakell's.

"I'm fine, I can walk back." Her brain clawed for space.

"No, I will escort you back to your room," he said firmly in her ear. Her legs felt wobbly as they made their way down the hallway.

Pecking her cheek, he whispered, "Sleep well, my dear."

As she opened her door, she didn't make eye contact. No way did she want to see all that loss in his deep, inky eyes again. No way! Selling her body to greedy men felt easy compared to being the sponge for someone else's anguish, as if the burning pain in him somehow melted the frozen pain she'd learned to hide.

Chapter Twenty-One

Still trying to recover from the lengthy travel, her emotionally charged time with Amare, and then two days of celebrating her birthday, Rakell really wanted to cancel her date with Jake. It wasn't that she didn't want to see him, but she felt unsure of herself; the edginess that had inhabited her in Patagonia still lingered. She'd wanted to tell Matt, but he and Jonathon had made plans that didn't make room for a Matt therapy session. So like so many times before, she stuffed it away. Compartmentalized the experience and the internal nagging about her unresolved life with it. She knew that seeing Jake would make her smile, but if she couldn't open up to him, the smile would be superficial, surface-level.

Rakell put on a pair of jeans, her riding boots, and a long sleeve button-up cotton shirt. Jake had texted her that he was on the way. Pushing the doors open to leave her apartment building, she saw Jake leaning against the passenger side of his truck. She craned her head toward the double doors of the apartment, worried one of the guys working the front desk might be watching, but she knew it was difficult to see out the smokey glass. She squinted, not seeing either of them near the doors, but still felt the need to be cautious.

He truly looked like he was from a different generation, with his straw cowboy hat, pale blue cowboy shirt with white snaps fastened over his wide chest, dark denim jeans, and dark brown square-toed cowboy boots that had definitely seen their share of Texas dirt. She wanted to leap on him, kiss him, then rip his clothes off.

Rakell smiled widely as her eyes raked over him. "Well, well. Don't you look yummy." A seductive tone rasped her voice.

His chest pulled in, a glitch in his breathing. "Hey …really? I'll take it. I'm thinking the same looking at you…yummy." He opened her door, and she climbed in the truck.

After jumping in the driver's side, Jake leaned over to kiss her on the cheek. Instinctively, she turned her head to the side, her eyes on the front door.

He pulled his head back, confusion taking over his features. "Huh? I don't get a kiss after...?"

Her face crumpled up, knowing she hadn't handled that right. "Jake, I just, well, I don't like the guys working here to know or make assumptions about my life, like…"

"Like what?" He shoved the gearshift into drive, pressing on the gas.

"I'm just private about who I see."

"Okay, but I didn't see anybody spying out the windows." It hit him that she'd instructed him to wait at the entrance of the parking garage the last time he picked her up, and a couple times now, she had come out the garage entrance. Who was she hiding him from?

He shook his head. *What's up with her? Hell, Jake, she doesn't know what's up with you.* Taking a slow breath, he said, "I missed you," the pitch of his voice giving away his need. He found himself reaching for reassurance with her, wondering if she missed him too. "A lot," he added.

"Glad to be home," Rakell said cautiously. She had wanted to grab him when she first saw him, but they had been right in front of her apartment, so she had restrained herself. Scolding herself, she thought how he could easily become a routine part of her life. He had that feel about him, like a slow Sunday morning made for relishing, *eking* out as much of the lazy feel of it as you can. But that wasn't her life. As an escort with a cover job, she led two lives, and that didn't allow for her to soak up moments with someone else. She had to be alert. *Have fun and move on,* she told herself. *You have goals—and in Dad's words: "Don't depend on any man, not me or any other man."*

She glanced over at Jake. "I always miss Austin when I'm traveling for work." She watched his expression shift, his jaw growing harder, the toothpick moving as he chewed with more intent.

Not really what he was hoping to hear, but he needed to let it graze over him. She was here now, and he was getting to take her to the ranch.

"Jake…that toothpick!"

"Bugging you?"

"I wouldn't say that exactly," she cooed… "it's just kinda hard to…think, with your mouth…"

He couldn't stop the twist of this mouth as his eyes darted over to her, the way she was crossing her legs, squeezing them together. "So, Sweets, I like keeping my mouth occupied…helps me control my thoughts." He grinned.

Jesus, the way he said that sounded dirty, her legs flexing as his deep voice ran the length of her thighs, teasing her groin. "Damn it, Jake," she said on a breathy giggle.

His eyes back on the road as he pulled the toothpick from his mouth, "just give me a chance to show you how useful this mouth can be…"

"Enough…" she yelled.

They both burst out laughing.

His parents were out of town, and it was Luis's day off, so Jake had agreed to feed the horses this morning and again this evening. It gave him a chance to bring wine, snacks, and a birthday cupcake out to his parents' gazebo, a party spot in the middle of the ranch. It was built on the highest point of their expansive property, which made for some relaxing post-ride evenings. There was a small barn structure, complete with a bathroom, and just outside of the gazebo stood a scattering of chairs and a large chaise lounge surrounding a massive firepit. Jake and his high school friends had spent many a Friday and Saturday night sitting around the firepit drinking beer.

It was the place where Jake and his sister Jenae had had their heart-to-hearts. He'd never forget the summer after he'd just turned seventeen and Jenae was home to intern at a law firm in Austin. He had missed her so much when she went off to college. Jenae had moved to Houston to attend Rice when he was fourteen, and it felt like a big ball of energy had been evacuated from the house. Before she'd gone off to college, he'd sneak in her room to get help with homework, and sometimes if he promised to do some of her chores, she'd even write his papers for school. She always made sure she misspelled some words so the teachers would be none the wiser. She had explained this to him, hands on her hips, her tone paired with the scowl on her face, after one of her papers he turned in got a *low B,* and he had dared to complain to her.

He wasn't observant enough to know when his sister needed someone—he just knew he needed her. Her second summer home, when she was twenty, he did sense something was wrong. Her affable self had become rigid, and her expression seemed bothered. During one of their family gatherings, Jake watched her face fall when one of his dad's brothers was ribbing her about when she'd be bringing a boy home. Later that night, he and Jenae grabbed a six-pack and took one of the four-wheelers to the fire-pit. After a couple beers, Jake threw it out there, saying what he'd been thinking for a few years: "So, Jenae, no one's gonna care if you like girls, for sure not me."

Jenae lifted her beer bottle, her face rosy from the fire. "Jake, I think you're going to turn out all right, despite all our fears." Her mouth turned into a shit-eating grin.

"What? Fears? Shit, do you know how hard it is to live up to you and Melissa with your perfect fucking school records? Dad never fails to mention that they never got a call from any of the *girls'* teachers, and they never caught the *girls* drinking, and the *girls* never streamed porn, and the *girls*…"

"Jake, you bought porn on Mom and Dad's TV? What? Okay, I take it back about you turning out—"

"Wait, I always refused to watch it with my friends, but last semester I got with someone…" His voice dropped low, his head hung, looking at his beer bottle. "I made a fool of myself because I didn't know anything, literally anything. Dad did a shitty job with the whole birds and the bees talk. Great, I know how babies are made and where they come from, but no idea how to get a woman to want to practice the act with me."

Jenae spit the beer she'd just swigged into the fire. "First of all, it's not Dad's job to make sure his *Romeo son* is good in the sack." She shook her head. "So you think porn will show you that? Believe me, you'll be utterly disappointed because no one acts like those girls do, unless they're being paid." She snickered. "Poor Jake."

He shook his head. "It's still better than not knowing how to even touch a girl, well, in a way that makes her feel good."

She leaned forward and said, "Jake, *I* can probably tell you how to do that better than any guy your age for sure, and definitely better than any porn video will. I have a girlfriend. She's in law school, so a little older, and she knows what she's doing…"

"Great, Jenae, how's that conversation gonna go?" Jake raised his voice to a falsetto squeak: "*Damn Jake you're so good, how'd you get so good at making me feel good?*" He cleared his throat, dropping his voice: "*Why, of course I learned from my sister, where else?* Hell, no, you ain't teaching me nothing about making girls want me."

Jenae laughed. "Making girls want you has more to do with what's happening up here…" She reached toward Jake and tapped his head. "Read, learn about the world, and keep being kind, they'll want you. Another thing is making sure they keep thinking about you past the first time, and they can't stop. That's how I felt after I was with Kim. I'd sit in class and just think about being with her again…because…"

"Damn, stop, okay. I'm cool with you liking girls as long as it's not the same girl I'm going for. I feel like you have homecourt advantage."

"No worries there, Jake. In no universe would you and I ever find the same girl attractive."

He smiled to himself, thinking about that night and how silly but open their conversation had been.

He rotated his head, taking in Rakell's profile, the small smile on her face as she stared out of the window. He hoped that he had something to do with that smile. Looking at her English riding boots, Jake remarked, "You good riding Western? Hell, if you can ride English, you can ride Western. We're only going on trails on the ranch."

"I should have asked, but I ride both. I haven't been in a Western saddle since I left Australia, but it's not a problem. I only have these riding boots." Rakell's eyes dropped down to the brand-new riding boots Amare bought her for Patagonia, which had replaced her old pair.

"They're nice. Super fancy. I hope you don't mind a little dust on them—this is Texas, after all." He wondered if they would ever get to a point where there wasn't an initial reluctance when they first saw each other, if it would ever be natural. It always felt forced at first, the conversation stilted, before they softened into being together. Once they did, though, it felt like he was with someone he'd been with for years.

"Dust is fine. I guess I should get some Western boots if I'm going to stay in Texas," she mumbled as if she were speaking to herself.

Jake grimaced, snorting. "You'd better" jumped out of his mouth.

Rakell whipped her head toward him, jolted by his tone. "Huh?"

He cleared his throat. "Nothing…just saying people are moving to Texas, especially Austin. Word's out it's a great place to live…that's all."

"Yeah…I like it so far," she said, looking out the window.

"So no reason to move, right? Unless…well, do you like your job?"

Her eyes were back on Jake thinking about how to respond. The thought of telling him she hoped to make it as an actress in Hollywood seemed ridiculous. "Yes, I mean, I guess it's sort of a way to make money now, but I hope to"—she caught herself—"learn more about the actual business side. Right now, I mostly work as an interpreter, sort of a liaison during transactions." Then her eyes shifted back and forth to take in the wide-open space before them as they turned off the highway onto a winding dirt road. "Wow Jake, is this all your parents' ranch?"

"Yep," he said as they drove by a large one-story ranch style house. "That's their place, but we're headed to the barn." He pointed down the dirt road.

"Looks like there's another barn on the side of their house."

"That's a party barn. Dance floor, bar, but it's all open. It's sort of barn-roof with no sides. Actually, it's more like a tent because they can zip the sides down in the winter, but they usually just put up heaters instead. My parents love to dance and entertain," he said proudly. He thought about how his mom had lured him into dance lessons in high school, telling him if he learned to move his feet on the field like Randall Adams (basically to dance), he'd be a better quarterback.

Tilting his head in her direction, he said, "I'd love for you to meet my parents…sometime soon."

"No, no—not ready for that." The words flew out of her mouth before she had time to formulate a response that didn't sound so defensive. *This is why escorts don't date* was all she could think, registering the huff of exasperation emanating from Jake.

"Um, okay. Just sayin' they're super nice people. You'd like them," he replied, slightly perplexed as he looked over at her staring out the window.

"I'm sure they are. I just meant that I'm not...well, we're not..."

"It's not like if I introduce you to my parents, it means we're headed down the aisle," he said in a strained voice, unsuccessfully masking his confusion.

Rakell reached over and touched his arm. "Sorry. I know. I just don't want to give off the wrong impression, like we're..."

"Got it," Jake snapped, not hiding his irritation, mad at himself for caring. This girl kept him shaking his head. Most girls were excited when he suggested meeting his parents. She literally seemed spooked by it, like it would seal their relationship, and it definitely seemed like she didn't want that to happen.

She saw him shake his head out of the corner of her eye. She hadn't intended to push him off that way. But her life was still just too complicated for parents. How could she make a real relationship work at this point in her life, dinner with Mom and Dad, smiling across the roast beef, passing the potatoes?

"So, Rakell, what do you do for a living?"

"Actually, I do quite well as an escort to billionaires. It's quite lucrative!"

How would that play out? Her story, with all its incongruencies, wasn't lost on her, but how did you tell someone that although you'd kept the company of men for years at only twenty-four, you were just starting to learn how to date as an adult?

She knew Jake was still huffy, exasperated. But meeting his parents was a big leap—or was it? More people to pretend with, to appear as someone she wasn't. She pushed that thought aside, thinking she just needed to make tonight right so they could both relax. She knew one thing for sure: Any time he was near, her nerves were on high alert, especially between her legs. The physical seemed easy to understand; he was objectively hot and clearly knew how to appeal to women, but the unidentifiable feeling was something else, something she'd only felt with her dad and Matt. Protection? Comfort?

Rakell snapped her seatbelt off and slid over, putting her arm around him. Laying her head on his shoulder, she said, "I really missed you, Jake. I'm not good at saying that kind of stuff, all that nice relationship stuff. You know...I've just done my own thing for a long time." She leaned in, her lips feathering against his cheek, softly pecking his jaw line toward his ear as he drove slowly down the dirt road.

"Whoa, watch it." He smiled, finally feeling the friction dissolve. "I think words just aren't your thing. You communicate better with your body," he whispered as her mouth moved from his jaw to his ear, then his neck. His lap responded to her lips on him.

Rakell's body arched forward, itching for him to touch her, craving relief from her angst-ridden state. Jake turned off the truck and snapped his belt off. He cupped her jaw in both his hands, his mouth moving onto hers. There was no hesitation from her as she opened for him, their tongues dueling as they both hungrily sucked up each other. Minutes passed before they pulled apart. "Definitely better with nonverbals," he whispered, pressing his forehead against hers.

She tilted her head back, finding it hard to pull away. "Are we going to ride?"

"Yep, I'd really like to ride," he said, a purposefully wicked look in his eyes.

"Really Jake? Junior high ranch boy humor?" She laughed, opening the door to the truck.

"Was that my inside voice? Ranch boy? Think that's some XX chromosome humor," he chuckled. "Eh no. Let me get that." he said, swinging his door open.

He ran around the front of the truck, getting to her side just as her feet hit the ground. "Hey look, that's my job, all right?"

The features of her face wrinkled up. "Jake, I can open doors," she sassed, putting her hands up and wiggling her fingers. "Look at these hands..." she taunted, then stopped, noticing the hardening of his jaw. Jesus, this was serious to him. What?

His hands cupped her chin firmly. "Let me do it. It's instinct to me, and it doesn't feel right when I can't..." He loosened the grip on her chin when he saw her eyes grow big. "Please, Rakell," he said, letting his hand drop away.

"All right, I..I..." She winced at the intense sincerity in his eyes.

Damn, he hadn't meant to squelch the passion and positive energy between them, but there were certain rules he lived by.

"Wait, I have something for you. Almost forgot, got distracted when you were seducing me." Ignoring her eye roll, he opened the door, reached into the back, and pulled out a wrapped box, which he put on the hood of the truck. "A little birthday present."

"Jake, you shouldn't have!" She cocked her head.

"Come on, open it. You need this if you're gonna live here."

Ripping off the wrapping paper, she saw that it was a hat box. Now she understood why he had texted her to ask what size hat she wore, telling her he wanted to make sure he had a helmet that would fit her. When she opened the box, she saw a heather gray felt cowboy hat with a lighter gray thin ribbon around its base. "It's beautiful," she said, pulling it out of the box and putting it on her head.

Jake moved forward in front of her, studying her as he adjusted the hat's angle on her forehead. "God, you make it look beautiful, that's for sure. Happy birthday," he murmured, dragging his rough fingertips over the crest of her ear before tucking her long hair behind it. Her sharp intake of air brought him back to the moment. The side of his mouth crested into a knowing smile—she was affected by him. He wanted to grab her shoulders, stare a hole through her, and demand she stop playing games. *Just let it happen, don't fight this*, he wanted to beg her. But could he really say, *Hey, don't protect yourself, I'm a good guy, I won't hurt you?* He wanted to believe that was true, but he couldn't be sure.

He took her hand, leading her into the barn. He saddled a large black horse that looked like a Thoroughbred-quarter horse mix. Aptly named Midnight, he was large and a bit feisty, sort of like Jake, Rakell thought, admiring the powerful animal. Jake then brought out a chestnut-colored horse, an Arabian-Lusitano mix named La Dame. Jake explained that she was his mom's second horse, so she didn't get ridden as much.

La Dame could be a little spirited at first but usually settled within a few minutes. Rakell assured Jake that she was an experienced rider and would be fine. She declined a helmet, choosing to wear the new cowboy hat instead.

Jake led them away from the barn. "How about a tour of the ranch?"

"Sounds good," she answered, gently turning La Dame to follow Midnight. The ranch tour took them almost two hours, and she was pretty sure there was still more she hadn't seen. His parents' property was an expansive ranch located in Dripping Springs, just outside of Austin city limits. Jake looked formidable on top of Midnight; he was a commanding rider, yet clearly sensitive to the horse, she thought, bracing for the hollow feeling that expanded in her chest when she remembered her high school days atop Blanco, her childhood horse. How carefree life seemed then, not knowing that in her future, a wildfire would rob her of the life she knew.

Chapter Twenty-Two

"Are you ready for a little break?" He pointed to a small barn-like structure in the distance. "We can get something to eat. Let the horses get a drink too." He steered Midnight toward the structure, which stood atop a small hill. Midnight picked up his pace, and La Dame followed suit, breaking into a light trot. "They know there's water and treats waiting for them!" Jake yelled back. "I'm going to let him go!" he shouted as Midnight broke into a canter. Rakell encouraged La Dame to race ahead. As they passed Midnight, she threw a hand up, waving good-bye to Jake. He raced up beside her, laughing. "Right here." He pointed to a couple of wooden poles near a large gazebo. They stopped, then he took the bits off and put halters on both horses. They drank from a small water tank before Jake tied them up. He then ran into the small building and came out with a bunch of carrots.

Jake guided Rakell inside and showed her the adjoining closed-in structure, which was basically just a bathroom and a small kitchenette. The rest looked like storage for outdoor furniture. He washed his hands before taking food and wine from the refrigerator. He set up the table in the gazebo, including a small plate with a cupcake covered in sprinkles. A lone candle poked out from the frosting.

She took off her hat, setting it on one of the chairs. "Jake, this is nice," she said. Then she saw the cupcake, and her chest tightened. The unexpected small gesture struck her as more meaningful than the countless gifts of jewelry lavished on her from her wealthy clients. This seemingly modest gesture, along with the cowboy hat, demanded more consideration than she expected from this rather straightforward guy. It felt like more than she could get her head around. "The hat, this… this…" Her hand waved over the table adorned with his presentation.

He studied her expression, the grateful surprise shaping her mouth before her full lips crested into a smile, her top lip pulling up too high on the right to accommodate her eye tooth. In those seconds, it occurred to him that her beauty went beyond that smile, her hair, the catlike green eyes, past her robust hips and breasts. It was in the way she appreciated this one-dollar cupcake he'd grabbed at the local grocery store or the sunset at the Oasis that made her so beautiful. Her expression registered to him as genuine, that unlike the women he'd dated in the past, she wasn't acting. But how could this matter to her when she'd already hinted at the rich men she'd been around as a consultant?

"Sit here," he said, patting the end of the chaise lounge as he sat. She sat beside him, still looking at the cupcake. "Happy birthday, beautiful." He kissed her lips lightly.

"Jake, thank you. This is so sweet, seriously." Rakell smiled. "I'm starving," she said, eyeing the food. She hadn't eaten all day, because she'd slept late due to her jet lag and her two-day birthday celebration with Matt and Jonathon. Matt had insisted that she fly directly into Houston from Argentina because he and Jonathon wanted to celebrate her birthday over the weekend: two days of drinks by Matt's pool, shopping with Jonathon (the best shopping buddy ever), and too much food. She had been pulled down by the fatigue, so she'd spent the day drifting in and out of sleep, forgetting to eat.

Jake handed her a stemless plastic glass filled with white wine. "Here's to you turning…?" He looked at her, realizing he didn't know how old she was. She looked young, and sometimes she struck him as naïve and inexperienced. But other times she came across as older, experienced, tough. He almost couldn't guess.

"Twenty-four," she said, taking a long drink of the cold wine. "Why, what did you think?" His stare wasn't lost on her.

He fought to control the features of his face, his shock. He'd always made a point of steering clear of younger women, preferring women closer to his age or older, women who understood themselves and knew what they wanted. He really wanted to stop playing games, which wasn't easy with younger people. Then it hit him—how could a twenty-three-year-old, who seemingly hadn't dated a lot, know how to suck a cock the way she had with him in his truck? None of it added up to him. An older boyfriend, maybe? Like, much older. But how would he broach that…*So hey, who taught you to suck dick like that?* He shook his head. Why did he care? He knew how to please a woman, and no woman had asked him, *How did you learn to do what you do, Jake?* He jolted back when he heard her lightly clear her throat.

"So how old did you think I was…?" She cocked an eyebrow, turning toward him.

"I wasn't sure, really didn't have a guess. In some ways, you seem so mature…" He leaned forward, reaching for a cracker and cheese, realizing she had noticed him staring at her.

"In some ways?" Rakell said, poking his side, her tone reeking of incredulous amusement.

"Most ways," Jake said, purposely trying to change the subject so he could hide his surprise and confusion. Sometimes, this girl seemed like she was closer to his age and had lots of experiences. Then other times, she said things that made him think she was sixteen and had no experience with men at all. "You ride really well. I can tell you grew up around horses. So you were raised on a ranch in southern Australia?"

"Like I said, outside of Adelaide."

"Do your parents still live there?"

"No, they sold it after I went off to college," she said in a clipped voice, leaving out the fact that the fire had left behind only scorched land and a dilapidated house. Rakell's eyes swept to the landscape, pausing on the horses they'd just been riding. The pain she worked hard to keep buried bubbled to the surface. The ranch, her dad trying to save her horse, her life in London, her decision to be an escort—all of it was intertwined. If she tugged on even one thread, the whole façade would unravel. *No, Rakell, disassociate*, she told herself, the mantra she lived by as an escort.

"Have you always lived here?" she asked, steering Jake's line of questioning away from her.

"Actually, my parents have had the land for a long time. Some of it belonged to my grandparents. My dad bought it from them, then he started buying the land surrounding it. We lived in the city limits until I was in junior high, then they built the house here."

"It's massive…beautiful land." Rakell looked around, taking in the soft, moist breeze, watching the surrounding oak and mesquite trees that formed a wall around them. She took another sip of her wine before lying back on the reclined lounge. "The breeze feels good." Her green eyes shifted up toward Jake sitting beside her. "I think I could fall asleep out here."

Jake took a sip of his wine, set it on the table, then moved up the lounge, lying on his side next to her, propping his head on his hand. "You're probably so jetlagged. Thanks for spending your recoup day with me." He leaned into her, moving his mouth inches from her lips. "Rakell, all I can think about is..."

His tone sounded like he was about to dive deep. *Please no, please.* Luckily, she knew the best way to shut a guy up. Tilting her head back, she reached behind his head, pulling him in. "Don't talk," she whispered, her mouth against his, nibbling his bottom lip, just feeling the moment, shoving back the memories of her ranch back home and everything that happened after the fire. She moaned, wrapping her other hand around his neck, kissing him with verve, sucking his tongue into her mouth. Her hands traveled down his neck to his shoulders, then frantically squeezed their way down his arms. Manically, she dropped her hands from his shoulders, her fingers scrambling to release the buttons on her own shirt. Her need was unabashed, but she didn't care; she craved the release he could give her.

Jake could feel her heat take him over. Her intensity was leading him to an uncontrollable edge, making it impossible to resist. He'd thought about her unceasingly during the past two weeks, replaying his time with her, his questions, his longing for her, her seemingly longing for him but always pulling back. Like a yo-yo, one minute she was in his grasp, the next swinging away. His hold felt tenuous. Her shirt opened up, revealing a gray sports bra, taut stomach, and a heaving chest. He spread his fingers over her abdomen, letting them tease the waistline of her jeans, then moved up under her bra. "Rakell, can I?" he said, his hand going to the front hooks..

"Yes." Her fingers released the hooks, not waiting for him.

"Jesus," he hissed as her breasts exploded from the constraints of the sports bra. "So fucking perfect." His hand spread out over the large mounds. "They look as beautiful as they feel." His hands kneaded the globes of flesh as she arched toward him. His mouth dropped to her chest, tracing a nipple with his tongue while his hand continued to massage the other breast, lightly pinching the pink nub between his index finger and thumb, plucking at it while his teeth gently grazed over the other the pebbled skin of her chest.

Pull the reins in, Jake, take this nice and slow, think George Strait in "I

Crossed my Heart." Show her that this is a slow dance, Jake. Reel this in gently.

Shit, her squeals, her thrusting hips, his need to see her, to *feel* her come, spurred him on. His impulsive cock switched the channel and then he couldn't hear George Strait anymore. Nickelback's "Animals" blared in his head. Nothing would stop him from gorging on those tits.

Jake jerked up, looking down at her big, begging green eyes, her mouth protruding with desire, her chest rising and falling rapidly. He used both hands to squeeze her mounds together, giving his mouth a small range to torture the rigid pink nubs, sucking and scraping, devouring the flesh squeezed between his large hands.

She thrust her chest forward as an almost pained whine slipped from her mouth between labored breaths.

"Tell me if it's too much, Sweets."

He got his answer swiftly as her hand reached behind his head, pulling it back down to her breasts. He continued without relenting, responding to her body's reply and her red swollen tips.

"Please…yes, please." Her hips rolled back and forth, her hand moving between her legs, squeezing her own sex over her jeans as his teeth alternated yanking on her rock-hard nipples while his hands kneaded the fleshy tissue. She was seconds from unzipping her jeans, slipping her hand below her panties, getting herself off. Too many men, over too many years, touching her only for their own pleasure, made Jake's attentive touch feel simultaneously sumptuous and explosive, the blue flame of fire coursing through her, heating her pelvis.

"Oh, God! I'm…!" she cried out as a quick spike of electricity shot from her nipples to her groin, igniting that flame, her eyes rolling back in her head. The brief intensity of the orgasm left her body pleading, a shock to her pussy making her whole groin ache for more.

His mouth slowed to gently sucking her tits and massaging her electrified flesh. Feeling her ripple under him shook him, making him want to feel more of her pleasure. As her body slackened, he moved his hands to her ribcage, his fingers absorbing the subtle feel of tiny bumps forming on her torso, holding her. His mouth laid slow, soft kisses on her lips. "Wow, Sweets. I want more of that," he whispered. He couldn't imagine what it would be like to be inside her, how her body would respond. He'd never touched a body so eager to release, so anxious to come that it would explode from nipple play.

Her nervous system eased back to the moment, recovering from the blow of her body turning on her, revealing her intense need. With the same sweetness, she kissed him back and whispered, "Take more, please." Her eyes implored him, looking into his steady blue stare.

"Sweets?" he asked, his fingers lowering to the button on her jeans. Rakell nodded her head. "Wanna do so much down here… so much." He was unzipping her jeans, pulling at them. Her hands joined his, pushing the denim down past her pale pink panties. He cupped her entire sex, struck by how wet her panties were. Jake looked up at her as she pushed her pussy forward, imploring his hand.

"Sweets, all this from your tits…you are so fucking sexy," he growled as he slipped his hand under her panties. "Fuck, you're soaked, I can't wait to…" His fingers moved through the folds of wet flesh covered with small wisps of wet hair. He could feel his cock throbbing against her hip. "…Be inside you," he hushed, pushing his middle finger deep into her vagina, exploring her tight walls. Her pelvis tilted to his hand.

"Oh, please…please," Rakell groaned, her hands swiping toward his crotch until her fingers found the hard shaft trapped under thick denim, stopping briefly on the snap of his jeans, then wiggling the zipper down.

He groaned, his cock stiffening even more. His distended balls felt like they were going to burst.

He lowered his head to her ear. "Can you take more? Two fingers?" She nodded her head, pleading. His voice was low and husky. "What I really want to do is shove my tongue up in that dripping pussy, slurp up all that cream and inhale until I can't fucking breathe."

"Please, I want…please, more," she whined, her voice sounding pained.

Jake slipped another finger deep into her, moving both fingers in and out as his thumb found her engorged clit, precisely working it in a circular motion. Her hips were rocking madly. "Lay still, Sweets. You're making it hard for me to finger-fuck you. You want that, right?" Lewd lust tugged at his voice, making it gravelly and darker than he had intended.

Her body registered his husky determined voice snaking over her skin. "Uh huh," she begged. Her hand pulled at his briefs, freeing his cock, stroking it sloppily, manically as a wild drive to come enveloped her sex.

"Fuck," he growled, feeling her hand roughly squeezing his cock. He drove his fingers deeper, harder, as his thumb flicked and circled her swollen nub. He moved his other hand under her shoulders, tilting her body toward him, giving his fingers a better angle, allowing her better access to his cock.

A prurient urge was taking him over. As the throbbing in his cock increased, so did his thrusting fingers. Clenching his jaw, Jake willed himself not to come yet. Yanking at the modicum of control that still lingered in him, he slowly pulled his fingers from her wetness, quickly sucking her juices before he moved her hand from his cock. "Not like this. I'll blow, and I want…"

Rakell's eyes popped open. "J-a-k-e…please…" Her voice sounded pained, and she shut her eyes, embarrassed. "Jake, I…"

"Shh…here's what's going to happen if you say yes," he said, his groin begging for a green light. "I'm going to pull these jeans and boots off, then bury my face in your pussy." His words came out choked, as if something was caught in his damn throat.

She sat up. "You don't want to just fuck me? We can, you did me a favor," she said breathily.

He'd already pulled her boots off, tilting his face away from hers, trying to hide the consternation her words caused. What the hell, a favor? Did this girl not know how amazing she was?

Kneeling on the ground, where her sock-covered feet hung just over the edge of the lounge, he looped his thumbs under the waistband of her jeans, yanking them down and bringing her lace panties with them. "That's fucked up, you hear me? No one's doing anyone favors here. Me watching you get off is not me doing you a favor; it's you letting me see you." His hands cupped her knees, then parted her legs slightly, inching his fingers up the inside of her thighs as he leaned forward, hovering over her pelvis. "Seeing you come like that will replay in my brain over and over. Believe me, I'll be using that visual. Tell me I have the green light to make this dripping wet pussy mine for dinner." His voice and eyes demanded that she respond.

His light touch dancing up her inner thighs felt like mini fire-crackers popping just beneath her skin.

"Tell me," he said, his fingers opening her folds, staring. "Do I?"

She crested her head up, stunned by the sharpness in his eyes as he focused intently on her pussy. "Yes, yes, I…I, but Jake—" she panted, trying to catch her breath.

He rested his sharp chin, on her pelvic bone, his hands prying her even wider, his hot breath coating her mounds. "Is that 'yes, Jake, please make me your meal'?" A cockiness oozed through his Texas drawl, watching her writhe from his touch, knowing much more was coming her way and he'd be the giver. Hell, he'd give this girl anything she wanted, even what she didn't know she wanted yet.

Her eyes half-mast, she absorbed his fierce expression with the sureness in his words. He knew exactly what he was going to do to her, and damnit if he wasn't gloating before he even got started, damn him, but she wasn't about to say no… hell yes, she wanted to feel it all.

"I want to taste more of that. Do you like getting your pussy eaten?"

The only time she'd found it enjoyable was with a woman, the French socialite whose husband had hired her to be the woman's fortieth birthday present. That was the first time she came from a mouth, and only with that client. If a client went down there, they usually didn't spend much time. Usually they'd just lick to see how wet she was before fucking her; clearly they didn't actually want to be there.

"Do you?" he pushed again, his voice gravelly.

"Not sure," she whispered, turning her head to the side as he raised his head up to look at her. "I think so?"

"Let's see." Jake could tell she felt embarrassed, and he wasn't sure she'd ever had someone please her orally. Again, he thought that was odd for such a bold, seemingly experienced woman. "God, I can't wait," he growled before pushing her knees up so her hips rolled back, taking his tongue and licking her to just before her asshole up her crack to her pussy, then sucking the whole of it in his mouth, his tongue finding her clit, sucking it. Her squeals spurred him as he thrust two fingers back into her sopping hole, his tongue lapping at her clit.

"Yes, Jake make me…oh… God!" she yelped as his mouth covered her entire sex, sucking in. "Oh my…"

He slid his fingers out and started lightly pinching her clit, feeling it grow from arousal. "On top of everything else, you smell like wildflowers and taste like vanilla ice cream drenched in some kinda sweet honey."

She forced back a giggle from his words. Such a little-boy thing to say. No man had ever expounded on her taste that way.

Then his fingers were gone, and he shot his tongue into her slit, stroking the entrance with his tongue.

He might come just from sucking and slurping on this amazing cunt, hearing her squeals and feeling the way her body torqued every time he pushed his tongue inside her.

Forcefully, he reached around and grabbed her hips. "You better lay still if you want me to keep fucking you with my tongue," he commanded, his mouth centimeters from her opening, his breath brushing over her lips. "Feel it, sweet girl, just lay back and absorb all of it, because this is just the beginning of what I'm giving. Got it?" His mouth encapsulated her inner lips, his tongue feverishly flicking her hard nub, while two fingers worked her insides. Relishing every bit of her, the fact that his hand and mouth were soaked with her juices, felt like a goddamn gift from the heavens. This, right here, pleasing her, that was his Holy Grail.

Her back arched again as a sharp cry flew out of her chest. "Oh my, I can't, I can't..." she continued, egging him on.

His mouth released her, and he said, "Oh yes you fucking can, and you will." His tongue lapped her from her ass to her clit, then he jammed his fingers in deep, searching for that spot as his mouth alternated sucking and licking her engorged nub. His chest swelled as the feel of her inner walls began contracting like a vise, and her cunt squirted liberally onto his fingers, followed by a sudden jolt and her screaming, pushing his head, pulling his hair.

"No, no, no...not again, oh please..." And then her words were lost to incoherent utterances mixed with low moans that sounded more animal than human.

Damn, he needed, ached, to be inside her. Now! He didn't give a damn if the horses needed to be fed, he thought, gently sliding his fingers from her and opening his mouth to release the suction of his mouth on her flesh.

He scooched up the lounge, wrapping his arms around her shoulders. He tugged her into him, holding her as her shudders eased into small muscle spasms against him. Her face snuggled into his chest, almost as if she were hiding. Fear pressed against him, striking him. Carefully, calmly, he asked, "Sweets? Just want to make sure I wasn't too..." He moved his hand, cupping her chin, tilting it up, practically forcing her to look at him.

When her eyes locked with his, she saw something that made her afraid for the future. He had the capability to shatter her heart. First by forcing her not to dissociate. Making it impossible for her to use her greatest form of protection from losing herself: never linking emotions to a man's touch, his words. This would be hard to fight, but she had to. She wouldn't join the leagues of women who had given up their dreams for a man. She owed that much to her father.

"No, no. You were..." Rakell drove her face harder into his chest, the rush of emotion seeming to overtake her. She didn't understand it; she just knew she wasn't used to her heart getting involved when it came to men. "It was great. I really needed it. I just..." She yanked on the reins of her emotion, taking on a business-like tone.

His jaw tightened at her sudden distance. The cocky asshole in him wanted to push her away and say, 'Yeah me too, need to get my rocks off now,' but the adult in him registered the fragility in her response, the coverup. He kissed the top of her head, knowing not to expose her emotion, wishing he understood why but being content to simply comfort, hoping this would pass soon, because he desperately needed his cock in her.

Their bodies were still intertwined, her shoulders finally softening against him as they languidly soaked in the calm surrounding them, so opposite to their frenzied physical crash fraught with inexplicable angst only moments before.

Chapter Twenty-Three

A voice familiar to Jake cut through their moment of calm connectedness. "Jake?! Jake?!" He could hear Luis yelling and the pounding of hoofs on the ground. Jake knew something was wrong—Luis was normally off today.

Rakell felt Jake jerk, and she sat up. "Who is that?"

"Luis," he said, quickly pulling up her panties and pants to her still trembling pelvis. "Go in the bathroom. He's almost here. Sorry."

Standing, Rakell frantically zipped and buttoned her jeans before scooting in the bathroom to pull herself back together. She hooked her bra, buttoned her shirt, and splashed water on her flushed face. She heard an older man yelling, speaking mostly in broken English with some Spanish words thrown in with his panicked speech. "Neo, Neo! Down! She's down!" he yelled.

She walked out to find a panicked Jake, rocking from one foot to the other. "Rakell, we have to go to the stables. Shit, I hadn't realized it was so late." He cursed to himself as he was jumping off the steps of the gazebo, sliding the bridle back on Midnight, then moving to La Dame.

"Jake, I got it. What's wrong?" She put La Dame's bridle on and mounted her, looking at Jake, then to the small man beside him. "*¿Qué pasa?*" she asked.

"*Hay una problema con Neo,*" Luis explained, speaking in a rushed but calmer manner as he pointed to the stable. "*Está echado.*"

"It's my horse, Neo. Something's wrong with him." He steered Midnight toward the stables. Since it was past feeding time, the horse took off. "Follow, but be careful, Rakell. They're hungry."

"Just go—I'm fine." She followed the two men galloping to the stables.

When Jake arrived, he ran to the stable at the far end. "Oh God, he's down. He's in a lot of pain."

Rakell heard Jake yell. The other horses were whinnying, hungry and picking up on Neo's distress.

Rakell led La Dame to her stall, then ran over to Jake, who was moving into Neo's stall. Neo was an impressive white horse but seemed so fragile at that moment, as he bellowed weakly, clearly in pain. "Oh, Neo." Jake's voice was strained with emotion.

She put her hand on his back. "It looks like he has colic." She grabbed the halter and rope that she saw hanging outside the stall door, then moved close to Neo, speaking in a calm voice. "Go call your vet," she instructed before turning back to the stricken animal.

Jake stood, not moving, eyes watering, staring at Neo. "I can't lose him. I can't. I just lost Gram. I can't…"

Slipping the halter onto Neo's head, Rakell glanced back. "Luis, can you feed the other horses so they don't agitate Neo more? Jake, please call your vet *now*." She spoke forcefully, hoping to connect to the boy who'd inhabited the man she had recently met.

Jake nodded, watching Rakell coaxing Neo to stand. "Come on, baby. Come on!" The horse resisted, but Rakell gently pulled up and back on the halter. "Stand with me. Please, baby."

Jake pushed open the stall door, running across the green space to Luis's home because there was limited cell coverage in the stables. He called the vet from a landline and left her a message begging her to come quickly, leaving his cell, asking her to text him when she got the message. Reception was spotty, but text messages usually went through at the stables. Then he ran back. The rest of the horses were quiet, busy eating. A sharp pang of guilt hit Jake. He had kept them waiting and hadn't checked on Neo when they first got there, thinking he would introduce him to Rakell after they were done riding.

Rakell's soothing tone met his ears. He slowed his steps, taking a deep breath as he approached Neo's stall, listening to her calm voice cooing, "That's it, baby. You're up. You're going to be okay. I know you're in pain, Neo, but it's going to be okay. Stay with me, mate." She spoke slowly, as if her voice could pacify the horse. When he saw her holding Neo's halter with one hand and gently stroking his neck with the other, trying to alleviate the horse's panicked pain, his chest constricted. He sucked his cheeks into his mouth, swallowing the emotion that rooted him motionless.

He saw a different girl now—not the sexy smartass he'd come to chase, but the deeply caring, capable woman he hadn't met until now. He craved to know her.

She turned when he cleared his throat. "Did you get in touch with the vet?" Her voice was steady.

"Left her a message." Jake moved beside her, touching his baby Neo, Gram's gift to him when he was twelve. He leaned and kissed Neo's neck softly. "Sorry, bud. I should have introduced you to Rakell here right away. Maybe we would have seen…"

"No, probably not. Colic is hard to spot. Jake, it's not your fault. He's older, his digestive system will probably start to have problems," she said, touching his arm, running her hand to his wrist, then intertwining her hand in his and gently squeezing. "He's probably going to be fine, but we need to walk him slowly until the vet gets here and can tell us if we need to haul him in."

Reluctantly, he let go of her hand. He opened the stall door as Rakell slowly led Neo out. They led him up and down the barn corridor, keeping a steady, slow pace. With a stiff throat, Jake told Rakell about his grandma giving him Neo for his twelfth birthday. "She would ride with me when she came to visit," he said, taking a deep breath. "I was sort of selfish about her when she and Grandpa came to visit. I demanded her time, and she gave it to me."

Rakell looked up at him, picturing him as a little boy riding Neo. "I can see how you'd probably be a pretty demanding little boy."

"I reckon I'm pretty transparent, huh?" he said, trying not to cringe at his own words. He was transparent, honest; he usually laid all of himself out to a woman.

She winced at the word *transparent*, knowing he was only seeing a sliver of her life. "So how did you come up with the name Neo?"

"Neo is short for Neapolitan. My grandma came up with it, because when she gave me Neapolitan ice cream for the first time, I think I was like four, I only ate the vanilla. Not just that once, but every time after that. She offered to buy me just vanilla, and I guess I said it didn't taste as good as the vanilla that was between the strawberry and chocolate ice cream." He heard Rakell giggle. "I know it's so silly, but my grandma kept buying me Neapolitan, and I kept eating just the vanilla, so when she bought me a white horse, she said, "I'm sure there's pink and brown under that white coat.""

"But you, Jake, are a vanilla man? Or the only person I know that could make vanilla complicated." Her lips turned up playfully as she nudged him.

"Hey now, watch it, you already compared me to a *Justa Burger*," he said, letting out a soft chuckle. Her presence softened the blow of this situation.

His hand found hers, needing to touch her. "I appreciate this…my grandma's death last December hit all of us hard. It's hard to describe how it feels to lose your biggest fan." He squeezed Rakell's hand.

"I can only imagine," she whispered, her throat constricting, thinking about her dad, her own biggest fan. "So have you always ridden Western?" she asked, shifting the conversation.

"Bareback and Western. I did some playdays when I was younger after getting a taste for rodeos. My dad entered me into one of those mutton-busting competitions, and I was hooked on rodeos, so my parents let me go to a few local playday competitions…barrel racing, stuff like that."

Rakell listened as they walked Neo back and forth, thinking Jake definitely had a side to him she hadn't predicted.

Jake's phone buzzed. It was Dr. Mortinson. *I'm on my way.*

When the vet arrived, she gave Jake a quick hug before shaking Rakell's hand. She looked to be in her mid- to late-fifties, with broad shoulders and muscular arms. Her black-silver streaked hair was pulled back in a ponytail. Rakell learned that Dr. Mortinson had been the family's vet for more than twenty years, which was one of the reasons she'd made the emergency trip out to see Neo. After a full evaluation, she suggested an anti-spasmodic drug and painkillers to help Neo relax. She recommended they keep Neo on his feet for another hour, giving time for the gas to work its way through him.

Finally, four hours later, just after ten, they put Neo back in his stall and waited, watching him until he appeared to be out of danger. Only then did Jake feel comfortable leaving. He texted Luis, who gave them a ride back to the gazebo. Jake packed up, giving Luis the leftover food. Rakell grabbed her new hat, and they headed to Jake's truck.

Opening her door, he watched her drag her legs into the truck, as if her limbs were made of cement. "Rakell, thank you for everything tonight. I guess it wasn't exactly the most relaxing birthday outing." Jake spoke slowly, feeling overwhelmed with emotion and fatigue, and the lingering horniness didn't seem to dissipate even in the midst of a crisis. He most certainly had an unhealthy craving for this girl. That was made obvious by the consistent chub when he was around her. His cock had partnered in this obsession. His heart and brain seemed to be fully committed to pushing him, clapping as he threw himself right over the edge.

"Glad to be there." Her voice was low, sincerity directing her tone. "I really love the hat. Thank you."

He jumped in behind the wheel, glancing at her, her head back on the seat, her eyes fluttering, trying to fight back sleep. As exhausted as he felt, he couldn't imagine how she must feel. Flying internationally, spending the weekend in Houston, and then tonight's drama. He wished they were at a point in their relationship where she'd just come home with him so he could hold her.

Rolling her head to the side, Rakell studied Jake's profile outlined by the glow of streetlights as they drove. The worry that had plagued him tonight was still etched on his strong features. She saw someone so kind and sweet when she looked at him now. She knew her perception was colored by his vulnerability and his willingness to be so open with her tonight. He had yanked at her heart and brought her body to a place she hadn't been. *I guess there are some men that are actually better than vibrators*, she thought as a pop of giggle left her mouth.

"What?" he mused, taking in her smile.

Her head facing him, she wondered if she should just say what she had been thinking. "Well, I was thinking that there really are some men, um you, who are better than my vibrator," she said, sounding lost in thought.

He let out a raspy laugh. "Jesus, I hope so. Was that a compliment?"

"Yes, yes. I was wondering, though…"

"Mmm…mmm." He tossed her a skeptical look, never knowing what would fly from her mouth, watching her sit up a little straighter.

"Where did you learn that...I mean, how...?"

Focusing on the road, purposely not letting her see him fight back a smile, he said, "I told you I grew up riding."

"Noooo...you know what I mean. How did you learn how to do all that?" Again, she had the fleeting thought that he might be an escort; he was good-looking enough and skilled as fuck.

"Be more specific, brave girl. Since this is the first time in my nearly twenty-eight years someone wanted to know how I came about my skill set in bed." He smirked.

She huffed, "You're an ass, you know that..."

He snorted. This girl pulled no punches. Damn, he liked that. "Mmm...mm, now *that* I've heard before...specifically what skill..."

She sat up defiantly. "The way you finger- and tongue-fucked me with the right amount of pressure, rhythm... how you made my cunt explode." Now she was fucking with him. She saw his eyes jump wide open, his eyebrows arching up, the amused shock on his face from her crudeness.

"Whoa...okay, so we're using that word. Damn. Sweetest cunt ever. Been wanting to say that all night ever since my mouth got to inhale that sweetness."

Reflexively, she crossed her legs, then uncrossed them, then crossed them again, squeezing her thighs together. "All right Jake, answer the question," she snapped, a small snicker following.

One horny girl, he almost said, watching her squirm from his words. "Okay. To answer your question directly, since you asked so directly, when I started at UT studying history"—he emphasized *history*—"I dated a woman who was in grad school, six years older. She knew what she liked, so if I was going to hang at her apartment and drink her liquor, she made it clear that I better learn quickly how to please her."

"So your girlfriend was brilliant."

"Yep, I tend toward the smart ones. That's not always the easiest route, but that is something that draws me." *Stop babbling, ask her, this is your opening.* "So you, how did you learn, you know...you said you hadn't really dated a lot, but..."

Her spine stiffened. She knew what he was inferring. And she had just asked him the same question, so she knew she'd have to answer.

He sensed her tensing, and again he wondered if she'd been taken advantage of. "I assumed an older boyfriend, sort of like my situation," he offered, giving her an out.

"Yes, someone older. But specifically what skill are you referring to?" she asked, adjusting her tone to appear relaxed, playful.

"Let me see, the way you 'cock swallow' like no other, a mouth trained to suck the fucking life out of a dude, taking my big cock almost to the root without literally choking…yep, those skills, Sweets, those amazing skills."

Her grin widened, listening to him. His tone, so gruff, smashed together with his illicit words, made her want his face between her legs again. She'd gladly swallow that huge cock if she got that in return. No piece of jewelry or fancy trip compared to where he'd taken her tonight.

"So do I get an answer, Miss Direct?"

"Yes, yes you do, Mr. Filthy Mouth." She covered her mouth, suffocating her own giggle, at his bark of laughter.

"Let's clarify, who taught me the term 'cock swallow'? As much as I wanna say 'cunt' when I think about your pussy, I refrain, so Sweets, the filthy mouth award goes to none other than you. And I'm here to tell you this country boy is eating it up, no pun intended. So give it up, the cock swallow skills…boyfriend?"

"Well, my friend Mandy in London showed me what to do with my tongue, then someone I saw, someone when I was younger, took the time to teach me. He had me kneel in front of a mirror when I sucked him off, and he gave me pointers about how to take it, you know, deeper." Sucking in a breath, she added, "Umm…you know, deep throat." She finished with a choppy gust of air, the confession making her edgy. Of course, she left out that Mandy was the friend who introduced her to the "escort business," and the older guy was a client, but she registered Jake's scrutiny as they drove in silence.

Jake's shoulders creeped up to his ears, listening to her, picturing it. He didn't realize he had swerved off the road until he heard the crunch of gravel beneath his tires. Yanking the wheel back, he turned the truck back to the road and centered it. His breathing taxing, he panted, "Holy shit!"

"What, what…?" she said, alarm ringing in her voice, her hands cupping her face. "Was that too—?" She shouldn't have told him that, but how else did girls learn?

"Sweets, that, that was—well I'm jealous of him. But whoever he is, he equipped a queen with wicked tools, and damn, I'm defenseless against all of it." He didn't look at her, but as he spoke, it occurred to him why he was so drawn to her. They were the same. She was his female match, plus some IQ points. They both enjoyed the basics, he could feel it. There was something extra about her, and of course about him, too, but their appreciation for the basics grounded them both. God, he needed to know her more.

"Mmm…I think you're pretty disarming too," she whispered, her head dropping back on the seat.

The truck seemed to crawl down the highway before exiting downtown. As much as fatigue tugged at him, he didn't want to see her jump out of the truck. The picture of her wrapped in his arms, sleeping beside him, kept making its way into his brain. The truck headed downtown toward her apartment, but with one turn, he could be headed to his house. "Rakell?" His voice broke as it jutted into the dark silence. "Just wondering if you, well…would you come home with me tonight?"

He swallowed, clearing the petitioning tone dominating his voice. "No pressure. I mean, I promise not to touch you." His cock twitched with his words, and his balls felt heavy as fuck, lead balloons swelling against stiff denim. *Stand down*, he commanded his groin. *I know, I know, I can jump in the shower before bed, we can do this, big guy, I swear.*

"Well…" she murmured on a breath.

Shifting his ass on the seat, scrambling for comfort, he realized it would be grueling to have her so close after the swirl of sexual and emotional tension tonight. *Damn. She's building a bridge between your crotch and heart. Breathe, Jake.*

"Um, why would I do that, then?" Her eyes were tiredly amused as she turned to look at him.

Jake felt his shoulders relax for the first time in hours. "Just meant I'd try—key word being *try*—to keep my hands off all the best parts," he said.

"Ah, so there are best and—"

He jumped in. "All are great. Just some respond better to touch," he mused.

Rakell took a quick breath in. "Stop, you're making me horny. On that note, I don't think it's possible for me to be that close to you all night and not want more." She was attempting to make him feel good, even as she was saying no.

"I'll put pillows between us," he said, looking at her smiling.

"Oh, perfect. That will do the trick. Not tonight, Jake. I need to sleep." Her heavy eyes peered out the window. Overcome by lassitude, she spoke more freely. "Haven't made it a habit of sharing a bed with anyone. Well, to sleep— it's usually just sex. I—well, I don't have a lot of experience with long-term relationships, you know the boyfriend-girlfriend thing," she rattled on. "I don't know if I could actually sleep with someone beside me all night. I'd like to try that someday. It sounds romantic." Her voice drifted off as her eyelids drew down over her eyes.

Jake had his answer, so he steered the truck away from Barton Hills toward the center of town, running her words around his head, not making sense of them. No doubt she was speaking with a lax tongue, just spouting her stream of consciousness, but he could tell by her tone that it was the truth. She had not had someone in her life that held her through the night regularly, yet a man taught her how to give a blowjob, had her on her knees watching herself in a mirror. He still had so many questions, but he needed to get his truth to her first before he started probing more. He'd been cautioned in the past by his family and friends to give people room, to sit back and let things evolve naturally, but that was tough for him. He always pushed, tried to move things forward. As his friends said, "He's going to Jake this."

He arrived at her place, stopped the truck, and jumped out. Opening her door, he leaned in and hugged her, thanking her again, not kissing her. She turned to get out of the truck, and his hand took hers, squeezing it. "It is. It really is."

He noticed her eyes shifting to the front door of the apartment complex nervously.

"Huh?" she said.

"It is romantic to hold someone all night, feel them sleeping against you." He smiled, leaning into her, gently pecking her lips. "Might even be better than sex."

Chapter Twenty-Four

"You need to get your head in this, Jake," Dwayne scolded as they racked their weights.

"I know. Just a little distracted."

"More than a little, dude. It's the Aussie girl, right? You're seeing her a lot?"

"Well, when she's in town. She travels a lot. She's in the Caribbean for business." A big grin crossed Jake's face. "That's when I hang out with you."

Dwayne grabbed his chest, acting like he'd been shot. "Brother, that hurts. I'm a consolation prize?"

"Dude, that's what I am to you, too, but you gotta admit we make pretty good backup dates," Jake replied, laughing.

"Well, what's the status? Is it just you two?" Dwayne asked as they moved to the chest press.

"I think so. I mean, it is for me, but not sure about her." Jake knew he sounded lame.

"Jeez, just ask her. I mean, tell her you want to be exclusive. I've never known a woman to turn down an exclusive chance with Pretty Boy Jake Skyler," Dwayne chuckled.

"Yeah, but she thinks I'm just Jake the gym rat."

"You haven't told her who you are yet? Jeez, no wonder you're not sure. Brother, that's your ticket. I mean, your personality is just okay." Dwayne put his hand in the air, fingers spread horizontally, shaking it back and forth. "I'll give you the handsome thing, but after that, your best shot is that you're a rich NFL player. You gotta use what you got."

Jake rolled his eyes. "Shit, if that's all I got, then I'm not sure I can keep her."

"Shit, that's more than most guys got. You know how many girls would kill for a chance with you? What am I saying? Of course you do. Seriously, Jake. I've never seen you try to hide it before. Anyway, it'll come out soon enough. Then she might be pissed you didn't say anything." Dwayne stood from the weight machine.

"You're right."

"So just tell her what you do. Hopefully she won't google your name and see the list of conquests that came before her and get spooked," Dwayne laughed.

"Thanks, you're making me feel super confident." Jake sat on the chest press to start his set. "I'm going to tell her when she gets back. At least this time, she's texting me back. Usually when she travels, I don't hear from her. It's total silence."

"After you tell her who you are, you have to say she's the only one you're seeing before she gets worried about being just another girl."

"I know, I know, you're right. I got it." Jake tilted his head toward the open incline press. "Let's get it while it's open."

Dwayne started loading the weights. "Three plates, big guy?"

Jake nodded. "What about you and Jenn?"

"Well, we're having fun." Dwayne threw Jake a slanted-eye look. "I've been meaning to tell you this...the other night, Cindy was at Jenn's house making homemade chicken fried steak. I guess she has her grandma's award-winning recipe..."

Jake sat, readying himself on the machine. "Okay, so why are you talkin' all sheepish? I mean, I love chicken fry, but that's not making me regret not dating her." Jake pushed up, straining against the weight, making it to ten reps before gently bringing the weight to its resting spot.

Once Jake got up, Dwayne sat on the machine. "Not thinking you'd be missing out on chicken fried steak, but what followed dinner and some shots? You are definitely missing out, 'cause that night was the start of something fun, something I'm looking forward to tonight while your ass is pining for some chick that doesn't even know you're..."

"What the hell, both of them? I thought we said no more of that..."

"You said that 'cause you got yourself in a few situations, but I never said that. Why would I, as long as they're okay, and they know

I'm heading back to Sacramento."

"Shit, and Jenn…?"

"It's a story…well, they know each other well…you gonna ask me how hot Cindy is in bed?" Dwayne started his set.

"Nope, don't care…"

"Bullshit," Dwayne spat with an exerted huff.

Jake shook his head. "I'm looking at the future. I just want…"

The clank of the weight slamming down startled Jake.

Dwayne's pinched expression bore into Jake. "You, with this shit? A relationship? You tried that with that actress, and look what happened. The whole time I knew it was BS, she's posting all this lovey-dovey shit, and she wasn't for you. You just wanted to prove to Coach and everyone else, hell, maybe even yourself, that you can be in something long-term, that you're not a player anymore."

"Get up, I know. I knew she wasn't for me, I knew it within…"

"A month…"

Jake sat. "Thanks, dude. I was gonna say three, but…"

Dwayne started rolling his shoulders. "Too heavy, need to go a little lighter. Okay, I knew in like three weeks. The second time I was around her, she was snooty as hell. I knew you two would be ending after Bye week when you brought her to your parents…remember that…?"

"Ugh…" Jake pushed. "Yep, how can I forget? You and Melissa have a habit of reminding me of everything. I know…shit…I just wanna have what my parents have. Don't you want that?"

"Finish the damn set." Dwayne put his hands on his hips. Once Jake finished, Dwayne pointed at him. "Sit your ass there and listen to me. Jake. No, I don't want what my parents had."

"Your dad was a good man," Jake insisted.

"Can you not talk? Yes, a good man, but drove a big rig for a living, so he was always gone, my mom was doing the family life thing on her own even before he died, then after that, she was doing everything. They didn't have what your parents have. They were too consumed with keeping their heads above water, always paddling against the stream just to breathe and pay the bills. There wasn't any time just to enjoy each other. No one sat around taking stock of their relationship or their kids. That's not what working poor or even lower-middle-class families get to do. So no, I don't see marriage and the kid thing as the end-of-the-rainbow shit."

Dwayne stabbed his finger in his own chest, his eyes boring into

Jake. "This is it for me. The NFL is not some job I'm doing while I build another life. This is *it* for me. My thing is to save money, invest like your dad tells me, but *this* is my pot of gold, in every way. I don't have anything after this is done. After this is over, when they won't let me catch a ball anymore, when I'm useless to them, you know what I am?"

With a deliberate inhale, he steadied his eyes on Dwayne. *Shit, he's worked up*, Jake thought. "Mmm...?" he murmured. It was rare to see Dwayne like this.

Dwayne bent forward, whispering, "I'm just another Black guy. Without football, I ain't nothing to this world, and if you think for one fucking second that I wanna have little Black boys that have to deal with all the bullshit my dad did and me—you're out of your mind, dude. No to that little dream!" He stood, turning away from Jake.

Jake jumped up from the machine. "Wait, Dwayne, shit! You've changed that..."

Dwayne spun around. "What the hell? You of all people... remember what your grandpa went through...moving from Morocco to France, marrying your grandma? Sorry, dude, I'm not trying to bring up Mimi, I know it's been hard...I'm just saying, it doesn't end."

At the mention of his grandma, Jake smiled, internally remembering how much she'd loved Dwayne. The time they went to see his grandparents in France and how she had doted on Dwayne.

He knew he needed to respond right to his friend, but what could he say? He stood there, at a loss for the next words, trying to find a way to tell Dwayne—what? *It will be okay?* "Dwayne, I know, but if you don't stand up..."

"No, Jake. You keep standing up for me, for Jordan, but I'm fucking tired. The difference is you can get in that old ass truck of yours to drive from here to Lubbock, not thinking about it. Not me. No, I get in my brand-new Mercedes, and I'm scared to death to drive across Texas without you or another white boy. And before you say shit about your heritage, look in the mirror—you're a tan boy with blue eyes. Once they see those, they just assume someone white was involved in your making. Not me, I'm Black as they come, and my boys would be too. No, not gonna do it. Not gonna worry about the next generation of *me-s*. So yes, I'm still doing the fun girl thing. While you're chasing your fairy tale, I'm just gonna live mine, okay?"

"Dwayne..."

"Dude, don't. I know how much it rips you up...but...fuck, try living it. It's far worse than standing up the way you do. I'd rather be you than me."

"Don't say that…"

"Just did, brother, and I meant what I said. Also, you're my brother, but you still don't get it. I can say this. It's not for lack of trying. You try, and that's more than I can say for most."

The cords on Jake's neck flexed as he struggled with his reaction. Dwayne rarely went off this way, and he sure as hell didn't go this deep. There was nothing for Jake to say, so he offered a silent acknowledgement, pinned to the place where he stood. Watching Dwayne turn, he had the urge to wail so loud the fucking world would shake. The fact that he and Dwayne could not see the same future because one had darker skin than the other seemed so implausible. He absorbed Dwayne's words and his fears, making Jake want to hit something. He knew Dwayne was right; it was easier to be the one that stood up for his friends than the one that had to face the reality itself. *Damn, I love you dude*, he wanted to yell to Dwayne's back.

As if he could read Jake's mind, Dwayne spun around, taking a couple long steps toward Jake while scanning the gym to make sure he hadn't created a scene.

"I know you're here for me," Dwayne said, his fist lightly hitting his own heart. "But if I were you, I'd worry about how you're gonna get laid after that fierce beauty learns you been lying about your fame. Tell her, pretty boy, just do it." He winked. "You got this."

Dwayne cracked a small smile before he walked away, thinking, *Jake, I'm not going to tell you the whole truth. I can't have you trying to fix me, it's too late for that. Let's just win a fucking Super Bowl…for my dad.*

He needed to talk to her when she came back. Dwayne was right about that—this game, hiding who he was, couldn't last forever. His justification—that he was an Austin, Texas boy looking for a normal girl, a Texas boy who just happened to play for the NFL—sounded newly hollow to him. *Hasn't that defined you, Jake? Hasn't the fame and money made it easy to welcome women into your bed? Hasn't it been easy to keep your promise to your mom and dad not to use "I love you" as a way to lure women, but instead be honest with women?*

He'd always laid it all out there. *This is who I am, I'm not looking to get serious.* These had been his exact words time and time again.

"I'll treat you right and make sure you have a good time, but I ain't lookin' for love," he'd drawl out his standard speech, looking into their big hopeful eyes, and they'd nod understandingly before running a hand down his chest to the bulge between his legs, cooing, "I understand, Jake. I'm here for you," or some version of that, so he'd gone with it. Did that make him a user?

His phone buzzed as he walked out of the gym. Climbing in his truck, he pulled it from his gym bag.

Rakell: *Miss you...* **Send**

Those two words from her changed his mood completely.

Jake: *Miss you more...* **Send**

Rakell: ☺ ...**Send**

Jake: *Still flying in tomorrow afternoon? I'll pick you up...* **Send**

Rakell: *I won't be much fun. Long flight...* **Send**

Jake: *Don't care, just want to see you...* **Send**

Rakell smiled, thinking about seeing him tomorrow. She was lying on the beach with a couple of the other potential *Sports Illuminated* models, waiting for the day's shoot to wrap. The days of shooting had been fun but tinged with an uneasiness. Nothing like displaying a more curvaceous body in a skimpy suit among a sea of thin models to make a girl question herself. More than once, she heard the wardrobe crew discuss her fuller body and how to dress around it, the camera crew positioning her just so to hide her hips. Her swimsuits were barely there, but some of the girls had suits that were literally painted on, so Rakell was grateful that at least hers covered her nipples. Lingerie modeling for catalogs was easier and provided more coverage, but the chance to be in *Sports Illuminated* was big for her career. It could help launch other modeling gigs and might help with acting opportunities as well.

Chapter Twenty-Five

Rakell shook her head, thinking about how Jake refused to meet her outside the airport, instead insisting that he come in. It was obvious that this guy got his way most of the time, but his approach was different than the billionaires she'd been accustomed to. Jake would work to get his way; they expected it. She pulled a small suitcase behind her through the airport, her heart beating. When she got to the top of the escalator leading to baggage claim, she saw him standing there, smiling. He gave her a small wave, a boyish gesture. She gulped in a breath as she stared at him. He was dressed in faded jeans, flip-flops, and a light blue linen shirt that he wore untucked. Loops of black hair sprung out around the edges of his baseball cap, and even from a distance, she could see the light shadow of stubble on his jaw.

Rakell felt the tug between her legs as she got closer to him. The Jake tug, as she'd come to think of it. Having people dressing, touching, and prodding her body for the past few days had left her crazily horny with no outlet. Sharing a room with another model made self-stimulation impossible. As the escalator approached the ground floor, she became almost giddy. Smiling, she returned his small wave. When she got to the bottom, she sprang off the last step, moving into him, hugging him as if they'd known each other for years.

Jake pulled her into his chest, squeezing her hard, his chest heavy, feeling like she'd been gone too long. She looked up at him. "Thanks for—"

Fuck, if someone recognized him, he'd be caught right here. He was sick of hiding, and he'd be ending this little charade tonight. She'd know the truth. His lips cut her off, moving in on her mouth, kissing, sucking her in, their tongues playing swords with each other, forgetting that swarms of people were moving around them.

Rakell gasped, pulling back. "God." A quick intake of air. "I should get my suitcase." Jake's hands didn't move from her back, the feel of her bare skin making him anxious to feel more of her. She had on a short denim skirt and a top that knotted between her breasts, exposing her mid-section. The thin material highlighted the fullness of her breasts as they pushed against the floral print. His body took it all in. She pointed, and he grabbed her suitcase, pulling it with one hand while he grabbed her hand with the other, escorting her to his truck.

As they started to drive out of the parking garage, Jake looked over at her. "You got some sun. As always, you look beautiful," he said, sounding like a nervous teenager. He wanted to ask her to sleep with him tonight, share his bed. None of these quick trysts followed by both of them scurrying to their separate corners. That wasn't how he pictured things with her. But it was starting to become a pattern. He wanted her to stay all night with him as much, or more, than he wanted to fuck her. He wanted both.

A stiff smile dominated his face like a mask, not revealing the true thoughts beneath the façade. Rakell wondered what was going through his head. "Thank you. You look pretty hot yourself." She tried to sound playful.

His steely eyes warmed at her words. "So you'll say yes, then?" His taut mouth moved into a sheepish grin as his eyes switched from her to the road.

"To what, a private strip-show?" she said, continuing to insert a playfulness into the charged seriousness exuding from him.

Jake snorted, caught off guard. "If that's what it takes for you to come to my place for dinner." He was thinking of the night, too, but held back. "James is gone for the next few days till Sunday, so I thought I could fix us dinner, more relaxed than going out."

"I...well, I haven't even been home yet."

"I know. Will your roommate care?" he asked, assuming she had to have a roommate, since she'd never let him come up or invited him in.

Jake's question made her jump, her eyes darting out the window. "What do you mean by that?" Her tone was defensive, her voice rising.

He blinked quickly, surprised by her reaction. God, he never knew what would set her off. He took a quick breath in, making sure he didn't match her tone. "Nothing. Just figured you had a roommate, making sure she wouldn't mind. Honestly, I was just trying to be considerate."

Rakell looked back at him. "I know, my roommate travels, too, but we don't bring people…" She was stalling, not sure where she was going with this. "We just have an agreement not to bring other people home. It's not a big deal if I don't go straight home. Not at all, but…" Rakell stopped, realizing she had just agreed to dinner.

"No buts," he cut her off. "I have great steaks, veggie kabobs, potatoes…and wine, of course."

"Mmm-mm…like, cheap wine? Remember how far that got you with the last one," she replied, muffling a giggle.

Jake arched his eyebrows. "Really? Well, I can show you the two bottles I bought, two French first growths. Where's that going to get me?" His mouth curled up.

"What? That's crazy. Don't spend that kind of money. Seriously, I'm just kidding. I can drink the cheap stuff." She sounded sincere.

"It's fine. I like nice wine too," he said, as he pulled into his driveway, "and I enjoy sharing it with someone who knows good wine."

It was shortly after five when they got to his house. His arm around her shoulders, he guided her inside the modest one-story home, a mid-century modern that he had transformed. He loved rehabbing houses, reselling them or renting them. But he loved the location of this house in Barton Hills so much, with its proximity to downtown, that he couldn't bring himself to sell it. Jake wanted to add a master bedroom wing to the other side of the one-story home. He was hoping to do that this summer.

Rakell could hear Dolly barking in the backyard when they walked in. Jake let her in, and both she and Jake petted her as she ran around at their feet. Then Jake let an excited Dolly back outside. "Go on, girl."

She smiled, watching him. He and Dolly were so intertwined, and it warmed her to watch him with her. "So is Dolly named after a particular superstar country singer?" she asked, the side of her mouth twisting up to expose her eye tooth.

"Yep, the one and only. And," he said, his eyes jumping to the back door, "this one lives up to her name: center of attention, and great voice, which, by the way, the neighbors have complained about. Mostly she's sweet and cares about the people around her, just like one of my idols."

"I like that. So did you listen to Dolly when you were young?"

"Yeah, my dad really loved her music, so I listened to her a lot as a boy. She's also my grandpa's favorite singer. My dad's dad, he grew up here before Austin was Austin. As a kid, I was into whatever my dad and Grandpa were. Well, still today, I can't get enough of Dolly." He walked toward the wine refrigerator.

"Wait a minute, your admiration doesn't have anything to do with her rack, does it?" Rakell turned toward him, hands on her hips.

Gulping the laugh bubbling up his chest, he blurted out, "I have no idea what you're talking about." His tone feigning innocence. "Do you want to start with champagne?" Jake pulled a bottle of Cristal out of a tall, stainless steel wine refrigerator in the kitchen.

"Bringing out the big guns. Way to change the subject, but yes, I'd love some." She looked at the bottle. "Are you celebrating something special?" she said, watching as he opened a three-hundred-dollar bottle of champagne on a Thursday night. She thought about his parents' expansive ranch, this champagne…had she ended up being attracted to the type of man she was trying to avoid? The family-money type who had no sense of the sacrifices most normal people have to make? But his truck and his home seemed modest, though even modest in downtown Austin was pricy. She'd make sure he knew she had her own money, her own means, that she didn't need anything from a man.

Pouring the foamy pink liquid into a tall champagne flute and handing it to her, Jake replied, "You, being home." She reached for the glass, but his hand lingered so that both their hands were touching the glass between them. His eyes were somber as he regarded her. "I really did miss you," he said, releasing the champagne flute to her.

She took the flute, hoping he didn't notice that her hand shook imperceptibly. "I missed you, too," Rakell said, looking at the glass, not him.

Well at least she said, "me," not Austin. That's progress, he thought, giving himself a little encouragement. He poured another glass before putting the bottle back into the refrigerator. He strode toward her, but she put up her hand.

His eyes narrowed. "Huh?"

Her hand still up, Rakell said, "Don't start kissing me and getting me all rattled before I toast you." She raised her glass. "To you, for showing me Austin. It's starting to feel like home." Smiling, she tilted her glass toward his.

He wanted to ask why none of her other dates had shown her Austin before. He kept that in his head, knowing she already seemed skittish about her past with men. He just smiled as they clinked their glasses together before sipping their champagne.

He added, "I hope so, but you need to live through an Austin summer before you declare it home." He smirked. "Some folks have a hard time with the Austin heat."

"Mmm...I think it's the Austin heat that's attracting me," she murmured, winking.

He stalked toward her, focused on her lips.

"Wait—one more thing. I want to take you out tomorrow night to dinner, my treat," Rakell said. She could feel his intensity making her lower stomach clench wondering if maybe they just fucked, got it over with, they could relax and just have fun.

Closing the gap between them, Jake replied, "Uh, no," his arm capturing her around the small of her waist. "You can tell me where we're going, but I'm paying." He leaned down, his face nearly touching hers, but she turned her head, avoiding his lips. "Hey!" he protested.

"Then I'm not going," Rakell said, her tone harsh. "I'm treating on the next date, or there won't be any more dates." She tried to break free of his arm around her, but he pulled her in tighter, sliding his hand down to her bottom, squeezing a cheek over her denim skirt.

"You...I swear." He swatted her bottom lightly then squeezed her ass cheek again. Her quiet moan teasing his cock. "You make me want to—"

"What?" Rakell taunted. The light pain from his large hand squeezing her bottom melted into arousal seeping between her legs. She pictured being bent over his kitchen table, him lifting her skirt and pulling down her panties as he jammed his cock into her, fucking her mindlessly as she rubbed her clit. She knew he'd let her. Hell, he'd probably love watching her rub herself while his cock pumped her from behind.

Setting the flute down hard on the table, Jake pulled her into him, one hand on her ass, the other on the back of her head, a handful of her soft hair filling his fist. His tight, possessive lips captured her full, pink challenging lips. He lightly bit her bottom lip, then pierced her mouth with his tongue, not waiting for an entry, forcing his tongue in. He sucked her mouth hard as his hand kneaded her ass, his fingers pulling up on the denim until his large hand was kneading lace-covered flesh.

Her head tilting back, her mouth open but not moving, Rakell accepted his entry, her hips tilting forward into him as she groaned into his mouth. She could feel him grow against her lower stomach. *God, just get this over with, get on with it.*

She jerked back from his kiss, her fingers going to her lips. "Jake," she chided, giving him a scolding glance.

Jake let go, his arm sliding off her waist, one hand pulling down her skirt. He knew he had lost control. He stepped back. "Sorry—I just, sorry. Shouldn't have been so aggressive." He spoke sheepishly, knowing he'd literally attacked her mouth. Damn, what this girl did to him. Handing her the glass of bubbly, he said, "Drink. The coolness will feel good on your lips. Do you want some ice?" He stepped toward the refrigerator, grabbed an ice cube, and moved toward her. "Let me," he murmured, before bringing the ice to her lip. Gently, he ran it along her full bottom lip. "Feel better, Sweets?"

"Better," she said, diverting her eyes from him before taking a long sip of her Champagne. She thought she might melt from the fire in his stare, there was so much going on behind his eyes. What she longed to tell him was that they should just fuck, get it over with. She didn't know if girls said that to guys when they dated. "I could use some more Champagne," she replied, sucking the last of hers down, feeling it work inside her empty stomach.

Jake pulled the bottle from the refrigerator, pouring her another glass. "Sorry again. It's just that you make me crazy." He touched her cheek. "Really crazy, but I know that's no excuse. So I agree to you taking me out to dinner…if you agree to going to a small dinner at Jordan's house Saturday night. Dwayne will be there," he threw in, knowing how comfortable she seemed around Dwayne. One of Dwayne's many gifts was using humor to defuse situations and disarm people. It seemed to work on Rakell.

She flexed her hip forward, her arm resting on it. "So you're bribing me?"

"Whatever I have to do, Sweets, that's what I'm gonna do. Bribe you or tie you up naked, make you come until you beg or agree…"

Her hand shot up. "All right, all right, no more, I'll go."

He laughed. "There's more than one way to get what you want in life." Turning, he put two large potatoes in the oven, then grabbed a tray of steaks and veggie kabobs from the refrigerator. She followed him outside to put the steaks on the grill. "How about we plan to eat in about forty-five minutes or so? I'll cook these slowly. We can throw the veggies on the last few minutes before these are ready."

"Sounds good," she said aimlessly, still caught up in his possessive kiss. The way he kissed her pulled at her insides. She turned, taking in his beautiful backyard: a pool with a cabana, lights draping from the live oak trees that surrounded the stone deck wrapping around the pool. "This is such a nice setup, like a complete living space outside, very cool," she said, pointing to the wooden-beamed outdoor veranda that opened to the steps leading to the backyard. At one end there was an outdoor kitchen where they stood, at the other an outdoor fireplace with sofa, chairs, and a coffee table. Between those spaces was a long wood-plank table that could probably seat a dozen people.

"Thanks, I do like how it came out. My dad's friend builds these when he's not busy being a principal. He worked with me on the design, then let me help him and his team build it. Learned a lot from him when we were making it."

"Wow, you helped build this, impressive...so you are...multi-talented aren't you..." she murmured, tilting her head and licking her lips.

"Back at you, beautiful," he said, and raised his glass before taking a drink.

"Do you entertain a lot?" Rakell looked at the long wooden table like she didn't picture this sort of skill as one he possessed.

"Well, kind of." Jake took her hand, guiding her over to the couch. "A few friends. Also, I have a pretty big extended family, and I like cooking." He sat on the couch, patting the cushion beside him, obviously for Rakell to sit next to him. Dolly took it as her cue and ran barking toward Jake. She looked up at Jake, who said, "Nope, girl, still not letting you up here. You know the rules" while pointing to a cushion against the outdoor wall. Dolly wagged her tail as she walked to her spot.

Rakell laughed. "Someone's possessive." She sat next to him, taking another sip of champagne, putting her legs over his and letting them dangle between them.

"So you built this to entertain friends and family?" Her eyes narrowed on him in jest. "You sure it's not the hordes of women you have over?" she teased, but there was some truth in her words, as she sensed this boy had seen his share of panties thrown willingly on the floor.

His deep blue eyes stilled on her. He was ready for just her; this was exactly what he needed to communicate with her. He needed to make that clear. "I want to talk to you about…"

She raised her hand to gesture stop, cutting him off, a mischievous glint to her eyes. "I want to talk to you, too. I think we should just fuck, get it over with, instead of all this crazy back-and-forth shit." She moved her hand between them, gesturing.

Jake blinked twice, his eyes shutting as her words hit him. Then they snapped wide open. "That's what you wanted to talk to me about?"

She put a hand on his chest. "Yeah. Currently I'm not fucking anyone else. I don't think you are, either, so we're both just walking around horny. Toys get old, so why don't we just fuck each other? We may end up liking each other more." She swallowed, suffocating the little-girl giggle bubbling up her throat, listening to her own words. She didn't know how to explain what she was thinking. "I mean, it just makes sense."

He snorted, "What the…" and took another drink, trying to grapple with her statement. Her request sounded more like a business deal than anything romantic. Shit, he knew he needed to improve in that department, but this girl was out-and-out void. "So how were you thinking this would go? Us just fucking, 'getting it over with,' as you said."

"Do you want me to be honest?" she asked, feeling bold. "I'm not that good at it but trying to work on it."

"Fucking…or being honest?" he asked, trying to decipher this girl.

Smiling, Rakell said, "The honesty thing. I'm really used to saying what I think men want to hear; it gets old. I think I'm pretty good at the fucking thing, though." Her eyes darted away, the corner of her lip lifting in a cocked smile.

Jake shook his head, not believing he was in the middle of this conversation. Someone had messed her up, some domineering asshole had gotten this girl all kinds of twisted up. "I'm sure you are." He cradled her chin with his long fingers, forcing her gaze upward. "I don't want you telling me what you think I want to hear. Do we have a deal?"

"I've been trying to be more upfront with you; maybe that's why it feels so tense," she explained, knowing that was only a half-truth. "Can

I have more?" She held up her glass.

He nodded, standing. She stood, too. "Maybe the tension comes from us liking each other. It's easier when you don't care. Does that make sense?"

"I don't know—I've never cared," she said flatly. But as soon as the statement came out, she wanted to grab it and stuff it back away. Even to her own ears, it sounded so devoid of emotion, while the truth was she'd never felt anything remotely close to this with a man she was so attracted to. She enjoyed him and felt like herself with him, like she did with Matt, but she also wanted to get to know Jake without clothes.

Jake turned his face to hide the perplexed look on his face. "Let's open up another bottle." He started to walk forward, his hand out, directing her to walk in front of him. From behind her, he asked again, "So how did you picture this going, us 'getting it over with'?" Trying to smooth over the coarseness in his tone. Her wantonness seemed to derail his judgment every time.

Rakell felt him staring at her from behind, looking her up and down. It turned her on. She really did just want to get fucked. If he fucked the way he kissed, she might very well explode. She spoke directly but a little lustily, knowing that's how men normally liked it. "Well, in there," she said, pointing to the door they were approaching, "I pictured you bending me over your kitchen table, yanking up my skirt, pulling down my panties, shoving your—"

"Jesus," he hissed, grabbing the door, opening it before she could, staring at her, fucking her with his eyes as she moved past. *So one minute she's pushing back on me, but the next she's suggesting I bend her over the table so we can get it over with.* He'd never heard a girl describe their first time having sex with a dude like a vaccination. Usually, women wanted to know it meant something. She confused him while at once turning him on.

"Grr…Don't make me crazy," he warned.

"Not trying to, just saying right here." She slapped the table. "Bend me over, shove your cock in me. Let's get it over with, then I won't be driving you crazy." Her eyes locked on him. "Do you have condoms here? I never fuck…"

His hand on the wine cellar door, Jake willed himself to block her words out. "I do, but that's not what's happening." He pulled out a bottle of white, staring at the label, looking at her standing next to the table. His breath speeding up, he stalked over to her. "Making me fucking nuts, that's what you're doing. Are you teasing me?" He took her glass and put it on the counter, pushing her gently from behind, his hand on her lower back.

Rakell bent over the table. "No, actually I'm not," she whispered as her chest touched the wooden surface.

His hands went to her hands, stretching them above her head onto the table. "Keep your hands here," he instructed, his voice raspy. "So, you pictured being bent over like this?" He leaned in, down toward her, so she could feel him through his jeans. His hand slid down the edge of her skirt shoving the material up. "Then me lifting your skirt up, exposing your ass?" His hand cupped one of her cheeks. "Then pulling your panties down so I can stare at your beautiful ass before I shove myself between your spread legs into that sweet cunt? You are going to spread them for me, right?"

"Yes, that's it," she replied, the pitch of her voice rising. "Yes…" She felt his hand pulling her panties down, letting them slide to her knees.

Dragging her panties off her legs, his hand twitched at the idea of spanking her. "You like this, your puss exposed to me like this?"

"Um, yeah."

"Really? Did you also picture getting spanked while I fuck you?" One of Jake's hands rubbed her ass while the other grappled with his jeans. He did not want to fuck her this way, not her, not the first time, but his cock begged for release, his balls inflated from the thoughts she put in his mind. *Damn her*, he thought, swatting her ass lightly, right on the crack. "Like that?"

"Ahh…" popped out of her mouth. Reflexively, her ass tilted upward, the sight of it making his cock jerk.

"Soo, do you like that?" *Hold on, Jake, slow down, buddy.*

"If you're into that, it's fine. Just not too hard," Rakell stated, again her tone almost professional, pushing her ass back to him.

"What? No, it's not what I like, it's what you like. What do you like?" His brain snapped into the moment, taking control over his cock. He grabbed her hips, pulling her up straight, off the table. Then he reached down, gently helping her step back into her panties and pulling them up before adjusting her skirt. "Hey, Sweets, it's about what *you* like. I want *you* to want this." He stroked her hair, then whispered in her ear, "Turn around—I think I know what you really like."

Rakell turned to face him, wondering if she had said something wrong to make him stop. Her army-green eyes wide, looking up at him, she responded, "I like what you like." Her submissive tone and her pathetic words scratched at her own brain, making her internally cringe. How would she ever shed the Marietta persona she'd cultivated during the past five years?

"Nope, that's not how this works. You're not here to please me. If we're together, it's because we both want it. Don't do this for me." Jake's voice was nurturing but riddled with concern, sending shivers up her back. "Come here," he said, taking her hand. "I want to see if you like something."

He led her to the living room sofa. She sat, and he bent down and pulled off her flip-flops. Sitting beside her, he could feel the tension in her body. He gently kissed her jawline until he got to her chin, then her lips. "*Rae*-kale, Sweets," he drawled. "Never do anything you don't want to do, okay?"

The intensity of Jake's eyes made water pool behind Rakell's own. "I don't. I mean, I'm not now." She put her hand on his leg. "Jake, sorry I'm not versed in the dating thing, what I should say or not, but I'm just so fucking horny, I can't stand it. I haven't…"

One corner of his mouth curled up. "So it's not me, you're just wanting to get off." His hands moved to the knot that held her shirt together. "I want to make sure that happens. Can I?"

Rakell nodded. "Yes. But I don't just want to get off. I want to get off with you. Both of us," she explained, a rawness in her tone, exposing so much. Her shirt opened, and his hands unsnapped her bra. Pulling it off, she sat beside him, naked from the waist up. He signaled for her to stand, and he shimmied her denim skirt down her long legs, along with her panties, her hands helping him.

Jake stared up at her, looking at her body, his eyes skimming from her face down to her breasts to her stomach, her hips. He relished the curves of her body; God, how he wanted to get lost in her. His eyes traveled to her pussy, covered in a narrow row of light brownish-blond curls, and landed on her legs. "I want to do so much to you, so many things I think you'd like." He rubbed the round, muscular globes of her ass. "You tell me if you like it, okay?"

"Um, okay." Her throat grew thick, and her pussy pulsed, seeping from his words. Then his hands tapped the inside of her thighs, coaxing them apart. Her legs spread willingly, wantonly, begging. Now her back was in the crook of the couch. He spread her legs, placing one foot on the floor and the other leg across the couch.

"Lean back against the pillow," he commanded, then took her hands, lifting them so they rested above her head. "Keep your hands behind your head while I play with this," he said.

His fingers explored the folds between her legs, opening her labia, finding her clit. "So what I propose is I find out what makes you tick." He slipped his middle finger in her all the way to his knuckle, then halted, letting her flesh absorb it. Willing self-control, he stared up into her eyes, watching the lids droop with the look of lust. "If there's something you don't like, makes you feel uncomfortable, tell me." Jake pushed his finger in more, eliciting a groan. "But if you like it, I want to know, okay?"

"Mm…mm," Rakell moaned, rocking her pelvis into his finger. "I like that." Her voice was low, lusty.

"Okay, good," he replied. "Another?" he asked, inserting another finger as his thumb rubbed her sensitive nub. "You seemed to like it at the ranch. Be honest, do you?"

"Yes, yes." Her hips moved forward onto his hand.

"So picture this: I get you off repeatedly. I experiment with this sexy-as-hell body, figure out what gives you pleasure. Once I figure that out, I'll have no problem pushing my way into you, deep, fucking you senseless, but…" He moved his finger sawing her pussy, finger fucking her slowly, easing his fingers in and out of her wetness. "But the first time I enter you, put my cock in this beautiful pussy, I'll be looking at those big green eyes, okay?" Jake's fingers were moving in and out of her faster now. "Okay, got it?" Damn, she felt so tight, so wet, so needy. Definitely a complicated twist for him. But right now, tonight, all he cared about was watching her soak up all the pleasure he could deliver. And damn if he hadn't been thinking about having her right here, with her legs splayed open, just like this.

"Yes, yes…oh God," Rakell cried, grinding into his hand. "Please, I want to, please," she screamed, her hips moving wildly. He used one hand to grab around her upper thigh, forcing her still while his fingers worked her, feeling her pussy walls pulsate around his fingers.

"Do you like it?" His voice dropped low, his fingers still deep in her. "You promised to tell me." Jake pushed another finger in part of the way. "So fucking soaked. You have no idea how bad I want to be in there, fucking that beautiful pussy. Tell me, does it feel good?"

"Yes, can't you fucking tell!?" she spit out as her body continued shuddering.

Jake removed his hand, steadying her thighs, gently swatting the side of her leg. "Hey, hey, nice, nice, you can say it nice." Mirth dominated his rough tone. "Three?" he asked, sliding another finger inside her.

"Yes, please, yes." Rakell pushed against him, screaming. "I'm coming again! Oh, God! Please, please, keep…"

"I'm not stopping anytime soon," he asserted as he continued to finger-fuck her, getting off on her absolute loss of control, the wild way her head twisted from side to side as she whimpered, his cock twitching every time she yelled, "Fuck me…Fu-…plea—" a trickled plea spilling out of her mouth.

He'd been with some experienced women, but no one as responsive as her, no one that felt like they had been in heat for years with no release. After she trembled in orgasm yet again, he gently pulled his fingers from her tight hole.

Rakell flushed, and her eyes glazed as she looked up at him. "Are you going to fuck me?" Jake's nervous system was alerted to the vulnerability ringing in her tone.

She was like an out-of-control horse; there was no way to stop the run home, so the rider just had to hang on for dear life. She seemed surprised, almost scared by her own reactions, as though she hadn't really felt this before.

He ran his finger slowly up her pelvis, toward her chest, his eyes boring into her. "Watching you come may be one of the most breathtaking sights I've ever seen." His finger traced her collarbone then gently moved up to her chin, running his moistened fingers on her lower lip, taking in her quick intake of breath. "You are getting under my defenses, beautiful…you aiming to do that?" His voice took on a strained quality. Firmly, his thumb rubbed along her lower lip as he added, "Trying to undo me…huh?"

Her eyes grew wide. "No, I don't want to…Jake, I…" She wasn't acting right now; there was no script that told her how to respond to the intensity stringing between them…the openness he seemed to display to her. "Jake…I…You make me feel so good, so, so… present…" The next part of the sentence she held in: *Rakell comes alive with you. You're bringing me back to me.* "I just mean that when you touch me, I'm here." Shutting her eyes, her thoughts escaping her brain, she threw the words out there. "I stay here, in my body, I don't pretend or go somewhere else, I mean mentally, I…"

Grappling with the statements that spilled from her, she put words to the *sense* he had with her, a feeling he couldn't pinpoint until this shrouded confession. He'd felt her shift before as if she was distancing herself when he touched her, as if fighting the emotional part of their interaction, only focusing on the arousal. He knew that he'd done that a million times before her, with so many women through the years. But it felt different with her, tangible, as if his neurons were intertwining with hers when he experienced her pleasure on full display. She was binding herself to him. God, he needed to know she would be his. But something in his brain, the logical side that he often overlooked, was blaring, *Slow down, man, you're gonna fuck this up if you run full steam ahead. Dance, Jake, dance, just like you do on the field, give yourself time to figure out the next move.*

He leaned toward her face, his hand cupping her chin. "Good, Sweets, because you have no idea how present I am right now, and I want you here with me…nowhere else." He pulled her bottom lip into his mouth, absorbing the slight tremble from her jaw.

Chapter Twenty-Six

The smell of cooking meat hit Jake's senses, jarring him from the trance of their connection. "Sweets, let me get you a robe," he said, slipping off the couch. He returned with a large white terrycloth robe. "Come here," he entreated, helping Rakell into it. He kissed her forehead. "I have to check the meat. I may have ruined our dinner because I was so busy getting lost in that sexy as hell body." He winked, walking toward the back door.

God, he couldn't wrap his head around this girl. Simultaneously so boldly sexy, so ripe with want, yet seemingly so new to pleasure. Every time she came hard, it seemed to shock her, like it was an experience she was trying to understand. He couldn't make sense of it. What he did know was that when her need was great, his heart overrode his cock, a feeling that was new to him.

Wrapping her arms around herself, taking a long deep breath, Rakell felt stunned, or maybe refreshed—she couldn't figure out which. But she knew she had never experienced anything like this in her life with anyone else. She longed for the loss of control, the hedonistic release as her body was consumed by his stimulation, rather than her body being used for someone else's pleasure. What she'd felt was so unlike anything she'd experienced as an escort; before, she'd always held back, making sure to keep her emotions in check. She wondered if it was always like this when you dated someone you liked, when you allowed them access to your body without a contract.

"Steaks almost ready," Jake announced, pulling two glasses out of the cabinet and handing them to her as he grabbed a bottle of red from the kitchen counter. "Are you hungry?"

"Starved," Rakell said.

"Do you want to change back into your clothes or stay in my robe?" he asked, picking up her clothes off the floor, then looking back to her. "'Cause you look pretty adorable in it."

Wrapping her hands around herself, she said, "Can I stay in this? I love the way it feels."

A small smile crossed his lips. "You can stay in it…" Damn, the word *forever* flashed in his brain. "You…as long as you want."

Something in his tone made her feel like she might cry. She hated that. She'd been so removed from emotion with men that his simple statement made her squirm.

"Let's eat," he said, walking toward the kitchen. She followed him, helping grab plates and glasses. He grabbed a bottle of the French he'd purchased, holding it up to show her, pronouncing the name perfectly. They decided to eat on the outdoor couch instead of the table. They sat side by side, eating and drinking.

"God, this wine is good," she said, her eyes resting on him. "Really, you should not have bought this."

Jake paused, summoning himself. He needed to tell her what he did, who he was. "Yes, I should have," he said, standing. He picked up his empty plate along with her half-empty dish. "You barely touched the potato. Are you one of those non-carb-eating beauties?"

Sheepishly, she said, "Um, just trying to cut back." It struck her that he seemed to enjoy, maybe even relish in, the fleshiness of her ass. *God, he should see all the models I had to compare myself to at the* Sports Illuminated *shoot.* "Let me help you."

He stepped away. "No, I got it. Don't cut back too much. You already look amazing, so don't fall into that trap," he said, walking toward the door.

Rakell wished that were true, but what he didn't realize was that she was trying to make it in an industry that didn't appreciate different body types. They gave a nod to plus size models, but normal, healthy women didn't seem to fit into a type. There was one standard—tall and thin, with emphasis on *thin*.

When Jake came back, he poured more wine. Setting aside the empty bottle, he sat beside her. She took another sip, definitely feeling the aftershock of the orgasms and the wine running through her blood, all of it making her want more. She turned toward him.

His eyes went to the opening of the robe, which had slid aside when she turned, exposing the side of her breasts. He stared at her as his hand reached into the opening of the robe, cupping one of her breasts, his thumb running over the nipple, feeling it harden from his touch. "So beautiful," he whispered, taking another sip of wine before setting the glass down, using his free hand to reach in and cup the other breast. Her chest moved toward his touch. "Damn, these feel so good. Your nipples are so sweet-looking, so pink and hard." He pulled the robe open as he dipped his head down. "I want them in my mouth again, okay?"

Rakell arched into his touch as he pushed her mounds together. He dipped his head to her breasts, moving his mouth back and forth, sucking, lightly biting, then soothing them with the flat of his tongue. "Jake, it feels so good. God, I just want…" Her words were lost in a soft moan as her head went back.

"Sit back and spread your legs." His tone edged on a demand.

"Um, Jake?" She leaned back against the couch.

"Spread your legs wide, please. I want to feel what you're thinking." His tone was thick, letting her know how aroused he was. He took her hand and planted it on his crotch. "You can tell what I'm thinking, right?" His hands lowered down her body, gently tapping the inside of her upper thighs. "Open up, Sweets, so I can feel what's going on in your beautiful head."

"Um, yes…okay." Her legs opened as his hand went between them, his fingers moving around her outer lips, then dipping, exploring the wet folds. "I can tell you what I'm thinking—that I want you to fuck me."

Jake's eyes fixed on her. He plunged two fingers into her slit. "What the hell? This pussy is always wet. What the fuck goes on in that dirty mind?" He smiled, his gaze intense as she looked away, moaning, like she was embarrassed.

"Look at me," he demanded, wondering why she seemed so shy, so new to this. But she couldn't be, there was no way. Rakell turned her eyes back to him. "I fucking love how wet you get, how turned on you are, how fucking crazy your body responds to my touch. Love it. Never turn away from it, because it makes me so turned on knowing how turned on *you* get." He pushed another finger in her, and she cried out.

"Please, Jake… please, please." He pushed his fingers in deeper as she pleaded, his mouth dipping to her tits again, sucking on her nipples as his fingers explored the tight wetness inside her. "Please…please,

Jake," she cried helplessly, as if she really was at his mercy.

Jake stilled his fingers, resting them deep inside her. He licked each nipple, then moved his lips to her ear. "Tell me what you want, Sweets. I'll do anything for you. If you ask for it, I'll do it." Tension coiled in his swollen cock and heavy balls as he watched her come undone yet again. He wanted nothing more than to lay her down and ram into her, fuck her madly, but he knew this time it had to be for her. Internally, he trembled, forcing control of his body.

Rakell turned her head to his mouth, biting his bottom lip, enough to pinch. "I want *you*, I want you *inside* me," she breathed, her hand touching the hand he had inside her, then moving back to the bulge between his legs, thinking how big he felt. "This, please. Do you want to be inside me?" she murmured. He gently slid his fingers out. Her pelvis flexed slightly, missing the fullness. She watched him as he sucked off his fingers.

"You know I do," he replied, standing, pulling her up by the lapels of the bathrobe.

Dolly brushed against his leg.

A breathy giggle jumped from Rakell's mouth. "Um, not sure your significant other approves of us leaving her here by herself."

"Well, she's going to have to live with it, unless you're into a ménage à trois that includes a furry babe."

"Ah, sorry, Dolly, not really into that."

Jake took Rakell's hand, marching her past the living room, down the hall to his room. He gently pulled her behind him, walking slowly but with a sense of urgency, his body leaning forward, focusing on the goal.

They walked across the threshold, Jake shutting the door behind them, turning on the light, then sliding the dimmer switch down so that a soft, low light filled the room. He didn't want it to be dark; he wanted to see and feel her, especially her eyes. Bringing her with him to the side of his bed, he sat on the edge, with her standing in front of him.

Rakell's stomach twisted, the rawness of her nerves responding to every look, every touch from him. She took in nothing about his room. They could have been anywhere. Her body was focused on him as he slid the robe off her shoulders, letting it careen to the floor.

Jake's eyes took her in, then closed for a second. "Rakell?" he asked, his hands at her hips, his thumbs resting on her hip bone, his fingers behind her, spreading, clenching as he moved her hips forward.

Her head lowered to look at him. "Yes?" Her voice was hushed.

"Do you have a picture? I mean, a way you thought it should be the first time we're together?" He'd learned from experience that some women had pictures, an expectation of romance, or a certain position, or something he was supposed to have done that he didn't do.

Her mouth twitched into a smile. "Well, I shared that with you already—fucked over the table. So I'll wait for my picture next time." He chuckled, but it sounded strained to her, like something was wrong. Leaning forward, she brushed her lips to his forehead. "Will there be a next time?" Her tone was neutral, like the answer didn't matter. She was not trying to sound needy; she was just wondering.

"What? Yes, yes of course," Jake said. He pulled her pelvis forward, kissing her belly. "Yes, that's what I want," he whispered against the flesh of her abdomen. There was an uncertainty to his tone, but it was only because he still wasn't sure what *she* wanted.

Rakell's fingers methodically unbuttoned the top buttons of his linen shirt. She then reached down, helping him pull it over his head. He guided her body to the side. "Lie down, beautiful," he instructed. She followed, lying on top of the blue cotton comforter.

Standing, his arms shaky, Jake undid his pants, sliding his briefs and jeans down his legs, his eyes fixed on her naked body. He watched her feet moving up and down the bed, her pelvis slightly arched, her body seemingly begging as she watched him. Excitement twisted into greedy need, jabbing through him. He pulled back on it. This had to be gentle. It had to be meaningful. She needed to feel that from him, he thought, coaching himself. He stood beside the bed, holding his rock-hard shaft while he rolled the condom down his cock. Rakell's eyes fixed on his cock as a low whimper spilled from her mouth.

Jake crawled onto the bed, lying next to her on his side, bracing himself with one hand as his right hand traced the length of her torso from her neck to the wet hair between her legs. Her legs instinctively opened to his touch, craving the feeling of fullness inside her. He drove two fingers into her pussy, and she cried out, "God, yes! Please!"

"I will, but I want to watch you come again," Jake said, his fingers working inside her then pulling out and flicking her clit. He moved between her legs, continuing to play with her clit. "Then I'll fill you up slowly, very slowly."

He dipped his face between her legs, his hands opening her farther.

She whimpered when she felt his tongue on her clit.

He sucked her swollen nub into his mouth. Rakell's hips lurched up, and her body jolted, quivering as she moaned, "Jake, I'm…" in a low, long whimper. It was a shallow orgasm, leaving her aching for more. "Please, now. Fucking fuck me now," she demanded impatiently.

Jake came down on her, his hands bracing him, his cock rubbing her inner thigh. He whispered, "Not yet, beautiful. That's for later. I'm going to make love to you first." He dipped his lips to hers, softly kissing her, staring at her intently.

Rakell's head sprang up, nipping at his bottom lip hard.

"Ouch! Damn, girl." He pulled back.

"No, you're fucking me! Not making love to me, you're fucking me first!" Her hands reached behind his neck, pulling him down while she forcefully kissed him. "Been waiting for this forever. Fucking fuck me, damn it."

"Jeez, you're on fire, driving me…" Jake pushed out between clenched teeth, trying to control himself. She made it next to impossible. He held his cock, wiggling the head around her pussy, then finding her slit and letting his cock lurch forward into her hole. She squealed, and he steadied himself there, just inside her.

Rakell's hips tilted up, egging his cock in. "More, more!" she demanded, her hands on his back, her nails digging in. Jake pushed himself in a little more but halted, feeling her snugness. He would definitely leave her sore if he moved hard and quick, like she was demanding.

"You feel so good," he growled. "So tight. Open your legs wider, let me in," he coaxed. "Going slow until I know you're okay."

"Please, I'm fine…please, keep going… push, I want to feel it completely in me," Rakell said, her voice faint, begging.

Jake began pushing in further, then stopping, then pushing, feeling her flesh give in. Rakell squealed with each push, then breathed and yelled, "Yes, please! Yes!" He was trying to look at her, make this mean something, but she was completely lost in her own body, in her own decadent pleasure.

Shoving it past her clenching walls, his cock cleaved her open as she wailed. Her cries were guttural, a commingling between pleasure and some kind of internal longing, flying into the air around them.

His cock continued to stroke her insides, sliding out so that the head was just inside her, slowly moving in deeper, then slowly out, her flesh giving in a little more each time, making it easier to move into her. He didn't care what she said; he was going slow, relishing this, no matter how hard her rapacity made it. He knew if he let go before her body adjusted, he'd regret his selfishness. Sliding further into her, Jake came down over her body, bracing himself on his elbow. "You feel so good... so, so good," he said, bending his head to kiss her nipples, feeling her shudder beneath him from the dual stimulation. He would do everything to her eventually. Never could he tire of such a responsive body.

Finally, Rakell's eyes focused, the pressure between her legs turning to full pleasure. She was glad he had moved in slowly, but now she was sure she could take him. "You feel so, so good too. I want to feel you deeper, harder. I can take it," she stammered out between heavy breaths.

"You sure?" Jake asked, furrowing his brows, "Because—"

"Please, I want..." She sucked in air hard, as his cock slid in deeper, his balls up against her ass cheeks. "Oh, God...oh God."

"More?" His tone was lusty, edgy, his body shaking with restraint, starting to lose control. She was making it almost impossible.

"Yes, harder!" she screamed, her fingernails raking up and down his back, daring his body.

Jake's body hurdled cock-first into the den of the dare, his cock pulling out, then crashing back into her again, his back dipping, his knees pushing on the bed, grounding him, giving his pelvis more momentum. He rode her with swift strokes in and out, finding a fast rhythm.

"Fuck, fuck. Oh, God!" Rakell screamed, her head shaking, her hands dropping from his back, grabbing the comforter, bracing herself. "Ohhhh, I'm..." she mewled, feeling her body give way.

"Rakell," Jake groaned, "let it go. Come, let it go." Driven to keep her going, he plunged deeper, circling his hips into her, putting pressure on her clit. She screamed harder, a sound generating deep in her chest, making him groan, charging his cock. He swelled inside her, throbbing, pushing in. The nut at the base of his cock dissolved as he came, shouting, "Fucking crazy about you!"

He was so caught up in his release he didn't hear her yelling, "Stop, stop! I can't anymore!" between ragged breaths.

Slowly, his cock emptied. "Shh, shh—okay." Jake stopped halfway inside her. "Sorry."

Rakell's eyes welled up. "I just can't come anymore... I can't." Tears pooling, she shrieked, "I can't!" water springing from her green eyes.

"Sweets, shh...shh," he whispered, pulling back and gently removing himself from her, crawling up onto the bed. He kissed her cheeks, tasting her salty tears, her sweat. "Just a minute." He turned, carefully pulling the condom off, reaching to the side of the bed, and wrapping it in a tissue. Turning back to her, he pulled her to his side, wrapping her upper body in his arms. "Shh, shh," he coaxed between heavy breaths.

Her body stilled, the tears drying up as she internally admonished herself for the swell of emotion that she seemed to be drowning in tonight. Again, it was overwhelming to her, and she didn't feel equipped to process or control it.

Rakell closed her eyes, sated but shaken by her response to him. How could it be like this? Shutting her eyes, she pushed away the nagging feeling of loss. She relished his tender touch as he softly brushed his fingers along her hairline, while feathering his lips against her forehead. As she lay intertwined in his arms, she was curious, wondering if it was always this consuming. The experience felt like getting knocked off your feet but landing on something soft, enveloping, a place you wanted to stay for a while.

"Hey, you?" Jake said, rubbing his hand up her back to her shoulder as he held her tight. He would have never predicted her reactions tonight. She strutted into a room, leading with bold independence, seeming almost detached at times. To see her become so vulnerable, so overtaken with emotion, confused him.

"Yeah, you?" Rakell replied, her voice strained, weak. Her throat was raw from screaming.

"You okay?"

"Mm...hmm. But I'm dying to finish the rest of that Bordeaux." Her eyes shifted upward, a sweet smile on her face. Jake smiled back. "I think I need to rinse off first. I'm a sweaty mess."

Looking her over, he saw that she was a lovely mess. "Me too," Jake said, moving off the bed, reaching for her hand. "How about a quick shower?" He pulled her up off the bed.

Her legs felt shaky. "Together?" Her confused tone matched her face, the way her eyebrow pulled down on one eye.

His hand was still holding hers. "Uh, yeah?"

Rakell turned toward the bathroom. "Um, no thank you. I think I've had enough intimacy for a night, maybe a lifetime." A weak laugh followed, and she felt his hand grab her upper arm, pulling her into him.

His eyebrows pinched together, his mouth straight. "What did you say?" With his hand firmly cupping her shoulder, he could feel goosebumps covering her skin on her upper arm.

"Nothing—just tired. I was kidding," she offered.

"Were you?" His eyes narrowed, studying her face. "Let's shower. It's not even nine yet. We can enjoy the wine outside."

She stiffened, pulling back from him. Submerged in the emotion washing over her, almost drowning in the unexpected high that came with his touch, she wondered how she could swim out of this. She tried to bury her reflexive instinct to get away.

"You go, I'll wait," she repeated, her expression confused, cautious.

Jesus, was this girl for real? *Let's fuck like porn stars, but showering is a little too intimate? Who the fuck has she been with?* The question thumped in his gut.

"Rakell, we just had incredible, mind-blowing sex. I was just inside you. We can shower together," His tone, authoritative at first, faded to a question. "...Okay, Sweets?"

"Um...okay, okay." Too many emotions collided in her, not aligning, making a mess of her mind. She breathed in deeply, trying to slow her thoughts. She didn't have to figure everything out this minute, this day.

They showered, Jake rubbing soap all over her skin, then slowly wiping her body with a washcloth as warm water sprayed over them.

I could do this all day, Jake thought, his hands gorging on her flesh, the voluptuousness and receptivity of it, making him long for more of her.

Rakell shut her eyes for a moment as he moved the washcloth down the small of her back to her ass. The feel of his washcloth-covered hand going into the crack of her ass, carefully wiping over sensitive private tissue was so sumptuous that it was almost extravagant, like something she didn't deserve. Her body soaked up his tender touch.

An unexpected mewl left her mouth as her body shivered.

Jake used his other hand to push on the small of her back, steadying her. He wished he could start all over again, ending in another heated fucking session, but he knew it had already put her on edge. He felt her inching back from him and remembered her words when he'd held her on the bed.

When the shower ended, she felt content, overflowing with sensuous pleasure. Relishing in the gratification, Rakell let herself believe she deserved it for once. She slipped his robe back on, asking him if it was okay. He smiled and said, "of course," nodding his head at her as if pleased that she had asked as he jerked on a pair of faded loose jeans and a worn gray T-shirt.

Chapter Twenty-Seven

Grabbing the other bottle of Bordeaux and an opener, they went outside to their spot on the sofa. Jake connected his phone to the outdoor speaker. Music spilled out around them. Rakell couldn't help noticing that there was a lot of Linda Ronstadt and Emmylou Harris on his playlist, artists he'd heard her perform at the bar. Also, Tricia Yearwood, Guy Forsyth, and Jace Everett—other artists he knew she liked.

She moved in next to him, closer. "Good taste in music," she said, giving him a knowing smile.

"Just paying attention, that's all." Jake twisted the corkscrew, popping the cork on the bottle and serving them both a generous pour.

Rakell picked up the bottle of Bordeaux, reading the label. "Chateau Haut-Brion 2003, a premier grand cru." She put the bottle down, her eyes intent, looking at him. She knew this bottle cost a lot. This guy…he made her feel so cared for. He really was putting himself out there for her. She had never experienced such sincere affection from a man she was fucking. Jake scrambled her brain, yanking at her heart.

He took a sip of wine. "So good, and your French pronunciation is excellent," he said, smiling and taking another sip. He wanted to add that his own mother was from France, but he kept it in, knowing that the more pressing matter was to tell her who *he* was.

"Jake, I'm concerned that you spent that kind of money. Honestly, I like wine, but I don't want you wasting money trying to impress me." Her tone was deliberate as she touched his cheek. "As you can tell, I like my *average* guy." She gestured to the bottles on the table. "So no more of this."

He didn't respond for a moment, not knowing how to tell her the truth, but also appreciating her genuine concern and her candid statement about her affection for him. It was so odd to feel this sincere thoughtfulness from a woman—much less a woman who'd kept him at arm's length until now. He leaned back, his eyes on her. He coaxed himself to be forthright, trying to squelch the anxious surge pulsing through his nervous system.

"You got me where you wanted me, so no more spending..."

"What, no, stop...please." Jake swallowed hard; she could see his throat stiffen. "Rakell, I didn't know this, I mean us...was going to happen tonight. Of course, I think about you, about being with you all the time, but this wasn't a setup." His tone was direct, earnest, his eyes set on her, making her want to squirm.

"I get it," Rakell said, her eyes shifting to the side, breaking his steady stare. "Actually, it was my idea, so it couldn't be a setup. Getting you in bed has been a semi-focus for me, let's just say, every night when I'm getting myself off." Her eyes still diverted from his, blinking, like she was embarrassed.

Jake had never heard a woman be so transparent about wanting sex in such a disarming way. Her words and the skittish little girl expression clashed, yet made him want to get his hands all over her again, feel her under him but mostly protect her...but from what?

Dragging the moist night air into his lungs before taking a long sip of the chewy red wine, he urged himself to open up. Face this head-on. He felt so edgy about what he needed to tell her. Usually, he'd be excited to tell a woman he liked what he did, how he could afford these wines and more, but her mixed messages made him unsure. "Rakell, I can afford these wines. I won't notice it financially. I...I...have money," he stammered, searching his mind, looking for the words.

Her spine stiffened at his confessional tone. "Okay," Rakell answered, hushed, her eyes growing wide. Was he about to tell her his parents supported him, that they were rich?

"I play football, professionally...NFL football," he blurted into the air as if throwing away a pass so he didn't get tackled. Every time he did that, he felt empty. It was a necessary strategy at times, but the coward feeling was real, and that's exactly how he felt right now, like a fucking coward.

Her eyes grew saucer-like, her eyebrows arching to his confession. Then she squinted, as if she'd figured something out.

After a lengthy beat of silence, he murmured, "What?"

She stood, taking her wine glass with her. She stepped away, looking at the craggy, twisted branches of the oak trees in his back yard, letting the impregnated silence hang around them. *What do I say? You lied? You didn't tell me who you were, even when I asked what you did for a living? But I didn't, can't, tell him my secret, so he's coming clean while I know...I won't, I can't. Even if I trusted him not to freak out, I don't trust that he wouldn't judge my choices, of course he would. Plus, you've signed NDAs, Rakell, you would be liable...ease back. Don't react.*

Ultimately, she couldn't say anything about herself, so his confession almost felt like redemption to her. *We are both liars, seeking a relationship without strings*, she told herself, but her body had connected to her heart, and the fear that accompanied that intense feeling rooted in her brain.

The sound of him clearing his throat as he stood abruptly caught her attention. "Rakell, please say something. I just..."

"Ohhhhh, just thinking about how that makes sense. I was wondering why all your friends look like meatheads," Rakell said, forcing the features of her face to soften, attempting to wipe away the fog of angst circling them.

A sigh escaped his lips. "Yeah, kinda a prerequisite for the job."

"Yeah, I suppose," she offered, trying to think if she'd ever heard of him, having just found out a few weeks ago that his last name was Skyler. "What team do you play for?"

"Sacramento Condors—they're a new team." He treaded cautiously. She wasn't smiling, but she wasn't backing away either; he was not sure what reaction he expected.

She swallowed a deep sip of wine, more than she had intended when she lifted the glass. "Why didn't you tell me that when I asked what you did?" Her tone was steady, resisting any judgment. After all, she lived much of her life in the shadows, and she knew she couldn't open up to him.

Jake's head bent, looking at the glass he was holding, his jet-black curls longer than when she first met him, flopping forward, veiling his face. He spoke into the glass. "I should have, but you said you wanted a normal guy, which I am, but I didn't know if you'd believe me if you knew that I'm a football player. So what I shared with you about the houses, also wanting to be a history teacher someday, that was all true..." He looked up, tucking a curl behind his ears, his eyes focused on her face. "I left out the NFL player part because...I guess I was trying to impress you with my *normalness*, because that's how I want to live." His lips pulled back into a slight smile.

After a few stilted moments, Rakell asked, "Are you famous?" Her tone was strained. If he was famous, there would be no way to stay under the radar. But if he was famous, wouldn't she have remembered hearing of him?

He put a hand on her shoulder. "No, not really. I mean, it's clear *you* haven't heard of me." Gently he wrapped his hand around her wrist, tugging her back to the couch. Mindlessly, she let herself be led, and they both sat.

A guilty look crossed her face. "No, I haven't. But as far as football players go, I've been singularly focused on Randall Adams," she said, shrugging her shoulders, "and he hasn't come calling yet." She let out a quick laugh, taking in his expression of mock anger. "I didn't mean that the way it sounded." Another jolt of laughter.

Jake set down his wine, grabbed hers, and put it on the table. Then he reached forward, yanking her onto his lap. She shifted so that her legs straddled his, pulling his robe shut around her, giggling.

He wrapped his arms around her waist, pulling her in, growling in her ear, "You really know how to build a guy up, don't you?" His hands moved to her sides, tickling her. "Don't you?"

She squirmed, trying to push his hands away. "J-a-k-e!"

"Fucking Randall Adams? Is that who you're waiting for? What about that *normal* guy shit you fed me? Huh?" His tone was playful but pointed.

Rakell put her hands on either side of his jaw. "Stop," she laughed, her head going back. "Okay, seriously though—you don't get much more normal and down-to-earth than Randall Adams. Do you watch his 'grounding' videos on TikTok? He has a degree in Eastern religious studies, and he…"

"Now you sound like my mom," Jake squeaked, attempting a poor imitation of his mom: "'…and he's so poised, and he goes into the wilderness butt naked to get in touch with the world, and he doesn't care about what others think…' Bullshit! Why the hell do you think he films all that down-to-earth shit? So people will say shit like that about him…"

It struck him then that his agent was right; *he* needed a full-time publicist, someone to help steer his public image like Randall Adams. He had to admit he admired the dude a lot, even though he was pretty sure that it was Randall Adam's decision not to give him a shot as backup quarterback to the Tornadoes when he was shopping around to leave the Seahawks. Rumor had it that Adams didn't approve of Jake's off-the-field reputation and all the drama that went with it. What about Randall's drama? People seemed to think his was okay.

People revered him for going naked into the wilderness; meanwhile Jake was on a video naked in a hotel room in Vegas which some stripper had graciously filmed, and suddenly he was seen as out of control. He wanted to get on Instagram after that and say, *"By the way, world, you're supposed to be naked in a hotel room, not outside."* Somehow his behavior appeared irresponsible, but when the "Zen Cyclone" did it, it was "getting in touch with the earth."

I definitely need a full-time publicist, he thought.

Jake tugged on her robe lapels, pulling her torso into him, rooting his face into the upper opening of her robe, using his teeth to open it wider. When she tried to stop him, he grabbed her hands, forcing them still by her side.

"Not fair," she chortled. "Oh my," she said, her head falling back as his mouth nuzzled in, finding a nipple and softly sucking.

His face still buried in the front of the gaping robe, he taunted, "Randall's not going to do this to you." He looked up, grinning. "Or, I should say, *for* you." His mouth targeted her other nipple. "Is he? No, because he's too busy laying butt naked in the desert making sure the sun shines directly in his asshole so he can connect with the fucking solar system or some other crystal earthy bullshit." His hands let go of hers, pulling the robe wide open.

"Jake, please." The arch of her back and the breathy plea gave her away. Her desire was the opposite of her words. "You're just jealous because he can be the big football player type and still show that he's deep and…"

"Stop. All this talk is going to make me soft, even with your hotness staring at me."

"Please, this is silly." She rolled her eyes, mocking him.

Tilting his head back, Jake dropped his hands. He directed challenging eyes at her, hands up, in surrender. "So is that, 'Jake, please keep going, make me come over and over'?" His mouth twisted into a small grin. "Or is that, 'Jake, please. Stop, I'm saving my wanton self for Randall Adams'? Which is it?"

Balling her fists, hitting him playfully on his chest, she cried, "Wanton? What the hell?"

He barked out a laugh, wrapping her fists in his large hands. "They use the word a lot in old western books. It means sexually lawless or unrestrained," he explained, pulling her hands away, again nuzzling his head between her large breasts. "Someone who can't get enough," he growled against her skin, making her squeal again.

"Thanks for the Webster Dictionary definition, mate! I know what the hell wanton means." Pressing her breasts into his head, her body begging for him to keep sucking on her nipples, in a husky voice, she whispered, "Do you like it—my wantonness?"

Lifting his head, Jake looked at her, wiggling his eyebrows. "Fucking love it, but pretty sure Randall would be too intimidated by all this." He laughed, then dropped her hands so that his hands were free, lewdly molding and squeezing her breasts as she moaned. "I, on the other hand, I've been praying for this." His hands pulled her breasts together as his tongue lapped at her nipples.

Responding to his swelling arousal beneath her bottom, she ground her hips into his lap, the cloth shielding his penetrating flesh from her opening. Her drive to feel him again deep inside her grew with the salacious, unapologetic way his body seemed to implore her own. She threw herself into his touch urgently, petitioning him to partake. In the past, she hadn't been present. Usually, her focus was on her own acting so the man would get off sooner and she could clock out for the evening, do her job and move on. But now with him, fully in her own body, she feared she couldn't fill the demand of her own need.

Rakell's moans grew louder, more demanding. "Jake, I want to...let's visit your room again." She jumped up from his lap, grabbing his hands. "Come on."

Her robe was open, exposing her whole body, making it impossible for him to resist, not that he was trying. Jake smiled, standing, grateful they were thinking the same thing. He walked behind her, letting her lead him, but as they approached the door, he grabbed her arm, spinning her around and pushing her up against the door. Pinning her hands above her head, he relished the way her mouth opened in a big O—surprised, yet so aroused. "J-A-K-E," she yelled between heavy breaths.

"I'm not waiting. Open your legs so I can fuck you until we both can't breathe," he growled, leaning his body into hers, soaking in the way her chest was heaving. *Yep, he had a bad girl on his hands. He needed her to be his bad girl, his, and nobody else's, just his. Fuck Randall Adams, Jake Skyler is your quarterback, you little minx. Jake Skyler is the only one that can handle this bad girl.* And with that thought, he held her hands in one hand as he hastily ripped his T-shirt off, then reaching into the pocket of his jeans, he pulled out a condom, ripping it open with his teeth.

"Oh my! Yes, sir, Mr. Skyler" rushed out of her mouth as she took in his ferociousness, the way his jaw hardened as he visually absorbed her body.

He let her hands go. "Keep them there, don't move," he said, rolling the condom on. Then his hands were on her hips, jerking her legs up as he pushed her body against the door. His rock-hard cock found her opening as he gripped her hips to steady her against the door.

Rakell's eyes widened as he pushed in deeply on the first stroke. She shouted, as if surprised, but then begged for more. He moved with long, fast strokes, his fingers digging into her ass cheeks, holding her hips up while he fucked her without restraint.

"Fucking love this pussy!" he yelled, looking down at her. "You like feeling this cock inside you, don't you?" Rigid lust dominated his tone.

"Yes, yes!" she screamed.

He steadied her gyrating hips, stopping himself most of the way inside her, and looked at her. Her eyes stared up at him, questioning. "Is it too hard, too much?" he asked, his voice suddenly gentle.

"Love the fullness. Don't stop," Rakell begged, almost crying.

Jake held her steady. "'Cause I love doing you hard, but I care. I mean, I'm crazy about you, so I—" Her hips bucked, arching from the door, and he held tighter. "Please...I want you to know that, that I care." His voice was shaking, edging on deep emotion.

"I know, but right now I need to come." She bucked again. "Come on."

Interrupted by her abrupt urgent force, Jake pumped again, his cock taking over as she screamed out, "I'm cuuuuminng!" She spurred him on with her mewling gasps, following her shrieking cry.

Thrusting in and out, his whole body worked toward the end goal until the tension in his balls released, spewing deep inside her.

Gently, he guided her to standing. Her head dropped to his moist chest. They fell limp, silent, both trying to catch up to their breathing until they could speak. "God, you are too much," Jake said into the moonlight kissed darkness. "In the best way possible," he added.

"I guess I could say the same for you." Rakell lightly touched his arm.

He pulled his robe around her, tying it, then hugging her again, he shifted her to the side so he could open the door. "Be right back." He motioned to the condom.

Moments later, he walked out into the living room, and she was sitting, head back on his massive leather couch, her hair splaying around her. God he really wanted to solidify this relationship. He thought about telling her then that he hoped they could be exclusive, only see each other, but he wasn't sure how to broach it.

Jake needed to proceed slowly, one step at a time until he was sure she wanted the same. He cleared his throat, watching her lids flutter open. "Hey, I'll get your suitcase out of the car," he said, starting to slip a leg off the couch, but then halted, noticing the perplexed look on her face even in the faint light from the kitchen.

What? This was too much. She'd just had the best sex of her life; she needed to go home, regroup. "Um, well, I didn't really plan on spending the night," she said tentatively.

He bent, hovering over her, lowering his face to hers, their noses lightly touching, his brows pulling in. "Well, I'm planning on waking up with you tomorrow."

"Not trying to fuck and run, but I'm not the type that needs to spend the night just because we had sex," Rakell said, an explanatory tone to her voice, her eyes fluttering open when he stood with a huff. "What?"

His face contorted, the muscles on his jaw ticked. "That's a fucking first," he spat out in disbelief. "Seriously, it's not a 'type.' It's called being normal. I mean, it's normal to spend the night with someone you're seeing, especially once you start having sex."

Rakell stood up, her hands on her hips. "Well, I'm not one of those girls that needs to feel loved and all that emotional stuff just because I'm fucking someone. So maybe I'm *not* normal." As she said those words, it dug into her that there was a lot of truth in that statement, making her wince with a jolt of sadness. Disassociating always made her believe she was stronger, more powerful than others, but at this moment it felt empty, gutless.

"Yep, figuring that out." Reaching forward, he pulled the lapels of the robe, dragging her into him. "Listen, Rakell…" His tone was directive, but he altered it when he felt her body stiffen in defense. "Let me just say I want you here. It will feel wrong if you don't stay," he explained cautiously.

She let out a barely audible sigh. "Do you have a guest bedroom?"

"What?" he replied, his face scrunching in irritation. "Yes, for guests, which you're not. You're my…you're here with me."

She made a purposeful pouty face. "So random guests are given more options than the girl that just fucked you senseless?"

Jake shook his head, disbelief racing through his brain. "First of all, I don't invite random guests to sleep with me in my bed; that would be weird. Second of all, *I* fucked *you* senseless, so I make the sleeping rules." He added, dropping his hands and turning toward the door, "I'll be right back with your suitcase."

Remembering that the only sleepwear she had packed was a Randall Adams jersey, the number twelve with a huge cyclone swirling on the front, Rakell asked Jake if she could borrow a T-shirt to sleep in. She changed into his oversized UT shirt and a pair of white panties, brushed her teeth, and met him in bed. He'd put on pajama bottoms and was lying under the covers holding the comforter open on her side. She slid in, and he pulled her close. She tried to act like she was used to it, affection after sex, but her nervous system couldn't ignore how odd it felt. She didn't know how she'd sleep with his arms wrapped around her, pulling her into his chest. She let him drop off to sleep, then slid out of his arms, moving sloth-like, not to wake him. She grabbed his robe and went to sleep on the couch.

Chapter Twenty-Eight

When Jake woke to an empty bed the next morning, he jumped up. It was six a.m. His eyes scanned to her suitcase, and he took a deep breath, half expecting her to have left. He found her in his robe, curled up on the couch with Dolly on the floor beside her, opting to sleep next to Rakell instead of her fluffy sheepskin bed. He rubbed Dolly's head, pointing to her bed, quietly urging her to it.

Then, slowly, he picked Rakell up in his arms, her face cradled on his shoulder as he carried her to his bed. She whispered that she was sorry but couldn't sleep. Helping her get out of the robe, Jake gently pulled her to him. "Lie on your stomach; I'll rub your back."

He kneaded her shoulders, then moved his hand up her shirt, rubbing her back, loving the sleepy moans escaping her mouth. His hand slid down to her white lace panties, gently kneading the flesh around them, under them, then the backs of her legs. Her thighs instinctively opened, his hand, moving under the white lace from behind, between her legs, finding slippery folds of flesh.

Rakell's moaning grew in intensity as she turned her head to the side. "Yes, that," she whispered before he glided a finger into her slit. "Yes, more." Her bottom curved up, angling toward his hand. Jake slid another finger in, watching as she pushed her bottom up, his fingers sliding deeper into her pussy, her knees moving under her hips as he finger-fucked her from behind.

Getting on his knees, Jake moved behind her as he kept his fingers inside her. Using his other hand, he guided the white lace thong down her legs, coaxing it over her knees. His fingers worked her, speeding up as she pushed and arched against him, her body letting him know she wanted more. He pushed another finger in her hole. She cried out, still begging for him to keep going. Watching her round ass rock back and forth on his fingers made Jake's cock grow stiff, and he almost winced in pain. She edged up on to her elbows so that her ass was in the air, her breasts floating in his orange T-shirt. He reached under her, squeezing the round flesh, pinching her nipples. He felt her pussy walls clutch his fingers, pulsing, then heard her muffled scream into the pillow as she came on his fingers, soaking them. The shuddering slowed, and he pulled his fingers from the clutches of her tight hole. Gruffly shoving his pajama bottoms to his knees, he scooted to the side of the bed, pulling them off and grabbing a condom from the drawer.

Jake heard her move from behind him. "Back on all fours, with that ass in the air if you want me to fuck you," he said hastily. He'd been picturing it the whole time his fingers worked her.

Immediately, Rakell complied, her elbows bent on the bed, her ass in the air, her head turned to the side, staring at his full erection, his hungry cock, protruding from his muscular body. He moved behind her. "Is that what you want, Sweets? For me to split your ass cheeks open and shove my cock into your pussy from behind? Because I'm fucking here for it."

"Please," she replied, urgent and rushed. "You know I do."

"Yes, I do—your pussy told me," he teased, moving behind her arched ass, holding her hips. "Pull the T-shirt off. I wanna see those tits bouncing when I pound you." His hands wrapped in front of her, bracing her as she pulled off the T-shirt, the sight of her tits spilling out and her ass in the air making him anxious to be inside her. "You tell me if it's too much, okay?" He was trying to sound controlled.

"Only if you don't stop in the middle and ask me if you should keep going," she snapped, her head turning to look at him kneeling between her legs, his hair mussed around his head, falling in his face, his blue eyes steeled, stubble framing his square jaw, his mouth tight. She felt his cupped hand lightly swat her lower bottom. "Oh, was I bad?" she goaded.

"Always. Not sure you know any other way." His hands tugged her hips as he jammed himself into her wet slit.

"Oh God!" she yelled. "Yes!"

Jake leaned forward, pushing his cock in deeper. He anchored his large hands around her breasts, filling his palms with her flesh as he let his cock slide in more, gauging her reaction. Rakell pushed her ass back, welcoming him into her hole. He rammed a little harder, finding her deeper parts, relishing her squeal, her fast breath. His hands still manipulating the flesh of her breasts, he dug even deeper, hearing her moan. He wanted to ask if she was okay, but he didn't stop. He listened to her and did what his body wanted, pulling out to just inside her opening, then thrusting forward into her deep space over and over, her screams intensifying as he rammed back and forth, driven on by the sound of his balls hitting the wet skin surrounding her hole and ass.

"Do you hear your wet pussy sucking up my cock?" he hissed, pumping her faster before he moved his hands back to her hips, one hand wrapped around to the front of her hips between her legs, finding the swollen nub as his cock stroked her internal walls. He needed her to come quickly; he could feel his cock pulling at his insides, jerking his semen out. His fingers stroked her clit. "Come, Sweets! I'm going to blow," he cursed under his breath, feeling the explosion as he kept pumping even harder, yelling as he careened into an orgasm.

"I'm…" Rakell's words were lost in guttural cries as she shook, begging Jake to stop, she couldn't come anymore. But he didn't. He kept working her clit, even as his pumping slowed with his spent cock. He wanted to yank every bit of tension out of her, turning it into pleasure. He fell onto her, his pressure pushing her hips into the mattress, her knees sliding down. He braced himself above her.

As his cock softened, falling out of her, he slid to the side of the bed, nudging her body to turn on her side toward him. Rakell smiled behind matted hair, and he brushed the strands away from her face, pecking her cheek. "Well, it's official—I'm addicted to that," Jake said, his hand caressing her arm as his eyes gestured toward her body. "Totally fucking addicted," he repeated, sliding off the bed to dispose of the condom.

"I'm totally exhausted. I guess this is one way to force me to sleep in your bed," Rakell whispered, smiling, looking at his face as he crawled into the bed next to her, thinking how crazy handsome he was, especially like this—messy, post-sex.

"Been found out. That was my plan." Jake winked, wrapping his arm around her, pulling her head onto his chest, rubbing her shoulders, feeling her limp body fold into his. Hearing her breathing steadily, he looked down. Her eyes were shut. A soft smile settled on his face as he fell off to sleep, holding her.

Chapter Twenty-Nine

Two hours later, Jake woke up, smiling again, feeling a limb against him. He kissed the top of her head. "Hey, you," he whispered, not sure if she was awake.

"Yeah, you?" came a muted sleepy voice as she looked up, her arms stretching out, then covering her yawning mouth with the back of her hand, a gesture that reminded him of a young child.

"Didn't you say you had a late morning meeting?"

"Mmm, yeah. I have a meeting, but not until after lunch, so I can catch up on emails and stuff from home before going in."

"Okay. Gym today?" he asked, sliding out from her arms and putting his pajamas on, hating to get up but knowing they both needed coffee.

"Yeah, either before or after work. Not sure."

"Be right back," he said as she shut her eyes again. He returned with two coffee cups.

Rakell sat up, pulling the covers up to her chest as he handed her a cup of coffee. "Thank you. You're the best," she said, her voice groggy.

"Remember that," Jake said, smiling.

She took a sip, the coffee slowly coaxing her awake. She wanted to be the one to pay for something, show him she wasn't the kind of woman that expected a man to pay. She'd do this, then make sure he knew this was casual. She really couldn't get involved, and now knowing he was one of those guys, those rich guys… he had skirted what he did so she wouldn't know that he was one of them. Her spine stiffened before her frontal lobe stepped in. *You haven't told him anything.* Maybe something casual, behind the scenes, would work for him too.

But could she do that with a guy like Jake?

Adjusting the features on her face to mask the internal war, she said, "So are you going to let me take you out tonight, Mr. Nineteen Fifties?" She smiled, then scowled jokingly when she looked at his stern face.

"Really? Just because I don't want you paying?" Jake said, sitting on the side of the bed. "I'll take being old-fashioned when it comes to that if you peg me as an evolutionary god for my bedroom skills. I should have counted how many times you screamed 'I'm coming!' since you've been here." A smirk was planted on his face as he cocked his head toward her.

"Okay, I'll give you that. But I'm still paying tonight, *and* I'll still let you keep proving your skills to me. I'm nice like that," Rakell replied, smiling at him over her coffee cup.

"If I give in to that, what do I get?"

Raising an eyebrow, she tried not to smile. "Um, let's see, cocky boy… a free dinner with a hot chick who likes fucking you? Not sure I'd be negotiating for more just yet."

"Got it. You're right—I should go with *lucky* right now." He stood. "Okay, hot chick who likes to fuck…I'm in."

"I said, 'hot chick who likes fucking *you*.' That implies something totally different," she corrected, then regretted it as soon as the tender, almost proud, look emerged on his face. She shouldn't have made it personal.

"I stand corrected. I like that even better," Jake said, smiling. "I can give you a ride, unless you'll let me make you breakfast."

"I'll take an…" She stopped at the sound of him clearing his throat "…the ride so I can get to the gym before work."

Jake texted her around four.

Jake: *Got an idea, call me…***Send**

An hour later, she called him. "Hey, you," he said, answering.

"Yeah, you?"

"I got an idea," he said and took a deep breath.

"So I heard," she teased, with an overly animated voice.

"And before you say no, I promise what I'm proposing is normal.

How about you pack for the weekend and stay over at my place while James is gone? Then we can have the whole weekend together," he finished, waiting out the disconcerted silence that hung on the line. He didn't want to beg, for Christ's sake.

"Um...I mean, I only live ten minutes from you. I can just run home, get ready for the next thing. I mean, I don't need to drag my stuff to your house," Rakell explained, trying to convince him and herself. Damn, this guy really was like sleeping under a weighted blanket, the heaviness comforting, lulling you to sleep, yet so difficult to get out from under. She wasn't sure if the security it provided was worth the suffocating feeling. A few more days, relishing being wrapped up by Jake? She could literally stay shrouded in the cocoon he seemed to create around them, away from the light of her life with his arms around her. *What the hell is the matter with you, Rakell?*

"I knew it would be a tough sell...but I wanted to try." More silence. "How about pack for tonight and we can go for a run tomorrow and maybe after that, brunch? Then if you insist, you can go back to your place?" he offered.

"That works," she said. He really was a master at getting what he wanted.

"Okay then, should I pick you up around seven? We can get there a little early and have drinks. They've got a fun drink menu."

"Sounds good," she said.

Rakell climbed out of the Uber and knocked on his door a little before six, wearing an orange sleeveless silk halter dress that fell to just above her knees, her hair loosely curled, wearing a bit of mascara and a light peach lipstick. She had her overnight bag in tow. Jake didn't answer, so she texted him.

Rakell: *Answer your front door, damnit...***Send**

Jake was getting out of the shower when he heard his phone buzz. He wrapped a towel around his waist, quickly moving to the front door. He looked through the peephole and saw her standing there, looking stunning.

"Well, hellooo," he said, eyeing her up and down, taking in the way the silk highlighted the fact she wasn't wearing a bra and gently hugged her hips. She wore strappy high-heeled black sandals, making her legs look even longer. "Not good at following directions, are you?"

"No Mr. Skyler, I'm not. Are you going to let me in?" Rakell said, her eyes perusing his body. He was still glistening from the spots that weren't completely dried, and he was wearing only a towel. He had shaven his dirty-boy stubble, which she had kind of liked, but his blue eyes seemed to dance as he looked at her, and she liked that. Those eyes alone made her wet, needy.

He opened the door wider, letting her move past him.

"Sooo…what's up?" he asked, his eyebrows arching.

She pursed her lips in a smirk, her eyes jumping with giddiness before her tongue snuck out the end, playing with her eye tooth. "Well, I read the menu at Justine's…I want everything, so I definitely plan to pig out." She didn't add that she'd been close to starving herself for months leading up to the *Sports Illuminated* swimsuit shoot, and she wanted to enjoy food before she had to be back on a regime.

"So you needed to show up an hour early and *not* wait for me to pick you up, to tell me that?" Jake said, amusement leading his tone. "You could have warned me that you were going to be gluttonous in a short text." He made quotation marks in the air with his fingers, proceeding with something that sort of sounded like a drunk Australian/British accent. "Jake and French food are my weakness, so I will not be able to get enough tonight. Therefore, overindulging in both." He chuckled at his own wit.

Her chin up challengingly, she raked her eyes over his bare chest.

The triumphant naughtiness her expression sported was not lost on Jake or his cock. Damn this girl, a subtle shift in the small muscles of her jaw, the glint in her eye, a not-so-subtle lick of her lips, and his cock couldn't help raising its hand like an eager student.

Rakell laughed, dropping her bag near the couch and walking toward him. "Exactly. Jake, you are such a keen observer. However, you're not getting the point of me showing up early. Let me make myself clear. I'm here to indulge myself with you first, because I may be too full later." Reaching forward, she tugged gently at the towel wrapped around his waist.

Instinctively grabbing the towel that was in danger of falling from his torso, he stepped toward her. "Damn girl, you are lusty. Wish I'd been the one to think of that." Wrapping his arm around her waist, he pulled her in, lowering his mouth to hers and kissing her firmly. Her moans accelerated his yearning. "So fucking horny, aren't you?" he said, breaking the force of their locked mouths.

"Mm…hmm. Are you complaining?"

Jake's hand slid over the silk protecting her breasts, feeling the freeness of the flesh under the silk. "Just wanna make sure I'm not being used, Ms. McCarthy, that it's more than just sex to you," he growled, pushing himself against her, so turned on by just kissing her, feeling her body firmly against his. "Well?"

"Not sure." Rakell nibbled at his bottom lip, tugging on the towel again. "Only one way to find out—keep having sex and see what happens."

His face scrunched up. "Huh, okay, that was not reassuring. You really are tough on a guy's ego." In his head, he was thinking, *Jake, you're letting yourself drown in this one, why?* Without effort, she was pulling him under. Shit, he could hardly get air, much less swim.

He was thanking the gods that she was here, that she hadn't backed away after his revelation last night. "Now…what do you have under that dress?" He reached behind her, pulling on the bow around her neck that was keeping the dress in place. As he did, he gently pulled it down over her breasts. "Oh…I see." Then he slid the dress down her stomach, past her bottom to her legs, exposing her completely bare body. He laid the silk dress on a chair. "Well, well…someone came prepared," he said, running his hand over her naked body. "Damn, you do come prepared," he hissed.

"Uh…mmm—Yes, I've been a little preoccupied," she stammered, her accent clipping her last word between forced breaths.

"I'll be right back." Jake ran down the hall, letting the towel drop. He returned with his erection sheathed in a condom. He led her to the couch, sitting and pulling her on top of him. "I love the idea of you riding me while I suck on these beautiful tits." His voice was roomy with licentious coarseness, so caught up in the visual of her straddling him. Damn if she didn't like "it" as much as him, and damn if he didn't love that about her, her unabashed desire of the flesh. He thought about the constant shift in her, lust driving her to open herself to him physically juxtaposed against the moments post intimacy of her retreating, seemingly stunned at times. What was that? Was she using him, just some guy to get off with? No, he knew the difference; there was something between them…something they both felt. It wasn't just him…was it?

Rakell straddled him, feeling his cock pushing up between her legs. He fisted his shaft angling his ass forward to the edge of the couch, then positioning her pelvis so that her hole lined up with his stiff erection. His large hands spread around her torso, bracing her body as he lowered her slowly onto him.

"Ahh, so big!" she yelped, her labia swollen from the vigorous sex they'd had over the last twenty-four hours. His cock bursting into her made her wince, but she craved the way he filled her up, how he relished her body as if he were present during every second of their interaction.

He steadied her, not letting her body drop down on him. "Easy, Sweets. Let me control it," he coaxed. "A little sore, huh?"

She nodded her head, her eyes big, the fullness of him only halfway in her, a comingling between pain and pleasure. She ached to ride him wildly, bob up and down on his cock, to come shrieking as he split her apart.

Jake leaned in, kissing her cheek. Still holding her hips tight, not letting her push down on him, he continued to kiss down her neck until he reached her breasts, then he sucked her nipples into his mouth, one then the other.

Rakell's head reared back. "Let me go...I don't care if it hurts. You feel so good...please." She cupped her breasts, arching them away from him. Dipping her head, she took a bite of the thick pectoral muscle on his chest. "Give it to me," she hissed, then pinched one of his erect nipples.

She heard his growl, feeling his hands reflexively tighten on her hips. "Damn it. Don't make me crazy, I'm trying to save you so I can have you all weekend, and you're trying to end us both." His voice was raised, almost lecturing.

Rakell shifted her hips, fighting against the hold he had on her. "Please, let me." She shifted her knees back so that her pussy dropped down on his hard shaft farther. "Oh, God! God!" she cried out.

"My wanton girl, can't get enough, can you?" As though to answer his question, her mouth made an O-shape as her neck crested back and her hips flexed on his cock. He let her slide down, loving the heat inside her as his cock edged its way farther up. He knew this was going to hurt, this angle with her swollen insides. She was going to regret her urgency.

He tried to slow her so they could ease into this, but her hips started to rock on his groin hungrily, sending his cock deeper and deeper, each small movement eliciting a whimper from her, followed by her begging, "Don't stop."

Jake shook his head. "Damn, those hips and that greedy little pussy. It's too much…" He followed with an acute grunt, letting her know he had given in. His hands palmed her ass, working with her hips to accelerate her motion.

Rakell's whimpers ignited into screams as nasty phrases flew out of her mouth, surrounding his ears, making containment of his own greed inconceivable. Madly, his hands manipulated her large breasts, his teeth and tongue unruly as they feasted on her flesh, driving her even more wild, increasing the ferocity of her thrusts.

"Fuck…fuck me…fuck me…I'm coming!" Her body convulsed as the spike of gratifying pain shot from her core, ripping through her spine. "Fucking come!" she demanded, her hands grabbing his shoulders.

Pushing his groin up, rocking back into her, Jake let himself go, let the gripping need for release swell, then spew from him, yelling, "Fucking crazy wonderful!" as his body trembled before shifting pace. His eyes shut, feeling his cock deflate. He pulled her into him, her head on his shoulder. "Sweets," he said, his hands gently rubbing her still spine as she breathed against him, "are you trying to kill us both?"

"We can die happy," she whispered. "I'm wondering how many calories we just burned." She laughed, knowing his face was twisting into a wry grin.

Rakell used a washcloth to wipe away the sweat between her breasts before re-dressing, adding panties and a white denim jacket to her orange halter dress and heels. She combed her hair, reapplied lipstick in the hallway bathroom, and waited for him in the living room. When Jake walked out in crisp, midnight-blue jeans, dressy black cowboy boots, a black button-up shirt with gray pinstripes, and his hair slicked back, a lone loop lying on his forehead, she couldn't help but stare. She was continually struck by how beautiful he was, and God was she ever drawn to him. The little boy with his wide grin and mischievous eyes intertwining with the steely-eyed man with a knowing smile came together in a way that made her both like him and want to fuck him.

Walking from the Uber to the front door of Justine's, Jake reached down, sliding his hand over her hip, feeling the edge of her panties under the orange silk. "Darn," he hissed, "panties?"

Rakell pushed his hand away. "I *told* you, I'm pigging out here. Nothing's happening tonight except me lying on the couch rubbing my belly." She giggled, almost to herself. It was in her hands. She got to decide when she wanted sex, what she desired, not what the man who paid wanted. If someone paid for it, she did it; if they didn't, she didn't.

This is what it's like to have control of my own desires.

This is new territory.

Liberating.

Leaning into her ear, he whispered, "God, baby. I love when you talk dirty to me."

"Screw you," she replied, smiling from ear to ear.

"Yeah, like that," he laughed, pulling out a barstool before helping her climb onto it. He slid onto the stool next to her.

Chapter Thirty

This time, Jake knew Rakell hadn't left. He went out to the living room, saw the blanket on the couch, then found her in the kitchen drinking a glass of water.

"Hey, Sweets, it's only five. Come back to bed." He slid his arm around her shoulders, his fingers gently caressing her skin. He loved the lace tank top and lace boy shorts she slept in.

The way he drawled out "Sweets," the tenderness in his tone, made her pull in. The intimacy of it was so raw. When she considered that he probably called all the women he slept with that with that endearing drawl, something dark roiled in her. She didn't have the right to ask him, to demand anything from him, but the idea of him and other women made her chest constrict.

Jake felt her shift away. "Hey, Sweets—you okay?" He didn't address the fact that she had probably been on the couch most of the night. In his ten years of steady dating, he'd never come across a girl who didn't want to share his bed at night, especially a girl he was having sex with.

Looking up at him, she answered, "I'm fine, just not a great sleeper."

"It's all right," he said, half awake, pulling her in tighter. He'd never dated someone that required so much processing, so much thinking about what her actions or words meant. He wasn't sure if that was because he hadn't cared enough before, or if she was just that jumbled up inside. He was unclear if the mystery was her or his feelings for her, suspending him in a cautious state, eroding his usual cool confidence. The feel of her breasts against his lower chest made him clench his jaw in restraint. He just wanted her back in his arms.

Rakell loved the feeling of her head buried in his chest. She licked his warm skin, her mouth close to a hard nipple, so she licked her way there, then sucked it in, hearing him groan, which made her suck harder.

"Damn it, girl. I'm just out here to get you back in bed. What are you doing to me?" he hissed as her tongue licked its way to his other nipple, taking it into her mouth and sucking it hard.

"I want you, and somebody once told me I'm better with nonverbals," she said in between sucking and licking his nipple, then moving her mouth around his chest, gently nibbling.

Cupping his hands on either side of her head, Jake pulled her head back, looking intently in her eyes. "Let's go back in the bedroom. I'm going to make love to you, and you're going to let me this time. No dirty talk, okay?" he said, a slight smile on his otherwise serious face.

She protruded her bottom lip. "Okay, but that doesn't sound like much fun," she replied, feigning annoyance, disguising her internal pull back from the word "love" and thinking again, *Does he talk this way to everyone?*

He barked out a quick laugh, taking her hand as he headed toward the bedroom. "Trust me—you'll still have fun."

They stood by the bed as Jake removed his boxer briefs, letting his erection pop out. Rakell stared at it: his smooth cockhead, the ridge of it, his long thick shaft, and his large balls. She felt her own arousal seep in at the sight of his. Then his hands were on her, pulling the tank top up, his mouth lapping a nipple while he massaged one of her breasts. She reached up and pulled the tank top off while he attended to her heaving breasts. He moved up, bracing her mouth with his, kissing her firmly but sweetly, letting her know that she meant something to him.

Rakell pulled back from the intimacy of it, then grabbed the back of his head, jerking him in, madly kissing him, jabbing her tongue in his mouth, moaning. "Fuck me," she hissed.

Ending the kiss with a peck on her lips, Jake cupped her chin. "Rakell, no. Let me control the pace. Let's do this slow, make it last." His eyes narrowed, piercing her needy expression.

A part of her wanted to run out the door, get far away from this. Shit, what was he doing?

"Deep breath," he said, one hand cupping her chin. His eyes were on her while his hand trailed down her abdomen, finding its way under her thin panties, reaching the wetness between her legs. "Oh, I can't wait to be inside you," he said, pushing his middle finger into her slit. "You feel so good, love this sweet pussy." His voice was husky, but this time, she noticed it was laced with adoration or something like it. She sensed that he was trying to make this time different; a shiver ran up her spine.

Bending, Jake slid her panties off her legs, his finger still in her. Then he stood, sliding his finger out. She gasped. "Shh...shh," he said. "Climb on the bed." He reached for his phone, and soon, slow jazz music started filling the room, the volume low, infusing the atmosphere. He grabbed a condom as he climbed up onto the bed to join her. Rakell just watched him. She felt almost as if she wasn't there, like she was watching another couple.

Jake came up on her side, kissing her cheek, then her mouth, then down her neck to her breasts. Then his lips were on her stomach, his tongue dipping into her belly button, feeling her muscles contract. "Please, Jake," she begged, her feet moving on the bed. "Please, just stick it in." Irritated urgency dominated her tone. "Fuck, come on. Why are you fucking with me?" Her head popped up, looking down at him.

He trailed kisses up her inner thighs as he moved between her legs, nudging them open more, looking up, the corner of his mouth tilting in a knowing smile. "Shh, just relax into this. It doesn't always have to be fast and furious, Sweets," he coached, his fingers separating the folds between her legs, studying her, thinking about what he wanted to do next. *I'm going to imprint myself on her.* Kissing in a sucking manner, his lips teased the skin surrounding her sweet hole, delighting in the soft mewls streaming from her mouth, wishing he could record her and listen to it over and over.

She'll remember this, he determined. *My lips on her soft skin, my nose nuzzling the top of her mounds.* Looking up at her, he murmured, "What's my favorite thing to eat, sweetheart? What do I crave, what can I not get my fill of?"

Her brainstem was alarmed by the care in his gentle touch, his intent eyes... no, no, she hadn't signed up for this, she was just having fun, she didn't know what the hell to do with this kind of attention. *Disassociate, disassociate, do not give in to this.*

"Ugh, you piss me off," she huffed, her head dropping back on the pillow. "What? Chuy's queso? Is that your favorite thing?"

His hot breath brushed over her sex as he let out a bark of laughter, then he rooted his nose into her folds. "Guess again, sweetheart," he growled before flattening his tongue on her clit.

Her back arching, she said, "O-M-G, rib-eeeye," determined not to give into him. "Daaaaamn it." Her back arched as his tongue thrust into her pussy.

Three times he fucked that sweet wet hole with his tongue, somewhere between aroused and amused, before pulling out and resting his chin on the top of her mound. "Wrong again. You're a smartass little minx, aren't you?" he challenged before his fingers slipped into her. "My favorite thing to eat is sweet, creamy pussy. Vanilla drenched in honey with some kind of wild berry pussy. That's what I think about even more than my mom's chicken cordon blue." He made his voice purposely dark.

She flung her head up. "Stop. You just ranked my pussy, or pussies in general, against a dish your mom makes. Wow, way to yank down the heat a few notches," she giggled. "In the future, don't compare any pussy to your mom's chicken."

Shaking his head, *damn this girl*, he swatted the side of her hip. "Lay the fuck down and let me eat," he said before his tongue dove into her, not holding back, the whole time saying how much he relished her body, how he wanted her to lay back and enjoy, that he was here to please her.

God, he made her feel cherished and on fire all at once. He was too close to reaching into her, seeing more of her than what she could show. *No, Jake. No, please, I can't let you in. Please.*

"Damn it, Jake," she yelled, her back bowing. "Fuck, pound me!"

What the hell does this girl have against being cared for? Someone hurt her, that much was clear. And right then Jake knew he wanted to be the one that *protected* her.

"I hate this fucking slow shite, mate. Put on some AC/DC and fuck me."

His low chuckle reverberated against the sensitive flesh between her legs. "Shh, Sweets, just trust me on this."

"Mm…mm, please. I just want to get fucked," she whined between heavy breaths.

"And you will later. I promise to bend you over the table tonight and fuck you like mad, but right now, I'm going slow, feeling you feel me." His fingers went deeper as his head bent down, kissing her outer sex. His tongue softly licked her clit as his fingers found a slow rhythm, moving in and out of her pussy. Her hips pushed against his fingers, her moans rising above the music.

Rakell shut her eyes. Her body hijacked her brain, feeling the sensation of his slow, deliberate movements through her nervous system as if he was playing an instrument. She desperately needed him to move past this.

Jake kept the same methodic pace until he felt her inner walls contract, then his tongue and fingers sped up, creating more friction as she wailed, her hips starting to flex. He used his other hand to steady her hips, slow her movements, so he could continue as she climaxed.

The slow heat boiled through her body, her chest arching, her hips trying to buck against his hold, her hands clawing the sheets, lost in the sensation. "It's too much...I can't!" she screamed, looking down at him, overwhelmed by his energy flooding her body. Paralyzed by conflicting emotions—fight or flight and a deep need to be encapsulated by him—she gave up, letting her head drop to the pillow.

Jake brought her off again until the wailing turned into low whimpers. Only then did he stop. Sheathing himself, then moving on top of her, he braced himself on his elbows. Slowly, at the same pace as the saxophone in the background, he rocked his cock into her. "Give me those green eyes now, look at me," he whispered, seeing her eyes skewed away from him. "Right now, right here, I'm going to make love to you. Look the fuck into my eyes," he commanded.

Pinned to the moment by his verve, she did as he directed but was still internally fighting not to connect her heart to his eyes. His intensity wiped her memory, and in those moments, Marietta disappeared. Rakell was present, a girl who grew up on a ranch in Australia, just a girl falling for a boy, a marvelously sexy, funny, sweet boy who rides horses too. *Oh God, this can't be happening, not to me, I'm not that girl. That girl's gone.* Her nervous system overrode her internal panic, and she melted into all the sensory pleasure being heaped upon her.

He captured her moans with his mouth, deliberately sharing the taste of her core with her. "Taste how your body loves it, how good your juices taste. Taste it, Sweets," he growled into her mouth, his tone still demanding. He would make sure she knew *he* was the one that made her squirt her essence on his tongue. *Him.* Finally, he could feel the tension, the demand, seeping out from her, letting him love her this way, even if it was just for this moment.

Opening her mouth to him, sensually matching his slow deliberate kisses, Rakell was giving herself to him in a way she hadn't done with anyone before. She tried to block the scattered thoughts that made her feel vulnerable, too exposed. She needed to turn her mind off and let her body be the guide. It felt so good, so sweet.

Nothing had ever felt like this before—

No penetration.

No touch.

No kiss.

Nothing.

She went with the music, rocking her hips slowly, feeling him touch her deeply, gently bumping up against her womb. The way he rotated his hips, creating a circular friction on her pelvic bone, coaxing her body into a climax that seemed to pull from her chest at the same time it erupted from between her legs, submerging her consciousness under a blanket of emotion. She lost herself, wrapping her arms around him, kissing him, urging him in closer.

Her rising moans pulled Jake in. He rocked his cock a little faster, desperate to come with her. He moved back and forth with long strokes until he burst deep inside her, spurting with three hard jerks, releasing everything he had inside him. *Everything.*

He clamped his eyes shut. The power exchanged, the walls between them disintegrating, he felt their forming bond through his whole body. He wasn't sure he'd ever felt anything quite so intense before…no, he knew he hadn't. This, this level of connection, was a first for him.

He brushed his lips on her cheek, then against her ear, whispering, "Now that was making love. Did you have fun?" His tone was soft and sweet, but he couldn't resist the question.

"Mm…mm," Rakell murmured, her fingers dancing on his upper biceps, feeling the strength in them, the sturdiness of him on her. She didn't want it to end, didn't want to be deprived of his lips, his touch, him inside her, or his force around her. She didn't want to give that up, yet her logical brain that had helped her survive years of living a double life waved the banner: DISASSOCIATE.

Jake remained on top of her, bracing himself until his penis slid out. Then he moved to her side, still kissing her face, listening to her murmurs. He wanted to say so much right then. He wanted to tell her he'd never done that with anyone else, never cared to express that much feeling through sex. But he didn't. While she felt real, solid, there was a precariousness about her that cautioned him. Reaching for his phone, Jake turned off the music. Both of them fell into a deep sleep.

Rakell woke up to him completely naked, placing a cup of coffee on the bedside table. "Here you go." He leaned down and kissed her forehead as her eyes fluttered between sleep and wake.

"What time is it?" she asked, her eyelids sliding back down.

"Almost nine. Do you want to go for a run then breakfast, or breakfast then fucking?"

"Let's skip all that other daily living shit and just fuck," she said, smiling with her eyes still shut.

"You really are bad," Jake laughed.

Her eyes fluttered. "So what's it going to be? If you're not up for it…?"

He set his coffee on the table and rolled her way, pinning her shoulders to the bed, then captured her shocked gasp with his mouth. Nothing about his kiss was gentle. Ferocity drove him, making sure she knew he wanted all of her. His mouth slid off hers, leaving her gasping as he bit lightly down her neck, her chest arching to his mouth as his teeth lightly scraped against her turgid nipple.

"Oh, God!" she wailed, her legs splaying open. She lifted her pelvis to his, trying to get friction against her clit.

Jake came down on her, pushing his rigid cock on her mons, his mouth leaving her nipple. "No, girl. You wanted to get fucked, right?" he spat out close to her ear. "Tell me…" he growled, his pelvis pushing hers into the bed. "Gonna bury this in you after you beg me to fuck you." Once again, her urgency, her boldness, the wanton nature she exuded took him over. "Ask for it," he commanded in a strangled voice.

"Fuck me," Rakell responded, a guttural demand.

He needed to hear his name, know that it was him she wanted, not just to get fucked. The thought kept entering his mind. Did she care who was doing the fucking? Did it matter that it was him, or was it just the act of getting off?

Rocking his hard cock against her pelvis, his thighs holding her in place as she squirmed beneath him, he commanded, "No...you need to say my name. Who do you want to fuck you right now. Who?"

"Oh my God, Jake... Jake...Jake, fucking fuck me!" she cried out. "Please," she added sweetly. His eyes caught her half smile. "Please."

"Get on all fours and hang on," Jake instructed. "You're a bad girl." He moved off her. "Now," he said, reaching for the bedside table.

God, his tone, his dominance made her even needier, more wet, achy. "Yes, sir, Mr. Skyler."

Jesus, this girl, he thought, ripping open the foil, sheathing himself. He kneeled behind her, his hands on either side of her hips, and slid his pulsing cock into her halfway, then more, then out almost to her opening, then back in. His strokes were jagged, harsh, so consumed by her insatiable desire. The feel of his balls hitting her outer lips tore at any sense of control he had. He thrust faster, harder, then reached under her pelvis with one hand, finding her hard swollen nub, pulling on it, rubbing it, as his cock sliced into her tissues. He drove it deeper, cramming himself into her as if the harder he pushed, the more permanent it would be. "Come, come," he urged, working her clit hard, jamming in and out of her soaking channel, her walls collapsing around his cock.

Her head swung back and forth as she screamed, "Fuck me! Yes...yes... harder!" Her hair whipped around her as she came. The whole scene made the pit in his balls boil up, ready to explode from the heat.

Now Jake wished he had put on AC/DC and was pounding her to some angry rock music. Next time, he told himself as his cock burst. He erupted deep inside of her, screaming, "Fuck, fuck! So, fucking good! Fucking love you!" His voice, his words spinning in the air around them as his cock came to a halt, undone, spent inside her.

Jake let his torso sag, bracing his weight on his hands. As her knees slid down, she collapsed to her belly. He pushed off with one hand, leaning onto his side. They were still, the only sound their weighted breaths, heavy between them. His throat constricted thinking about his words. Shit, he hadn't said *that* to a woman since he was twenty-one, and that had not turned out well, so he'd promised his mom and dad he'd only say it if he knew for sure.

Had he really just said "love"? She couldn't keep doing this, she thought, caught between a jolt in her heart and the cynical knowledge that some men would say that when they were in the throes of an orgasm. Hell, they would say anything, even "I want to marry you" or "You're all I've ever dreamed of." She'd heard men yell it passionately, then watched minutes later as they jumped up to hurriedly get dressed before rushing home to their families.

He rolled off the bed, discarding the condom in his bathroom, relieving himself, washing his face, brushing his teeth, buying time before he had to go back in there and face her. He wondered if she had heard him clearly. Shit, he shouldn't have said it. He had to move past it. That felt so disingenuous, but he had to. He cleared his throat, gearing himself up to portray a nonchalantness...not an easy tempo for him.

Rakell was lying on her side, facing away from him when Jake climbed back onto the bed. He sat against the headboard, sipping coffee. "Hey, you."

"Yeah, you?" she mumbled.

"Are you hungry?"

She turned, looking up at him. "I'm definitely getting there, but I need to shower."

"Of course," he said. "Me, too," he added, his eyebrows arching.

"Well, I'm going first. Single showers this morning." She smiled. "I can't take any more of this," she said, waving her hand between them. "I call a sex truce."

He laughed. "So who can't keep up with who now?"

She sat up, throwing her hands in the air. "I give up—you win."

Jake gave a wry smile, staring at her breasts. "If that's the case, you better cover those up, 'cause all I can think about is sucking them into my mouth."

"Ugh," she said, sliding off the bed, grabbing his robe, and throwing it on quickly. She felt his rakish stares on her as he loudly licked his lips.

"I want to do bad things to that body," he said in a throaty tone, followed by a hearty laugh.

"Stop. Stop!" she said, pointing at him.

"What? I'm just looking."

"You are eye-fucking me. Stop it," she demanded playfully,

grabbing her overnight bag before walking into the bathroom and shutting the door.

After showering, Rakell put on short denim shorts with slightly frayed edges and a flowy flower-printed thin cotton top with short sleeves, along with a pair of brown leather sandals. She quickly blew-dry her hair. Once it was mostly dry, she stacked it on top of her head in a messy bun. When she walked out to the living room, Jake was already showered and dressed. Petting Dolly, he looked up when he heard her enter. "See, Dolly? Daddy's got a beautiful girl," he murmured, standing. He moved forward and hugged her. "Hey, the place we're going for brunch, The Wayback, is kind of halfway between here and my parents' house. Would you be open to me inviting them?" he asked, his hand still lingering on her upper arm.

Rakell didn't have to answer; Jake could tell by the way her shoulders stiffened involuntarily. She swallowed thickly, her eyes popping wide, like he'd just told her aliens would be joining them.

"Up to you," he said, trying to gently back away from the request.

"Can it just be us? Not trying to be selfish, but I'm sharing you tonight, so can we just…"

"Yep, no problem—they're probably busy anyway. I just know how much you're going to like them, and vice-versa." He tried to sound casual, but there was an edge to his tone. He wasn't walking on solid ground, and his nervous system picked up on it, making him unsteady, overly cautious. He'd normally handle this with a woman he was seeing by calling her on it. His family was the center of his life, so any woman that avoided meeting them wouldn't fit in his world.

"I'm sure. I'd love to meet them someday," she said unconvincingly.

Jake cocked his head, a somber expression crossing his face. "Rakell, it's normal when a guy likes a girl to introduce her to his parents. Again, it doesn't mean we're signing some contract."

Rakell let out a breath. "I know, it's all…well, it's all great." Pressure felt like it was building behind her eyes. "I'm just easing back into the whole dating thing," she explained, wanting to move away from the topic.

"I guess I'm confused by—well, I thought you *hadn't* been dating…or is that just recently?" he asked, gently, thinking maybe she'd had a serious relationship a long time ago. That might explain some of her reactions, especially if it had ended badly. Maybe that's why she moved past it every time he ventured there. So odd; he'd literally spent God knows how many first, hell second, third and beyond dates listening to the details about the last dirtbag past girls had been with…which was always a fun conversation, especially when the previous dirtbag shared some of Jake's same qualities.

A puzzled expression crossed her face as she thought about how to summarize the last five years of her life. "I just don't really like looking backwards…but no, I haven't really had a long-term boyfriend. More like the opposite. I've been so focused on what I needed to get done for school when I was in London and now work that I haven't really had any kind of long-term relationship." She touched his upper arm, squeezing his bicep. "So just not in the know on how these things should go. Can I—"

Jake interrupted, quickly kissing her cheek and wrapping his hand around her upper arm. "Should I slow down?"

"Mmm…maybe?" she said, dropping her eyes from his, wondering if he was capable of that, if it was part of Jake's biological make-up. Obviously, this guy had always gotten what he wanted in life. He definitely wanted her. But what did that mean? Could she push him back so they could just have fun? Would he be okay with that?

He kissed her cheek again. "I'll try. Let's go—I'm starving," he said, sliding his hand down her arm, intertwining his fingers in hers.

The Wayback was the kind of place you willingly let hours slip away. It made her want to stay all day. Jake ordered the Wayback Breakfast: two eggs, thick-cut bacon, grits, and buttermilk biscuits. Rakell opted for the leek quiche. They drank Rose Gold Rosé while they walked around the countryish grounds. Eight cabins stood among blue bonnets and live oak trees blanketing the landscape. It had taken them only twenty minutes to get here, but it felt like they were in a different place, a different time.

Looping her arm in his, Rakell said, "Um, that breakfast. Don't you have to stay in shape when you play football?" She nudged him.

"Yep, but I got someone helping me work it off, so I reckon I can splurge," Jake chided, lightly pushing her. "You could stand a few more pounds yourself, so you should splurge too." His hand squeezed her bottom.

"What? Seriously, no one has ever told me that." Her head spun away. Her weight, and needing to control it, constantly occupied her thoughts. She knew that if she were ever going to move from catalogue modeling to the big time, it would mean losing more weight.

"Hey, I'm serious—you look great. Please don't get caught up in the whole 'skinnier is prettier' thing. It's not healthy. I hate what it does to women." His tone was almost admonishing.

Snapping her head back to look at him, Rakell shot back, "What the fuck? I don't need you telling me what my body should or shouldn't look like. I'm trying to..." She abruptly swallowed her next words, clenching her jaw, her eyes staring off.

Jake flexed his arm, pulling her closer. "Hey, hey...I'm not...I'm just saying—"

She cut him off, realizing she had overreacted yet again. "I know...it's just..."

Leaning down, he kissed her forehead. "Sorry," he whispered, thinking that having two sisters should have taught him that you never, ever talk about weight with a woman. Not to mention the array of models and actresses he'd dated that obsessed over their weight to the point that going out to dinner seemed like a chore.

Rakell pulled back on her anger; he didn't know her goals. "Trying to knock me out of competition, keep me to yourself?" She angled her hip into him as they walked, playfully knocking him off a step.

Jake smiled, flexing his arm, yanking her into him. Turning, he reached behind her neck, tilting her head up as he laid his mouth on hers.

She invited him in, and they stayed that way for a long moment. "Such a nice day," she said.

Jake pulled her hand up to his mouth, kissing the top of it, his eyes moving over her face. "I think the key is to start off on the right foot...in bed."

"Well, at least we got that part right."

"Damn, that was kinda harsh. Don't think that's the *only* part we got right," he said, opening the door to the café.

She laughed. "Didn't mean that the way it sounded."

"Perfect timing," the waiter said, putting their food down as they approached the table.

"Man, that is a lot of food." Jake's eyes took in his breakfast. "Gonna need to work this off later," he said, his eyes jumping up to Rakell.

"You don't have to eat it all," she replied, smiling.

As they ate, Jake told Rakell about how he'd met Jordan and Delilah. Well, the version of the story that didn't make him sound like a jerk.

He left off the fact that the first time he met Delilah was after Jordan had pulled him out of a bar, drunk, just as Jake was about to leave with two women. He'd always remember that big paw on his shoulder. "Boy, I've blocked for you before, saving your ass, and I'm about to do it again. Let's go," Jordan had said, pulling on Jake's arm, telling the girls he was sorry but that Jake was in no condition to be going home with them. Jake had protested a bit, but Jordan wasn't the kind of man you argued with. Even at twenty-two, Jordan was wiser and more grounded than most older men, with the fierceness and strength of youth.

The next morning, Jake had woken up on Jordan and Delilah's couch to them arguing in the kitchen. Delilah was saying Jake wasn't worth salt, just a stupid player with a football in his hand. Jordan assured her that if he could keep his act together, someone like Jake could go far. "He's just immature, cocky. But inside, he's really a good kid, *really* good. I just couldn't watch him get himself in trouble last night," Jordan had explained. At the time, Delilah had been in her second year of medical school, and Jordan was a senior at UT.

"So wait—I thought Jordan was an emergency room nurse at St. David's?" Rakell asked, confused when Jake explained that Jordan and Delilah broke up shortly after he was drafted by the Miami Dolphins. Jordan's stint with the NFL hadn't come up before. Rakell figured it was because that would have been too close to the truth Jake had been concealing. "I guess if Jordan and Dwayne played for the NFL, that would have...well, it would have been harder to keep up your charade..."

"No..." Jake put his hand up, then pointed to his mouth, finished chewing, and took a drink of water. "Okay, hey, I mean, I just wanted to be able to tell you without it coming out another way," he implored, looking at her.

"Yeah, makes sense..." she mumbled, shoving the bitterness to the back of her brain. "So, Jordan?" She shifted, thinking she needed to figure this out. They both were not who they said they were, and now his truth was out there, but hers...no way could she reveal it. She nodded for him to continue.

"He went to nursing school after he played for Miami. He was a first-round draft pick out of UT. He's a superstar...was even before he went to Miami, but he never let that get to his head. Well, maybe a little, but not like most guys would have. He played for Miami for five years, got hurt, then left the team. After that, he moved back to Austin to be with Delilah, who was finishing her medical residency around that time. He could have been a Hall-of-Famer, but he chose her instead. They've got a great love story." Jake smiled, remembering the twists and turns that finally brought them together.

"He seems happy." She almost added, *he chose 'the things that matter,'* thinking about Antone's and their first kiss. She would never again hear those lyrics without the sensory input of his lips manifesting on hers. There are certain things your nervous system will never un-feel, especially when the senses join forces, Jeska's and Guy's voices swirling in the air, the spicy smell emanating off Jake, his hands growing firmer on her hips as he tugged her close, the cool moistness of her own sweat covering her chest, the tingling in her groin as she advanced her mouth on his...all imprinted, forever captured and linked with that song.

"Um *Rae*-kale?" Jake whispered leaning forward. "You okay, Sweets?"

"Yes, I was just lost." She swallowed her next line, *lost in that song, our song.* "So it sounds like Jordan has been kind of like a big brother to you," Rakell said, taking a sip of the rosé.

"He's definitely been there for me every step of the way. Sometimes he's had to shake me a little to help me get my head on straight, and that would piss me off, but I'm grateful he did. Plus, I got

Jasmine, their baby girl, out of the deal. I'm her godfather," he said, visibly puffing out this chest. "So definitely the winner in this relationship."

A tenderness she'd heard when he had talked about his grandma the evening he'd almost lost Neo took over his voice when he talked about Jordan and his family.

She smiled, looking at him, wishing she could introduce him to Matt and his family. They were the closest thing she had to a family of her own. She still talked to her mom in Australia maybe once every few months, but there would always be a wall of anguish between them. It had become a chore to call her mom. The bitterness her mother felt toward Rakell seeped into her tone when they talked, especially when her mom drank (now seemingly on the daily). When Jake asked again about her parents, she brushed aside the questions, saying it was hard to talk about them because they were so far away and there was such a big time difference.

As they climbed back in the truck, Jake explained that he was responsible for bringing the wine for the dinner party at Jordan's house that evening. Rakell probed Jake to find out what people would be wearing and how big the party would be. She learned that Dwayne would be there with the girl he had been seeing, and three other couples—all players from UT and their wives. "Did you bring something for tonight, or do we need to stop by your place to pick stuff up?" Jake asked, driving toward downtown.

"Yes, I need to go home. But should I grab my bag from your house first, then meet you back there or…?"

"Let's just go by your place and grab stuff for tonight," he pushed, not wanting to be away from her.

"Jake, are you going to let me breathe?" she chided.

"All right, I'll drop you off and pick you up later." His face was impassive. "Catch up on that breathing shit, cause you're mine tonight and tomorrow, got it?"

"Do I have a choice?" Her tone was amused.

Grinning, he said, "No, not really. The weather is supposed to be beautiful, just like today, and there are some beautiful wineries around Austin. I already arranged for a car to drive us to a couple of them; we can start with Fall Creek. They have some pretty nice wines. So grab stuff for tomorrow, too." They pulled up in his driveway. Dolly met them at the door, anxious to see Jake. "Down, girl. Jeepers," he said, walking to the back door.

Rakell grabbed her overnight bag, wondering how this was happening so fast. She felt sucked into something she only imagined for her future life but couldn't have right now, not knowing when or how to put the brakes on without ruining everything. Like the feeling of ending a great vacation, one that invigorated your spirit, but having to return immediately to work. A reality that was hard to face.

Chapter Thirty-One

Rakell took a quick nap before getting ready. Feeling refreshed after resting in her own apartment, she chose a black leather skirt with an off-the-shoulder blue and black striped silk blouse, simple silver hoops, and black open-toed medium-heeled booties. She opted to wear her hair straight. Jake texted that he was on his way, so she grabbed a small black purse, transferring a few of the contents of her everyday purse into it. She felt anxious about tonight, about meeting Delilah and the other wives as Jake's date. She wondered what he'd said about her to them.

Matt! She had to tell him about Jake, who he was. Shoot, Matt only knew him as the hot guy from the gym. Would it matter to Matt if they kept their affair low-key, and how could that happen with Jake? He didn't seem capable of low-key.

Matt didn't answer when she called, so she left him a message. "Hey, want to talk to you when you get a chance. Turns out the guy at the gym is a football player. I really like him. Ugh, bad timing. I know Jonathon's in town, so if you guys are busy, we can talk tomorrow night. Love you."

She faded off at the end, her gut knotted up, thinking about Matt. But she'd spent so many nights alone while he and Jonathon became closer and closer, and of course she wanted that for him, but what about her?

She texted Jake and asked if he could pick her up in the parking garage below the complex, giving him the code. George was working the front desk today, and she didn't want him to see her leaving with the overnight bag. He knew her and Matt well enough to ask questions, and although she was pretty sure George had figured things out, she didn't want to be obvious.

He was waiting for her in the parking spot by the elevators when she walked out with her bag. He jumped out of the truck to open her side.

She was stunned by how handsome Jake looked in his black tight jeans, black boots, and silver and cobalt blue button-up dress shirt. God, this guy was all-consuming, she thought, looking at him. She could understand how he got anything he wanted in life, especially when it came to women. She was getting the distinct feeling he was *not* used to being told no, not unlike so many of the men who she'd been an escort for over the years. In Jake's case, it was due to his kind, charismatic personality, those eyes, and that smile. A slight shift in his features and his look could go from dark and edgy to little boy—then mix in his sexual prowess, and let's not forget he's an NFL player, and that Americans revered sports like no other. This guy had his way with women because of who he was, as opposed to so many of the men she'd worked for who got their way because of money and power.

His smile grew wider as she approached him. "Damn, girl. Trying to do me in? Black leather!" He whistled, and she rolled her eyes, yet internally soaking it up. She'd never had a guy out-and-out whistle at her. He grabbed her bag and threw it behind the seats, then helped her in the truck, eyeing her up and down before leaning in and kissing her deeply.

Pulling out of the parking lot, he said, "Gonna stop by the house quick, 'cause I forgot the wine."

When they pulled into his driveway, he shoved the gearshift into park and left the engine running. Reaching into the back, he grabbed her bag. "I'll drop this off, so you can't change your mind," he joked, knowing there was an air of truth to his statement.

"Jake...I'll help..."

"No ma'am. Keep your ass in that seat, 'cause I wanna get there early and damn that skirt is distracting. Not sure I can keep my hands to myself." He nodded at her knowing smirk. "You know exactly what you're doing," he barked, jumping out of the truck.

They arrived at Jordan and Delilah's house fifteen minutes early because Jake wanted to have some time with Jasmine before the babysitter, who lived next door, took her for the evening. Jake introduced Rakell to Delilah, who gave her a hug, and said hi to Jordan, who was just finishing setting the table. Jasmine ran to Jake, yelling, "Unc J! Unc J!" He picked her up in his arms, kissing her cheek, saying how much he missed her, loved her, that she was his girl. Watching them together pulled at Rakell so much that she had to look away from them; it made her want to cry, though she didn't understand why.

"Delilah, it smells so good," Rakell said, walking into the kitchen. "Can I help?"

"Yes," Delilah said, smiling. "You can open some of the wine you guys brought and pour us both a big glass. I'm going to need it tonight with six cocky football players talking shit in my house," she laughed.

"I'm not sure what to expect," Rakell said softly.

"Imagine a room full of men who've been told how great they are their whole lives, add in alcohol, and, well…" She talked while stirring something on the stove that smelled delicious.

Rakell opened the bottle of white wine. "Well then, let's get a head start."

"That's what I'm talking about, girl," Delilah said, taking the glass of white Rakell handed her. "You'll be fine. I already heard you don't take Jake's shit or feed into his ego. I love it. He's a great guy, but these superstars are used to getting everything they want."

"Yep. I didn't really think about that, but I can see it," Rakell replied, trying to hide her confusion. Superstar? He hadn't made it seem like that to her.

Rakell immediately liked Delilah. She was the kind of person that drew you in. Not only was she attractive and smart, but she also owned her saucy sassiness, making no apologies for the slight gruffness that came with it. Her laugh could open up the coldest person, Rakell thought, as they continued to talk in the kitchen before the other guests arrived. She could picture Delilah setting Jake—hell, setting *anyone*—straight.

Before the other guests arrived, Rakell ran to the bathroom. When she reached into her purse to reapply her lipstick, she saw that Matt had texted her earlier.

Matt: *Got your message. Let's chat tomorrow. What's his name?*…**Send**

She texted back before slipping the phone back in her purse.

Rakell: *Jake Skyler…* **Send**

Dwayne showed up as she was coming out of the bathroom. She recognized the girl he was with from the karaoke bar. Rakell saw Dwayne introduce Delilah to the petite, attractive brunette wearing a short red dress and heels.

"Well, well. He finally wore you down." Dwayne smiled, looking at Rakell. "Rakell, this is Jenn," he said, squeezing her hand. Rakell and she shook hands. Looking at Jenn, she wondered if this was Dwayne's Austin off-season girl. She was starting to put the pieces together of these two, who played for Sacramento—a team she'd never heard of— but returned to Austin for off-season. Oh yeah, they played ball in Sacramento, but they played the field in Austin. The picture started to take hold in her brain. Shit, was Jake thinking she was his off-season girl? Was that what these two did—return to Austin and hook up with a different girl during off-season, then left? She wasn't sure how long an American football off-season lasted, but maybe he was planning on ending it with her as soon as he was done in Austin. So once again, was she some man's *trinket* until he was ready to move on to the next trinket? For free? She shook away the thought.

Other guests began arriving. Rakell met three other guys that Jake and Jordan knew from UT along with their wives. Two of the couples had kids and were talking about how happy they were to be away for the evening. Jake and Jordan returned after taking Jasmine next door.

Jake gave hugs all around, then looked at Rakell and asked, "Did you guys meet my girlfriend?"

Rakell's head swiveled in Jake's direction. *What the hell?*

One of the guys, Chris, looked at Rakell, smiled, and said, "Yep, but we heard 'friend,' so you might be jumping the gun, buddy." He laughed, gently hitting Jake on the arm.

She had indeed introduced herself as Jake's friend before Jake and Jordan returned.

Jake looked uneasy but laughed. "Guess I gotta work on that." His eyes shifted back to Rakell, the cords in his neck flexed as if he was trying to pull back from whatever he really wanted to say. Rakell could feel her face heat up, flushing. It seemed like the room grew quiet, all eyes on her. She saw Delilah's sharp brown eyes shift to Jordan, who shrugged. "Rakell, can you follow me? I need a little help," Delilah said across the living room, shifting toward the kitchen.

"Of course." She followed Delilah, grateful for the invitation.

When they turned past the wall from the living room to the kitchen, Delilah put her arm around Rakell. "Girl, you know these guys are going to give you shit all night because they're poking at Jake, right?"

Rakell nodded her head. She knew then that Delilah was someone she could trust. "I know. I just…the whole girlfriend thing, I mean…"

"Jake's never worked this hard," she said, her arm dropping off Rakell and grabbing a pot. "Can you hold the bowl?" Rakell picked up a large ceramic bowl, holding it as Delilah scooped stew into it.

"I need to talk to Jake. I thought we were just having fun. Not sure I am ready for the whole girlfriend thing. I just found out a couple days ago that he's a football player. I thought he was just a normal guy, a gym rat sort of guy," she explained.

Delilah finished scooping the stew into the large bowl, put the pot down, and looked at Rakell, her eyes intent, serious. "He's a big deal in the football world, but a good guy. I know he has a reputation, but I've known him for a long time, and I can vouch for his character. He got caught up in the whole NFL player bullshit, like all of them. Even Jordan did for a while." Delilah scrunched up her face, shaking her head quickly. "But he wouldn't be my daughter's godfather if he weren't top-notch. With that said, you won't meet anyone quite as intense. To be loved by Jake is to be loved by a force of nature." A wide grin spread across her face as she pulled some corn biscuits from the oven.

"Yes, he is intense." Rakell nodded, stilling the features of her face, trying to hide her reaction to the word *love*. Then she forced a smile. "Direct me. What's next?" she asked. Rakell took the bowl Delilah gave her to the table, then she came back, grabbing the rolls and a big bowl of rice to set on the table. Walking slowly back into the kitchen, she tried to gather her thoughts. "Delilah, when you said he's a big deal…I mean, how big?"

Delilah turned around. "You really don't know, do you?"

Rakell shook her head, mild queasiness churning inside her. "I just thought…"

"You know Randall Adams, Drew Brees, Tom Brady? Well, Jake's the next level below. If he keeps going like he has been the last couple of years, he'll be one of them. He's just trying to stay out of the limelight. The media hasn't really been his friend, so I think he's aiming for low-key. I'm pretty sure he thought being in a long-term relationship with that actress would help his case, but that strategy backfired."

Rakell's agitation grew listening to Delilah, as if her neurons were battling each other. She let out an audible sigh.

Delilah pulled a large pork roast from the oven. Rakell reached to help her as they set it on the counter. Delilah looked at her sternly. "If Jake's pushing things too fast, stand your ground. He'll get it. He may not like it, but he'll get it. Most women cave to him. I think you get why." A low, guttural laugh left her mouth as she turned to grab a platter.

A forced, uneasy laugh jumped from Rakell's mouth. "Yep, I get it. I think I need more wine," she said, reaching for the bottle.

"I'm feeling you," Delilah concurred, extending her glass. "Their world…it's a different world. Dwayne's a good guy, but he's made it clear nobody is long-term in his head; he's having fun. I told him that's fine as long as the women know that. But I believe Jake when he says that he wants a normal girl, an Austin girl he can…okay, damn, I'm talking too much."

"Oh, yes, a normal…girl," she said, taking a quick sip of her wine, the weight of Delilah's words piling on her chest like heavy bricks… lies, her lies, his lies, the whole fucking lie.

"You two having a party in here without us?" Jake said, walking into the kitchen, Jordan behind him. Jake moved into Rakell's space, his eyes landing on her lips. "God, I love that mouth," he whispered, lowering his lips to hers and quickly pecking.

Her mouth opened like she was going to say something, but she stepped back. "Shh," she teased, covering her uneasiness.

Jordan narrowed his eyes on Jake. "Okay, Jake. Enough with the heat." Then he turned to Delilah. "What can we do?"

"Take the roast to the table," Delilah directed, "and salad." She nodded toward the refrigerator.

"We need more plantains. Jake can't keep his paws off the avocado dip and plantains," Jordan said, opening the refrigerator and pulling out a large bowl of salad. "Jake, grab the roast."

"Can't help it. They're so good." Jake's eyes were on Rakell. She looked preoccupied. He moved close to her, leaning in, kissing her mouth gently.

She looked at him, wondering how the hell she was going to deal with this and not make a mess of it.

"Get drink refills. We're five minutes from sitting down," Delilah called toward the living room, and Rakell picked up two bottles of wine, bringing them to the table.

A bubbling boisterousness pervaded the atmosphere around the table. Jake made sure Rakell sat next to him, sensing that she might be feeling overwhelmed. He was well aware that this crew could do that to anyone. He loved that she and Delilah seemed to hit it off, and she was engaging with the other guys' wives. He could tell Rakell knew her way around a party socially and didn't have a problem engaging with people she didn't know.

"So, Rakell, you said you worked at Waterman Consulting, right?" Tiffany, the wife of one of Jake's UT buddies, asked.

Rakell's head turned toward her. "Yes, but I mostly act as an interpreter because I don't…"

"Oh, I was just asking because I'm pretty sure I went to high school with one of the Watermans…I think she was a couple grades older than me. Isn't it the Watermans who own that famous ranch between Houston and San Antonio?"

Grabbing her wine, Rakell took a swig. "Not sure. I don't know much about the family; I just work there. I don't…"

"No biggieee," she said with a twangy east Texas drawl. "I was just wondering because they are one of the Texas elite families. *Texas Monthly* does a story on them whenever they put up a flippin' Christmas tree or buy a new dog or another plane. Basically, they're in the news a lot…so you would probably know…"

"Ah, um, I just, well, I'm not in a very high position." The words sputtering from her mouth sounded to her own ears like those of a lying fool. Her face flushed.

Tiffany tilted her head. "Honestly, it's not a big deal at all. I was just pointing out a common thread," she said, her eyes slanting at her husband.

Jake cleared his throat. Leaning toward Rakell, he whispered, "Hey you, you okay?"

"Yes, sorry, just hard to describe what I do." *Jesus, Rakell, that sounded ambiguous*, she thought to herself. "Well, because I'm not really part of the business side…I just…"

She felt Jake's hand touch her leg before gently cupping her knee under the table. "You're fine. No one is judging your profession, so breathe. You don't have to impress anyone."

"Hey, pretty boy!? Pass the rolls!" Dwayne shouted from across the table. Jake shot him a side-eyed look before he obliged.

Rakell registered the look, too. The scurry of eyes shifting around the table, with each passing minute, increased her anxiety, making it hard to eat, even though the food was amazing. "So this 'pretty boy' thing sounds like it has stuck." Clearing her throat, she struck an indifferent tone. "What's the story there?" Her voice stayed steady, feeling all the eyes find her across the table. She swallowed the anxiety scratching its way into her vocal cords.

"It's a stupid thing," Jake responded, thinking about the other women he dated and how they got a kick out of it. Many of them were seeking media attention themselves and made sure they had pictures of Jake with them on social media within days of a first date. He could tell Rakell was not liking this at all.

"So how did you get that nickname?" she asked, her voice walking a tightrope, clearly unsteady, loud enough for some of the other people at the table to hear. Her question prompted snickers from a few of the guys.

Jake took a big bite of pork, purposely not answering.

Her anxiety twisted into frustration. Rakell let her fork drop to the table beside her plate. Turning her head from Jake, she redirected the question to Dwayne. "Dwayne, how did Jake get his nickname?"

The activity at the table stopped—no clanking of utensils on plates, mouths stilled mid-chew—as eyes shifted from Dwayne, to her, and then to Jake.

Out of character, Dwayne looked like a deer caught in headlights.

Jordan rearranged the features of his face, clearly somber, as he looked toward Rakell. For a moment, his gaze jumped to Jake, then he shifted back to her. "Jake made some questionable choices many years ago, so the media coined that name, and it stuck. It's long behind him, but as good friends will do"—he looked around the table—"these guys won't let him live it down."

Jake looked at Jordan, nodding and mouthing, *Thank you*. In diplomatic Jordan fashion, he'd skimmed the top of Jake's transgressions.

Let it die, Jake thought, hoping Jordan's explanation was enough to squelch further curiosity. But if she looked him up, all of his shit would be in her face. Damn it! When you're drafted, they should make your twenty-one-year-old self look into a crystal ball so you won't fuck your thirty-year-old self up.

Twisting internally, Rakell picked up her fork, begging herself to act, to do as she'd done hundreds of times as Marietta: smile graciously, make small talk, look at her client adoringly. Even if their buddies just laid it out on the table that you're with a *tombeur*. So what if you're *not* getting paid, but you've still managed to end up on the arm of a wolf? She moved her food around on the plate before reaching for another swig of wine. *Why the hell does it matter? You're in this for sex, and he's great. Stop, just enjoy!*

Jake gently nudged her. "Hey you..."

She smiled, that automatic phony upturn of her lips that she'd trained herself to do, her doe eyes looking up at him. "Great meal," she whispered between closed teeth.

Jake visibly winced. *Damn it, Jordan's explanation didn't assuage her.* He could tell she was still hanging on to it.

The conversation moved on to kids and daycare. Delilah and another wife worked full-time, so they talked about the juggling act of motherhood with professional life. Then the conversation moved to the UT football team. "Hey, Jake. I heard Coach Mark's following you to Sacramento. Is that right?" Chris, one of Jake's UT buddies, asked.

"Yep, so stoked about having him. He'll be our offensive line assistant coach. It'll kinda be fun having him yelling at me again," Jake laughed, and a couple of the other guys joined in.

"I think you guys have a shot this year. You and Dwayne were on fire last year. Getting to the playoffs as a new team is a big deal," Chris commented.

"Dwayne was on fire for sure. He caught anything I threw, and there were some shit throws in there." Jake smiled, looking at Dwayne.

"Sure were," Dwayne laughed, grabbing the bottle of wine, filling his and his girlfriend's glasses. "But let's be real, brother—you're starting to heat up, and the media's all over it. They can't get enough of you. Meanwhile, I'm sitting here like, 'Hey, pay attention to me'," he said with a loud bark of laughter as he gently pounded his chest.

"Yeah, right," Jake shot back. "Give me a break. They love you. Especially that little hip roll you do after a touchdown."

"You'll have to show me that," Dwayne's girl, Jenn, said in an overly sultry voice.

"Damn, we have to go. Check please," Dwayne chortled.

The whole table laughed. Jake smiled at Jenn, thinking about what Dwayne had told him at the gym. Usually, he'd be intrigued by their arrangement, but this girl next to him had snagged his heart, and he was focused on knowing her.

Delilah stood, starting to clear plates, but Jordan made her sit, motioning for all the guys to stand and help. They did.

Dwayne stood, grabbing a few plates. "We are not letting you clean up, too. Not after that amazing meal." The guys cleaned up, and the women moved to the living room.

Rakell answered a few more questions about what she did and how she and Jake had met at the gym. She had gained her footing with her answers and story until Jenn asked, "So why did you move to Austin from London?"

The heat crept up her chest. When she opened her mouth to answer, nothing came out. Rakell cleared her throat, but before she could even get a mutter out, Delilah put her hand up in Rakell's direction. "Do not answer that. We all get following somebody to a new place only to find it's not going to work."

Jenn jumped in. "So true. That's why *I'm* in Austin. I moved from Boulder, but now I'm in love with this city. So I guess I'm stuck with that hunk in this hot city." Her eyes scooted toward the kitchen as she laughed.

Rakell nodded, her heart slowing as she forced the edges of her mouth into a soft smile. Why had she stalled like that? Why hadn't she just said, "Work, for work, they recruited me because I speak four languages"? This was why escorts didn't date; the complexity of keeping up with the lies was overwhelming.

As they finished up cleaning in the kitchen, Jake tugged on the edge of Dwayne's sleeve. "Hey, Dwayne, about our conversation at the gym...I..." It had crossed Jake's mind so many times and he wanted Dwayne to know he got it, that he understood.

Dwayne started shaking his head. "Damn it, I knew it was eaten' at you. Stop. I got some shit off my chest. We don't have to talk everything out. I'm not looking for goddamn roses from your ass...just wanted to vent. So a little word of advice, quit lookin' at me all longingly. It's fucking weird."

Jake jerked his chin to the side, scowling, his lips pursed in question. "What the hell? I wanted to say sorry that I didn't think about your perspective, not make out with your ass."

"Sorry for what? You'd be apologizing for history. Dude, stop. Let people go off. I was just blowing off steam at the gym, needed to rage a little. You don't have to solve everything, and you lookin' at me with those blue sparkly puppy dog eyes is not going to help you tonight. You finally snagged the girl, yeah *that* girl, and if you keep this up, she's gonna figure out it's *me*...it's been me all along...hasn't it?" Dwayne stepped away from Jake, his lips curling. "Well I got news for you...I'm not into the emotionally labile type. Nope. I prefer my partners to have thicker skin."

"Fuck you," Jake snapped, following Dwayne out of the kitchen.

Dwayne snickered. "Stop, if you don't want folks to think we got something going on."

When Dwayne and Jake joined the group in the living room, Chris suggested they get some pictures, since it seemed like this only happened once a year. They took some of just the guys, then Dwayne said, "Rakell, go over and sit by Jake, preferably on his lap, so I can get a picture of you two."

A few eyes moved to her, but she just sat, her body stiffening.

"That would be great," Jake said, looking at Rakell. "Sweets, come over here." He stood, sensing her reservation now that everyone seemed to be looking at them, and added, "Or I'll come over there." He started walking toward her.

Rakell abruptly stood, her hand out, like she was stopping Jake. "No, no. I don't want to be in any pictures. No, not having something posted. I don't do social media, and I don't want a picture as your girlfriend...I don't..." She sounded flustered and on the edge of tears.

Shit, Jake thought, *what just happened?* He slowly drew in a deep breath as he approached her. A fog of disquiet began to settle in the room. His brain scratched around for something to say to move the group's attention away from her.

"I don't blame you for not wanting to be pictured with that mug," Dwayne said, jumping in and trying to lighten the situation. "Hey— Jordan, Delilah, Chris, Amy..." He started directing another picture, moving past the tenseness in the room.

Thank God for Dwayne—sometimes. Jake's eyes narrowed, his body tensing as he struggled to make sense of her reaction.

He looked at Rakell, confusion twisting his face. "Okay

then…so…" He wracked his brain for something to say besides what was right there, the words sitting on his vocal cords, restless to jump out with, "What the fuck was that about?" but he was determined not to make a scene and ruin the night. It wasn't his style.

Summoning his father's mild demeanor, he softened his expression. "Guess I need a better stylist," he said, winking at her, trying to squelch the awkwardness that she'd flung into the room. Walking toward her slowly, like he would a spooked horse, he closed in on her. Her face flushed pink, turning red, as he approached. Putting his hand on her shoulder, he whispered, "Hey, you? You okay?"

She took a quick breath. "I don't want my picture taken with anybody…" she spat out.

Any semblance of how his dad would proceed dissipated as it hit him. *She's fucking lying. There's someone else, and she doesn't want him to see her with me. Fuck!*

Gritting his teeth, he made a deep sound in his throat and shot out, "Damn it! What the fuck is going on? Worried about someone seeing us, someone that I should know about?"

The muscle on the side of his jaw ticked, his eyelids lowering as he cocked his head slightly, watching her chest rise and fall quickly. Stretching his arm forward, he grabbed her wrist, pulling her around the corner into the hallway.

"Jake. Please."

"Tell me now, 'cause I won't be humiliated in front of the fucking world again."

She backed up against the wall, jolted by his intense anger. *The world, huh?*

He stepped forward, a leg on either side of her, willing himself to slow his breathing. His head dropped, bringing his forehead to hers. "I'm already insane about you…but I can't go through that again." He snapped in a gruff whisper so his voice wouldn't travel into the living room.

Squeezing her eyes shut, she insisted, "Please. I just don't do social media, and once a picture's been taken, there's no guarantee it won't end up there." She hoped it made sense to him.

His hot breath smothering her, his eyes boring into her skull, he said, "Fine, fucking fine…don't take a picture with me." He popped his head back, his eyes unceasing, one hand going to the wall next to her head. "Just don't make a fool out of me…that's something I can't let go of." Then he pushed back, spun around, and walked past the laughter filling the living room. *Damn it.* He had to get a drink, regain some composure before engaging. He waved Dwayne off, pointing to the kitchen, motioning he was getting another drink.

She bent forward, sucking in a long breath, slowly letting it go. Then she walked into the bathroom. Looking at herself in the mirror, she thought, *How can I do this?* She knew she needed to smooth this over with Jake, to say…what? She wasn't sure.

When Dwayne saw her emerge from the hallway, he raised his eyebrows, signaling her, discreetly pointing to the kitchen. She moved past the large dining room table, noticing Jake's black cowboy boots, heels dug into the floor, toes up, as he leaned onto an elbow against the kitchen island. He didn't look up from the large glass of red wine he held when she entered.

How do I do this? she wondered. *The same way you have the few times Matt has been upset with you.* That happened when Matt thought she had put herself in a precarious situation with a client or she refused to take an expensive gift Matt wanted to give her. It occurred to her, as she moved around the island, standing opposite Jake's large frame, that Jake would be easier to melt than Matt.

He huffed, hearing her. What the hell was he supposed to say— *Damn it already, what the hell is up with you? The mixed messages, the facts that don't add up, what the hell? I wanna know what the hell's going on inside that beautiful brain. Who the fuck hurt you? 'Cause I'd like to twist off his goddamn head.*

With her hands on the counter behind her, she arched her torso forward, making sure her chest was protruding toward him, her wide, open eyes entreating him. He remained fixated on the red liquid in his glass, tension emanating throughout his musculature.

"Jake, I didn't intend to put you off, and I, well I'm not trying to humiliate you or…I just don't do the social media thing, mate." She intentionally pushed her Australian accent into her words, making it bloom within her voice.

Finally, he straightened up, cocking his head as he took in her ample cleavage and the way that tooth scraped across her lip. "Not fair. You know that, right? This isn't the way adults talk through things," he muttered.

"Ooooh…sorry sir, didn't realize the old man has a preferred way of making up. I know my preferred way, and it's quite adult," she cooed, desperate to smooth over the tension.

He stood, taking her in while trying to process, feeling unsettled by how she could ricochet from one emotion to another. Despite feeling disoriented by the events of the night, her sultry tone had his cock in a chokehold, making it impossible to ignore. *Your weakness for this woman has no limits.*

She could feel the heat radiating from his torso. Her big eyes peered upward to take in his face. *Jake, I'm so confused, my life is not what you think it is. You are more than I thought, and I am more than you know. Matt, I owe Matt, I don't know how to do this, Jake, and do you truly care about me, or am I your off-season Austin girl? But what right do I have to ask anything of you?*

Watching him fight back something, the features in his face shifting, she could visibly see the muscles in his shoulders relax.

He put the glass down, his eyes hooded. *What the hell, Jake, you just going to cave again, or get to what's driving her, why she's bouncing all over the place?* He had an Achilles heel when it came to women, but with her, his whole person was an unprotected target; he couldn't seem to stop her from penetrating him. Shifting his legs, he said, "I'll tell you what, I'll let you get away with it this once. Mostly 'cause I like the way 'sir' sounds rollin' out of that gorgeous mouth of yours. It's filled with all kinds of promises that I'm pretty sure you're good for, darlin'." He matched her cheesy, exaggerated accent with the one that came so easily to him.

"So tell me. What are you promising, darlin'?" He laid it on thick.

Two catwalk-like steps and she was inches from his torso. "Well, sir, Mr. Skyler, we can start with a pash, then I'll treat you to a gobby," she said, her fingers running up and down his biceps, "then we'll have a naughty." Her eyebrows popped up as "naughty" sauntered off her lips.

"Not even sure what all that is, but damn if you don't know how to make my body respond," he muttered in a low voice, almost to himself, before sucking in a quick breath at the feel of her hand cupping him. He heard footsteps in the dining room and swiftly removed her hand, still holding it. He lowered his chin, kissing the top of her head. "Truthfully, it's probably sound advice to stay off social media, but for us players, if we do it right, it can help with endorsements. I wasn't going to post anything about us. Promise…" When he settled himself, he could acknowledge that it was kind of refreshing to be with someone who wasn't chasing the spotlight. But her reaction seemed to be more than just an aversion to social media, and it left a heavy, churning sensation in his gut. He made a mental note to search for her name on social media, considering what could have been posted to make her so leery. Maybe a past boyfriend? The thoughts started trickling through his head. She was extra sensitive, so maybe there was something *really* bad out there.

The guests started saying good night, hugging and getting ready to leave, complimenting Delilah's meal and exclaiming over how nice it had been to catch up. Rakell hugged Dwayne as he left. He made a point to tell her he'd see her at the gym and that they had to chat in order to plan something for Jake's birthday in a few weeks.

Jake's birthday? One hot weekend and now she was planning a birthday celebration?

Then Jake thanked Delilah, giving her a big hug. Delilah reached out and hugged Rakell, whispering in her ear, "Hang in there. You two make a nice couple." She pulled back, winked, and added, "If you ever need me, I'm here."

"Thank you so much." Rakell squeezed Delilah's arm, smiling, masking the emotion that was lying just beneath the surface. She grabbed her purse and walked out with Jake, her phone buzzing repeatedly.

"Someone's trying to get a hold of you," Jake said casually.

"Yes, yes," she said, grabbing her phone and glancing at all the messages from Matt.

Jake opened her door and helped her climb in before jumping in the truck to begin the drive home. "Everything good?" he asked, keeping his tone neutral, ignoring the anxiety emanating from the passenger side. Her ragged edginess agitated the angst in his bloodstream as she distractedly looked at her phone, then out the window.

Chapter Thirty-Two

Rakell stared down at the texts from Matt.

Matt: *Jake Skyler, like 'THE Jake Skyler??' UT, now NFL Jake?*...**Send**

She scrolled to the next one.

Matt: *He's not an 'under the radar' guy. Read this*...**Send**

He included a link to a newspaper article titled "Pretty Boy Stepping Up." She knew Matt and could tell he was furious. God, how had she not seen this sooner?

She scrolled again.

"Skyler and Dallas Cheerleader, Samantha Graves. Skyler's back at it." She clicked on the link to see a picture of Jake, with his hands up the back of a woman's skirt.

Her breath hitched.

Another article, *"Jake 'pretty boy' Skyler known for dancing on the field apparently takes his dancing skills off the field as well."* Rakell didn't click on the link...just saw something about him and two strippers.

She couldn't take any more.

Matt: *One more thing*...**Send**

Rakell stared at the picture Matt had sent. It was Jake with a famous movie star hanging on his arm.

"Everything okay?" Jake repeated, this time not masking the concern ringing in his voice. Jake shot a quick glance at her as she sat glued to her phone.

She looked up. "Why did you lie when I asked if you were famous?" Her voice was coarse and shaky, like she was swallowing all the anger bubbling in her chest.

Jake thought it would be easier if she just screamed at him, instead of this. The barely contained anger, laced with disbelief, brimming with distress, exuding from her voice. It was as if she'd just learned he'd been cheating on her. The hurt rung out in the truck. Damn it!

"Hey, come on…I didn't lie. I asked you if you knew who I was, and you said no. My point was, if you don't know me, how famous could I be?"

"That's a crock of shite. You knew what I meant." Her pitch was rising, her accent thickened with anger. Her jaw jutted out, her eyebrows screwing together as she stared at him.

Jake kept his eyes on the road, sucking in a slow breath through his nose, coaxing himself not to escalate with her. "Rakell," he said apprehensively. "Honestly, outside of Austin, people don't recognize me. I mean, a little more in Sacramento now, but when I played for Seattle, no one knew who I was because I was a backup quarterback. Now maybe that's starting to change. But in general, it's mostly here in Austin, 'cause I'm a local guy who made it big," he explained, waiting, enduring the pregnant silence that seemed to stretch on before briefly glancing at her then back to the road.

"*Rae*-kale?" he ventured, tenuousness threading his voice.

Her head dropped into her hands. *How the hell did I get here?* "Um…sure…. okay," Rakell huffed, popping her head up, crossing her arms over her chest. "So dating famous actresses, models, and an array of NFL cheerleaders—that's just what average Austin boys do all the time?" Her tone was overly derisive, piercing.

"Where did you hear all that? Is that what all those messages are about?" His voice strained, his fingers tightening on the steering wheel.

Whipping her head toward him, she said, "Yeah, I got to find out all about you from social media. You didn't let on any of that to me. You—you painted yourself as some, some normal…" Her voice was escalating. She stopped herself, clenching her jaw, blood pounding in her temples. Logic began taking a backseat to the ping-ponging ball of emotions bouncing around her. Anger, fear, jealousy, and sadness swirled through her; how could she just hang out with a famous NFL playboy? Did she even have a right to the anger and jealousy rippling through her? Wasn't she doing the same thing to him? She wasn't about to tell him what she really did to make money.

Frustration mixed with regret unfurled in his gut. He'd been cornered by his own past, no way out. Damn, he'd finally met *that* girl, and it was unraveling. Jesus, but she wasn't being reasonable. "Normal, average…that's what I want. That's the life I lead when I'm not…"

"Not what? Courting the who's who of Hollywood and famous models…fucking everything with pom poms? So…okay, normal guy shit is banging a cheerleader from every team? That's one way to win, I guess."

His neck stiffened, his head snapping toward her. "Damn it, *Rae-kale*, what's that got to do with anything…? That's in the past…"

"Bullshit! That's who you are, and you led me to believe you were some normal ranch boy from Austin. Average! You're anything but average…" She turned, looking out the window, hugging herself.

Get yourself together, you're hiding so much from him. You want the same thing he does, just a normal life, and this is just supposed to be for fun. She had a niggling feeling that someday she'd file that under "the lies we tell ourselves to get through things we can't make sense of or we don't have answers to, because we don't have enough life experiences to categorize the experience."

The regret of his past started choking him, the realization that all those dalliances with no strings attached, indeed had strings that could cost him this girl. Trying to settle himself, he sucked in a long breath through his nose and slowly let it escape his mouth. Then her words jammed into the base of his spine.

"You tricked me! For what? You can obviously fuck any girl you want, anyone! So why lie? Why lead me to believe…that…" Her words were screeching out of her mouth almost without air.

Jake snorted. "Led you to believe what? That I'm a normal guy who's crushing on you?" His voice started to rise. "Is that what I led you to believe? 'Cause that's the fucking truth!" His hand pounded the steering wheel. *Fuck, Jake. Reel it in,* he admonished himself, hearing his high school coach's words in his head: "Bury that temper, Jake. It clouds your judgment and doesn't do anyone any good."

Her head snapped toward him. "Stop with the normal-guy bullshit…please!" Her breathing was rapid, frenzied, as if she were running from something.

"No…I won't. I *am* a normal guy. I'm being called a liar because I didn't lead with, 'Hey, I'm a famous NFL quarterback. Wanna date me?' That makes me a liar?" He shook his head. "Fuck, I was trying to…"

Rakell shut her eyes briefly, her head dropping into her hands, trying to catch her breath. "I just didn't want that. I mean, I just wanted normal for once, for my first boy..." er words trailed off.

"What? What did you say? Your first...what?" His voice came out stunned before he purposely softened it.

"I mean, here in Austin. Except, I mean..." she mumbled into her hands.

"Rakell, Sweets, please..." he drawled out, his tone coated with molasses slowing his speech down, desperate to reach her.

She looked up. "I'm so tired and probably have had too much wine. Can you just take me home?" Her tone was defeated.

"No, that's *not* how this works," Jake said, trying not to sound pissed. "We are not going to argue and end like this tonight. That's not going to happen."

Rakell whipped her head toward him, her chest pounding, anger roiling in her. Then she stopped herself, drawing in a long breath. "I'm just tired, I just need to..."

"Your bag is at my house anyway," he said matter-of-factly, willing himself to regain composure.

"I can get it tomorrow." She trailed off, her voice now faint. She had backed herself into a corner with him, and the only way out was to blow the whole thing apart, but she didn't want to hurt him or ruin the memory of what they'd had. However briefly they'd connected, he'd altered her way of seeing men and generated feelings she had never experienced before. Feelings she didn't want to let go.

Jake kept driving, passing the turn to her house. "At the very least, we're going to my house to get your bag and talk. If, after that, you want me to take you home, I will, but not like this. I'm not dropping you off like this," he said with surreal calmness directing his voice, almost as if he was coaxing someone off a ledge. As he pulled into the driveway, he looked over at Rakell. Her face was blank. "*Rae*-kale," he drawled out, "this is something we can work through." He turned off the engine, quickly jumping out to open her door, trying to get to her door before she jumped out. He'd made the point that he opened doors, he was trained to do that, and she'd made the point she knew how to open her own door. *What the hell.*

It occurred to her as her hand went to the door handle that he'd been working to pronounce her name correctly, but when lust or emotion got a hold of him, he reverted back to his Texas drawl. Her mouth curled up reflexively thinking about how much she liked how he said her name and how he drawled out "Sweets." She'd miss that. She'd miss him.

Rakell didn't respond. She knew it wasn't something they could work through, which had more to do with her situation than his. Even if she wasn't an escort, would she really want her first real boyfriend to be a famous NFL player who obviously had a long string of women before her? She had sworn that after this year, she'd shed herself of wealthy men who thought of little but themselves. So here she was, mixed up with intense feelings for another guy with money, fame, and power.

But this—Jake—seemed different. He did seem like he cared. Her head roiled with all his contradictions: Jake, a boy from Austin she had connected to. Jake, the NFL superstar whose antics were detailed in the media. Could she even trust herself? She had no experience dating, getting to know men, really getting to know them. She knew men through one lens only: that of an escort.

They walked in the house, neither one speaking. Jake asked her to sit outside with him. It was only ten, and the night air was finally starting to cool down. He poured her a glass of red wine. She asked for water, and he brought that to her, too, and then sat beside her on the outdoor couch. He tried to figure out where to start, how to move this forward.

"*Rae*-kale," he said, his hand on hers as he spoke. "I know, when you read stuff about me, it's going to seem like...well, like I'm a big player. That was true my first few years in Seattle."

Abruptly, she stood, her back to him. "I am fine whatever your answer is, but I just want to know this: Am I your Austin off-season girl? A fling until you go back to Sacramento, you know, a little *Austin heat* that you and Dwayne seem to drum up so easily?" Her voice was steady, but she couldn't yank all the emotion out of her tone. She just needed to know if she could trust herself in the future.

She heard him stand behind her. No words were thrown into the air as they stood motionless for a moment that seemed to stretch on. He almost couldn't stand it, forcing back the urge to grab her and fuck her mouth with his tongue, making her know she belonged to him. *You,*

you, make me different, make me want to re-write my past, please see that.

"I, well, I reckon the best way to explain it…" he stammered.

"Just say it, Jake! 'Yes, Rakell, that's what you are—a girl to pass time with.' Please! I am way too tough to let someone like you, or any man, make me feel less than." She gulped. She hadn't read him right after all. She'd thought he really cared, that she was something more, even if she couldn't return it. For a while, she'd felt comforted knowing that someone like Jake cared for her. That when she left the industry, she could find someone like him. Now she questioned everything.

Lean in with the truth, Jake. There's been way too many lies clouding this. Stop now.

"Maybe at first I thought…" He could see her ribcage pull in and heard the charged puff of air escaping her mouth. "Listen, damn it!" He stood back, though his instinct was to grab her, to force her to hear him.

He lowered his voice. "*Rae*-kale, give me a chance to speak before you react, please. Okay, yes, I saw you and thought, *Fuck she's hot.* And yes, at first, I figured we'd have fun for a few months. But within a short time, I realized that I wanted it to be more. That you liking me without knowing who I was meant that I could be the person *I* want to be. I—honestly, if all I was lookin' for was off-season fun, I would have moved on earlier." He tightened his jaw, because the words resting behind that sentence were, *You're way too fucking difficult for an 'off-season' fling.*

But there was honesty, and then there was getting yourself killed.

She turned, looking at him with her hands on her hips.

He put his hand up. "Let me tell you who I am. When I started in the NFL, my head was full, I had a lot of money, and women were there. I mean, I was an idiot. You can ask Jordan. But I changed once I moved to Sacramento. I've been trying to get my head in the game completely. And, well, I've been looking for the right person, someone who would be interested in me for me—a normal guy." Finally, she stopped staring at the ground and looked at him. "Someone like you. A normal girl." His eyes focused on hers.

Her lips crested into a small smile. She liked the "normal" tag, even though she knew life after the fire, for her, could not be described as normal. Nothing had felt normal after that. Damn, did she ever crave that. "Not sure I'd peg me for normal," she said instead. She wanted him to stop explaining. Every word made her feel hollower. His truth made her deception more acute and painful. No matter his past, he led with good. But would he be able to see that *she* was good, despite her past? As she stood there, looking at him, all of the justifications she'd told herself a million times over about becoming a high-end escort seemed nonsensical.

"Not quite *normal*, normal," he teased, moving toward her. "But exactly what I'm looking for." He pecked her cheek. "Exactly," he whispered in her ear.

Shutting her eyes, trying to absorb the soft touch of his lips against her cheek, she said, "Obviously, we don't really know each other, and I was just…" She wanted to tell the truth: She had not been seeking a serious relationship but had been hoping for something enjoyable, something fun, generated from her own desire, rather than contractually fulfilling the desires of others. Of course, she liked him. A lot. More than she had planned to. But her life wouldn't allow for that now. The fear of opening up to him kept her silent; she couldn't share anything about her job or her clients. She had to back out. She needed to break this off before things got even more complicated.

She gently fell into him, his touch making her want more, more, before the end. She slid her hand to the back of his head, her fingers intertwining with his hair. She brought his face down to hers, attacking his mouth with hers, purposefully being rough. She could feel the hesitation in him, but she pushed past it, deliberately forcing her tongue into his mouth until she could feel him give in. She felt his arousal rising as his fortitude softened.

Rakell pulled back from his mouth, leaning in toward his ear. "Don't forget, I'm much better with nonverbals," she whispered. Then she gently bit his earlobe as she rubbed up and down his hard chest, one hand sliding down to his crotch, loving the feel of the hardness growing there.

"I'll say," Jake grunted, thinking that this girl only had one communication style. "So you're staying?"

"Mm…hmm, if you're going to take care of me." Her tone was lusty yet laced with innocence.

"I can do that." Jake yanked her on top of him, sliding her blouse down and unsnapping her strapless bra, then moving his hands to her breasts. "I'll start here." They both groped at each other before he took a deep breath. He stood, bringing her to standing as well, turning her to slowly unzip the back of her skirt, undressing her, leaving her standing in her black lace thong. With his hands on her hips, he slowly turned her to face him. Then he stepped back, his eyes perusing her naked body as she nervously shifted her legs back and forth.

"Jake?" she said, her voice raspy, a comingling of confusion and ache.

He shook his head as he took her in. "God, you're beautiful," he said, his hands moving to her ribcage, wanting to take her, lay her on the outdoor couch, and drive into her. It seemed to be what she wanted as well, but he knew he needed to draw this out, let her know she meant something to him. *Fuck*, he thought. He loved her.

"Let's get in the hot tub," Jake said, pulling his shirt off and quickly shucking his pants and briefs, tossing them on the couch with her clothes.

"Jake? I'm dying," Rakell said, staring at his erection. "Are you sure you...?" One side of her mouth twisted up creating a crooked smile. Anxious lust tickled her crotch, making it impossible to keep still, her fingers on her thighs, fidgeting.

"Yes, let me grab some towels." She watched his near perfect body stride toward a cabinet near the house. He walked back and gently took her hand. "Leave the panties on so I can focus on enjoying the night with you, drag it out a bit."

She followed him toward the pool where a waterfall cascaded from the slightly elevated hot tub. The night air still held a grain of warmth, but a delicate breeze was diminishing it, making the hot water feel delicious on her feet as she sat on the edge of the hot tub. She watched his tan-skinned muscular form lower itself into the water and move between her dangling legs, his hands on her thighs. God, she'd miss this, his touch, the slow deliberate power of his hands as he kneaded her flesh. A comingling of tenderness and possessiveness dominated his actions.

"Mmm," she whispered, smiling at him, her legs parting to fit his torso. He commanded her while simultaneously nurturing her, and every nerve fiber in her body became alert to his touch. She couldn't help pondering the difference between him and the other men who'd touched her. Jake made it obvious that pleasuring her was a priority. "I love the feel of your hands on me." The breathy words rushed out of her mouth as she arched her torso responsively, her hands on the deck behind her.

Jake's eyes absorbed the excitement displayed in her body, her arched back pushing her erect nipples upward as her legs splayed open. "And I love my hands on you—we got a symbiotic thing going on here," he said, slipping a finger under the thin strip of lace covering her crotch, pushing his middle finger into her, relishing her moans.

"Yes...yes," Rakell whispered, arching a little more, letting him know that she wanted to feel him inside her.

He slipped another finger in her, stirred by her earnest craving of him. He groaned pleasurably, curving his fingers slightly inside of her wet pussy, reaching toward her upper walls, searching for the spot that he knew could make her whip her head back and forth, screaming. The more she moaned, the harder it became not to just pull her forward, rip her thong off, and let his cock dive into the place it wanted to be. God, he wanted to skip all this—the effort of trying to figure each other out, the back-and-forth games—and just claim her. Let her know she had a future with him.

Sliding his fingers out, ignoring her pleading whimpers, his powerful hands fisted the black material on either side of her crotch and yanked forcefully, ripping the delicate fabric, pulling it from her, tossing it onto the deck.

Rakell jerked, feeling the tension along her hips and hearing the rip of fabric. "Jake!?" she yelled, sitting up to face him. "Oh my God...did you just—?" Her eyes darted to the pieces of black lace, then back to him. Her mouth was tight, her eyebrows pulled in. "What the fu—"

"Shit, was that too caveman? I mean, I was trying to be..." His hand went back to her knees, studying her serious face.

"I've never had anybody do that. I mean...I *think* it was sexy." Her nose scrunched up, before her face broke into a huge grin, her hand going to her mouth to stop the laughter gurgling in her throat. It was too late, an odd blend of a snort and giggle flew into the air.

"Wait, wait—that played out waaay sexier in my head. Didn't really see it as a comedy routine, but okay," he mused, happy the weight of the night seemed to dissipate with her laughter.

He joined her, his head dipping between her legs as a gruff burst of laughter jumped from his mouth. "You said 'sexy,' right?" Jake pushed out before another burst left his mouth.

"Yeah, super fucking sexy...you Neanderthal." She couldn't stop giggling. "Not sure I can get back into the mood after that display." Her head dropped down as her fingers yanked his hair, pulling him up to her mouth, still giggling as she moved her mouth onto his, pecking his lips through a smile.

"If it fucked up the mood, I'll never do it again, and I promise to buy you a dozen more pairs," he said.

"No, I loved it, *really*," Rakell said, sliding into the hot tub and wrapping her arms around his muscular girth. "You goof." Her head tilted back as she laughed again.

She had a feeling that these moments with him now would result in future heartache. His flinty blue eyes steadied on her, and his hands encompassed her hips, pulling her to him. *I'll miss you.* Not just the sex, but the connection she felt in that moment: a link between them that seemed more real than anything she had experienced before.

The joy of this moment would end. Tomorrow, she'd be left with the memories. Would it be better to have these memories to accompany the pain, or would it have been better to have stopped it before more of their threads wove together?

She couldn't stop herself; she didn't want to stop herself. She craved him, this. The laughter, his touch, his intensity, his nonstop questions, and of course, the sex. Would she experience anything like this with another man in the future? She *had* to walk away, didn't she? She couldn't risk what it would mean to try to make this continue with Jake, could she? She absolutely couldn't betray the commitment she had made to Matt. Could she tell Jake the truth? Let *him* be the one to walk away? Inadvertently, she shook her head.

"Hey, you? Are you okay? Honestly, I didn't mean to freak you out." Jake leaned into her, his lips brushing up against her forehead. He tried not to register the feeling of her naked body against his, imploring his body to remember that tonight he was walking on thin ice, unsure still of what may be roiling around in her brain after the headlines she'd read earlier that evening. No matter what he said about it, he knew it would always sound like a defensive reaction.

He knew all too well that if the truth was not revealed up front, then every bit of what was said afterward seemed weak, questionable. He could only hope that they'd move forward, and he'd have a chance to show her the authentic Jake, the person he knew himself to be. Flawed, yes, but not the star-seeking womanizing buffoon he'd helped the media create.

Rakell's top teeth lightly touched her bottom lip as she smiled, her big green eyes meeting his. "Jake, I'm fine. Just a little distracted by *this*..." As she spoke, the fingers of her right hand trailed down his abdomen before wrapping around his hard shaft.

A low, mournful sigh emanated from deep inside him, surrounding them. It was almost as if he were in pain. But her intimate touch made him feel absolved; he was getting a second chance at his girl.

"Too hard?" she asked, stroking him beneath the hot water that bubbled around them, her whole hand encapsulating his wide, stiff shaft.

"God, no. Just right, Sweets. As always, just right." His head went back as he reveled in the feeling of her controlling his cock, him. "Perfect. God... like that," he groaned. "I want you..."

She moved a bit to the side, still stroking him. "I want to feel you in me," she said, purposely letting her breasts brush against his lower chest as she cupped his cockhead in her palm. "Just this. No...no barrier." Her eyes caught his chin shift as his spine reflexively extended back, his hand covering her hand around his hardened penis before pulling them both away.

His chest sucking in at her words, Jake intertwined his fingers with hers. Steam rose from the water around them. His other hand cupped the back of her head, tilting her to face him, registering an attentiveness molding her expression as she clearly studied his reaction to her request.

For several seconds, their eyes remained locked on each other. The air around them stilled, and she became keenly aware of the cool night air brushing against her skin, making her nipples rigid. She waited, steadying the buried tremble that threatened to surface. "Jake?" she muttered.

His fingers wiggled from hers, his hand running up her arm before his thumb and index fingers gripped her chin, his fierce blue eyes intent on her. "Rakell...we both said we've never...why now, why me?"

Her jaw trembled imperceptibly, his hand absorbing it. She fought to hold her stare to his, to keep the swell of emotion pushing against them back. "I...um. I trust you. I want to experience that feeling, and I want it with you. I'm on the pill, and I'm clean."

"I trust that...of course, I know. You know that I am...well, I've never...plus the team doctors test me for everything all the time." He smiled, the intense blaze in his eyes softened. "I want to feel that with you, too." His mouth broke wider, that little boy smile emerging through his serious face. "Are you sure?"

"Yes, I wan—" Before Rakell could finish, his mouth was on hers, her lips soft and emotive.

Sucking up her low whimper, his hands reached around to her full bottom, fingers digging into her firm flesh. The internal flame that had been smoldering all night ignited, fleeting thoughts flashing through his mind. *This is not smart. You've never done this before, risked it for a night of pleasure. What if she gets pregnant?*

God, Rakell pregnant, with my child?

He wasn't sure he'd care.

No, he'd be happy.

His hands clenched her ass harder as his lips grew more aggressive. "Wrap your legs around me," he growled, a low gurgle emanating around his words, a primitiveness inhabiting him. His brain was wiped blank. Nothing else mattered. Just her, just this moment, as he hoisted her up around him.

"God I can't wait to feel you around me. Move my cock into you now." His tone was demanding; all control had evaporated with her sweet appeal to feel him inside her. Her tremulous, dulcet voice as her eyes seemed to beg for it yanked on any threads of fortitude he'd had left, unraveling the pledge to himself. He would bury himself deep inside her, fully exposed.

Rakell did as he requested, wedging her hand between them, helping to aim his cockhead to her slick hole, her ass bobbing on the top of the hot water, her pussy flexing as his bulbous head pushed in. She grabbed his shoulders with both hands, pulling herself onto him, a lustful mewl rising from her throat as his hard cock penetrated, opening her to him.

Jake jerked her flush against him, her tits smashing against his hard torso, his cock etching through her wet flesh, his balls pinned to her crack. He held her there, squeezing her ass, his eyes pinching shut as she bit into the warm flesh where his neck and shoulder met.

"Hard, fast...let it go..." she urged into his ear.

"Jesus!" His spine shifted, edging himself just a bit farther into her. He drove into her, then forcefully grabbed her hips, sliding her up and down his manhood as she dug her hands into his shoulders for support. "I love how goddamn good you feel...I didn't know...I have to have you like this every time..." His own words didn't register in his brain. He had the fleeting thought that he might be leaving marks on her ass, yet his body kept going without frontal lobe guidance.

Rakell angled her pelvis, shifting it rhythmically, engulfing his bare cock. The unadulterated feel of his hard staff burying into her was more than she had imagined, the intense naked pressure erupting into a pleasure so surreal, yet so tangible. It was something she would never forget, their two systems intertwining in such a way that it seemed the neurons were communicating without thought from their hosts.

"Kiss me," she urged. "Please…" And his lips linked with hers as his fingers continued to dig into the flesh of her hips. "Yes, mmm… sooo good," she mumbled against his full lips.

Jake sucked in her moans, her whimpers. "I'm going to come so deep in you, are you sure?" he asked, groaning into her open mouth.

"Yes…" Her tone was definitive, but he heard the thread of a plea in her voice. "Yes."

He kept pumping her. "I can never go back after feeling you. I have got to have this forever. Come, Sweets. Come. That-a-girl. Give it all to me, all of you." His thick voice cut through the cloud of steam in the night air, swirling around her, almost catching her up in another life—not her own, but one of a girl who'd finally found *that* one. The forever one.

She rocked herself, letting her breasts scrape against him, friction building throughout her. The word *forever* made her wince, despite it exuding from her own consciousness. She blocked it out, focused on absorbing what was happening, wanting to capture it. Then the friction ignited, the two winding up together, bursting from deep within her as if a string of firecrackers were popping just below her skin's surface.

She howled, a sound that didn't even register to her ears until seconds later. It didn't sound like her; it was as if it were from an animal. She felt his hardened cock thrust back and forth, moving within her with such concentration. He burst deep inside of her, shooting his semen into her womb. The intensity of his movements, mixed with the gravelly roar that seemed to come from his chest, caused a rippling orgasm to emerge again, shooting through her spine, making her arch and cry out.

Forever blinked like a strobe light in her brain, a part of her wondering if she could have that in her future, a forever with a man like Jake.

Jake held her to him tightly, their breathing ragged, her head to his chest. Once he softened, he slowly removed himself from her, sliding his hands to her back, then one hand up cradling her head, his fingers intertwining in her semi-damp hair. "I love you" crept to the tip of his tongue; he had to swallow hard to keep it locked inside. Rakell had splayed herself to him, almost begging him into her core. He wanted—no, maybe *needed*—her to be the only woman he experienced this way. Because as he stood in the hot tub, pulling her up with him, gulping the cool air, recovering from the most intense physical-emotional experience he'd ever had, he was sure that she was *the one*. He snuggled his arms around her more tightly with that realization, exhilarated and terrified all at once.

Finally, releasing their wrought embrace, the mental and physical connection having bonded them together, making it difficult to pull themselves apart, they moved into the house. After a quick, hot shower together, fatigue coaxed them to bed. Jake engulfed her in his arms, her damp hair to his chest.

"Rakell, I know that my past may seem overwhelming, maybe even threatening," he began as he felt her head move against him. He gently cupped the side of her head, tilting her face so her eyes met his. "But I can assure you that I never saw a future with those women, and they didn't see me that way either. I was always honest about being a player—not that I'm bragging. I'm just saying I made a point not to lead anyone on. The important part of this long explanation"—a combined laugh and sigh left his mouth—"is that I don't want what you saw in those headlines. I have no desire to be with a famous Hollywood type or a model. That's not me. It's not what I need or what I want."

Her hand went to his chest. "Jake, it's…"

"No, please. I want you to know if I never had to go to LA again, except to play ball, I would be happy. I hate all the glitz, the parties, the bullshit that is LA and the Hollywood people. So many normal people get caught up in this fucked-up spiral of Hollywood. It's not good, and I've seen some good people follow that twisty path up, then spiral all the way down. I don't want a girl like that. It's not for me."

"Jake, I have…I have goals and some of those goals…" she stuttered, desperate to find the words to make him understand how much he had come to mean to her, how complete he was beginning to make her feel. He needed to know how special he was, but her future dreams were Hollywood. "I want to… I need you to know how good you make me feel, and I, I know this feels different. I just…"

Her throat convulsed, the words shriveled in dark fear, settled to the bottom of her gut. *What is he doing to me? Every kind word, possessive kiss, intent touch, and act of concern… Oh God, he is undoing Marietta and only Rakell will be left behind. I'll have to figure out who I am. Who is Rakell without Marietta?*

His blue eyes poured into her saucer-round eyes, thinking about how many women he'd bedded, knowing that wasn't intimacy. Intimacy had to be rooted in honesty, the security of knowing you could unveil yourself to someone and them to you. That deep, settled sense of knowing that your dreams, your fears, and all the in-betweens, would be handled with care.

That was intimacy.

He wanted that with her. He would dive deeper into her dreams, her fears, and show her he could be trusted with all of her. He wanted to be privy to what was going on in her head.

He shifted on the bed, his arms encircling her back, his hands absorbing the tremble within her torso. Bending his forehead to hers, he whispered, "I want you, all of you, not just this." He ran his hand down her side to her hips. "I want to own your dreams, your fears, your secrets. I will work to be that person you trust with all the things that run through that beautiful head, knowing that I'm safe…"

Watching the tears trickle down her face, he kissed the salty liquid, knowing he would be there for her. Whatever it was, he would take it on. "I want to embrace all of you. I want *you*, period."

She laid the palm of her hand gently on his cheek, searching his eyes, his face.

I hope you understand the choices I have had to make.

THE END

Nylix Minxes

Join the Nylix Minxes, THE naughty book club! The Naughty Book club is free and gives you access to exclusive content. **Bookstagrammers** & **BookTok** friends, we have special material for you to create your unique *Austin Heat* reels using actual video footage and pictures of actor James Joseph Pulido and other models/actors involved in bringing this series to life. (The videos and pictures will be updated periodically; you will be notified via email when new footage is uploaded.)

Get new content, character backstories, and be the first to know when the next book in the *Austin Heat* series is released. Receive information about new *Austin Heat* merchandise.

I can't wait for you to read all the extras...reserved for Nylix Minxes. Get your lipstick ready, *you naughty little minxes!*

www.Amarinylix.com

More Austin Heat!

Austin Heat: THE ONE…That Got Away

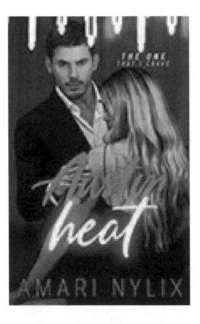

Austin Heat: THE ONE…That I Crave

Acknowledgements

Thank you to the community of Austin for embracing this fun, saucy series. The reason Austin has a reputation as one of the most creative, exciting cities in the nation is not only because of its stunning skyline, vibrant music scene, enticing bars, or fabulous food. It is also because of its people. So cheers to you!

A special thank you to the following Austin businesses: Lift-ATX, The Driskill Hotel, and Chuy's Tex-Mex Restaurant.

Guy Forsyth and Jeska Bailey, your music is on a constant loop in my house and mind. "The Things that Matter" plays a key role in this book.

Jon Hamrick: Your art continues to take my breath away. Thank you for creating such a fun logo for my naughty book club. The bookish minx is adorable...I want to be her!

The Media Team
Dharmesh Bhakta, Caleb Pickens, Rebecca McDowell, Brook Amber, and Ashly Cantu: You all inspired me, but it is the laughter that I will never forget!

A big shout out to **Mesh Bhakta** for the captivating photos that are melting panties throughout the world and **Caleb Pickens** for the cinematic videos that have the world breathing a little heavier.

A big hug to Rebecca McDowell. You didn't know that "helping" with my social media would lead to creating movie trailers....did you? I love our long, late-night talks about everything from tequila, sexting, careers, and love 😊!

The Modeling and Acting Team
James Joseph Pulido: You said "yes" to some cover photos and videos, but it was so much more than that...you infused life into Jake's image and made words come off pages into scenes that are filled with

emotion. You are not only a beautiful model, but a skilled director and gifted actor, as well as a kind human being.

Jessica Gonzales: You were a game changer…your beauty is only surpassed by your heart!

J.D. Holeman: You, my friend, brought your A-game! Thank you!

Coach Mark Hambrick: Thank you, dear friend, for jumping in… and for making the sacrifice to wear burnt orange for this project.

Erynn LaRae and Chiara Stock: Thank you. Your smiles lit up on camera.

Neopolitan and his mom, Kathy Thomas: Neo, you are a gorgeous horse with a lively personality! Such an alpha! Hugs to Kathy for all your help!

The Editorial Team

Kasi Alexander: Thank you for your willingness to jump on board in the final hour. You helped decrease my anxiety!

Jennifer Imrie: I appreciate your eye for detail. Your knowledge of grammar is not surpassed.

Alyssa Goody (@editorgoody.qualityreads): I am so grateful for all of our long conversations about this project. You have a gift for editing, and I so appreciate all of your input.

Christopher Skowronski (@thecwolf): My number one line-editor; the first to see everything! I still haven't found a synonym for c@%*head, that's your job darling. And yes, there is such a thing as a *slow burn* 😊!

Alexis Washam (Verto Literary): First, thank you for taking on this project. You forced me to go deeper with Rakell, truly making me dig into her character, as well as the other characters in this series. Darling, I am letting everyone know that *you* are directly responsible for all the sex scenes that ended up on the cutting room floor.

Research Team
Bill Delaney (CSR: Chief "Spice" Researcher): Have you ever had a better job? You finally found your calling, darling, and the *pay* is great too!

Tara Delaney (CFR: Chief "Feels" Researcher): Darling, you do get on my nerves with all the sensory, nervous system, and psychological talk, but it has made the connecting scenes that get the reader to all the spice that much more intriguing.

PR and Marketing Team
She-She Media (@sheshemedia): My Austin cheerleaders!! You three were the first to read this as a book. Thank you for your feedback! Your enthusiasm keeps my imagination going late into the night. Darling Suzanne, please tell your "teacher friend" I listened.

Get-Red-PR Books (@getredprboooks): We appreciate your guidance during this process. Your company's understanding of the complicated publishing world has been invaluable.

Author Buzz (www.authorbuzz.com): MJ Rose, you have been a wealth of information! We are so grateful for your insider knowledge as a best-selling author and a marketing guru who has helped so many authors get their voice to the masses.

Early Readers
Bookstagrammers and BookTok readers: Thank you for reaching out and asking to read this book. It has truly been a pleasure getting to know some of you personally. Read on, you darling Minxes! I adore your spicy suggestions.

To all my dear friends who encouraged me to get this series to the masses, love you, darlings! I'm up for tequila and a lil' dirty talk anytime.

The Cover Story

Dear Readers:

You *must* trust your gut! I am so grateful I listened to that voice blaring in my head during the creation of these covers. Jake has become part of my psyche, as have all the characters in this series. I knew I wanted Jake on the covers as he is the energy behind this series.

When I started looking for models and speaking with photographers, I kept hitting a dead end. I didn't see Jake in any of the photos suggested to me after describing the character. I believed that if I went with someone who didn't epitomize *the* Jake that I had come to know so well over the past few years, I would be giving up part of him in my mind. I finally decided I would opt for a more artistic cover, a graphic of a martini glass.

The week I made that decision, I came across a black and white photograph of James Joseph Pulido in New Mexico wearing a black cowboy hat. I stared at that photo for a few long, memorable minutes before I showed the photograph to my husband. He didn't hesitate. "Damn, that's Jake. Who is that?" A few days later, I wrote an email to James's agent, February 25, 2023, not knowing if it would even be answered. *I will never forget that email!*

Once James agreed to fly to Austin, I contacted my good friend and amazing photographer, Darmesh Bhakta (Photo by Mesh), who was able to grasp my over-the-top vision. He and his team worked tirelessly to bring to life an extensive list of photos and videos. The results are stunning: gorgeous covers and steamy videos that tease.

The most extraordinary part of this experience is not how much James Pulido looks like my vision of Jake. No. It is how much James *embodies* "pretty boy" Jake Anthony Skyler. Jake first came alive on these pages in 2020 when I wrote the first draft of this book, so to actually meet the character I thought only existed in my head was *surreal*.

So here you have it…(actor/model) James Joseph Pulido as *Jake!*

About the Author

Amari Nylix tells sordid stories revolving around tempestuous love affairs. Inspired by the secret liaisons of Old West villains, heroes, and the temptress women who lure those powerful men into their webs. She particularly enjoys it when the men's armor is ripped away, exposing their soft underbellies known as their hearts. She relishes in the men's pursuit of the soft, feminine kitten, only to find themselves shocked when she turns out to be a wanton minx.

Years of traveling the globe, studying her human subjects as they let their emotions draw them into sticky situations, taking notes along the way, led her to write stories that taunt. Amari delights in sharing her torrid stories of heart-wrenching, epic love that begin with the desires of the flesh and evolve into affairs of the heart.

In the *Austin Heat* series, Amari works closely with bestselling author of both non-fiction and fiction, Tara Delaney 😊. Tara has extensive professional experience in behavior and nervous system development, while also having studied how early trauma impacts our responses as adults. Tara is responsible for trimming back Amari's numerous spicy scenes, allowing room for all the *FEELS*.

They have a productive, albeit contentious, working relationship. Tara insists that the only way to draw readers into characters is through their hearts and minds, while Amari insists that readers only slog through *"that stuff"* to get to the spice.

Disclaimer: Ms. Nylix is NOT responsible for your increased water bill due to the number of COLD showers required to get you through this steamy series.

www.amarinylix.com
IG: @author.amarinylix
facebook.com/author.amarinylix
TT: @author.amarinylix

Made in the USA
Coppell, TX
05 December 2023

25406526R00188